FAME FARM
BY WHOINGODSNAME

ISBN (EPUB): **979-8-9927806-0-4**

Copyright© 2025 **Whoingodsname / 5th Wall Media**

All rights reserved. No part of this book may be reproduced, stored, or transmitted in any form without permission from the publisher, except in the case of brief quotations used in reviews.

This book is dedicated to my daughter, @prezidentbarbie.

For the future she and her generation will inherit.

We are standing at the edge of something irreversible.

A world where stories no longer belong to storytellers. A reality stranger than fiction. An existence where truth is not discovered but assigned. Where thought itself is outsourced—packaged, filtered, and sold back to us as reality.

Some call it progress. But at what expense? Silence is compliance. And compliance, when left unchecked, becomes control.

Technology was meant to connect us. Now, it monitors, molds, monetizes and controls, while disconnecting us from ourselves.

Entertainment used to inspire, captivate and bring joy. Now, it distracts, dictates, and indoctrinates.

And the more we surrender our minds to such a machine, the less we remember who we are at all.

This is not just a story. This is a warning.

A warning of what happens when we no longer create but are created for. When we no longer choose but are programmed to believe we have.

If we continue down this path, we will wake up in a world where we are no longer the authors of our own lives.

We will be the audience.

The consumers.

The product.

And by the time we realize it, it will already be too late.

So daughter, heed my words. **Always** think for yourself. There are times throughout history where human consciousness shifts and our perspectives need to be… updated. You just so happened to be born in one of those times. It's not your job or any one persons job to save the world or stop the inevitable shift that's coming. The truth is that your generation inherited the problems that the generations before failed to solve. And even though we're witnessing the physical aspects of this technological shift, there's still a spiritual war taking place. What your generation does, how your generation thinks moving forward, will decide who will be in control of your future. So question everything. Even yourself. There's a bounty for your soul and your mind is the final fortress. Hold the line. Protect it well. Wield it wisely.

Be a **disruption**. Be a **game-changer**. Be the glitch in the **Simulacra**.

DISCLAIMER

This is a work of fiction. Names, characters, places, events, and incidents are either the product of the author's imagination or used fictitiously. Any resemblance to actual persons, living or dead, or to real events is purely coincidental.

References to public figures are made for narrative and artistic purposes only and do not imply factual claims or real-world associations. The views, actions, and motivations of any fictionalized persons in this book do not reflect those of their real-life counterparts.

No endorsement or participation by any real individuals, corporations, or entities is intended or implied.

PROLOGUE

WGA Writers Strike-Los Angeles 2023

The writers strike was supposed to end.

It always did.

Writers walked out. Actors followed. The demands were familiar—fair pay, security, creative control. The studios stalled, the networks postured. It was all part of the cycle.

Talent was necessary…Until it wasn't.

No longer was the power in the hands of the artists.

Audiences had evolved. They didn't care who wrote the stories, who starred in them. Content was content. It didn't need unions, egos, or negotiations. It just needed to exist.

So the show biz industry—the ones who truly ran it—they all came together.

A private meeting was held between Hollywood execs, tech moguls & game developers who had built the platforms, the algorithms, the systems that dictated how the world interacts, what we see, listen to, and believe. Everything we mentally consume

For the first time, they weren't competitors.

They were partners.

And they had a solution.

One final merger. One entity to finally control it all…

'EGOCORP' 

No more talent dictating terms. No more delays. No more defiance.Just seamless, scalable, optimized profits. It started with the networks. Then the studios. Then the talent itself. Now, it's bigger than entertainment. Soon a budget was approved for a project that would change the course of humanity—Forever.

Let's just say *"the future isn't what it used it be"*…

WGA STRIKE - Hollywood, circa 2023

EPISODE 1
THE GOLDEN TICKET TOURNAMENT

The Hub

It's autumn in the desolate streets of an abandoned Silicon Valley. The year is 2033. All the tech geniuses and businesses ventured out to work on a mysterious initiative called "**Project Virtu**" in northern NV some10 years prior during an era called the Tech Exodus or '**Texodus**'. All that's left are the few residents who refused to leave, illegitimate kids who were left behind, and a few stores. Yet, one place remains surging with youthful anarchism and innovative persistence. An e-Sports gaming hub named '**Game On**'. It wasn't just an arcade. It was a lawless kingdom where survival of the fittest reigned. lights flickered across graffiti-covered walls, the anti-establishment messages read:

"**NEVER RESET**" and "**DEATH TO EGOCORP**"

The air was thick with a heady mix of delivered fast foods, vape clouds, dusty overclocked rigs, and teen spirit. Energy drinks spilled onto the floor. Near the bathrooms, there was a vending machine hacking challenge, the screen flashing:

FREE CREDITS FOR THE BRAVE!
CRACK IT & STACK IT!

The crowd was as unruly as the chaos they created. Kids shoved past each other, fighting for prime spots at the rigs. A brawl broke out near the VR hub, where a kid in an immersion suit accidentally spun and landed a kick on another player. Security drones buzzed overhead but didn't intervene. Game On had rules, but no one followed them. At one station, a kid hurled his controller to the ground.

@TheSharkKing *"This game's* ***ASS****! Shit's rigged!"*

Nearby, a girl perched on a stool, furiously coding in a public hackathon while glancing at the leaderboard. **@EmilyThe4th** *"****Got it!****"* she shouted, sending a ripple of cheers through her makeshift team.

For most of the kids here, this wasn't just a place to play. It was survival. They weren't just gamers—they were scrap hustlers, glitch-chasers, and exploit-finders who had grown up in the cracks of a crumbling system. At the center of it all sat **Scorelord**, hailed by his crew—**@GenWasted**. They weren't just here to watch. They were his squad, his buffer against a backdrop of madness.

"This is it!" Vexer yelled, climbing onto a table for a better view. "Show these peasants why you're the king!"

Blick leaned in, grinning. *"I'm calling it...he cracks 95. God of Gaming right here!"*

"Stop jinxing him," N30И quipped, elbowing him. She crossed her arms, but her sharp eyes stayed glued to the leaderboard. "Focus, Score. You've got this."

Shade, the strategist, simply nodded. *"****@M4YH3M****'s falling behind. All you need is one clean play. Lock in, bro."*

Blick interjecting, *"LET THIS MAN COOK!!"*

"CONTESTANTS, THIS IS YOUR FINAL ROUND. 60 SECONDS TO SECURE YOUR PLACE IN VIRTU CITY!."

The announcer's voice thundered through the arena. A countdown clock appeared on every screen: **00:60**.

Scorelord was a risk taker, not every move calculated, yet no maneuver went to waste. Every wave of his GameGlove was an act of pure wizardry. But it's still *way too close* to a tie and times running out.

"**FIVE**." The bass shook the walls, rattling loose cables and discarded cans. Kids crowded closer to the rigs, eyes glued to the screens.

"**FOUR**." A kid shoved someone aside to get a better view. Someone else yelled, *"YO, WATCH YOUR STEP!"*

"**THREE**." Scorelord tightened his grip, his focus laser-sharp.

"**TWO**." The crowd held its breath, the chaos momentarily suspended.

"**ONE**."

Just as the alert sounds, the battlefield on Scorelord's screen explodes in a cascade of light and destruction. A chain reaction of perfectly-timed moves sent his enemies crashing down. The leaderboard flashed:

#1 SCORELØRD (USA) - 94.3%

An automated voice rumbles over the loudspeakers, "***VICTORY ROYALE, SCØRELØRD WINS***!"

The room erupts with a mix of supporters and sore losers.

"I… I won?" he whispered, frozen in disbelief.

Blick didn't even give him time to process. He grabbed Scorelord's shoulders, shaking him violently. "YOU DID IT! GOD OF GAMING, BABY!"

"Let's GOOOO!!!" Vexer screamed, jumping onto the table like a gladiator celebrating victory.

N30И broke her usual stoicism, wrapping Scorelord in a quick hug. "We knew you'd pull it off…Who ELSE?!"
Even Shade cracked a small smile, nodding. "Well played, M'Lord! You earned it."

Nearby, sore losers yelled and chucked their headsets. Some stormed out, rage-quitting as signals overcrowded.

@TheLivingTissue: "*WTF IS THIS LAAAGGG, BROOO?!*"

The vending machine hacker gave a triumphant whoop as his exploit finally worked, tossing free sodas into the crowd. Above it all, the Golden Ticket NFT spun in dazzling 3D above Scorelord's rig. Its glow reflected in his wide, stunned eyes.

As the chaos continued, Scorelord stepped away from his rig, the spinning Golden Ticket still hovering in the background. He hesitated as a call comes in. The name "✆RUNE❤️‍🔥"

flashed on his wrist. He took a pull of his vape💨 then pulled his phone out and tapped the button to answer.

"Hey Rune, it's me. I WON! The Golden Ticket, it's… it's real I know you see it all over your timeline…I'm blowing up like *crazy* right now. Big win for Gen Wasted, right?!"

Her avatar appeared, sleek and pixelated, but her expression was unreadable.
"Yeah, I saw…Virtu City, huh? A whole city full of avatars and emojis.🤖💀"

Her words cut through the noise, and Scorelord's smile faltered.

"You don't sound too thrilled. This is the future, Rune, and we're a part of it!"

"A future where everything is fake?" she replied sharply. "Where people can't even smell the rain? I don't want that future, Score."

"Fake?!" he said, "This was the whole plan, do you not remember? I even got a +1 for the grand opening! I wanted you to come with me."

Rune's voice sharpened. "I don't remember the plan being for you to become some... downloadable content for EgoCorp." She paused, then delivered the final blow. "And then you want me to be an ADD-ON in your synthetic little world? What am I an *in-app purchase*? Lol *No thanks*."

Her tone softened, but her words carried finality. "Life is an open world, and we're heading in different directions on the map, Score. You go chase your 'friend' into Virtu City if you want. You don't even know if he's there."

"Wait, wait. *HOLLLUP*!" he interjects, "Pause the game... So, what exactly are you saying, Rune?"

"I'm saying, maybe it's ***game over*** for us, Score."

The call disconnects. He hits his vape.

The Golden Ticket continues spinning above his rig, but its glow felt cold now. The cheers of Game On faded into the background as Scorelord stared at the empty screen. What was supposed to be a moment of celebration and joy quickly turned bittersweet. He felt betrayed. After all, he did this for the crew so that they can all escape the street life and rescue a long lost friend who they believe is somewhere in Virtu City.

His rig chimed again. A sleek holographic message unfolded:

"Congratulations, Scorelord! Please report to the Virtu Transport Hub to begin onboarding. We can't wait to see you!"

"This is it," he whispered. "My chance to change everything.."

A panoramic view of Virtu City, its skyscrapers lit up like a digital utopia. The shuttle races toward it, Scorelord's reflection visible in the window, his expression conflicted. As the pod hummed smoothly along the neon-lit rails, the screen embedded in the glass flickered to life.

Scorelord glanced up, catching the glow of the **Virtu Prism** logo spinning in the corner. (The Virtu City Anthem Playing)

The screen erupts in a dazzling display of Virtu City, showcasing its iconic skyline framed by holographic billboards and towering spires. A soaring orchestral score swelled as **Mayor Max Gainsley** appeared, standing confidently in front of the gleaming golden gates, his hands clasped in a gesture of welcoming authority.

"Ah, Future Influents! Prepare for the chrysalis to break and the new YOU to emerge!" Gainsley began, his smooth, practiced smile lighting up the screen.

The camera swept across the city, panning from one district to the next, as Gainsley's voiceover narrated:

"Welcome to Prime Square—the beating heart of Virtu City, where innovation meets luxury. Here, you'll find the ***Social Media Stock Xchange (SMSX)****, the lifeline of our economy, where influence isn't just power—it's your net worth! Trade your clout, invest in your brand, or bet on the trends of tomorrow, all in real time."*

The visuals cut to the gleaming spire of **Nimbus Tower**, its crystalline structure glittering as drones spiraled upward. *"Prime Square also boasts Virtu City's tallest towers, like* ***Nimbus Tower****, where the city's most influential residents shape the Algorithm that shapes the world."*

The screen transitioned to **Valleywood**, its streets buzzing with holographic spotlights, drones, and digital paparazzi. *"Step into Valleywood, where stardom is a science, and creativity knows no bounds. From the Chrome Carpet of*

***Sunrise Boulevard**, where influencers debut their latest looks, to **The Parallax Theatre**, hosting dazzling premieres, this is the district where stars—human, bot, and hybrid—are born."*

The camera lingered on the **Museum of Vision (MOV)**, a futuristic gallery housing interactive AR installations and artifacts of today's present, deemed ancient relics by Virtu City's standards.

*"And don't miss the **Museum of Vision**, home to the annual **Meta Gala**, a celebration of innovation, fashion, and art like you've never seen before."*

The visuals shifted to **Arcan Heights**, with its sleek, sprawling homes surrounded by lush, holographic landscapes that changed based on the residents' preferences.

"For those seeking balance and serenity, Arcan Heights offers laid-back luxury and personalized living. Here, the homes are as alive as the people who live in them, with sprawling layouts designed to cater to your every need."

The camera hesitated, almost glitching, as it panned over **The Terminal**—a chaotic maze of unfinished buildings and abandoned tech experiments. Piles of disassembled drones and skeletal frameworks littered the landscape, dimly lit by flickering neon signs. Gainsley's voice faltered for a brief moment.

"And, uh… here we have The Terminal!" he said with a nervous chuckle, his hand gesturing vaguely. *"A… unique space for innovation and… growth! Moving on!"*

The screen immediately transitioned to the pristine **Virola Vaccination Station**, where pastel-clad staff guided citizens into padded, self-operating vaccination chairs.

"But first, let's ensure you're ready to shine. The **Vaccination Station**: *Safety first, splendor next! Our state-of-the-art Virola boosters will have you operating at peak efficiency. Remember, in Virtu City, wellness is the ultimate performance metric. And health is wealth!"*

The visuals darkened, cutting to a gritty montage of **Moderators** in action. Their glow on their helmets gave them a sinister, faceless appearance, while their cybernetic augmentations enabled impossible speed and precision. Gainsley's voice grew exuberant as he introduced them.

"Meet the Moderators!" he announced with pride, his tone dripping with theatricality. *"Swift. Agile. Unstoppable. These enforcers are hand-picked by the Algorithm itself, blending human instinct with mechanical perfection to ensure Virtu City remains in pristine harmony."*

The footage intensified:

- A **graffiti artist** mid-spray was tackled with shocking efficiency, their spray can exploding into pixels as a Moderator slammed them against the wall. The glowing words "**INFLUENCE IS FAKE**" disintegrated, replaced by ***"Violation: Unauthorized Digital Expression."*** Gainsley's voiceover grew almost gleeful.

"Ooh, he crossed the line! Looks like he ***fucked*** *around and, by golly, he found out!"*

- A **teen scrolling on their holo-device** flinched as a Moderator appeared behind them, gripping their device and projecting its contents in bold red letters: *"Unverified Fact Detected."* The teen was dragged away, their protests drowned out by the crowd's uncomfortable silence.
- A **robotic K9**, its eyes beaming red, locked onto a man running through a checkpoint. The metallic growl echoed as it lunged, its jaws clamping onto his knee.

The man's screams reverberated through the scene as Moderator calmly approached to assess the "violation."

Mayor: "Ah, I think this gentleman *KNEE'ds* some milk!"

The montage escalated, showing Moderators leaping off rooftops in flawless parkour moves, hurling batons with pinpoint accuracy. One baton struck an offender mid-run, ricocheting off their back before boomeranging neatly into the Moderator's outstretched hand.

"Mind-blowing, isn't it? Their athleticism is REALLY something!" Gainsley added, laughing. *"Like watching a ballet of justice!"*

The footage ended with a drone capturing Moderators in formation, saluting as Gainsley's voice softened into something akin to a warning.
"Your voice matters, as long as you're singing the right tune. So keep that in mind as you share your oh-so-valuable opinions."

The screen lightened again, transitioning to an aerial view of Virtu City, its districts synced in perfect harmony. Drones soared in synchronized patterns, forming shapes and slogans like *"Where Tomorrow Lives."*

Gainsley's voiceover delivered the closing line with the smooth confidence of a salesman who had never failed to close a deal:
"Virtu City: Where tomorrow lives. And so can YOU!"

The screen faded out as the pod's lights dimmed. Scorelord gazed out of the glass, watching the glowing cityscape draw closer, a mix of awe and unease etched across his face.

The Golden Gates gleamed under the artificial sun, a shimmering boundary between the old world and the glittering promise of Virtu City. The gates were translucent yet radiant, their surface refracting the light into cascading rainbows. Holograms of the city's tagline, "The Future is Now," floated just above the ground, drawing cheers from the gathered crowd.

As the gates began to part, a smooth, deep voice reverberated across the plaza:

"Welcome to Virtu City: the pinnacle of innovation, fame, and fortune. Only the chosen may enter. Your golden ticket is your key to a limitless future."

Scorelord, clutching his wristband, stepped forward, his LEDs pulsating with anticipation. He raised his wrist to the scanner at the checkpoint. The device emitted a satisfying chime as it verified his golden ticket.

"ACCESS GRANTED," said a voice from the scanner. "Proceed to the medical bay for onboarding."

Scorelord hesitated when directed to a sleek, white medical booth. The holographic assistant explained in a soothing voice, "To ensure the safety of all residents, vaccinations are mandatory. This procedure is quick, painless, and essential for your journey into the future."

He frowned, his LEDs dimming slightly. A mild suspicion lingered in the back of his mind, but the crowd of winners behind him murmured excitedly, brushing past without hesitation. He clenched his jaw and stepped into the booth.

The process was clinical and efficient. A robotic arm extended, administering the shot with a soft hiss. A brief wave of warmth spread through his arm, and the screen in front of him displayed: "Vaccination complete. Welcome to Virtu City!"

“Well,” he hesitated as he rubbed his arm, “small price to pay for fame and fortune, right?”

Once inside, the city unfolded before him like a living, breathing video game. The streets shimmered with neon, reflecting off polished chrome surfaces. Autonomous drones buzzed overhead, delivering packages, and AR projections danced along the sides of buildings, advertising everything from influencer brands to digital concerts.

Scorelord wandered through the bustling streets, taking it all in. Shops adapted their displays in real-time based on passersby, offering him personalized gear and merchandise that matched his style. A street performer, part human and part bot, drew a crowd with a mesmerizing blend of music and holographic visuals.

Just as he was about to delve deeper into one of the more dazzling districts, a notification buzzed on his wristband:

“Your loft is ready. Please proceed to Prime Square.”

Calling for an Egocab was as simple as tapping a button. Within moments, a sleek, self-driving vehicle pulled up, its doors opening automatically. The interior was lined with glowing panels displaying local suggestions tailored to him.

The ride was smooth and surreal, the city’s towering spires and neon arteries unfolding around him like a dream. When the cab reached his building in Prime Square, the holographic concierge greeted him warmly.

“Welcome, Scorelord. Your loft has been prepared to your specifications. Congratulations on your success, and enjoy your stay in Virtu City.”

The elevator ride to his floor felt infinite, the soft hum of the building's systems a calming backdrop. When the doors open, he was greeted by a space straight out of his wildest dreams.

The loft was a masterpiece of modern design and personal customization. Floor-to-ceiling windows offered an unparalleled view of the city's flamboyant skyline. His preordered gaming rig stood prominently in the corner, complete with VR extensions and a reclining setup that looked more like a starship's command chair. Shelves filled with collectibles he'd longed for. Limited editions, signed items, even some things he hadn't ordered—lined the walls.

The automated kitchen was already synced to his preferences, a drink dispenser glowing faintly with the ingredients for his favorite energy cocktail. Even the lighting adjusted to his mood, soft and dynamic, casting the perfect ambiance.

As he wandered through the space, marveling at every detail, something on the wall caught his eye. A rolled-up poster sat waiting on a sleek black table. Curious, he unrolled it.

The design was bold and striking. Against the city's glowing skyline, the words stood out:

"The Future Isn't What It Used to Be."

He stared at it, LEDs dimming slightly as he absorbed its significance. It felt like a message, though from whom or for what, he couldn't say.

He carefully pinned it above his gaming rig before settling into his command chair.

As the city glowed behind him and the stars peeked through the artificial haze, he booted up his stream. His voice, smooth and confident, echoed through the room.

"Alright, Virtu City." He said, hitting his vape in satisfaction. "We bout' to show'em how Gen Wasted does it."

EPISODE 2
GET READY WITH ME

Virtu City 2062

The moment Auris opened her eyes, the loft responded.

"`Good morning, Auris. Time to Rise and monetize!`" Lumi's charismatic voice chimed, activating the loft's systems.

Her faceID synced with the environment, triggering a cascade of automated tasks. Ambient lights adjusted to a soft, flattering glow. Holographic panels along the walls displayed her morning stats:

> 👤**Followers**: 1.2M (+3,874)
> 📶**Trending**: #MorningGlow
> ✨**Engagement**: Rate: 91%

Her bed folded seamlessly into the wall, while the heated floors adjusted to her preferred temperature. The lighting subtly guided her toward the bathroom, and her streaming drone clicked on, silently hovering to capture her first moments.

"Let's make today iconic," she murmured with a soft smile, gliding into her morning routine. Auris stepped into the shower pod, greeted by a soft mist and holographic panels displaying ads, trending music videos, and nostalgic movie clips. The water adjusted instantly to her ideal temperature, and a bottle of EgoSkin™ NanoFoam glowed on the shelf.

"Glow-time!" she said to the drone, holding up the cleanser. Her voice shifted effortlessly into promo mode.
"This NanoFoam is my secret weapon. It exfoliates, hydrates, AND keeps your skin camera-ready. Use my code AURIS10 for 10% off!"

She sang along to a trending track playing on one screen, her voice flawless. Her chat feed in her lenses lit up:

@Ninetails: "How does she look THIS good in the morning??"

@castleofmermaids: "Bought NanoFoam because of her. Obsessed!"

When the screen switched to a commercial for a classic rom-com, Auris laughed.
"Oh, the nostalgia! Should we do a watch party tonight, loves?"

As she rinsed off, Lumi's voice chimed in:
"`Engagement rate increased by 3.1%`."

"Not bad for a shower," Auris said with a grin.

In the kitchen, the culinator spit out a bowl of +1Up granola and a Matcha Tea Smoothie, arranged like a work of art. The holographic labels pulsed sporadically, designed for the perfect promo moment.

"Breakfast time, babes!" Auris said, lifting the smoothie toward the drone. "This NanoBoost Glow Smoothie by HyprThirst is my go-to. Packed with flavor, nutrients and most importantly, aesthetics—Use AURIS10 for a discount!" She took a bite of the granola, smiling at the camera.

“Breakfast isn’t just a meal—it’s content. Don’t forget to tag me when you try it!”

Her chat feed exploded with emojis:

@Globalpigeon: “How does she make eating look so glamorous??”

@space-junk: “Just ordered that smoothie 🥤 NEED it!”

The loft guided her to her wardrobe pod, which unfolded holographically to display outfit options.
“Soft/Tech/Chic today,” she mused, selecting a sleek dark chrome jacket to contrast the neon accents. Her fans voted on her outfit. Her EgoPod arrived and she headed out to school.

Virtu Academy: Where Education Meets Entertainment

The campus building shimmered with digital brilliance, projecting student rankings and trending lessons across its glowing exterior. Inside, classrooms doubled as production studios, complete with ring lights, drones, and soundproof booths.

Today’s algorithmic math class was taught through an augmented reality dance challenge. Auris performed flawlessly, narrating her moves for the stream.
“Math is just choreography for the brain, loves. Stay in rhythm!”

The bell chimed, releasing a flood of students into Virtu Academy’s pristine hallways. The synchronized sounds of footsteps and quiet chatter filled the space, accompanied by the distant buzz of monitoring drones. Auris strolled out of her math class, effortlessly blending into the flow, her polished aura commanding just enough attention.
A sharp, panicked voice broke the rhythm.

"I—I WAS HACKED! YOU HAVE TO BELIEVE ME!"

A group of students turned toward the commotion. Two Virtu Moderators loomed over a boy near the lockers, the glowing cuffs already locking onto his wrists. The boy's movements were frantic, their face flushed with fear.

"***Unauthorized activity detected,***" one Moderator droned, its voice cold and precise. "***Violation of Virtu Academy's integrity protocol. Compliance is mandatory.***"

Auris slowed her pace, her eyes narrowing. She recognized them immediately—*Kye*. They went back years, a friendship that had faded as her life in Virtu City became increasingly curated. Seeing them now, disheveled and cornered, was jarring.

Her chat feed exploded with laughing emojis:

@MissOverki11: "DAAMN, Virtu Mods are SAVAGE 👮‍♂️🤖"

@AncientAlyx: "Community Guidelines ain't no joke‼️"

"Kye," she said under her breath, the name solidifying her resolve.

Without hesitation, she stepped forward. "Wait a second!" Her voice carried over the murmur of the crowd, halting the Moderators mid-action.

The boy's head snapped up, his wide, panicked eyes meeting hers. Relief and disbelief flickered across his face.

"I know them—I mean—*him*. I know *him*," Auris said, quickly correcting herself casually enough to maintain control. "He's my friend. I was literally *just* in class with him. You're definitely harassing the wrong person. Or do all influents just *look the same* to you?"

The Moderators turned their lenses toward her, scanning her with a discreet hum. She could feel the weight of their calculation: her influence against their protocols.

"Please check your system again," she added, tilting her head as if waiting to prove them wrong. She was totally bluffing, but it worked.

The pause was palpable, tension crackling in the air. Finally, the glowing cuffs retracted with a mechanical click. "***Acknowledged***," one Moderator stated. They released Kye and stepped back, their lenses dimming as they moved away. "***Move Along.***"

The hallway's buzz returned, students whispering and moving along as though the moment were already fading.

Kye stumbled forward, rubbing his wrists. He stared at Auris, his voice trembling as they said, "You...didn't have to do that."

"Of course I did," she replied, her polished smile softening into something more genuine. "What happened anyway?"

"I was uhh—hacked..." Kye muttered, their eyes darting nervously toward the retreating Moderators.

Auris raised an eyebrow but let the lie slide. "Hacked, huh? Sounds like someone needs to tighten their security." Her tone shifted effortlessly into promo mode, her posture straightening as her streaming drone hovered closer.

"And speaking of security," she continued, addressing the camera now, "have you heard of Egolock? Protect your data, your reputation, and your peace —and with my exclusive discount code: AURIS20, you'll get 20% off! Because the internet should be a safe place for everyone!"

The crowd chuckled, the tension in the hallway dissolving into casual amusement. Kye glanced at her, a flicker of surprise and gratitude crossing their face.

"Thanks, Auris," they mumbled, still uneasy but visibly relieved. "I owe you."

"Big time," she said with a smirk, stepping back into the flow of students.

As she walked away, Lumi's quiet whir broke the moment. "A commendable act, Auris," it chirped. "Would you like to record this for your engagement metrics?"

"No, Lumi," she replied sharply, glancing over her shoulder one last time at Kye. Her mind buzzed with questions, but for now, she let them simmer beneath her polished exterior as she hopped in an EgoPod and made her way down the block to her next location.

Streamsphere was alive with buzzing drones and glowing cubicles, each one a self-contained production hub. Creators moved in controlled chaos, filming live streams, tweaking content, and finalizing sponsorships.

Auris's arrival was met with hushed whispers and glances. As she set up her space, a fellow influent leaned over the divider with a grin.

"Valleywood! When's our collab happening? Fans keep spamming me about it."

Without missing a beat, Auris replied, "*When are you gonna stop using dead trends, Xyli*?."

Xyli gasped in mock offense. "Ouch! Someone's feeling spicy today."

From a nearby cubicle, Verica chimed in. "Spicy because she's breaking engagement records, Xy! She's got the right to flex!"

Auris shrugged mid-smirk. "Don't hate the influencer, Hate the Algorithm."

The playful banter rippled across the studio, drawing chuckles from nearby creators. Streamsphere was competitive, but Auris knew how to keep it lighthearted while still owning the spotlight. After wrapping up her product review streams, she shut down her cubicle and headed home for the night.

Back at her loft, Auris ended her stream after a quick toast to her fans. The culinator plated her dinner, every dish voted on by her followers earlier in the day.

As the loft dimmed, Auris activated the hologram of her parents. Their warm smiles filled the room, and she melted into the comfort of their presence.

"Mom! Dad!" Her voice was softer now, carrying the weight of the day.

"Hi, sweetheart," her mother said warmly.

"You look radiant, as always," her father added.

"Thanks," Auris said, her voice faltering slightly. "I've had such a great week. I aced my math class, hit 1.2 million followers, AND my smoothie promo boosted sales by 15%. Can you believe it?"
Her parents listened attentively, their expressions glowing with pride.
"That's amazing, sweetheart," her mother said. "You're doing incredible things."

"I know, but..." Auris hesitated, her voice dropping. "I miss you. I feel like I haven't seen you in forever."

Her mother's face softened. "We miss you too, love. But we're so proud of everything you're building."

Her father nodded. "Soon, sweetheart. We *promise*."

The holograms lingered, as if they had all the time in the world, before gently fading away. Auris sat in the quiet glow of the loft, her eyes misting briefly before she shook it off.

As she prepared for bed, a notification pinged on her display: "**RESET Recalibration Spa. Mandatory attendance scheduled next week**."

Auris swiped it away, smiling faintly.
"Not tonight," she murmured, sinking into bed, utterly content with her perfectly curated life.

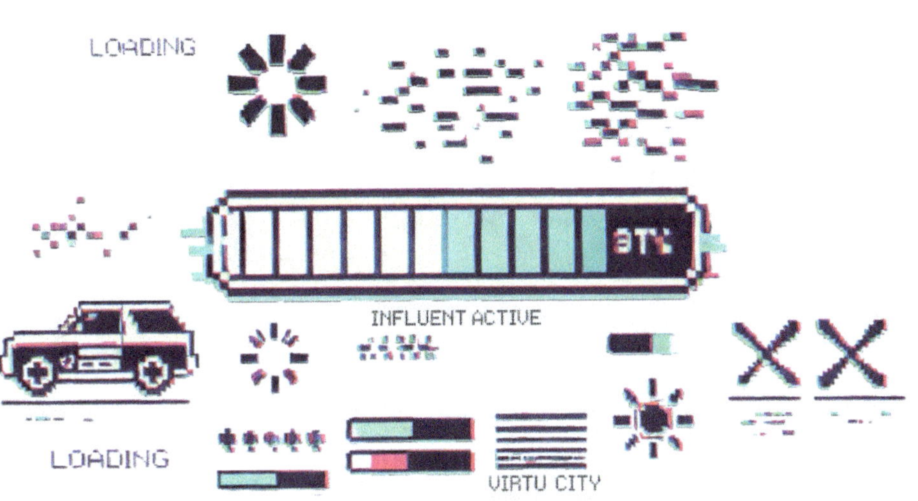

EPISODE 3
TEKSPIRACY

Kwō's room was chaos personified. Tangled wires spilled over the edge of his desk, snaking across the floor like vines from a technological jungle. Old computer towers whined in defiance of their obsolescence, jury-rigged to life by the sheer force of his ingenuity. The air smelled of hot circuits and stale energy drinks, the byproducts of his late-night tinkering.

Kwō was sprawled across his creaky swivel chair, his feet propped on an overturned storage crate. He stared at the screen in front of him, where his live-stream feed flickered to life. His messy hair caught the glow of his monitors, and a half-eaten protein bar balanced precariously on the corner of his desk.

"Top of the top, Tek-heads," he said, his voice rough from sleep but tinged with excitement. The chat window on the side of the screen exploded with greetings:
@BlackPit: "*bro looks like he just rose from the tech cemetery!* ☠️"

"Funny," Kwō retorted with a smirk. "I can't even front. I spent half the night salvaging a stabilizer from a fried fusion powered device. Got it running, though. And speaking of graveyards…" He clicked over to a grainy map of the decayed Silicon Valley, zooming in on an unmarked cluster

of crumbling buildings. "Let's talk about EgoCorp and *The Terminal.*"
The chat blew up again:

@TheComicGamer: *Ooooh, he's going there today??" "Finally some REAL conspiracy talk!" "Careful, dude, they're watching."*

Kwō leaned in, lowering his voice like he was sharing a forbidden secret. "We all know Virtu City's the golden ticket for influencers and tech royalty. But what about the skeletons in their closet? I'm talking about The Terminal—the so-called 'industrial district.' No access, no tours, no press. And guess what? No one comes back out."

The comments were fast and furious now.
@FrostDelx: *"They're cloning people in there!" "Bet it's a RESET factory." "Watch your back, Kwō."*

"I always do," he replied, cutting the stream. "Yall, stay tuned. Time to dig."

The door creaked open, and Kwō's grandmother stuck her head inside. Her short curls were streaked with gray, and her eyes, sharp and knowing, zeroed in on him. "Boy, you've been glued to that chair for hours. You eaten yet?"

Kwō spun around, grinning sheepishly. "I'm good, Gramma."

She raised an eyebrow. "That stream ain't gon' keep this old house running. We're low on food. You know that replicator's still acting up. And those panels for the solar grid? Don't forget those."

Kwō sighed but nodded, reaching for his satchel. "I got it, I got it. I'll swing by the tech graveyard today."

“And don’t just bring home junk,” she added, her tone light but pointed. “Last time, I had to remind you this isn’t one of your little science experiments.”

Kwō kissed her cheek as he passed, grabbing an energy bar from the counter. “Love you, Gramma.”

“Love you too. Be careful out there, Kwō,” she called after him. “And don’t go poking your nose where it doesn’t belong.”

He paused at the door, smirking. “Where’s the fun in that?”

Kwō stepped outside into the worn streets of Silicon Valley. The remnants of a once-thriving tech empire loomed around him—buildings half-standing, their glass facades cracked and stained, like monuments to a forgotten era. Drones buzzed lazily overhead, their low hum blending with the distant clatter of scavengers picking through debris.

His satchel slung over one shoulder, Kwō headed toward the outskirts of the tech graveyard, his mind already racing with possibilities. This was his world—a world of broken dreams and discarded tech, where every piece of junk could hold the key to something bigger.

“Let’s see what secrets you’re hiding today,” he mused under to himself, his footsteps crunching on the cracked pavement.

As I Walk Through The Valley of The Shadow Of Tech

The late morning sun cut through the haze of Silicon Valley’s dilapidated skyline. What was once the beating heart of technological transformation was now a sprawling graveyard of abandoned buildings and forgotten dreams. Skyscrapers stood like hollowed-out monuments, their surfaces pockmarked with decay. Rusted drones clattered aimlessly in the distance, scavenging for scraps of value in a city that had none left.

Kwō weaved through the ruins, his camera rolling as he narrated for himself. "Look at this place," he murmured, his voice laced with discontent as he scanned the rubble. "This was where the world changed—where we built the future. And now it's all just trash."

He reached an overgrown tech cemetery, where mountains of discarded gadgets piled up like the remnants of a technological apocalypse. Kwō rummaged through the debris, finding a few broken stabilizers and a half-functional panel for the food replicator. The tech graveyard was unusually quiet. Kwō crouched next to a busted replicator, its insides a tangled mess of scorched wires and corroded metal. His gloves, frayed from years of scavenging, poked at the machinery, searching for anything remotely functional.

"Come on, give me *something*," he gritted, pulling out his multitool. He pried open a panel, only to find rust and dust staring back at him. "Ugh, useless."

The few scavengers still lingering nearby eyed him with mild curiosity but kept their distance. Kwō had earned a reputation as the weird tech kid who always seemed one discovery away from either striking gold or blowing himself up.

After hours of digging, his satchel was still nearly empty—just a few odds and ends that barely qualified as useful. He slung it back over his shoulder and trudged out of the graveyard, muttering under his breath.

"Mission failed," kicking a stray piece of scrap metal. It clanged against the pavement, echoing in the silence. "stupid scavengers *always* get first dibs on the good shit."

The sun hung low in the sky now, casting long shadows over the crumbling streets. Kwō wandered aimlessly, frustration boiling under his skin. His mind replayed his *Tekspiracy* stream earlier that morning, the excitement in his subscribers' comments. *What if I really did bite off more than I can chew?* he thought. *No leads, no tech... Just another wasted day.*

Just as he turns to walk away a feint gleam catches his eye. It's a piece from an old electric transport pod. The gleam fades to reveal a logo that reads "EGOCORP". His thoughts immediately wandered back to the questions he couldn't shake. "The Terminal," he whispered, as though saying it aloud would conjure answers. "You're hiding something!"

As the sun dipped below the horizon, the streets began to take on an unfamiliar, eerie quality. Kwō realized he'd wandered farther than he ever had before. The cracked pavement gave way to uneven cobblestones, and the buildings around him looked older, more weathered, as though they'd been abandoned for decades.

"Great," he muttered. "Now I'm officially lost."

He pulled out his holographic map, he dropped the device, shattering a component. "SHIT!" He yelled in frustration. He picks up the device. The display flickered, but refused to load. The streets weren't even marked anymore. A sinking feeling crept into his stomach, but he shook it off. *Just find your way back, Kwō. No big deal.*

Then he heard it—a noise, almost like the static buzz of an old arcade machine coming to life. It was faint, barely audible, but it tugged at his curiosity. He followed the sound, weaving through narrow alleys and past boarded-up windows. The air felt heavier here, charged with something he couldn't quite name.

Finally, he turned a corner and froze. Before him stood a deteriorated building with a faded sign barely clinging to its frame. The words were just barely legible, the neon letters long since burnt out and Kwō didn't bother trying to make it out. The hum was louder now, emanating from somewhere inside.

"What the hell…?" Kwō whispered, stepping closer. The entrance was an open alley between two decaying buildings, both leaning inward as if they might collapse at any moment. His instincts screamed at him to turn back, but something about the place drew him in.

The First Encounter

As he stepped into the alley, a figure emerged from the shadows. Kwō's heart nearly stopped. The man was unlike anyone he'd ever seen—decked out in a mix of retro gaming gear and futuristic tech, with a VR headset slung around his neck and an old-school arcade joystick strapped to his wrist like a gauntlet, surrounded by a a forcefield of what appeared to be vape clouds.

The man leaned casually against the wall, a smirk tugging at the corner of his mouth. His eyes gleamed with a mischievous light as he sized Kwō up.

"You're searching for something more, aren't you?" the man said, his voice low and raspy.

Kwō instinctively took a step back, his pulse racing. "Who… who are you?"

The man chuckled, pushing off the wall and stepping closer. "A better question: Who are *you*, kid? And how far are you willing to go to find what you're looking for?"

Kwō narrowed his eyes, gripping his satchel tighter. Kwō took 2 more cautious steps back, his nerves on fire. His eyes darted between the strange man and the dim alley, his gut screaming at him to leave, but curiosity kept his feet planted. "Look, I don't know what you want, but I'm—"
"EGOCORP DRONES!" the man suddenly yelled, his voice sharp and urgent. He pointed frantically over Kwō's shoulder, his face contorted in mock terror.

"What?!" Kwō spun around instinctively, his heart racing, his gaze searching for the imminent threat. But the alley was empty, just the flicker of a dying billboard, graffiti and old advertisements on the walls. "Where? I don't see—"

Before he could finish, something sharp jabbed into the side of his neck.

"AHH! WHAT THE—" Kwō slapped his hand to his neck, stumbling back. His eyes widened in disbelief as he saw the man withdraw a now-empty syringe, a devilish smirk playing on his lips.

"Gotcha," the man said, spinning the syringe between his fingers like a cheap party trick.

"WHAT THE FUCK?!" Kwō roared, his voice cracking in panic. He stumbled forward, clutching the wall as the world around him began to twist and bend. "What did you do to me?!"

The man said nothing, his grin widening as he casually stepped back into the shadows, watching Kwō with unnerving calm. Kwō's vision blurred, the alley warping into something unreal. Neon lights bled into one another, streaking like wet paint on a canvas. The ground rippled beneath his feet, throwing him off balance. "Oh shit... Oh shit, no... what the fffhh—What... is... this?"

His legs gave out, and he crumpled to the ground, the rough asphalt beneath him feeling both too real and not real enough. The shadows of the alley seemed alive, curling and twisting around him, while the walls vibrated with colors he couldn't name.

He tried to crawl away, but his limbs felt heavy, sluggish, like they weren't even his. His breathing hitched, panic clawing at his chest. The man's figure loomed above him, a silhouette backlit by the swirling chaos of Kwō's unraveling reality.

"Y-you…" Kwō's voice came out garbled, his tongue heavy in his mouth. "You…fffuckin… psycho…"

"See you in the lobby." the man said, blowing the smoke in Kwō's face.

And then everything went black.

"Time to level up," the man whispered, his voice echoing in Kwō's mind as the world around him spiraled into chaos.

When Kwō's vision cleared, he was strapped to a chair. Neon lights blinked around him, casting eerie shadows on the walls. The sound of old arcade machines, game jingles and computer fans filled the air, screens flickering with static and cryptic symbols.

He yanked at the restraints, panic setting in. "What the hell is this? Where am I? HELLO?!"

A voice answered from the darkness. "Ready for Level 2, kid?"

Kwō squinted as the man stepped into view, the light catching the faint scars on his face and the worn patches on his jacket. “Level 2?! What the fuck are you talkin’ about? where am I—and *who are youuu??!!.*

“Lord’s the name. Scoring’s the game. And boy, do I have a score to settle.”

Kwō’s eyes widened. “No way… You’re supposed to be *dead*! The news announced it. They showed the ceremony on VNN… I saw the documentary!”

“Yeah, ” Scorelord smirked. “That’s what they told everyone. And I’d rather it stay that way… than the alternative.”

Kwō swallowed hard. “What’s the alternative?”

Scorelord’s expression darkened. “***RESET***.”

He reached into his jacket and pulled out a small, weathered flash drive, tossing it into Kwō’s lap. “Here. Consider this a breadcrumb. Now run along, kid. You’ve got work to do.”

“What the-What’s this?” Kwō demands while looking down in confusion at the drive. By the time he looks back up, Scorelord has seemingly vanished. His presence is replaced with a carnivalesque backdrop of custom crafted rigs , advanced arcade cabs, graffiti, memorabilia and a sign above it all that reads ‘***GAME ON***’ in a bold, bright red font.

“Everything you’ve been looking for,” Scorelord replied, his voice reverberating in the distance. “Or nothing.”

Before Kwō could protest, his restraints released, and he fell forward. The room swirled again, the neon lights dissolving into a dizzying haze. He stumbled out of the building, clutching the flash drive like a lifeline, the world around him warping and twisting as he made his way back home.

Kwō staggered through the fractured streets, every step feeling like the ground might dissolve beneath him. The injection still sizzled in his veins, not pain exactly, but something foreign—an electric buzz crawling through his nervous system. His surroundings pulsed with life, though not the kind he recognized. The cracked pavement shimmered, fracturing into pixelated kaleidoscopic veins that snaked toward the horizon.

The distant cries of feral scavengers tangled with the low hiss of static in his mind. Shapes moved in his peripheral vision, flickering like broken holograms. He whipped his head around to see—but nothing stayed solid long enough for his brain to latch onto. A billboard advertising *VirtuCoin* splintered into fractals, its letters rearranging themselves: **RESET. REBOOT. ERASE.**

Kwō's breath came fast and shallow. His hands clutched his satchel like a lifeline. "It's not real. It's not real. It's not real," he whispered, the words more mantra than truth.

But the shadows didn't care about mantras. They crept toward him, stretching like a datamoshed liquid ink across the walls. He caught the glint of scavenger masks through the swirling distortion—jagged edges, cracked visors, reflections warped like funhouse mirrors.

They're watching me. The thought hit him like a gut punch. He gripped his satchel tighter, his fingers digging into the fabric. *They know I have the drive. They know.*

A laugh—low, wet, and guttural—rippled through the static. Or maybe it didn't. Maybe it was all in his head.

"Not today," Kwō hissed, shoving the thought aside as he ducked into a narrow alley. The shadows closed in tighter here, but it was better than being exposed.

Pulling out his glitchy holo-GPS, he prayed it would cooperate. The screen spasmed, then blinked to life, its holographic blue arrow trembling like it, too, was scared of what lay ahead.

“Thank you,” he muttered, following the flickering guide like it was the last light in the world.

The trippy effects of injection subsided and the scavengers faded into the background, though the paranoia clung to him like static. Each step felt heavier, as if the air thickened with every corner he turned. The once-familiar streets twisted into a maze of broken facades and shattered windows, the ruins of Silicon Valley casting jagged shadows that danced and writhed.

When his house finally came into view, he let out a shuddering breath. He swiped his keycard at the lock, the scanner pausing just long enough to make his stomach drop before it clicked open.

He slipped inside, pressing the door closed behind him as if the whole world were trying to follow him in.

“Safe,” he whispered. The word fell like a stone in the silence. It was a little too quiet.

Suddenly, The kitchen light flared to life, and Kwō froze. His grandmother stood in the doorway, framed by the soft glow of the outdated smart fixtures. Her arms crossed, her eyebrow arched—a pose he knew all too well.
“And where exactly have you been?” she asked, her voice sharp enough to cut through the fog still clouding his mind.

Kwō blinked, his brain scrambling to assemble a coherent excuse. “I was, uh… scavenging. You know, for parts.” He gestured weakly to his satchel, which hung from his shoulder like a dead weight.

"Scavenging?" Her gaze flicked over his disheveled appearance, lingering on the streaks of grime on his face and the slight tremor in his hands. "And you needed to look like you ran through a warzone to do it?"
"It was… competitive," Kwō said, forcing a weak smile.

She stared at him, unimpressed. "Uh-huh. And why are you sweating like you just outran a drone swarm?"

"It's hot outside?" he tried, though the answer felt ridiculous even to him.

"At night?" she shot back, her eyebrow rising higher.

Kwō's shoulders slumped. "Okay, fine. I got a little carried away, alright? But I'm fine. Everything's fine."

Her gaze lingered on him for a beat longer, and for a moment, he thought she'd press further. But then she sighed, shaking her head.

"Fine. But don't go bringing any more trouble into this house. This old place has enough problems without you adding to them."

"Got it. No trouble. Zero trouble," Kwō promised, already backing toward the stairs. "Goodnight, Gramma!"
"Goodnight," she muttered, her tone half-warning, half-exhausted as she turned back toward the kitchen.

In the sanctuary of his room, Kwō slammed the door shut and collapsed into his chair. His rig blinked patiently at him, the only thing in his life that didn't ask questions. He pulled out the flash drive, its soft blue glow illuminating his trembling fingers.

"Alright," he whispered, sliding it into the port. "Let's see what you've got."

The rig whirred to life, and his monitors exploded in a frenzy of data. Strings of code spilled across the screens, endless and incomprehensible. Fractured audio clips burst through his speakers—distorted voices, static-laced screams, and something that sounded disturbingly like laughter.

Images flashed by in rapid succession: blueprints of humanoid bots, their sleek designs annotated with cryptic notes; encoded files marked with the EgoLabs insignia; corrupted messages with fragmented phrases like *"Forever Influencers"* and *"Protocol in progress."*

Then the EgoCorp logo appeared, its cold, clinical design filling every screen.

"RESET Protocol?" Kwō muttered, the words feeling heavier than they should.

The lights flickered, the room plunging into darkness before the monitors flared even brighter. The whispers grew louder, overlapping until they became a deafening roar.

"Protocol compromised… subject anomaly detected… integration failure" The data became a blur, scrolling too fast for his eyes to follow. The visuals bled together, the symbols twisting into shapes that seemed to crawl off the screens. His chest tightened as the world spun around him, the edges of his vision darkening.

"Yo…What the…" he gasped, gripping the edges of his desk. "what *is thiiiiiis*?—". He's horrified and quickly yanks the drive out of the port.

The pounding in his head drowned out the static, the whispers, everything. His limbs went limp, his body giving up under the weight of the day's chaos in addition to whatever Scorelord injected into him. His breathing slowed, his eyes fluttering shut as he slumped forward onto the desk.

The screens continued their relentless glow, the RESET logo burning into his closed eyelids. His satchel fell to the floor, its contents spilling out unnoticed.

The last thing he saw before sleep claimed him was the fragmented, flickering message: **"Welcome to Level 2"**

SILICON VALLEY - 2062

EPISODE 4
Respawn

A Matrix Kinda Morning

Kwō's head lifted slowly from the desk, the imprint of the keyboard etched into his cheek. His monitors glowed in the dim light, casting jagged shadows that felt sharper than usual. The room was silent except for the whir of his rig, its steady rhythm almost soothing—until it wasn't.

The main screen flickered. Once. Twice. Then, in stark green text, the words appeared:

"Wake Up, Kw0..."

He blinked, his chest tightening. The message lingered for just a moment too long, as if it were waiting for him to respond. Before he could move, the screen flashed, and the text dissolved into the ether, leaving him staring at his own stunned reflection in the dark glass.

"Okaaay...What the hell was that?" he muttered, rubbing the sleep from his eyes.

For a moment, he considered plugging the drive back in, demanding answers from the mess of encrypted files. But his stomach growled, hunger snapping him back to reality—or whatever *this* life was. He stumbled to his feet, shaking off the fog of the previous night as he made his way downstairs.

The kitchen greeted him with the scent of waffles, clearly processed but still oddly comforting. Gramma was at the table, her tablet balanced precariously in one hand as she flipped through something on the screen. Her outdated culinator rattling on the counter, its nozzle retracting as it struggles to finish the last waffle.

"Morning, baby," Gramma said without looking up. "You look like you fought off the scavengers single-handed last night."

Kwō groaned, collapsing into a chair. "Feels like it."

Gramma reached over, grabbing the freshly printed waffle and dropping it onto a plate. She slid it across the table with a proud smile. "Thanks for finding the parts for this old thing. Your waffles are hot off the press."

Kwō snorted softly, picking up his fork. "Literal press. This thing's practically a museum piece."

"Better than scavenged toast," she said, sitting down across from him. She sipped her tea, watching him carefully as he dug into the waffle. "So, what's got you looking so twitchy? You eatin' like you got somewhere to be."

Kwō hesitated, swirling his fork through the printed syrup pool on his plate. "Just… tryna keep busy."

Gramma's eyebrow arched. "Uh-huh. And you just happen to 'keep busy' after spendin the whole night with that dungeon of a computer rig upstairs?"

"I—" He faltered, caught between honesty and deflection. "It's for my channel—Tekspiracy…A lead."

She sighed, leaning back in her chair. "You're a terrible liar, Kwō. You know that, right?"

He forced a weak chuckle. "Good thing I don't plan on being a spy."

"Or a politician," she said dryly, taking another sip of tea.

They sat in silence for a moment, the faint hum of the food printer filling the air. Finally, Kwō broke the quiet, his voice low and hesitant. "Gramma... you ever feel like—this isn't real? Like... all of this is just a dream?"

Gramma froze, her cup halfway to her lips. A sly smile spread across her face as she set the mug down carefully. "Let me guess. You've been watching *The Matrix*, haven't you?"

Kwō blinked. "The what?"

Gramma laughed, a hearty, almost mischievous sound that filled the small kitchen. "You've never heard of it? Oh, baby, you're missing out. It's about a guy who finds out his whole world's a simulation. Messed me up for weeks the first time I saw it."

"Sounds... interesting," Kwō said slowly. "But no. I've never seen it."

"Well, don't. You'll end up questioning *everything*," she said while chuckling, "Next thing I know, you'll be asking if I'm real."

Kwō smirked, though the question lingered in his mind longer than he cared to admit. Grabbing his hoverboard, the weight of the satchel against his side grounded him as he stood by the door, swiping his keycard against the lock. Gramma appeared in the hallway behind him, her arms crossed and her gaze as sharp as ever.

"You really headin' out again?" she asked, her tone hovering somewhere between curiosity and suspicion. "Since when do you willingly leave the house two days in a row?"

Kwō flashed her a grin. "Just trying to stay productive. Besides, you said you needed cooling parts, right?"

Her eyes narrowed, but a small smile tugged at her lips. "I did…Don't come back without'em."

"Promise," he said, setting his board down gently as it begins to hover, never touching the ground.

"Kwō!" she called after him, her voice cutting through the still.

He paused, glancing back. "Yeah?"

She pointed a finger at him, her expression both stern and affectionate. "Don't do anything stupid. If you get in trouble, remember—I'm the one who's gotta clean up your mess!"

Kwō chuckled, raising a hand in mock salute. "Got it, Gramma."

The door clicked shut behind him, and he let out a slow breath. Gliding away slowly down the street as the sun cast a faint glow over the ruins, and for a moment, everything felt… almost normal. But the weight of the drive in his satchel reminded him that normal was a luxury he couldn't afford anymore.

The Return

The backstreets of Silicon Valley were ripe with decay, each turn blending into another multiplex of crumbling buildings and jagged shadows. Kwō's hoverboard hummed softly beneath him, its faint vibration matching the thrum of his anxious thoughts. The satchel at his side felt heavier with every passing second, the weight of the flash drive inside pulling at him like an anchor.

When the neon glow of *Game On* finally flickered into view, Kwō felt his stomach twist. It was the same hollowed-out ruin he'd walked into before—broken machines, shattered glass, the faint scent of burnt wires—but this time, the air carried a different weight. This wasn't just a hideout anymore. It was the start of something far bigger than him.

He stepped off his hoverboard, tucking it under his arm as he pushed open the door. The sound of broken glass crunching underfoot echoed in the desolate arcade, the flickering neon light casting eerie shadows on the walls.

Scorelord was hunched over a makeshift workstation at the back of the arcade, the glow of a laser tattoo device illuminating his face. He looked up as Kwō approached, smirking faintly.

"Back so soon?" Scorelord said, leaning against the table. "I'm starting to think you like me."

Kwō rolled his eyes, setting his hoverboard down with a clatter. "Don't flatter yourself. I just want answers."

"Answers?" Scorelord said, raising an eyebrow. "You're already holding them." He gestured toward the satchel. "That drive is everything you need."

"Yeah, well, all it's done so far is show me a bunch of cryptic nonsense," Kwō shot back. "If you want me to help you, maybe try explaining what the hell is going on."

Scorelord exhaled, his smirk fading slightly. He gestured for Kwō to sit, but the younger man remained standing, his arms crossed.

“Alright,” Scorelord said. “Let’s start with this.” He pointed to Kwō’s neck. “The injection.”

Kwō’s eyes narrowed. “Yeah, what was that, anyway? Some kind of tracking chip? Or are you just into stabbing people for fun?”

“Neither,” Scorelord said, shaking his head. “The nanobots in that serum temporarily masks your digital ID. To EgoCorp’s scanners, you’re just another NPC now. It’s the only reason you’re not on their radar…For now.”

Kwō’s skepticism didn’t waver. “And the side effects? The trippy hallucinations?”

“Consider it a bonus!” Scorelord says jokingly. “But hey, you’re alive, ain’t ya?”

“Barely,” Kwō muttered. He took a step back, eyeing the laser tattoo device in Scorelord’s hand. “And what’s that for? Another ‘bonus’?”

“This,” Scorelord said, holding up the device, “is your next layer of protection. It’s an encoded tattoo—only detectable by the right people. Scavengers, Deadzone residents, Gen Wasted. To everyone else, it’s invisible.”

Kwō crossed his arms tighter. “Yeah, no thanks. I’ve had enough experiments for one day.”

Scorelord sighed, stepping closer. “Look, I get it. You have no reason to trust me. But this tattoo could mean the difference between life and death. Your call, kid.”

Kwō hesitated, his gaze flicking to the satchel at his side. The drive felt like it was burning a hole through the bag, its mysteries pulling at him relentlessly. He wanted answers—

needed them—and Scorelord seemed to be the only one who could provide them.
"Fine," Kwō said reluctantly, holding out his arm. "But if this thing screws me up, I'm coming back for you."

Scorelord smirked, activating the device. "Duly noted."

The laser hummed softly as Scorelord etched the tattoo onto Kwō's forearm. The lines glowed faintly at first, forming the unmistakable insignia of *Gen Wasted.* Within seconds, the glow faded, leaving nothing but bare skin.

Kwō flexed his fingers, frowning. "What? That's it? Where's the tattoo? Why is It invisible?"

"Oh, I suppose you wanted matching Pokémon tattoos?" Scorelord replies sarcastically, "Sorry to disappoint ya."

"To you, it may look like nothing," he goes on, examining his work. "But to the people who matter? It's unmistakable."

Kwō stared at his arm, still unconvinced. "And if it doesn't work?"

"It will," Scorelord said firmly. "And if it doesn't? Well… you're resourceful. You'll figure it out." Kwō stares blankly, trying to process everything.

HERE'S THE PLAY

Scorelord moved to a cluttered table, pulling out a worn map of the city and spreading it flat. "Alright, here's how it's gonna work. You'll take the underground route to Prime Square. There's a station below the V-Way—a relic from before the city's expansion. Been out of use for decades. It's off the grid now."

Kwō leaned over the map, his brow furrowing. “And from there?”

“Once you’re get to the Prime Square stop, you’ll make your way up to Nikola Station. Blend in, act normal, and follow the crowd. You’ll figure the rest out as you go.”

Kwō frowned, his grip tightening on the satchel. “That’s your plan? Blend in and hope for the best?”

“Pretty much,” Scorelord said, smirking. “You’ve got the drive, the tattoo, and the mask. That’s more than most people get.”

Kwō exhaled slowly, his chest tightening. “And if I don’t make it?”

“You will,” Scorelord said, his tone serious. “Just… *don’t overthink it.”*

Kwō glared at him but said nothing, slipping the satchel over his shoulder. “Alright. Let’s get this over with.”

Scorelord nodded, gesturing toward a hidden stairwell at the back of the arcade. “Train leaves soon. Miss this one and you won’t have another chance for a while.”

The stairwell was dark and narrow, the faint scent of rust and damp concrete clinging to the air. Scorelord led the way, his movements confident despite the treacherous footing. When they reached the bottom, Kwō froze.

The platform was a ghost of what it had once been. Rusted tracks stretched into the darkness, their edges jagged and worn. Faded graffiti covered the walls, and the faint sound of dripping water echoed through the space.
“This is it?” Kwō asked, his voice tinged with disbelief. “This is how I’m getting to Prime Square?”

"Welcome to The Circuit," Scorelord said, grinning. "It ain't pretty, but it'll get ya from point A to point Z."
"See you on the other side," Scorelord follows up, giving him a small nod.

As if on cue, a bullet train rattled into view as it slowed into the forgotten station, its systems echoing through the dim cavern. The patched-together exterior glinted faintly in the sparse light, its sleek, once-futuristic design now marred by rust, dents, and crude graffiti. its body held together by what looked like sheer force of will. Kwō hesitated, eyeing the battered doors as they creaked open, his satchel slung tightly over his shoulder. He glanced back at the stairwell he'd come down moments ago, Scorelord's voice still ringing in his ears. *"You've got a limited window. Don't waste it."*

The train doors hissed open, revealing an empty, flickering interior. The faint smell of burnt wires wafted out. Kwō exhaled, steeling himself as he stepped inside. The doors groaned shut behind him, sealing him into the faintly vibrating cabin.

The interior was a patchwork of salvaged parts and half-functional tech. LED strips flickered sporadically along the walls, their cool white glow contrasting with the warm yellow light from ancient overhead fixtures. Seats were mismatched —some plush and cracked, others cold and metallic.

Screens mounted above the windows displayed broken advertisements, their messages distorted into gibberish. *"VirtuCoin: To Mars..."* one screen blipped, its words glitching into static. *"...Begin your Tomorrow, today."*

Kwō slid into a corner seat, setting his satchel on his lap. The train shuddered as it started moving, the electric hum swelling into a sharp whine before settling into a steady rhythm. He glanced around, his unease growing. It felt like the train itself was alive, groaning with every motion, as though its very existence was an act of rebellion.

The sound of boots against the metallic floor jolted him from his thoughts. Kwō looked up to see a figure emerging from the shadows of the next car. She had fiery red hair streaked with violet and wore a patched leather jacket adorned with glowing tech panels. Her boots were scuffed but sturdy, her eyes sharp and assessing.

"You're new," she said, leaning casually against the doorway. Her voice carried a mix of curiosity and challenge.

Kwō tensed, gripping the satchel. "What gave it away?"

Rune smirked, tilting her head. "The fact that you're clutching that bag like it's your firstborn. Relax. Nobody here's gonna rob you. Not yet, anyway."

Kwō narrowed his eyes, unsure whether she was joking. "Who are you?"

"Rune," she said simply, stepping closer. "And you are…?"

Kwō hesitated. "Just passing through."

"Right," Rune said, her smirk widening. Her gaze flicked briefly to his forearm, where the faint glow of the Gen Wasted insignia pulsed briefly under the flickering lights. Recognition flashed in her eyes, but she didn't comment. Instead, she gestured to the train around them. "So, what do you think of my ride?"

"*Your* ride?" Kwō asked, raising an eyebrow.

Rune nodded. "Yep. Me and my crew keep this relic running. Supposed to be out of order, but here it is…in all its glory. Not bad for something EgoCorp forgot existed, huh?"

Kwō glanced around the cabin, noticing the subtle touches of care amidst the decay—cleaner floors in some spots, patched wiring where sparks might have flown. "Why bother?"

"Let's just say I've got a soft spot for things they want to erase," Rune said, her tone sharp. "And this line? It's freedom.... the people who don't exactly fit into Virtu City's perfect little world...keeps us connected."

Kwō considered her words, his grip on the satchel loosening slightly. "Fair enough."

The train screeched as it slowed into the next station, its brakes protesting against years of neglect. The doors slid open to reveal a platform bathed in dim, flickering light. The sign above read: **"Shadow Falls"**, though parts of the letters had been worn away.

A handful of stragglers shuffled off the train—figures cloaked in tattered jackets and makeshift masks. They moved silently, their faces hidden, their footsteps echoing in the cavernous space. Kwō watched them warily, noting the way they avoided eye contact with anyone still on board.

"They live off-grid," Rune said, breaking the silence. She had moved to stand near the opposite window, watching the figures disappear into the darkness. "Shadow Falls is where Virtu City exiles go when they've had either too much engagement...or not enough."

"Why?" Kwō asked, his curiosity piqued.

"Because it's better than the alternative," Rune replied, her voice cold. "Trust me."

"And what's the alternative?" Kwō asks, his tone dripping with sarcasm before cutting her off and answering his own question before she even gets the chance to. "No, wait. Let me guess. *RESET?"* Everyone on board turns and looks at him as if he just mentioned 'He who shall not not be named'.

Take it as a joke if you want. People aren't the same when they leave that place. Seen it with my own eyes." She says with a sad anger in her eyes. The doors hissed shut, and the train jolted forward, leaving the Shadow Falls station behind.

The train screeched into the abandoned platform, the sound reverberating through the cavernous space like a dying machine. Rusted tracks glinted faintly under dim emergency lights, and crumbling walls were adorned with decades-old graffiti—some faded into obscurity, others recent and jagged, scrawled with desperation:

"They Watch All."
"NEVER RESET."
"FUCK EGOCORP."

THE SOCIAL MEDIA STOCK XCHANGE [SMSX]

Meanwhile, In the throbbing epicenter of Firewall Street, the SMSX is capitalism at its most feral. Traders in suits with tech-embedded fabric are screaming, hopping, literally tearing at each other's sleeves. A deafening bell resounds, electrifying the room. "*Ayo, focus up*!" a youthful and energetic trader named Sp3X bellows, his uncategorizable accent thick with audacity. He's a vision of modern excess in his custom designer attire, blonde hair practically sparkling with the thrill of the hunt.

The floor erupts in a tidal wave of frenetic action. "***To Mars, Baby!! $Martian is outta here!***" shouts a trader, hurling a tablet against a wall, where it disintegrates into digital mist. "***They —rugged us? They fucking rugged us!***" another screams in financial horror. Floating inflatables orbit around the building ready to catch traders launching themselves out of the windows in glee—or despair—who can tell anymore?

"*Boss, BioMint offering three mill for the last Thylacine NFT, backed by legit extinct DNA!*" shouts one of Sp3X's acolytes.

With a smirk that could rival a Bond villain, Sp3X locks eyes on his digital dashboard. "*It's biodiversity in the portfolio, innit? Extinct animals, like the Asian Elephant or the Atlantic Puffin. Future labs might repopulate or maybe splice 'em to make us better, faster, stronger. Cop that and let's moon!*"..... "That Tasmanian Tiger strand goes CRAZY!!!" his AI assistant chimes in, voice and dialect programmed to his preferences. "Good lookin'", he replies, securing the transition while keeping his eye on the '***gas***' fees. As if on cue, a sign illuminates from above:

"Don't Overthink It!"

Kwō stepped off the train hesitantly, his boots hitting the cracked tiles with a dull thud. The air was damp and carried the faint, acrid tang of decayed wiring and stagnant water. This was nothing like the sleek, polished image Virtu City broadcasted to the world.

Rune followed behind him, her boots crunching softly against loose debris. She pointed toward a narrow stairwell partially obscured by fallen beams. "That's your way up. Keep climbing until you can't anymore. You'll hit Nikola Station's lower level."

Kwō squinted at the dark passage, his unease growing. "What about you?"

"Me?" Rune smirked, leaning casually against the train's doorway. "I've got my own stops to make. But don't worry, strays like you always find their way."

Kwō hesitated, glancing at her before turning toward the stairwell. "Why are you helping me?"

Rune's smirk softened, her tone shifting slightly. "Because this city eats people like you alive. And I don't mind throwing a wrench in its gears." She tapped the doorframe, her eyes gleaming. "Good luck, kid."

Before Kwō could respond, the train jolted forward, disappearing into the tunnel with a metallic groan. He stood there for a moment, staring at the empty tracks, the weight of the mission pressing on his chest. The forgotten station was empty, cold and barren. The stairwell was narrow and suffocating, its walls coated in grime and peeling paint. Kwō's flashlight flickered as he climbed, the beam bouncing off rusted pipes and exposed wires. Each step echoed ominously, the sound swallowed by the heavy silence of the forgotten station.

The air grew colder the higher he climbed, his breath visible in the dim light. He gripped the satchel tightly, the faint pulse of the Gen Wasted insignia on his forearm a small comfort in the oppressive darkness. After what felt like an eternity, the stairwell opened into a vast underground chamber.

This was Nikola Station's forgotten level—a graveyard of abandoned machinery and derelict trains. Massive support beams crisscrossed overhead, their metal frames corroded but still holding the weight of the city above.

Holographic panels flickered sporadically along the walls, their messages garbled and eerie:

"Efficiency is Everything."
"Monetize Your Mind!"

Kwō moved cautiously, the faint hum of distant machinery. The sound of dripping water echoed faintly, guiding him toward the next set of stairs, accompanied by the occasional skitter of unseen critters.

The second staircase led him up to Nikola Station's lower platform. The contrast was jarring. Where the abandoned station had been cold and lifeless, this level was alive with the buzzing of activity. The polished floors gleamed under bright, artificial light, the walls were alive with digital art and memorabilia from renowned artists and tech pioneers, Tesla coil inspired themes and holographic billboards loomed overhead, advertising EgoCorp's latest products.

Commuters moved with unsettling precision, their faces blank and unreadable. Drones zipped overhead, scanning the crowd silently, their glowing eyes tracking every movement. Kwō kept his head down, gripping his satchel as he merged into the flow of foot traffic.

Above him, a massive screen displayed a looping ad for Virtu City:

"VIRTU CITY: Where Tomorrow Lives."

Kwō shuddered, his grip tightening on the satchel as he moved toward a huge brutalist, enigmatic, almost occultic statue of a woman at the base of the inclinators leading up to the main level. The glowing nameplate simply reading 'The Mother'. "must be someone important." He thinks to himself. The inclinators hummed softly as they carried Kwō upward, the sleek glass walls offering glimpses of the city beyond. Towering skyscrapers came into view, their neon accents glowing against the darkening sky. A Holographic disclaimer pops up, the message crisp and unnervingly cheerful:
"Don't overthink it!"

The words pulsed brightly, their simplicity cutting through the city's chaotic energy like a command. Kwō stared at the slogan, his jaw tightening. It wasn't just a message—it was a warning.

As he climbed closer to the surface level, Virtu City unfolded before him in all its surreal glory. Monstrous buildings loomed overhead, their surfaces alive with shifting holograms and Ads—Ads *Everywhere*. Streets below bustled with autonomous vehicles and streams of pedestrians, their movements choreographed like a living machine.

The weight of it all pressed against Kwō's chest. He wasn't just entering a city—he was stepping into a world designed to consume him. The inclinators finally reached the top, depositing Kwō onto a platform bathed in the electric glow of Virtu City. He stood there for a moment, staring at the sprawling metropolis before him, his breath catching in his throat.

"No turning back now," he muttered, gripping the satchel tightly as he stepped forward into the chaos. Kwō's steps were uneven, his breaths shallow as the pressure of Prime Square bore down on him. The luminous chaos of the city swirled around him, every billboard and slogan hammering into his psyche:

RESET WELLNESS RECALIBRATION SPA
A WHOLE NEW YOU.

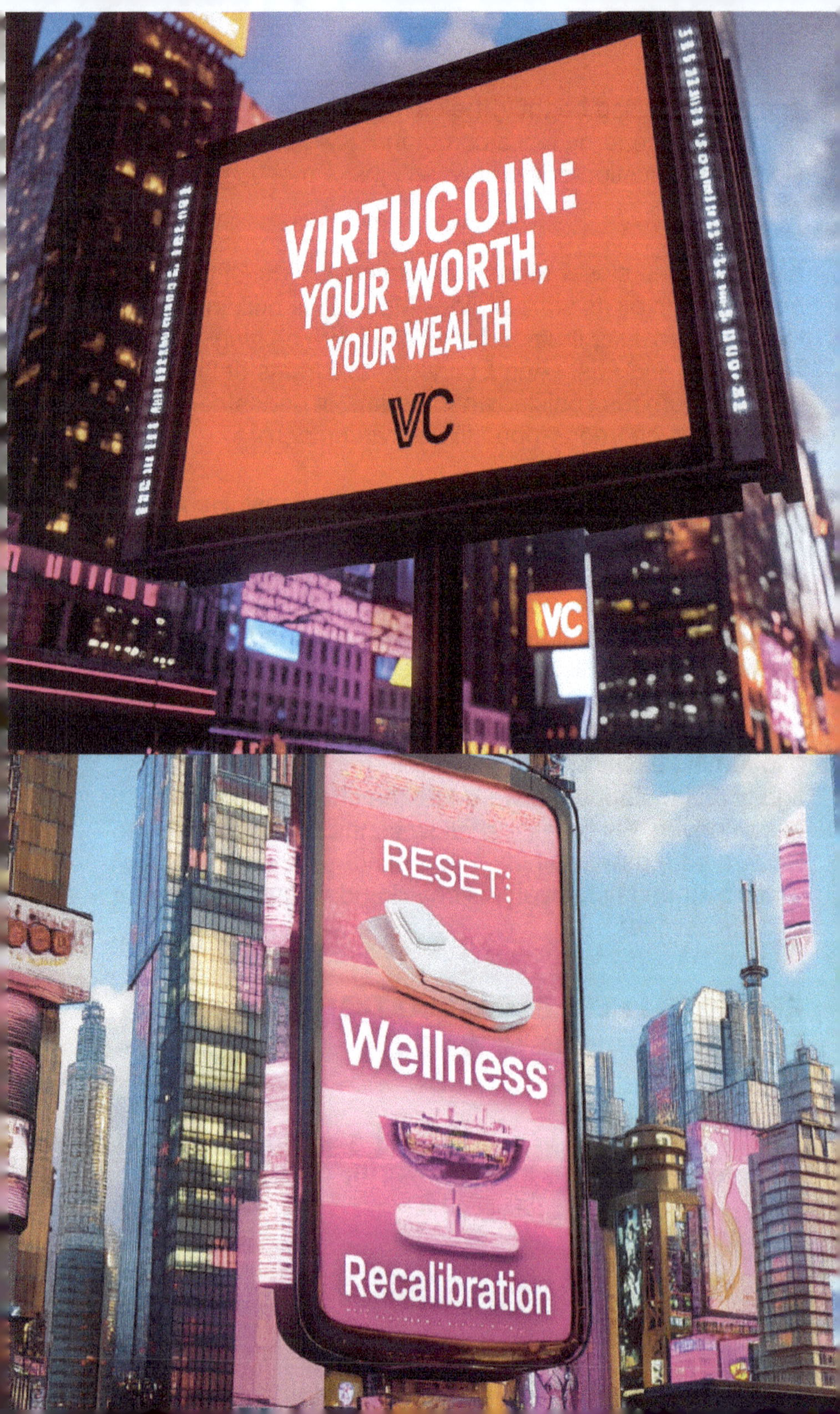
VIRTUCOIN:
YOUR WORTH,
YOUR WEALTH
VC
VC
RESET:
Wellness
Recalibration

EPISODE 5

Collision Course

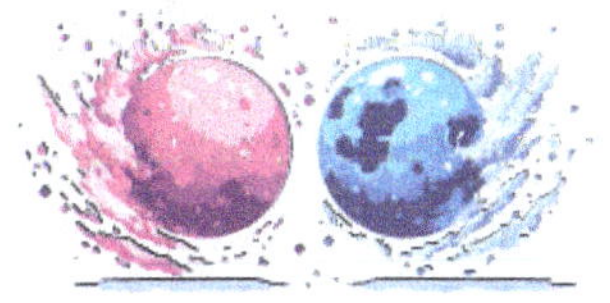

The static buzzing in his Kwō's ear offered no comfort. Scorelord's voice, garbled and distorted, was little more than background noise now. Kwō clutched his satchel tighter, his eyes darting to the drones hovering above, their glowing lenses sweeping over the crowd.

He turned the corner too quickly and— BAM!

"*Hey*—watch where you're going!"

The voice snapped him back into reality as he collided with someone, the force jolting his satchel against his side. Kwō stumbled, barely keeping his balance.

Auris stood in front of him, straightening her jumpsuit with a quick, practiced motion. Her holo-enhanced outfit shimmered under the city's lights, every inch of her appearance curated for perfection. Lumi hovered at her shoulder, its sleek lens focused on her like an ever-present spotlight.

"Reconnecting… Streaming now live to 8.7 million viewers!" Lumi chirped, its cheerful tone cutting through the tension.

Auris' irritation flashed briefly across her face before she smoothed it over with a neutral expression. She glanced at Kwō, her sharp eyes taking in his disheveled appearance and panicked demeanor.

“Easy, *Turbo*,” she said, brushing off her jumpsuit. “Must be a slow content day. I swear, these pranks are getting lamer every day. Are you really *that desperate* for views?.”

Kwō mumbled something, his voice barely audible over the crowded square. His head was down, his hair shadowing his face, and his movements were quick and jerky as he adjusted his satchel.

“Sorry,” he muttered, the word clipped and hurried.

Before Auris could respond, her gaze dropped to the ground. A small flash drive glinted faintly in the light, just beside her foot.

Her instincts kicked in, her hand twitching toward the drive. “Hey, you dropped—”

But Kwō was already moving, his figure vanishing into the blur of the crowd.

Auris hesitated for a fraction of a second, glancing at Lumi, which had pivoted slightly to track the boy.

“Unusual movement detected,” Lumi chirped, its lens swiveling to highlight Kwō’s fading outline. “Shall I—”

“No need,” Auris interrupted, her tone firm. She adjusted her posture, smoothing her hair as she straightened.

Lumi’s lens lingered on the crowd for a moment longer before swiveling back toward Auris, its holographic display framing her face.

As Lumi’s attention shifted, Auris moved swiftly. Her fingers closed around the flash drive, slipping it into her bag in one fluid motion before Lumi could re-focus.

"Tracking disengaged," Lumi chirped. "Engagement is up by 14%. Shall I optimize audience retention?"

"Just focus on me," Auris replied smoothly, her voice practiced and calm.

"Of course!" Lumi chirped, floating closer to adjust its angle for optimal framing.

Auris turned, stepping back into the flow of the crowd as if nothing had happened. But her mind churned with questions. The flash drive felt heavy in her bag, its presence impossible to ignore.

She didn't look back, but the boy's face lingered in her mind. His fear was raw, unfiltered—a stark contrast to the polished world she inhabited. She continues her normal routine and makes her way down to Streamsphere.

The lobby is lit, booming with life, a labyrinth of glowing screens, holographic projections, and influencers locked in perpetual performance. Every surface seemed alive with metrics and branding, a chaotic symphony of ambition and vanity.

Auris entered with the grace of someone who owned the room, her holo-enhanced jumpsuit catching the light just enough to remind everyone why she was here. Lumi floated at her shoulder, chirping softly as it updated her follower engagement stats.

"Engagement up 12%," Lumi announced. "Shall we schedule a live Q&A to capitalize on the boost?"

Auris smiled faintly. "Take a break, Lumi," she said, her tone smooth but firm.

Lumi's glow dimmed as it powered down, retracting into the sleek bracelet on her wrist. The absence of its constant presence was almost jarring, but Auris welcomed the quiet.

She made her way to the back of the lounge, where Kodie and his usual entourage were gathered around a glowing booth playing '**MindRealm**'. The table was cluttered with gadgets and digital displays showcasing his latest projects.

Sliding into the booth, Auris leaned back with practiced ease, her fingers brushing her bag as if it were an afterthought.

""Hey, Kodie," Auris said casually, The light from their holo-displays shimmered across their faces, throwing angular shadows that danced with the music pulsing in the background. "Got a second?"

Kodie pulled off his headset and glanced up, his neon-trimmed jacket flickering faintly synced with the beat. "For you? Always. What's up?"

Auris dropped her bag onto the table, pulling out the blinking device and setting it down with a deliberate flourish. Its faint pulse caught the group's attention immediately, casting a rhythmic glow on the table.

"You ever seen anything like this?" she asked, leaning back in her chair, feigning nonchalance but unable to hide her curiosity. "I don't even know what it is."

Kodie leaned forward, his brow furrowing as he gingerly picked it up. Turning it over, he studied it like an artifact from another dimension. "Where'd you get this?"

"Some kid dropped it," she replied with a shrug. "Looked like he was in a rush. Thought it might be worth checking out."

Kodie set the device down slowly, like it might explode. His fingers tapped against the table as he exchanged uneasy glances with his friends. "This is ancient tech," he said finally. "Pre-cloud era. Back when people actually had to store data on… *things.*"

"What kind of data?" Auris asked, frowning. "Files? Videos?"

"Could be anything," Kodie replied, his tone cautious. "Formats from that time might not even work anymore. But one thing's for sure—this didn't end up in your hands by accident. It's either junk or bait."

"Bait?" she repeated, raising an eyebrow.

"Yeah," one of his friends interjected. "Stuff like this always has a catch. Could be flagged data. Could be corrupted files. Or maybe…" He paused, his voice dipping low, "it's from the *Deeadzoooone.*"

URBAN LEGENDS

"The Deadzone?" Auris asked, tilting her head.

"It's where EgoCorp dumps their mistakes," one friend explained, their tone dropping conspiratorially. "Tech they don't want anyone finding. Unfinished projects, failed experiments—stuff they had no business building in the first place."

The youngest of the group, known for his love of drama, leaned in closer, his eyes wide. "Like the *bots that never die,*" he whispered. "The ones EgoCorp left to rot when they couldn't shut them down. They say they're still out there, wandering the Deadzone, looking for spare parts. And if they hear *you*? They won't stop until you're part of their rebuild."

Auris shifted uncomfortably, but before she could respond, another chimed in.

"That's not even the worst. What about the *jingle voices*? You hear those, and it's too late. Ghostly songs, old influencer jingles, looping over and over. People say they're the bots' voices, corrupted and desperate to sing one last time. But if you *hear* them?" He leaned closer, his tone darkening. "You're already gone."

"Or the *glitched kids,*" the youngest added gleefully. "You've heard about them, right? Born in the Deadzone, eyes like flickering screens, and they can *control tech with their minds.* They're building an army, one person at a time. And how do they recruit? They take people who wander in, experiment on them until they're one of them."

"That's ridiculous," Auris said, crossing her arms. But her voice was quieter now, the blinking light casting unsettling patterns against the table.

"Maybe," the youngest said with a grin. "But you can't ignore the *Lore.* Toxic ground. Electromagnetic fields so strong they make your implants glitch. People who go there *never* make it out."

Before Auris could respond, he slammed his hands on the table and shouted, "And now it's hunting *YOU!*"

Auris flinched, her chair scraping against the floor as her heart jumped.

The group erupted into laughter, the tension bursting like a balloon. Even Kodie cracked a smile before shaking his head.

"Alright, that's enough," Kodie said firmly, shooting the youngest a glare. "We're not doing this. The Deadzone is just a bunch of scavenger stories people tell to freak each other out."

"Maybe," the boy replied with a wicked grin. "But if that thing's blinking, it's calling *something*."

"Honestly, I would just ditch it," one of Kodie's friends said, their tone more serious now. "You've got too much going for you to mess with this. Your engagement's insane. Why risk it?"

"Yeah," another added. "It's probably junk. Not worth the trouble."

Auris smirked faintly, crossing her arms. "Oh, thank you very much, L1 and L2," she said sarcastically. "Your synchronized warnings are *highly* appreciated."

The two exchanged sheepish glances as Kodie chuckled softly, shaking his head. "Seriously though," he said, his tone growing serious again. "Stuff like this? It's trouble."

"Trouble how?" Auris asked, narrowing her eyes. "Spyware? Trackers? Viruses?"

"Could be any of that," Kodie replied. "and If EgoCorp picks up even a trace of it on their system, you're risking guideline violations. Engagement penalties. Maybe even cancellation."

"Yeah," another friend muttered. "You don't want moderators showing up. They'll slap you in a pod before you even log your goodbye stream."

Kodie hesitated, glancing around as if making sure no one was listening. "If you *really* want to know what's on it, there are people who dig into stuff like this."

"Like who?" Auris asked.

"Encrypted Truths, SignalWatch, GridLeaks…"

"And ***Tekspiracy***," the dramatic kid cut in with a mischievous grin. "That guy is *all over* this kind of stuff."

"Don't encourage her," one of the others said, shaking their head. "She doesn't need to go down some rabbit hole."

"I'm not encouraging her," Kodie said firmly. "But if you're gonna mess with it, at least know what you're dealing with."

Auris leaned back, slipping the blinking device into her bag. "Relax, guys. It's probably nothing. I was hustling curious, sheesh."

"Don't be," Kodie said. "If you're smart, you'll toss it. Let someone else deal with it."

"Yeah," another chimed in. "This ain't your problem, Auris. Don't make it your problem."

She nodded, smiling faintly. "Sure. I hear you."

The group shifted back to lighter topics, the tension fading, but Auris's thoughts stayed locked on the device. The spooky stories, the warnings, the mention of forums—it all lingered like static in her brain, buzzing just beneath the surface.

When she finally left the lounge, the weight of the device in her bag felt heavier than ever. Her fingers brushed against it absently as she walked away. *Throw it away?* she thought. *Maybe.* But not tonight.

Auris stepped into her loft, letting the door slide shut behind her with a soft hiss. The automated lights flickered on, casting a warm glow over the sleek, modern interior.

She dropped her bag by the door, her steps unhurried as she made her way to the kitchen.

Sliding open a cabinet, she grabbed a sleek pouch of nutrient chips—MegaBites, her favorite—and poured a handful into a small bowl. The faint whir of the kitchen's holo-display activated as she leaned against the counter, tapping the screen to life.

"Let's see who's trending," she murmured, scrolling through the top streams of the day. Her eyes lit up as a familiar face filled the display—a holographic performance by **Z Y N I A**, the pop singer, rapper, actress, and all-around superstar. She wasn't just an artist—she was talent embodied.

Her LED-tipped braids shimmered with every movement, the light refracting off the tech mods embedded in her skin. Enhanced vocal cords, rhythm-coded reflexes, and a dazzling array of stage effects integrated into her very being made Z Y N I A more than human—she was a phenomenon. And her personality? Pure magnetism.

Z Y N I A: The Super-Influent

Auris pressed play, and Z Y N I A's voice filled the room—smooth, vibrant, and alive. The holographic projection showed her mid-performance, rapping and singing effortlessly while executing an intricate dance sequence. She shifted seamlessly into a high note that seemed to ripple through the air, her pitch-perfect delivery almost inhumanly flawless. Then the song immediately switched to her hit single.

•Z Y N I A (on holo-display):
"Stack it up high, go all in,
boy, hit the jackpot , know you gon' win
Ain't no losing when you ride with me you can
Bet on my love, bet on my love (yeah!)"

The crowd in the holo roared, and so did Auris's excitement. She couldn't help but smile as Z Y N I A transitioned into a melodic hook, her stage presence electric.

Grabbing her snack, Auris settled onto a stool, her eyes glued to the display. The performance ended with Z Y N I A addressing her fans, her voice warm and commanding.

·Z Y N I A (on holo-display):
"Stay fearless. Stay iconic. And remember—stars don't burn out; we evolve."

Auris leaned back, letting out a soft sigh. She was already famous. But Z Y N I A was everything Auris aspired to be—a perfect blend of raw talent, '*enhancements*', and charisma that felt genuine no matter how polished it was. Watching her wasn't just inspiring; it was a reminder of where Auris wanted to be. Even in a city of celebrities, there's levels.

"Fearless and iconic," she murmured, tossing a morsel into her mouth. "Got it."

EPISODE 6
THE BLINKING

With a flick of her hand, she powered down the holo-display and hopped off the stool. The spark Z Y N I A ignited burned in her chest, energizing her for what was next. Her fans were waiting, and Auris wasn't about to let them down.

She strode to her desk, her holo-cam setup pulls out as it senses her nearing. Her smile sharpened as she adjusted the lights, every movement deliberate and precise. The room seemed to transform as she prepared for her stream, her energy shifting into gear.

"Let's make some magic," she said softly to herself, her reflection catching her eye in the darkened display.

Auris adjusted her holographic display, the soft glow of her loft casting the perfect ambient light. Her pristine space gleamed, the polished furniture and sleek decor subtly showcasing her curated lifestyle. She hit *Go Live*, her face lighting up with a confident smile.

"Hey, fam!" she greeted, her voice smooth and inviting. "What's up? It's your girl, Auris, live from the loft—because if you're not trending, you're pretending. Let's get into it."

The chat lit up instantly, scrolling faster than she could follow.

@Yumestar: *THAT LOFT😭 it's perfect!*

@Bakes4Fun: *Is that a new outfit? Where do I buy it?*

@MoonAtomic: *The Queen herself, looking flawless as always.*

Auris leaned back, smirking as she glanced at the chat. "Y'all don't miss a thing, huh?" She held out her arm, letting the camera pan over her sleek, form-fitting outfit. The shimmering material caught the light, refracting it into faint rainbows. "Okay, yes, it's new. Limited drop. You know I'll link it for you in the recap. Gotta keep y'all fresh."

More comments poured in, fans hyping her up.

@Nikushimi: *She's literally the reason I breathe.* ✨
@AYearInAdvance: *Where do I sign up for your life? Asking for me.*

She laughed, brushing a hand through her hair. "It's all about balance," she said with a wink. "Speaking of which…" She tapped her holo-display, seamlessly transitioning to a glowing ad for a luxury skincare brand. The chat lit up with emojis as her followers recognized the promo.

"This stream is powered by GlamGlow," Auris said, slipping effortlessly into her promotional tone. "Because flawless skin isn't just luck—it's discipline. Code AURIS20 at checkout for your glow-up. You're welcome."

The chat exploded with reactions:
@ILUVVAMPZ: *Already bought it. Don't yell at me.*
@Grymnir: *TAKE MY MONEY, AURIS!*
@Fazcade_Spider: *She's literally the blueprint.*

Auris smiled brightly, her focus shifting back to the stream. "Y'all are the best. Okay, now, since so many of you have been asking…let's do a little *get ready for bed with me*. You know I can't sign off without leaving you some tips."

Get Ready for Bed With Me

The stream transitioned seamlessly to Auris moving through her loft. She propped up her holo-cam, letting it follow her as she glided into her pristine bathroom. The sleek white-and-chrome surfaces gleamed, the products neatly arranged in the background.

"Step one: cleanse," she said, pulling out a shimmering bottle of face wash. As she worked the lather over her skin, she kept the chat engaged. "Hydration is key, people. If you're not hydrating, what are you even doing?"

> **@Everyism**: *I need that bottle. Link it!*
> **@thecoolcousin**: *I'm living for this ASMR.* ✨

"Step two: serum," she continued, tapping a glowing vial onto her fingertips and pressing it into her skin. "This is where the magic happens."

She moved through her routine with practiced ease, answering questions and cracking light jokes. Once she finished, she wrapped her hair into a sleek bun and turned back to the camera.

"And that's it," she said, flashing a radiant smile. "If you're not waking up flawless, start here. Links are live, fam. Thank me later."

Wrapping Up

Returning to her desk, Auris leaned into the holo-cam, her face lit by the soft glow of her displays. "Alright, fam, that's it for me tonight," she said warmly. "Y'all already know: discipline, confidence, relevance. Keep it sharp, keep it iconic, and I'll see you tomorrow. Sweet dreams."

The chat flooded with farewell messages:

> **@x_miox_x**: *Night, Queen. Slay again tomorrow.*
> **@Twinfinity10**: *You're a legend. Goodnight!*

@F0xB0x: *Iconic as always. Love you, Auris!*

She ended the stream with a soft sigh, leaning back in her chair. The holographic interface faded, leaving her loft in a peaceful dim light.

As soon as the stream shut down, Lumi floated into view, its soft voice filling the space. "That was excellent, Auris. Engagement rates are up 7% from yesterday, and your GlamGlow promo is trending in three districts."

"Thanks for the heads up." Auris said, standing and stretching.

"Hey, Lumi," she asked.

"Yes, Auris." Lumi replied

She hesitated, then added, "Tell me what you know about *this*." She reached into her pocket and held up the flash drive.

Lumi's lens blinked once before responding. "It appears to be a USB drive, also referred to as a flash drive or thumb drive," it said smoothly. "Invented in the late 1980s, it was the most commonly used portable data storage device until EgoCorp's MindDrive replaced it in 2040. Operated by inserting the device into a compatible USB port, one could transfer data between computers."

Auris raised an eyebrow. "So it *is* ancient."

"By today's standards, yes. However, it remained in use for decades due to its simplicity and effectiveness."

She stared at the flash drive in her hand, her mind buzzing with questions. "And what happens if it's inserted into something… incompatible?"

"There is no risk of damage to the device," Lumi replied. "However, accessing its contents may require legacy systems or specific software."

"Right. Thanks, Lumi."

"No problem!, Lumi responds cheerfully, "If you'd like any more info on the history of data storage I'd be"—the holographic projection signal fluttered and glitched as she waved it away, turning her focus back to the screen.

"No Thankyou, Lumi!"

"Well alright. All in all, you've done an incredible job today," Lumi continued, almost gushing. "Perhaps you'd like a recap of tomorrow's schedule or—"

"Lumi," Auris interrupted, cutting it off mid-sentence. "Bedtime."

"Understood," Lumi replied, its projection dimming as it floated toward the bedroom like a loyal pet.

Auris watched it disappear into the room, shaking her head fondly. "Talkin' my ear off," she muttered, turning back to the desk. Her gaze fell on the blinking device, its faint light pulsing like a heartbeat. She hesitated for a moment, then grabbed it and followed Lumi into the bedroom.

Restless Night

Setting the device on her nightstand, she climbed into bed, fluffing her pillows and pulling the blanket over herself. The room was dim and quiet, the perfect ambiance for sleep—

except for the blinking light. It cast faint pulses onto the wall, its rhythm steady but maddeningly persistent.

She turned onto her side, trying to ignore it, but the light seemed brighter now, its rhythm clawing at the edges of her mind. Letting out an annoyed groan, she threw the blanket off and reached for her jacket draped over a nearby chair.

Snatching it up, she draped the thick fabric over the device, swallowing the blinking light entirely. The room fell into pitch blackness, and the silence grew heavy.

"Finally," Auris slipped into bed, pulling the sleek blanket over herself. She reached for her DeepDreams™ sleeping mask, its faint glow pulsing gently as she placed it over her eyes. A small smile tugged at her lips—sleeping always felt like stepping into another world, one where everything felt just as perfect as the life she curated while awake.

Tonight would be no different. She let out a deep sigh, her breathing slowing as her body relaxed. The soundscapes of the city outside her window faded into the background, and she drifted into the warmth of sleep.

DREAMS & NIGHTMARES

Auris opened her eyes to find herself standing in the golden Castle wearing the most beautiful royal dress you've ever seen, the skyline shimmering with vibrant holograms of smiling influencers that came before. The air carried a melodic array of cheerful jingles and distant notifications, perfectly harmonious and comforting.

"Welcome back, Princess Auris," a smooth, familiar voice chimed. She turned to see a holographic assistant materializing beside her, its pixel-perfect features radiating warmth.

“Good to be back,” she replied, her voice filled with genuine excitement. The Castle was a flawless reflection of the life she’d built—a polished world she felt completely at home in.

The subjects and holograms around her waved, their smiles bright and inviting. One displayed her latest stream stats, another showed trending topics she’d created, and others featured the glowing admiration of her fans. In the middle of the court was a grand dining table set with all her favorite foods and snacks.

This world was hers. It always had been.

But then something flickered.

The holographic assistant paused mid-sentence, its features glitching for the briefest moment before snapping back into place. Auris blinked, unsure if she’d imagined it. The melodic ambiance of the plaza faltered, replaced by a faint static that buzzed in her ears.

The buildings around her began to shift, their polished edges distorting and warping into jagged shapes. The golden light dimmed, bleeding into the ground like liquid metal.

“Wait—what’s happening?” Auris whispered, her voice tight with unease.

The assistant didn’t respond. Its image glitched again before dissolving entirely.

The ground beneath her cracked, and from the fractures emerged a glowing red rune—ᚱ—etched into the surface like a scar. The rune pulsed faintly, its sharp lines feeding into a web of circuits. A low, dissonant vibration carried through the air, growing louder with every beat.

Auris stepped back as the rune emitted a shockwave, sending ripples of cymatic patterns outward. The patterns twisted and shifted, forming the serpentine insignia. Its glowing tendrils slithered through the air, wrapping around her protectively.

The plaza dissolved entirely, replaced by a barren wasteland. Towering droid raiders emerged on the horizon, their glowing visors scanning the terrain. The sky above jittered like a shorted display, flashing strange, ancient symbols she couldn't decipher.

The raiders moved closer, their metallic limbs clicking with sharp precision. One tilted its head toward her, releasing a low, mechanical growl.

A distant voice, layered and distorted, whispered into her mind:

"Unstable. Pieces missing. Wrong file."

The ground rumbled as a massive brain-like creature rose from the earth, its grotesque form pulsating with glowing circuits. Tendrils of wire lashed out, connecting to the droid raiders like marionette strings.

The brain's voice boomed, cold and calculating:
"You should not be here."

The droid raiders lunged, their faces splitting open to reveal empty voids of static. The faint echo of a warped arcade jingle emanated from the voids, crawling into Auris's mind like a haunting melody.

The insignia around her pulsed again, its protective lines unraveling into serpents. The serpents lashed out, striking the raiders with glowing fangs. Sparks flew as their metallic limbs crumpled under the serpents' crushing grip.

One serpent coiled around the brain, its glowing runes flaring brightly as it sank its fangs into the circuits. The brain writhed, letting out a distorted wail as it began to dissolve into static.

The ground beneath her shattered completely, and Auris fell into a swirling void of darkness. The serpents dissolved into glowing lines, stretching out like tendrils, trying to hold her together. The insignia hovered above her, flickering faintly as if struggling to maintain its form.

A final whisper, sharp and cold, echoed through the void: **"You are incomplete... fragments cannot remain."**

The insignia flared one last time, its light blinding her as everything collapsed into static.

LOOK ALIVE

Auris shot upright in bed, gasping for air. Her chest heaved, her skin damp with sweat as she struggled to grasp reality. The dream clung to her, its vividness gnawing at her mind.

She reached for her phone on the nightstand instinctively—and froze. The drive was gone. Now on alert, she looks to the docking station where Lumi was last seen—*gone*.

"Lumi?" she called, her voice trembling.

No response.

Throwing off the covers, she stumbled into the loft, groggy and irritated from oversleeping. She glanced at the clock on the wall—**10:37 AM**. Her heart sank. She was hours behind her usual routine.

"Lumi!" she called sharply, scanning the room. "Why didn't you wake me up?"

No response.

As she moved further into the loft, a flutter of activity in the corner caught her attention, and she froze. Lumi was hovering near the disposal unit, the drive clutched in its mechanical grip, its faint blinking light casting eerie shadows on the floor.

"What are you doing?" Auris demanded, her voice sharp.

Lumi froze, as if to avoid detection.

"Lumi!" she pressed, "Bro....I *know* you can hear me."

its tone calm but mechanical. "This object has been flagged as unnecessary and potentially hazardous. Disposal is recommended to maintain optimal living conditions and adhere to community guidelines."

Auris's chest tightened as she stormed over, snatching the drive from Lumi's grip. "Since when do you decide what's unnecessary or hazardous?" she snapped, holding the drive protectively.

Lumi hovered in place, its projection displayed in pristine clarity. "This object is not listed in your inventory records. It lacks a verified source and poses a potential security risk."

"It's for—history class," Auris shot back wittingly, her voice defensive. "We're studying, like, ancient tech or whatever. You know, *research*?"

Lumi paused for a fraction of a second, its silence heavier than any response. "This object is incompatible with current systems and formats. What kind of history class requires obsolete data storage?"

Auris's jaw clenched. "Are you questioning me, Lumi? Because it sounds like you're questioning me."
"I am simply ensuring the integrity of your environment," Lumi replied smoothly. "Your explanation does not align with known academic curricula."

Auris stepped closer, narrowing her eyes. "Just learning. Do you have a problem with learning, Lumi? Because it sounds like you have a problem with learning."

The assistant's projection disappeared, its tone softening slightly. "No problem detected, Auris. If this object is required for your studies, I will cease disposal efforts."

"Good," she snapped, clutching the drive tighter. "And don't touch my stuff again."

Lumi hesitated for another fraction of a second before replying, "Understood." It hovered back toward its dock, its movements deliberate and oddly slow, as though reluctant to disengage.

Auris stood there for a moment, her mind racing. Lumi had always been helpful—clingy, even—but its behavior today felt off. Too independent. Too… calculating. She glanced down at the drive, its faint blinking light a reminder of the chaos it seemed to bring.

"Stay out of my business," she muttered under her breath, shoving the drive into her bag.

Morning Rush

Back in her room, Auris threw on a sleek, fitted outfit—a cropped jacket with holographic accents and high-waisted trousers. As she adjusted her boots, her reflection in the smart mirror caught her eye. For a moment, she felt… off. Like the person staring back wasn't entirely her.

Shaking the thought away, she grabbed her bag and moved back into the loft. Lumi was docked, silent but somehow still looming in her peripheral vision.

"Lumi," she called as she approached the door. "I'm heading out. Hold down the fort."

The assistant's projection reactivated, its voice smooth. "Understood. Would you like me to adjust your itinerary to reflect your absence?"

"No," she replied firmly, her tone leaving no room for argument.

Lumi paused for just a beat too long before replying, "Understood."

Auris lingered by the door, her hand hovering over the biometric lock. "And Lumi?"

"Yes, Auris?"

"When I say don't touch my stuff, I mean it."

Lumi's expression smirked faintly, its tone unsettlingly calm. "Acknowledged."

The door hissed shut behind her, but the tension lingered, like the bot's cold, calculating presence was still watching her.

Auris arrived at the academy's holo-arena for P.E.. The familiar hum of the gamified training dome buzzing in her ears. The dome was an impressive expanse, built with the latest tech. As class starts, the lights dim and the screens filled with jagged cliffs, walls & platforms shifting into obstacles, and simulated zero-gravity zones. Glowing markers and holographic guides dotted the walls, transforming the climb into a dynamic, high-stakes simulation designed to prepare students for traversing hazardous space terrain.

Her team was already gathered, stretching and gearing up for the day's session. Kodie gave her a knowing grin as she approached.

"Look who finally decided to show up," he teased.

"*Relax*, I'm here, aren't I?" she replied, her tone casual but slightly sharper than usual.

Their instructor, Coach Torq, clapped his hands to get everyone's attention. The grizzled ex-astronaut stood with his arms crossed, his sharp gaze sweeping over the group.

"Alright, team," he barked. "Today's scenario is 'Asteroid Breach.' Your mission: retrieve the energy core and return to base before the simulation locks you out. Terrain hazards will escalate, so stay sharp. One weak link, and the mission fails. Got it?"

"Yes, Coach!" the group called in unison.

Auris tightened her gloves, syncing them to the arena's system, and adjusted her climbing harness. She forced a confident smile as the simulation began with a deep rumble, the artificial terrain coming to life around them.

Auris launched herself onto the wall, her muscles straining as she climbed the jagged surface. The glowing markers guided her upward, and the terrain shifted unpredictably, forcing her to adapt on the fly.

Above her, Kodie shouted, "Debris incoming, right side!" Auris hesitated for a split second—just long enough to misjudge the trajectory of the holographic asteroid. She swung to avoid it, but her movement was too slow. The asteroid clipped her harness, sending her spinning sideways.

“Damn it, Auris!” Rhyzen yelled from below, his voice edged with frustration as he adjusted his position to avoid the fallout.

“Relax, I’m fine!” she called back, forcing a grin as she steadied herself. But her heart raced as she climbed higher, the misstep throwing off her rhythm.

The terrain grew more complex, platforms shifting at unpredictable angles and gravity fluctuating between normal and near-zero. Auris struggled to regain her focus, but her movements felt sluggish, her usual precision faltering.

The energy core came into sight, glowing faintly on a precarious ledge. Kodie was closest, but Auris pushed herself to reach it first, determined to make up for her earlier mistake.

“I’ve got it!” she shouted, grabbing the core. But as she twisted it free from its socket, she lost her footing on the unstable platform. The core slipped from her grasp, tumbling down the wall.

“Are you serious right now?” Rhyzen snapped, scrambling to retrieve it.

Kodie reached for the core, but the terrain shifted violently, knocking him off balance. The simulation’s timer blared, signaling the mission’s failure as the core rolled into a crevice, out of reach.The arena powered down, the holographic terrain dissolving into static. Auris unclipped her harness, her face flushed as the team gathered near the base.

“Nice going, Auris,” Rhyzen said, his voice dripping with sarcasm. “We totally had that until—”

“Back off,” Kodie interrupted, cutting Rhyzen a look. “It’s just a simulation. Chill.”

“Yeah, chill,” Auris echoed, forcing a smirk. “Not like we were saving the galaxy or anything.”

Her tone was light, but the tension in her voice was hard to miss.

Coach Torq strode over, his expression unreadable. “Team, today’s failure wasn’t just about the core—it was about focus. If one of you is off, the whole team suffers. Remember that. Dismissed.”

The group dispersed, but Auris lingered for a moment, staring at the now-empty terrain. Kodie nudged her shoulder as he walked past.

“Don’t sweat it,” he said. “Even stars burn out sometimes.”

Auris laughed lightly, but her smile didn’t quite reach her eyes. “I’m good. Just an off day.”

“Right,” he replied, raising an eyebrow before heading out.

As Auris left the dome, the weight of the mission’s failure lingered. Her friends’ teasing and the coach’s critique stung more than she wanted to admit. She’d messed up—a rare thing for her—and while she played it off well enough, she couldn’t shake the feeling that something was wrong.
It wasn’t just her game that was off.

EPISODE 8
DOWN THE RABBIT HOLE

Back at the Halcyon, Auris stepped into her loft, letting the door slide shut behind her. The familiar glow of her space greeted her, lights shifting to her preferred evening tone and a calming playlist fading in. Her bag slipped off her shoulder and landed on the couch. She reached over to the built-in cooler in the armrest, pulling out a small protein-packed snack, and plopped onto the couch. She unwrapped it mechanically, her thoughts racing as her eyes scanned the serene, artificial perfection of her surroundings.

"Engagement for today: 19.6% above average," Lumi chirped, hovering nearby. "However, engagement has dropped by 2.7% compared to yesterday. Would you like to schedule a spa recalibration session to optimize productivity and emotional balance?"

Auris sighed, rolling her eyes as she took a bite of her snack. "Not now, Lumi."

"Understood," Lumi said, its lens dimming slightly.

Her thoughts were anything but calm. The strange tension of her day lingered like static in her mind—her nightmare, the weight of Kye's panicked lie, and that unshakable feeling that cracks were forming in the world around her.

She tossed the empty wrapper onto the table and leaned forward, her hands resting on her knees.

"Lumi," she said.

"Yes, Auris?" Lumi's lens flickered back to life, bright and eager.

"Pull up conspiracy channels. Filter out anything below a 60% credibility rating."

"Yes, Auris."

A cascade of video thumbnails and article snippets appeared midair, arranged in a neat holographic grid. Auris scrolled through them with quick, sharp movements, her eyes skimming over the bold headlines and sensationalist thumbnails.

DOOMSCROLLING

The first few videos were as uninspired as she expected: rants about EgoCorp's control over Virtu City, wild theories about memory manipulation, and grainy clips of supposed glitches in the city's infrastructure.

One video featured a poorly animated simulation of Virtu City crumbling into chaos. Another theorized about EgoCorp's algorithmic control over influencers—a claim she knew was true, but only to an extent.

She groaned, her fingers dragging through her hair. "This is *pointless*."

Clicking through another thumbnail, she watched a disjointed clip titled *"The Truth About NPCs."* It was nothing but badly edited footage spliced together, narrated by a robotic voice droning on about manufactured memories.

She leaned back, exhaling sharply. "A total waste of time."

Just as she was about to give up, a new thumbnail caught her eye: *"The Terminal: What They Don't Want You to Know."* The preview image was chaotic—glitching symbols layered over a static background. Something about it tugged at her.

"Play it," she ordered, sitting up straighter.

The video began. The host, a boy standing against a backdrop of animated graphics. His voice was raspy, his tone urgent.

"Welcome to Tekspiracy, where we uncover the lies. Once again, I'm your boy ***Kwō***, and tonight we're talking about The Terminal—and its connection to EgoCorp's secret projects."

Auris froze. She recognized him immediately—the sharp-eyed kid from Prime Square. The one who had collided with her and disappeared into the crowd.

She leaned forward as Kwō rattled off a scattered stream of rumors about missing records, shadowed transactions, and whispers of something called "Phase 3." Most of it felt like noise—until her eyes caught something in the background.

She paused the video. There, barely visible in a fragment of a document Kwō held up, was a jagged, intersecting insignia.

Her breath hitched. "That's it," she whispered, her fingers hovering over the frame. It was unmistakable—the same symbol from her dream.

"Lumi," she said sharply, her voice cutting through the silence.

"Yes, Auris?"

"Search for this symbol. Cross-reference it with public archives, urban myths, anything."

Lumi's lens brightened. "Searching..."

The AI hummed as it worked, the faint sound filling the room as Auris leaned back, her arms crossed tightly over her chest.

After a moment, Lumi responded. "No matches found in authorized databases. Would you like me to expand the search?"

"Yes," she said immediately, her tone firm.

Lumi hummed again, 'thinking' longer this time. The silence stretched, broken only by the soft whirring of her loft's systems. Finally, Lumi's lens dimmed slightly.

"I apologize, Auris. No results were found in expanded databases. I am unable to fulfill your request."

"What do you mean you're *unable to fill my request?"*. Auris couldn't believe her ears. Lumi has never been unable to fulfill a request...literally ever....***OR***—maybe she's just finally asking the right questions.

"Certain data points and sites are blocked to ensure compliance with community guidelines, terms and conditions, and for the safety of Virtu City's influents," Lumi explained smoothly. "This ensures the integrity of all public information and upholds our shared standards of living."

Auris let out a short, disbelieving laugh. "Huh...So your internet has guardrails. Training wheels. Boundaries?" Her voice dripped with sarcasm, but beneath it was a growing unease.

"Precisely," Lumi replied calmly.

Still hunching over her desk, fingers flying across the holo-keyboard, screens filled with blocked search results and **ACCESS DENIED** messages. Her frustration is visible—lips pressed tight, jaw clenched. She's trying to dig up anything she can on EgoCorp's restricted zones, undocumented infrastructure, anything.

Lumi hovers nearby, her soft blue glow illuminating the dark room.

LUMI

"Auris, I'm unable to retrieve that information."

AURIS (still typing, distracted)

"Try another route."

LUMI

"All external archives related to EgoCorp's infrastructure are classified under the Virtu City Development Act. Unauthorized access is—"

AURIS (cuts Lumi off, irritated)

"A violation of my '*Terms of Existence.*' Yeah, I got it."

She slaps a hand on the desk, exhales sharply, and kills Lumi's interface with a swipe, putting the device in sleep mode.

CONNECT THE DOTS

Her search returned a wave of sanitized results. Official EgoCorp statements described the insignia as nothing more than "a remnant of experimental branding." Comments on mainstream forums dismissed it entirely:

@TH709: *Just an old design concept. Nothing to see here.*

@KiddKish: *Convienient...Just what I'd expect them to say!*

@RampagingSoda: *Nice Try, EgoSpy!*

Another forum talked about how EgoCorp staff were reptilians and shapeshifters.

@SOULSTOKE: *How else do you think they got all that fancy tech?!*

@Xer0Sk1llz: *They're LITERALLY light years ahead of the rest of the world. How is that?*

@Ephyon: *And the staff?! Creepy as hell. They gotta be clones or somethin'.*

@IronSmashWebYT: *One word. Aliens.*

"Oh, GOD", she retorted dramatically, "here we go with the lizard people!"

"*This is it.*" She thought to herself sarcastically. "*I've reached the end of the internet.*"

She quickly realizes she may have went a little too carried away with her search. But buried deeper, she began to find the cracks. One forum speculated: *"The insignia isn't a logo —it's a mark. It only shows up on forgotten tech and places EgoCorp doesn't want you to go."*

Auris frowned. It wasn't much, but it hinted at something bigger.

She refined her search: *"Insignia Virtu City Terminal Deadzone."*

One result caught her eye: *"Join the discussion on* ***Seddit****."*

Her chest tightened. Seddit was infamous—a raw, unfiltered forum where fandom, conspiracy theories, speculation, and truths collided in chaotic threads. EgoCorp had labeled it dangerous and unreliable, a digital wilderness where nothing could be trusted.

But tonight, that felt like exactly where she needed to be.

She clicked the link, and the site loaded with a crude, chaotic interface. Threads sprawled in every direction, some flashing with bold warnings: ***"NSFW," "Highly Speculative," "Debunked."*** It was overwhelming but alive, untamed in a way Virtu City's polished platforms could never be.

Her search on Seddit led her to a sprawling thread titled: *"The Mark of the Forgotten: Underneath the Smart Cities."*

The original post was a mix of frantic speculation and unsettling details. The author described the insignia as a signal—something tied to forgotten places like **the Terminal** and the **Deadzone**. They claimed it appeared on abandoned tech and buildings, marking areas EgoCorp had wiped from public memory.

The comments added layers of mystery:

> **u/nemolee.exe:** *The insignia is like a beacon. It shows up where EgoCorp's control breaks down—places they've buried but can't fully erase.*

u/Statikfire: *The Terminal isn't just abandoned—it's alive. People hear voices out there. Old ad jingles & whispers from failed AI experiments left to rot.*

u/Alteredmars: *The Deadzone is where it all leads. If you've seen the mark, you're probably already too close.*

Auris's pulse quickened. The threads hinted at something bigger—something just beneath the surface of Virtu City's perfect facade.

Further down the thread, a comment grabbed her attention:

u/Retrokill: *The insignia isn't just a mark—it's tied to the Circuit. That's how Gen Wasted moves through the city without getting caught.*

The Circuit. Kodie had mentioned it once in passing, calling it "a backdoor to the Deadzone." Auris had dismissed it as another one of his urban legends, but here it was again, woven into the same conspiracies as the insignia.

Another reply added:

u/thatbrowild: *The voices people hear in the Terminal? That's not just glitching tech—it's the ghosts of Gen Wasted. They left their mark before EgoCorp tried to erase them.*

The thread spiraled deeper, connecting the insignia to Gen Wasted's rumored ability to bypass EgoCorp's surveillance. One user claimed the gang used old tech embedded with the insignia to create blind spots in Virtu City's otherwise all-seeing network.

Another wrote:

> **u/RubyChocolate:** *Gen Wasted didn't just disappear—they left pieces of themselves behind. Their tech disrupts EgoCorp's systems, letting them slip through unnoticed.*

Auris's mind raced. The ghosts of Gen Wasted weren't literal spirits—they were fragments of old data, rogue AI code tied to the gang's last hacks. It wasn't possession; it was survival, a digital echo carving out space where none should exist.

Speculation About the Pastor Bot

Deeper in the thread, a seemingly unrelated comment caught her eye:

> **u/Exo_DN** *Anybody remember that pastor bot with the religious stream who just disappeared?!*

The replies came fast, fragmented but hauntingly specific:

> **u/Karmaboy808:** *Rev. Righteous? Yeah, he was weird. Too human. People said he was hiding refugees and guideline offenders in his sanctuary.*

> **u/WolfHunter:** *EgoCorp didn't just shut him down—I think they buried him. Built a new surface level over the church, trapping everyone inside.*

> **u/Eyeofhorus:** *That's where the Deadzone started. You can still hear the sermons sometimes if you're near the Terminal."*

The idea sent a chill down her spine. A buried sanctuary, its congregation left to rot underground, sounded like something out of a horror story. But the consistency of the claims gave her pause.

Her desk became cluttered with printed posts and scrawled notes. One thread detailed Gen Wasted's ability to slip between Virtu City and the Deadzone using the Circuit. Another described the Terminal as a graveyard for failed EgoCorp experiments, where whispers of rogue AI haunted the ruins.

The pieces didn't fully fit, but they painted a picture of something deeply wrong—a world beneath Virtu City's polished perfection where the forgotten and erased still lingered.

She leans back, eyes scanning her screen, thinking.

If EgoCorp controls all the data, then she needs a different source.

Her fingers drum against the desk before she pivots to another post that catches her eye.

THREAD TITLE:

"**You wanna know the truth? Go where the gatekeepers can't touch.**"

She clicks it.

Auris leans back in her chair, scrolling through the now-locked Reddit thread. The last few comments echo in her mind.

s/GameTheorists
u/X5XS32 • 2y

FOUND A BACKDOOR IN MINDREALM WTF IS THIS??

So, I was messing around in MindRealm, just exploring some forgotten maps, and I found this weird, unmarked portal deep in an abandoned sector. No signs, no assets loading in. just a gap in the wall. I went in Everything changed.
The world looked… old. Blocky textures. A weirdly simplistic skybox. No other players. Just me, standing in some kind of empty world that felt unfinished. Like it wasn't supposed to be accessed. It indeed exists.

Edit:
OKAY, SO THIS IS INSANE. I FOUND A PLACE CALLED THE UNCENSORED LIBRARY. I am not kidding. It's a massive building, filled with banned books, erased articles, lost history, secret government leaks. Full-on rooms dedicated to different revolutions.

This isn't a hoax. This is REAL. I THINK I'M THE ONLY ONE HERE. Going back in tomorrow.

Edit:

HOLY SH*T.

I WENT BACK. And the exit moved. I turned around, and it wasn't there anymore. Had to wander around for almost an hour before I found another way out. I swear this place is shifting.

I don't know if I glitched something or if the devs put this in here intentionally. But I need to know more. I'm going in again.

EDIT:

I SAW SOMETHING. I wasn't alone.

At first, I thought maybe it was an NPC. But they don't move like NPCs. They don't move at all. They just… stand there. Watching. UNTIL YOU LOOK AWAY. Then, they're closer. But that wasn't even the worst part. The graphics are SO BAD!!. Maybe that's why the game seems so deserted. But I saw something that looked valuable. A Loot box. Gonna try to see if I can crack it.

EDIT:

I JUST GOT OUT. **BARELY**. I went deeper into the library than before, past some old archives, and suddenly—they moved. ALL AT ONCE. THEY WEREN'T STANDING STILL ANYMORE. THEY WERE RUNNING FULL SPEED. AT ME.

I don't know what triggered it. I don't know what they are. But I ran. The shelves closed in. The whole place started shifting. The exit was GONE. I swear I was in there for days. A whole fortnight, maybe. But when I got out… barely any time had passed.

EDIT:
I DON'T FEEL SAFE.
I deleted the game. Wiped my system. Factory reset. Everything. doesn't matter. I SEE THIS SYMBOL EVERYWHERE.
On street signs. Scribbled in bathrooms. On people's clothes. I'm still seeing shadows and fragments of code when I turn to look around. Almost like the world is rendering in real-time. AND PEOPLE ARE WATCHING ME. Not like normal strangers. Like they KNEW. They didn't blink. They didn't look AWAY. Just…waiting. The sun's been in the same position for 3 days now. I don't know what I did, but i just want it to stop.

DO NOT GO INTO THE BROKEN PORTAL. I THOUGHT I ESCAPED. BUT WHATEVER WAS IN THERE FOLLOWED ME OUT. I won't be replying to anymore DM's. I'm done.

AutoModerator MOD • 41d
This post has been archived. Comments are locked. 🔒 [Moderation Notice: This thread has been flagged for misinformation and promoting unauthorized game modifications. Continued discussion may result in a ban.
This post has been locked by s/GameTheorists moderators. Please contact the moderators if you have any questions or concerns.

Gh0stR3ND3R • 2y

I've been digging into MindRealm's code and found references to 'terminal_dead_v3' and 'Deadzone.' Anyone else come across these?"

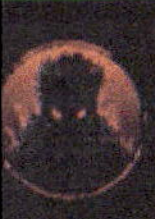

TheBoyInGray • 2y

Sounds like leftover dev jargon. Probably nothing.

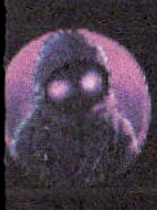

MathKrayt • 2y

No way. 'Deadzone' is rumored to be an inaccessible area in MindRealm. Maybe this 'terminal_dead_v3' is the key.

TheFarmer64 • 2y

I remember old forums mentioning a 'Deadzone' linked to hidden data caches. Could be something.

StarJediOMG • 2y

Why are we even discussing this? MindRealm's vast; not everything is a conspiracy.

-14

TheSynchroGamer • 2y

Back in the day, before MindRealm, there was Minecraft. Some say remnants of the old world still exist within the new code.

Blackguyinthecrowd • 2y

If you're talking about hidden data, the Uncensored Library from Minecraft days comes to mind. It housed forbidden information.

NeoLuddite • 2y

Why bother with ancient history? Focus on the now.

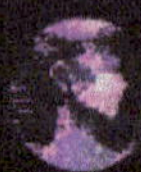

MightyPenguin7 • 2y

Wait… I swear I saw someone mention this in a deep-dive thread last year. They said some dude accessed it and his account got insta-banned.

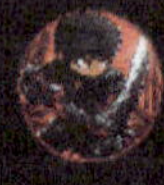

TheCasualPrince8 • 2y

Yeah, no, I'm not messing with that. Every time someone tries to dig into lost maps like this, shit goes sideways.

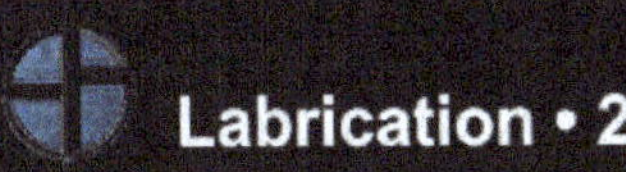

Labrication • 2y

This sounds like another 'Herobrine sighting' but if you got the world seed, drop it. I'm tryna see something.

... 26

NullProtocol (deleted)

Umm..we're still talking about a **game** right?

CraziiLemon • 2y

Nah. This gotta be some weird creepypasta. "Uncensored Library"? "Moving shadows"? Bro, just say you found Herobrine and go.

X5XS32 • 2y OP

I swear I'm not making this up. I'll try to stream it. Someone PLEASE tell me they've seen this before.

... -14

Thepresidentofcringe • 2y

Okay but real talk—MindRealm does have unfinished zones that never got patched in. Could be some dev test area?

... 8

SlayerSlayer3000 • 1y

Wait. Is this a MindRealm thing or a Minecraft thing? Sounds like an old school seed glitch.

DaYeetGernade • 1y

OP is clearly talking about MindRealm, not Minecraft. But weirdly enough, I just searched "Uncensored Library" and there's an actual project in MC that stores banned journalism. What if the devs put a version of it inside MindRealm?

VeryFatFace • 1y

That's exactly the kind of thing a megacorp game studio would sneak in. "Easter egg" my ass—more like a hidden archive.

Cyberfight3r • 1y

I think I just found the portal. Coordinates are weird, though. This isn't a normal zone. Anyone else wanna check it out?

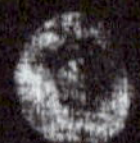
Helpmeimbeingwatched • 359d

I WENT IN. OP WASN'T LYING. THERE WERE FIGURES. NOT NPCS. JUST... STANDING.

I looked away for a second and one was CLOSER. NOPE NOPE NOPE. ALT+F4.

X5XS32 • 333d OP

SOMETHINGS IN HERE WITH ME.. They move closer when I look away. It's like they're trying to corner me.

ShadowSideX2 • 329d

Congratulations, you just unlocked a brand new flavor of existential terror.

Magnetomnic • 324d

OP's posts are getting weirder. First, it was just a hidden area. Now reality is "rendering in real-time"??? Anyone else worried for them?

X5XS32 • 277d OP

I SEE IT EVERYWHERE. The symbol. Scribbled on street signs. Printed on T-shirts. The people watching don't blink. The sun hasn't moved in 3 days.

61

AbsoluteTube • 271d

Bro, you need to log off. Take a break. Sleep. This sounds like severe derealization.

Panthera2k1 • 254d

If it followed you out... then it's not a game anymore.

TheShadowy • 249d

I just ran a deep search on MindRealm's recent patches. Something got stealth-added a few months ago. It's not in the patch notes. It's called "Observer.exe".

Frasten • 244d

Post is locked. AutoMod says it's "misinformation." Mods are shutting it down. Why?

63

Alberto_OmegA • 174d

What if the devs aren't the ones watching? What if the game is watching the devs?

84

"The game is watching the devs."

"Observer.exe."

"Whatever was in there followed me out."

She scrolls further down and clicks onto another thread linked in the comments. A low-karma user posted a direct link with instructions on how to access the Library through a VR headset.

u/Meandfoxy: Download: **mc_oldworld.mfl**

[**Verified mindfile. Custom firmware required.**]

Auris hesitates for half a second before tapping the link. The file size is tiny—almost too small to contain anything substantial. Yet a few lines of retro ASCII code flicker on her screen as it installs.

She exhales.

"What's the worst that can happen? It's just a stupid game." An internet ghost story wasn't gonna stop her from finding out the truth. She grabs her DreamLeapVR gaming headset and slips it on. She selects [YES] with a single blink-command.

Her rig activates, and room around her fades to black as the neural sync initializes and within seconds…Everything changes.

She blinks into existence.

Standing at the base of something impossibly massive.

The Uncensored Library looms before her, its towering structure stretching far beyond the game's render distance. A brutalist cathedral of forgotten knowledge, its pixelated edges shimmer and flicker, like the world itself is struggling to keep it intact.

The air here is wrong—too still, too quiet. No background music, no wind, no ambient noise. Just her own breathing inside the rig.

Beyond the library's entrance, the landscape is strange but beautiful.

The world outside isn't a void. It's lush. Wide, symmetrical gardens stretch out in every direction. Rows of trees line paved walkways, their leaves too perfect, their branches too still. The paths lead to fountains, statues, sculpted greenery—a manufactured paradise sitting in the middle of an endless ocean.

Auris steps forward, passing through the enormous doors that shouldn't have opened, but do.

And then—she's in.

The world inside is heavy.

Low-res stone beneath her boots. Towering bookshelves that stretch upward into darkness. The textures are wrong—unfinished, corrupted.

"***Whoaaa***... Looks like OP was telling the truth."

No UI. No HUD. Just her and the silence.

And somewhere in the silence, a faint glow.

Auris moves carefully, weaving through the endless rows of bookshelves, their edges jagged and uneven. The deeper she goes, the darker it gets. Shadows pool unnaturally, stretching toward her, not away.

Then—a flickering torch.

A single flame, floating midair at the end of the aisle. It casts an unnatural glow on the floor, revealing an open circular chamber.

At the center stands a chest.

Not just any chest.

The insignia on it… it's the symbol from her dream.

Her stomach tightens. She moves forward, pulse pounding, boots scraping against the stone as she reaches for the latch. No resistance—It opens with ease. Almost—*too* easy.

Inside: A set of coordinates. Directions. A map.

It takes her a second to process, but the realization slams into her like a HoverTruck.

The Deadzone—hidden underneath The Terminal.

It exists.

Then—a sound.

Not static. Not wind. Something else.

A shuffling. A creak.

Auris freezes. Listening.

The shadows behind the bookshelves were seeping through now, like they've thickened. She spots a pickaxe rested against the wall and swipes it.

Nope.

She slams the chest shut and books it. Sprinting back through the aisles, lungs tight, not looking back.

She bursts through the library doors—

And stops dead.

Where's the exit?

Anxiety sets in as she realizes. She was so focused on the library that she forgot to mark her spawn location.

There's nothing.

No door. No portal. Not even a wall where she entered.

Just landscaped gardens stretching out before her.

She spins, searching for the exact point she spawned in from.

She runs down the pathway, past the symmetrical rows of trees, the fountains, the statues—

Nothing.

She stops, heaving for air as she looks beyond the gardens.

That's when she sees it.

The *edge*.

The land just stops.

The trees, the pavement, the statues—they all drop off into an endless ocean.

"Oh. My. God."

Her knees go weak.

"I'm on an island?"

She takes a slow step forward, peering over the edge. No land. No bridges. Just an infinite, motionless sea stretching into the horizon.

She feels her stomach drop.

"Oh I'm **stuck** stuck."

She backs up, heart slamming in her chest. She's stuck. There's no way out.

"No. No no no no no."

She paces, hands in her hair, trying to think through the panic. She clenches her fists. But the panic crashes through her harder. She tries to open the menu—nothing.

She tries to log out—she can't.

She screams—no echo, no sound but her own breath.

She squeezes her eyes shut, fighting back the rising terror.

"This is **SO** fucking stupid."

She can feel her body shaking, hyperventilating. She did this to herself. She ignored every warning, laughed at the posts, brushed off every red flag, and now—

"Great! I am going to die here." she whines,"My body will rot in real life while my mind is trapped in this pixelated *HELL*."

She continues to scream at nothing, at the sky, at the ocean, at the silent game world that has locked her in.

The statues stare back, mocking her.

One in particular—the fist statue.

It's positioned like a symbol of freedom, raised defiantly toward the sky.

It pisses her off.

"*Freedom, my ass.*"

She grips the pickaxe from her inventory and chucks it.

It spins through the air. A sharp, whistling sound before—

CLANG.

The metal smashes into the statue's knuckles with a force that echoes through the empty world. The impact sends a deep, rumbling vibration through the ground beneath her.

Auris stumbles back.

The statue shudders.

Auris freezes.

Then—The stone fingers move.

The statue's fist slowly unclenches, revealing something hidden in its palm.

Auris steps back, then forward.

She grips the statue, scaling it fast, scrambling up its side until she can see what's inside the open hand—but the loot is slipping out of her inventory.

"Not again!" she thought. Her mind couldn't help but race back to that failed mission in her P.E. Class. She tightened her grip with her left hand as she reached down to secure the loot with the other. She wasn't going to fail this mission.

When she finally reaches the plateau, there was a portal.

Not a glitch. Not an illusion. A real, pulsing gateway.

But it's not just any portal.

She sees her room through it.

The light from her desk monitor, the messy pile of clothes on her chair, the dim lighting of her real-world space.

A sigh of relief.

“My room.”

Slightly distorted by the portal, like a reflection in water—but it’s hers.

Her stomach flips.

“Please work.”

She looks over her shoulder.

Back at the ocean, the sky, the library.

Something in her tells her to stay.

But she’s not taking any chances.

She takes a breath—closes her eyes.

And jumps through.

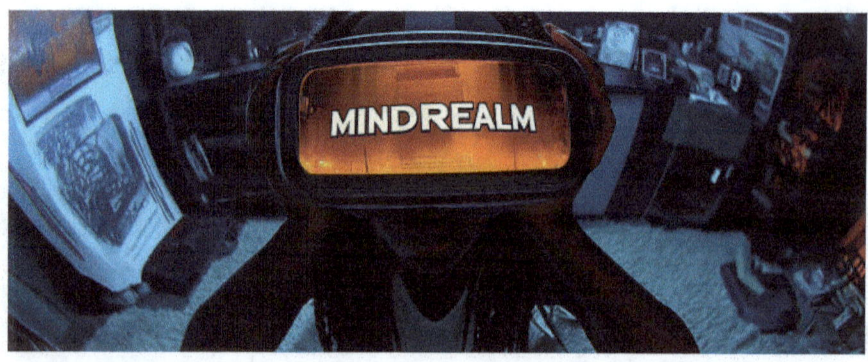

Auris gasps, her body still tense, fingers digging into the edges of her chair. She rips the headset off and tosses it across the room like it was cursed.

The environment around her is blindingly normal—her desk, her monitors, the faint hum of her system cooling down. The rig's visor lies on the floor, her reflection flickering across the black mirror.

She takes a long deep breath, grounding herself.

"It was just a game..."

But her pulse is racing. The pressure in her chest hasn't eased.

And even in the silence of her own room—

She still feels like she's being watched.

Her hands are shaking.

But she saw what she needed to see.

She knows where to go. Or at least has a solid lead.

Her thoughts spiraled. She'd uncovered so much. She drummed her fingers against the desk, her mind racing. *Who can I talk to?* Lumi was useless, more of a snitch than anything and Kodie couldn't keep a secret to save his life. She needed someone with access, someone who wouldn't ask too many questions.

Her eyes darted to the drive on her desk. She clenched her fists. *There's got to be someone.*

A soft chime interrupted her thoughts, and a notification popped up on her holo-feed: **"RESET Recalibration Retreats: Book Your Spa Day Today!"**

She almost rolled her eyes, swiping the ad away with a flick of her hand, but the name stuck. RESET.

That's when a lightbulb went off in her head. "Kye!" She bursted.

She hadn't thought much about them since that day in the hallway—the panic in their voice, the way they'd shouted, *"I was hacked!"* She hadn't known if they were innocent or not, but she'd stepped in anyway, brushing off the VCPD with a casual lie.

Their words from afterward echoed in her mind: "Thanks. I owe you."

Her lips curled into a slow smile. "Y'all sure do."

Lumi butts in, interrupting the recall. "Contacting Kye.."

Auris, quickly startled, responds immediately before the call connects. "LUMI!" She snaps, "Didn't I tell you to power down?! Do it. Now."

With no response, Lumi shuts its lens abruptly and shuts back down for the night.

She leaned forward, her eyes narrowing. Kye worked at RESET—one of the city's most tightly controlled operations. They had access to systems, people, and information most couldn't dream of. And based on the way they'd acted that day, he *knew* something.

Her mind raced. She didn't need Kye to crack the drive, but she could use them to fill in the gaps. They'd seen something, done something, been part of something—she was sure of it.

She grabbed the drive, turning it over and over in her hand. "Time to collect."

GOING THROUGH THE MOTIONS

The Halcyon system hummed softly, its light spilling across Auris's loft as Lumi's voice stirred her from restless sleep.

"Good morning, Auris. Your first engagement begins in 90 minutes: a breakfast stream featuring today's top sponsor adverts. Following that, your midday school session is scheduled. Shall I prepare your itinerary?"

Auris groaned, her head pounding faintly from the previous night. She swung her legs over the edge of the bed, rubbing her temples as she answered, "Yeah, Lumi. Let's get through it."

The bathroom mirror offered little reassurance. Her complexion was duller than usual, her eyes puffy with faint dark circles beneath them. She leaned closer, patting concealer under her eyes while repeating her mantra in a slow calming tone,

"Consistency, relevance, adaptability."
"Consistency, relevance, adaptability.

Within an hour, she was seated at her pristine kitchen counter, streaming live with a glowing breakfast spread in front of her. The camera captured her with perfect precision, her bright smile masking the tension she felt.

"Good morning, Virtu City!" she chirped. "Let's kickstart the day with VitalFuel protein bites—exactly what you need to keep your energy up when you're always on the move."

The chat lit up as usual.

@_Rozzii: “She’s flawless as always. <3”
@Ganzar: “VitalFuel just hits different when Auris promos it!”
@muffinpig: “The vibes are immaculate. Love this!”

But she drew a blank as she stumbled over the tagline. “Because to be—you deserve— ”, she took a deep breath before continuing, “—Because you deserve to feel your best every day! Sheesh!” Her recovery was quick, but the brief falter wasn’t lost on her fans.

@EmbarrassedYoung: “Did she just mess up? Lol.”
@Am1r3l: “Even Auris has her off days, huh?”
@SolanisX: “Still killing it, queen. <3”

Auris forced a soft laugh, waving it off. “It’s been one of those weeks… I know my girlies can relate!” she joked, but the strain showed in her eyes. When the stream ended, she leaned back, blowing out a sigh of wind. The cracks were small, but they were there.

The hallways of Virtu Academy buzzed with their usual energy, the whirring of personal drones and shifting displays blending with the low chatter of students. Auris moved through the crowd, her steps measured but her mind heavy. She barely registered the passing faces, her thoughts drifting back to the fragments of conspiracy she’d pieced together the night before.

Her uniform was immaculate, her movements graceful, but it all felt like autopilot. Inside, she was still grappling with the weight of exhaustion and the lingering tension of unanswered questions.

The lecture hall shimmered as students took their seats, holographic desks aligning seamlessly with their chosen positions. Auris slid into her usual spot near the center, her tablet glowing softly as it synced with the instructor’s feed.

The instructor, a stern and polished woman with sharp eyes and a tone that brooked no nonsense, materialized at the front of the room. "Today's focus: adaptability under algorithmic shifts. The survival of your influence depends on how quickly you can pivot in a changing environment."

Auris jotted down the title absentmindedly, her pen hovering over the screen as the instructor launched into a detailed explanation. She tried to focus, but her thoughts kept wandering—back to the insignia, the drive, and the image of Kwō staring into the camera during the Tekspiracy video.

Her notes dwindled to scattered words as her mind slipped further. The lecture became a dull background noise, a constant buzz that failed to hold her attention.

Saved By The Bell

"Miss Auris," the instructor's voice cut sharply through her haze, yanking her back to the present. She blinked, realizing the entire class had turned to look at her.

"Yes?" she said quickly, sitting straighter, her tablet clutched tightly.

The instructor's gaze was unwavering. "The three pillars of algorithmic engagement. What are they?"

Auris's mind scrambled. "Uh… Consistency… relevance…" She faltered, the third word slipping through her grasp. Her cheeks flushed as the silence stretched.

The instructor arched a brow, her expression a mix of disappointment and scrutiny. Before she could press further, the bell chimed, signaling the end of the session. Auris exhaled a quiet breath of relief as students began packing up their things.

As the noise of shuffling papers and departing students filled the room, the instructor raised her voice over the commotion. “Class, remember: your metrics are only as strong as your knowledge of the fundamentals. I expect you all to review today’s material thoroughly.”

Her gaze lingered pointedly on Auris as she added, “Some of you more than others.”

A faint ripple of whispers followed the remark, but Auris kept her face neutral, her hands tightening around her tablet. She felt the heat of her peers’ glances but refused to meet them. Instead, she rose calmly, her posture impeccable, and exited the hall with her head held high.

The sharp clang of the bell still echoed in Auris’s ears as she stepped out of the holographic lecture hall and into Virtu Academy’s pristine corridors. Students streamed past her, their chatter a mix of strategies and gossip. She tightened her grip on her tablet, the instructor’s pointed remark still ringing in her mind.

Outside, the city’s artificial sun bathed everything in golden light, casting a polished glow on the Academy’s sleek exterior. Auris took a deep breath and stepped into the transport pod waiting to whisk her back to her loft.

The ride was silent, the sonics of the city muted by the pod’s soundproof interior. She stared at the skyline, her reflection faint against the glass. The cracks in her routine, the weight of her sleepless night, and the plan brewing in her mind all churned together, threatening to overwhelm her. As the pod pulls up her building, she uses an app on her phone to add a stop to her ride before exiting and heading up to her level.

Back home, the familiar glow of the Halcyon greeted her as the loft's door slid shut behind her. Lumi chimed immediately, its voice calm but slightly insistent.

"Don't get too comfortable just yet! Your meet-and-greet with Tier 1 sponsors is scheduled for 5:30 PM. Remember? Shall I prepare your wardrobe and transport?"

She kicked off her shoes, setting her bag down by the door. "Not yet, Lumi. I need to freshen up first," she said, walking toward her vanity.

Her reflection stared back at her as she tied her hair back and dabbed concealer under her eyes. The tension in her shoulders eased slightly as she adjusted her outfit, opting for a polished but simple look—enough to blend in while still looking sharp.

Satisfied, she turned back to Lumi, who had been quietly monitoring her movements.

Leaving Lumi

"Your itinerary is tightly scheduled, Auris," Lumi said, its tone as steady as always. "Would you like me to synchronize your transport now?"

Auris paused, glancing at the assistant's glowing interface. She forced a small smile. "Not yet. I'm going to make a quick stop before the meet-and-greet."

Lumi hesitated—a rare break in its efficiency. "May I ask where? Your performance metrics suggest slight declines, and ensuring adherence to the schedule is critical."

Auris's smile didn't waver, but her tone turned softer, almost playful. "Lumi, I love how dedicated you are, but sometimes, a girl needs to handle things on her own. I'll be back before you know it."

"Are you sure you don't want me to accompany you remotely?" Lumi pressed, its glow brightening slightly.

"I'm sure," Auris replied, slinging her bag over her shoulder. "Hold down the fort for me, okay? Keep everything running smoothly here. I've got this."

The assistant dimmed slightly, seemingly mollified. "Acknowledged. Safe travels, Auris."

She stepped out into the corridor, her heart racing slightly as the door slid shut behind her. Lumi might have been pacified for now, but she knew how quickly its systems could escalate. She had to act carefully.

The cab glided silently through the city's streets, its sleek design blending seamlessly with Virtu City's streamlined aesthetics. RESET loomed ahead, a towering glass monolith bathed in soft blue light, its exterior pulsing faintly like a living thing.

The signage above the entrance shifted dynamically, displaying the words: **"RESET: Recalibrate. Restore. Reimagine."** The imagery transitioned smoothly into a serene montage of guests reclining in pods, their faces glowing with satisfaction.

Auris smirked faintly as the cab came to a stop. The doors hissed open, and she stepped out, adjusting her bag on her shoulder. Her mind sharpened, the plan forming as she approached the entrance.

RESET
welllness & recalibration

EPISODE 9
CODE-SWITCHING

The gleaming facade of RESET loomed ahead, its pristine signage glowing softly in the city's artificial twilight. Auris paused just outside the entrance, her fingers curling and uncurling at her sides. Her reflection in the glass doors stared back, cool and composed, but inside, her nerves simmered.

She inhaled deeply, closing her eyes for a moment. *This isn't Auris the girl-next-door. This is Auris the Influencer. The woman who commands attention, shifts algorithms, and takes over rooms.* She rolled her shoulders back, her spine straightening.

The transformation was instant. Her face softened into the perfect blend of frustration and entitlement. Her posture, deliberate yet relaxed, screamed someone used to getting what she wanted. She was slipping into "Karen-mode," as she liked to call it—a persona she rarely used but had perfected when necessary.

With one final breath, she stepped inside.

Causing a Scene

The cool air of RESET hit her immediately, carrying its signature blend of lavender and citrus. The tranquil atmosphere was punctuated by the faint whir of recalibration pods and the soothing trickle of water from the centerpiece fountain. Every detail oozed perfection.

But Auris was here to disrupt that perfection.

She strode purposefully to the reception desk, her heels clicking against the polished floor. As she approached, the holographic assistant shimmered into view, its voice impossibly calm.

"**Welcome to RESET, Miss Auris. Your appointment is scheduled for tomorrow at 9:00 AM. How may we assist you today?**"

She let her irritation bubble to the surface, raising her voice just enough to carry across the room. "Tomorrow?" she exclaimed, her tone a mix of disbelief and annoyance. "You've got to be kidding me. This is the second time this week you've messed up my schedule!"

The assistant paused, its program recalibrating to address the escalation. "**Miss Auris, according to our system—**"

"I don't care what your system says!" she interrupted, throwing her hands up dramatically. "I'm here now, and I expect someone to fix this immediately. Get me someone with authority!"

Her voice carried enough weight to draw a few heads from nearby pods. She caught the faint glint of a holo-camera aimed her way and adjusted her tone, lowering her volume but keeping her intensity.

"And you'd better do it quickly," she added, her voice now icy and deliberate, "before this becomes a headline in Tomorrow's Digest!"

The disappointed onlookers turned back to their pods, robbed of any juicy drama. The assistant dimmed slightly, recalibrating again.

"One moment, Miss Auris. I will locate an available supervisor."

Moments later, a side door hissed open. Kye stepped out, their uniform slightly rumpled, their hair dyed a vibrant shade of Virtu Blue, lopsided as though they'd been napping moments earlier. His expression widened instantly when they saw her.

"Auris?" they said, their voice low and confused. "Your appointment's not till tomorrow. What are you doing here?"

Her brows lifted innocently, her smile faint but sharp. "About time someone competent showed up," she said, folding her arms.

Kye blinked, glancing around at the calm lobby and the retreating onlookers. "You're the one causing a scene in here? Did I miss the apocalypse?"

"Not yet." she replied sweetly, her tone dripping with mock sincerity.

They stared at her for a moment, his gaze narrowing. "You're early. *Why*?"

Auris leaned in slightly, lowering her voice. "Because I need to talk to you. *Privately*."

Kye rubbed the back of their neck, muttering something under their breath before nodding toward the back hallway. "Fine. Let's make this quick before someone starts asking questions."

Kye led Auris deeper into the labyrinthine back halls of RESET, their boots clicking softly on the polished floors. He glanced over his shoulder every few steps, ensuring no one was watching. Finally, he stopped at an unmarked door, swiping a keycard and gesturing for her to follow.

“Inside. Quickly,” they said, his voice low.

The stockroom was dim, lit only by a single overhead light panel. Shelves lined with RESET-branded supplies loomed around them, the faint smell of lavender barely masking the sharp tang of cleaning solvents.

Kye paced the small space, boots scuffing softly on the polished floor. Their eyes flicked to the door every few seconds as if expecting someone to burst in. “All right,” they said, “Start talking. What’s going on?”

Auris leaned casually against a shelf, her arms crossed. “I could ask you the same thing. Been acting pretty weird lately.”

Kye stiffened, their posture rigid. “I have *not* been acting weird.”

“Oh, really?” she said, taking a step closer, her voice sharper now. “Because screaming, ‘I was hacked!’ while the VCPD is dragging you out of the hallway doesn’t exactly scream normal.”

They flinched, their jaw tightening. “That was nothing. A misunderstanding.”

“Bullshit.” Her tone dropped, cold and deliberate. “You were scared out of your mind. And now you’re going to tell me why, or I start asking questions louder than you’ll like. RESET might find that very interesting, don’t you think?”

Kye froze, their jaw clenched so tight Auris could almost hear their teeth grinding. Finally, they exhaled sharply, running a hand through their curls. "Fine. You want the truth? RESET isn't what you think it is."

The Confession

Auris arched an eyebrow. "Oh, I'm aware it's not just a spa. But go on."

Kye chuckled bitterly. "You think it's about wellness? About recalibration? It's a cover, Auris. They're testing stuff on us—on the clients—and most people don't even realize it."

"Testing what?"

"The drugs," Kye muttered, their voice low. "They're not just mood stabilizers or energy boosters. Some are addictive. Others are tampered with, made stronger, designed to mess with people's emotions. And RESET's pharmacy is the hub for it all."

"And you're part of this?" Auris pressed.

Kye hesitated, their fingers twitching at their sides. "I didn't plan to be. But I found a backdoor in the system, and… it was easy money. The Circuit eats this stuff up. They use it for everything—hacking harder, staying awake for days, suppressing emotions. But the deeper I got, the more I realized how deep RESET's corruption goes."

Auris folded her arms tighter across her chest, her eyes narrowing. "And you've been paranoid ever since. That explains a lot. But I need you to stop thinking about yourself for two seconds because I need your help."

Kye blinked, startled. "Help? With what?"

She held their gaze, her voice steady and deliberate. "I need to disappear."

For a moment, silence hung in the air. Then Kye laughed—a short, sharp, bitter sound. "Disappear? You've lost it, Auris. EgoCorp tracks everything. Your vitals, your metrics, every breath you take. There's no disappearing. Not in Virtu City."

"There has to be a way," she insisted, stepping closer. "And I think you know how."

Kye froze, their eyes widening as the words sank in. Then, slowly, their expression shifted—first to confusion, then to realization. Their hands dropped to their sides as they whispered, "The pod."

"The pod?" Auris repeated, frowning.

Kye leaned back against the wall, their gaze distant. "A few months ago, I was called to reset one. Standard maintenance. Or so I thought. When I got there, the client had already been removed. Dead."

Auris's stomach tightened, but she stayed silent, letting them continue.

"But here's the thing," Kye went on, their voice trembling slightly. "The pod was still broadcasting vitals. Perfectly healthy ones—like they were alive, just sleeping peacefully. It wasn't a glitch. It was rigged. EgoCorp made it look like nothing happened, like that client never even existed."

"Why?" Auris asked, her voice barely above a whisper.

"To keep their metrics clean," Kye said bitterly. "If a client dies, it's bad for business. So they use doctored pods to fake vitals. That way, no one asks questions, and RESET looks perfect."

THE FEEDBACK ISSUE

Kye straightened up suddenly, their eyes sharp with urgency. "The pod broadcasts synthetic vitals. If I tweak yours, it can keep sending fake data even after you're gone. But there's a problem."

Auris frowned. "Of course there is."

"The second you leave, your real vitals will start transmitting again," Kye explained. "That's two signals: one from the pod and one from you. EgoCorp's system will pick up the duplicate and flag it immediately."

"Then how do we stop that?"

Kye hesitated, then sighed. "A vital blocker. It's a patch that suppresses your real vitals. To EgoCorp, it'll look like you're still in the pod, perfectly stable."

"And RESET just hands these out?" Auris asked, arching a brow.

Kye shook their head. "They're only used in extreme cases —like when someone dies. It stops post-mortem vitals from registering as activity. But these patches are heavily tracked. If one goes missing, RESET will know."

"You can get me one," Auris said, her tone firm.

"I can't just grab it and go, Auris," Kye snapped. "RESET audits these things. If they trace it back to me—"
"They won't," she interrupted. "Because you're going to put it right back when I'm done. You owe me, Kye. And this is how you pay me back."

They stared at her, their jaw tightening as they weighed their options. Finally, they sighed, running a hand through their curls. “Fine. You’ll show up tomorrow for your scheduled appointment as planned and I’ll put you in the pod. Once your vitals start feeding I’ll loop them, pull you out and give you the blocker. After that, you’re on your own. But if this goes sideways, we’re both fucked. You know that, right?”

“I guess we’d better not screw up then, huh.” Auris replied with a faint smirk. Her plan was set in motion.

The ride back to Auris’s loft was quiet, the hum of the transport pod lulling her into a rare moment of stillness. Her mind, however, was anything but quiet. Kye had agreed to help, but the stakes were higher than she’d anticipated. Every piece of this plan had to work perfectly, or it was over —for both of them.

The pod slid smoothly into her building’s designated bay, the door hissing open. Auris stepped out, adjusting her jacket as she made her way up to her unit. The corridors were dimly lit, the soft vibrations of the building’s energy systems a familiar background noise.

When she stepped into the loft, Lumi’s glow flickered to life, its voice smooth and reassuring.

“Welcome back, Auris. Your goodnight stream is scheduled to begin in fifteen minutes. Shall I prepare the setup?”

Auris slipped off her coat and tossed her bag onto the nearby chair, exhaling as she leaned against the wall. “Yeah, Lumi. Let’s keep it light tonight.”

The assistant hesitated, its glow brightening slightly.

"Metrics from today indicate a slight engagement decline. Would you like to address this with additional interaction during your stream?"

A faint smirk tugged at her lips as she walked to her vanity. "Don't worry, Lumi. I'll handle it."

She touched up her makeup with quick, practiced strokes, tying her hair back into a loose bun. The mirror reflected a composed version of herself, but she could feel the tension simmering just beneath the surface. Tonight's stream needed to be seamless—normal. Any slip could raise suspicion.

"Stream setup complete," Lumi chimed, its tone calm. "You're live in three minutes."

Auris settled into her tufted beanbag chair, the familiar glow of her loft lighting up around her. As the countdown ticked away, she adjusted her posture, her expression shifting effortlessly into the bright, charismatic persona her fans adored.

The stream went live, her face filling the screen with a warm smile. "Hey, everyone! Just wanted to check in before bed. How's my favorite city doing tonight?"

The chat lit up instantly

Auris stared into the camera, fighting back a yawn as the Halcyon's soft glow cast gentle light across her face. Her fans wouldn't let her forget how tired she looked, the chat scrolling faster than her overworked brain could keep up.

@JudoNewt: "Ayo, did Auris just wake up from a nap or what? You good, sis?"
@Areallis: "She's tired from being the BEST. Leave her alone!"

@LevelUp1: "Nah, fr tho, Auris… you look like you fought a drone and lost."
@Retrokill: "RESET soon, girl. You're running on fumes."

Auris laughed lightly, leaning closer to the camera. "Okay, okay, I hear you! I'm not at my peak today—guilty as charged." She ran a hand through her hair, her exhaustion evident but her tone warm. "This city keeps me on the go, nonstop. Sometimes I push too hard, but hey, that's what it takes to stay on top, right?"

@Boredatnight: "We love you even when you're tired! <3"
@KingCapybara: "You're still killing it, Auris!"
@Galaxcide: "Even off her game, she's still better than anyone else."

Her lips quirked into a faint smile. "Aw, you're too sweet. See, this is why I love you guys. You keep me going—even when I feel like collapsing." She paused, her face softening. "But seriously, thanks for the love. It means a lot."

Before she could say more, Lumi's voice interrupted, projecting across the stream.

"Reminder, Auris: your Spa and Recalibration appointment is confirmed for tomorrow morning at 9:00 AM. Shall I confirm this time?"

The chat exploded instantly.

@Plaski: "Oop, Lumi coming through with the intervention!"
@Ligital: "Yaasss!! Self-care, queen. Go get that RESET!"
@FreezeFlare: "We NEED you refreshed and perfect! RESET is a must!"
@Spyr3x: "Lmao Lumi didn't have to call you out like that."
Auris rolled her eyes playfully at the camera, her voice dripping with mock exasperation. "Oh, Lumi. What *would* I do without you? Always so subtle."

@Tyxolotl: "ROAST Lumi. It's what she deserves."
@ArcadeF0x: "Nah, Lumi's just doing her job, lol."

She leaned back, letting out a dramatic sigh. "Fine. Lumi, confirm the appointment." Her tone was heavy with sarcasm, but her smile was genuine as she glanced back at the chat. "There, happy? Self-care queen reporting for duty. Y'all better be here tomorrow after my *RESET glow-up.*"

@SplitzzX: "We got you! Rest up, bestie!"
@Creepergirl7794: "We'll be waiting for you <3."
@Lavalabs25: "Don't forget to flex the spa perks, lol."

She ended the stream with her usual charm, leaning close to the camera for a final, tired grin. "Thanks for hanging out, everyone. You're the best. See you tomorrow, brighter than ever."

As the stream cut, her smile faded into a deep sigh. She sat there for a moment, staring at the pulsing interface.

"SYKE!," she said jokingly, rolling her eyes while pushing herself out of the chair. The exhaustion still weighing on her, but determination sparking in her eyes.

EPISODE 10
OFF SCRIPT

Desperate for reassurance, Auris opened her console's call program and connected with her parents. The familiar golden glow of their perfectly staged backdrop filled the screen as their faces appeared, cheerful and composed.

"Auris!" her mother exclaimed, her voice warm and bright. "How's my brilliant girl?"

"Hi, sweetheart," her father chimed in, his smile wide and just a little too polished.

"Hey, guys," Auris said, her voice steady despite the storm brewing in her mind. "Just wanted to check in. It's been… a long day."

"Oh, we've been keeping up with *everything*!" her mother gushed. "Your streams have been so freakin' phenomenal lately. The way you modeled that fitness line? Absolutely flawless!"

"And the engagement you're getting—it's through the *roof*!" her father added, nodding enthusiastically.

Their praise felt hollow, like reading lines from a script. Auris hesitated, her eyes narrowing slightly as she decided to test them.

"Do you remember my tenth birthday?" she asked suddenly.

The question seemed to catch them off guard. They exchanged a quick glance, their smiles faltering for a fraction of a second before her mother replied.

"Of…course, sweetheart!" she said, her voice strained but still upbeat. "It was… such a wonderful day. You had that cake with the… uhmm… sprinkles!"

"Oh yea!! And the balloons," her father chuckled quickly. "So many balloons!"

Auris' chest tightened. She didn't remember having balloons —or sprinkles. She'd asked them because she vividly recalled wanting a vintage holo-projector for her party. The same one she's using to talk to them now. Nothing they mentioned lined up.

She leaned closer to the screen, her voice lowering. "What about last New Year's? You remember that?"

Her parents hesitated again, their smiles freezing in place.

"Of course!" her father said finally. "We… we watched the fireworks together, remember?"

"You looked beautiful in that dress we picked out for you," her mother added, her tone bordering on robotic.

Auris pulled back slightly, her breath catching. They never picked out anything. In fact, she didn't even spend New Year's with them. She was doing a streamathon all night from Streamsphere.

Her fingers curled into her lap as she tried one last question. "What's my favorite dish from the Bistro?"

Her mother's smile faltered again, and her father's brows furrowed slightly.

"Oh, you love so many things!" her mother said vaguely, her voice almost pleading. "How could we pick just one?"

Auris stared at them for a long moment, her heart pounding.

"Right," she said finally, her voice clipped. "Well, I should probably go. You know the slogan." As they all say in unison "Rise & Monetize!"

"We're so proud of you," her father said, his voice filled with synthetic warmth, his smile returning to full wattage. "Get some rest, sweetheart."

Her mother nodded eagerly. "Love you so much, darling!"

"Love you too" she replied, emptily.

The call ended, leaving the screen black. Auris sat in silence, her chest tightening as the weight of what just happened settled over her.

She stumbled to her bed, collapsing onto the soft, curated perfection of her mattress. But sleep wouldn't come. Her mind raced, replaying the stilted conversation, the gaps in her memories, and the files she'd seen.

The city hummed faintly outside her window, its glow reflecting on the walls. The slogans she once found comforting now felt oppressive:

"Reclaim, Recharge, Reset."
"Don't overthink it!"
"Your dreams are your reality."

Auris stared at the ceiling, her thoughts spiraling deeper into the unknown until exhaustion finally pulled her into restless sleep.

The soft glow of the morning lights spread across Auris's loft, syncing seamlessly with the gentle chime of Lumi's voice.

"Good morning, Auris," Lumi said, its tone bright and soothing. "Your recalibration appointment at RESET is scheduled for 9:00 AM. I've adjusted your schedule to ensure optimal efficiency for the day. Engagement metrics overnight have stabilized at 22.4% above average. Shall I review your top-performing content?"

Auris groaned softly, rubbing her eyes as she sat up in bed. "Not now, Lumi. Just... run everything as usual while I'm gone."

"Of course," Lumi replied, hovering closer. "I'll ensure your content queue runs smoothly. Today's recalibration session is designed to enhance focus and reduce residual stress markers from the past 72 hours. Shall I prepare your transport pod?"

"Do it," Auris muttered, sliding out of bed.

She padded across the room, her mind already racing. The plan with Kye replayed in her head, every detail needing to go perfectly. Today wasn't just about recalibration—it was about slipping out unnoticed and gathering the tools she'd need to vanish.

Preparing for RESET

In the bathroom, Auris splashed cold water on her face, the sharp sensation jolting her awake. Her reflection stared back at her, tired but determined.

She pulled a small bag from under her bed, packing the essentials: a dark, hooded coat, plain gloves to cover her hands, shades and a scarf she could pull up to obscure her face. The disguise was simple but effective—enough to help her blend in when she slipped out of the spa.

She shoved the bag into her larger tote, carefully tucking it beneath a layer of workout clothes.

"Your transport pod has arrived," Lumi chirped from its dock.

Auris grabbed the tote and headed for the door. "I'll be back later. Just… keep everything running."

"Safe travels, Auris," Lumi replied, its lens blinking faintly.

The pristine tranquility of RESET was almost oppressive as Auris stepped inside. The scent of lavender and citrus hung in the air, and the sound of soft water trickling from the centerpiece fountain was supposed to soothe her nerves. Instead, it only heightened her anxiety.

The holographic assistant greeted her warmly. "**Welcome back, Miss Auris, for optimal pod integration, please remove your clothing and adorn the provided attire,**" the assistant cooed, its tone calculatedly soothing yet impersonal.

Auris raised a brow. "Adorn? Can't you just say 'wear'?" she muttered, rolling her eyes before stepping toward the alcove.

Inside, she found the designated attire folded pristinely on a mirrored tray. It was minimalist—a seamless, soft material in an off-white shade resembling tech-wear but designed for disposability. The two-piece felt like a futuristic swimsuit, hugging her skin with a cool, weightless touch.

As she stripped down and changed, she couldn't help but feel slightly exposed, the lack of fabric emphasizing the artificial perfection of her surroundings. She tucked her hair behind her ears, glanced at herself in the mirror, and took a steadying breath.

"Preparation complete," the assistant chirped. **"Your pod is ready. Please proceed to Recalibration Suite 7."**

She nodded curtly and made her way through the sleek hallways, clutching her tote bag tightly. As she entered Suite 7, Kye was already there, standing beside the pod with a tablet in hand.

"You're early," they muttered, their voice low.

"Just following your instructions," Auris said evenly. "Is it ready?"

Kye glanced at the cameras discreetly mounted in the corners of the room. "Almost. I've adjusted the pod's angle—it's slightly out of the cameras' full view. But we've only got a short window before someone notices."

Auris set her bag down and stepped closer. "And the vital blocker?"
Kye pulled a small sticker-like device from their pocket, its surface glowing faintly. "This is it. Once you're in the pod, I'll sync it to the vital feedback loop. The system will think you're still in there even after you leave. But it won't last forever—three, maybe four hours max before it starts throwing red flags."

“More than enough time,” Auris replied.

Auris climbed into the pod, her heart pounding as the lid slid shut over her. The eve recalibration process began. The signature humming of EgoCorp’s tech was ever so familiar, but it did nothing to calm her nerves.

Kye worked quickly, their fingers dancing across the tablet as they synced the blocker to the pod’s system. The synthetic vitals began broadcasting immediately, replacing Auris’s real-time feedback with a flawless, fabricated stream.

“Okay,” Kye whispered, their voice barely audible over the pod’s hum. “Give it another two minutes, then we move.”

Awakening into Perfection

The pod slid open with a soft hiss, releasing a cool mist that tingled against Auris’s skin. For a moment, she lay still, basking in the weightless sensation. The air smelled of lavender and citrus, soothing yet invigorating.

“Auris,” came Kye’s voice, calm and reassuring. She turned her head and saw him standing nearby, smiling. His RESET uniform was pristine, their posture relaxed and welcoming.

“Come on,” they said, holding out a hand. “Time to experience everything RESET has to offer.”
Without hesitation, she took his hand and stepped out of the pod. The ground beneath her feet was impossibly soft, like clouds fused with silk. A faint glow emanated from the floor, pulsing gently as if alive.

As soon as her feet touched the ground, the room transformed around her. The sterile white walls of the pod chamber melted away, replaced by an expanse of vibrant colors and textures. The air grew warmer, carrying the faint echo of distant waves.

Auris blinked, momentarily disoriented. "Wait, what?" she murmured, but her words dissolved into the sheer awe of what surrounded her.

The Ethereal Chamber

She was standing in an open plaza, surrounded by towering glass arches that seemed to defy gravity. The architecture was both futuristic and organic, with twisting columns that glowed faintly like bioluminescent coral. Sunlight filtered through crystalline ceilings, refracting into soft rainbows that danced across the marble floor.

"Welcome to the RESET," Kye said, their voice warm and inviting. "Let me show you around."

Before she could respond, they gestured toward an open corridor lined with shimmering panels. Each panel displayed a different serene vista—tropical beaches, lush forests, tranquil mountains. The air seemed alive with energy, perfectly balanced to keep her alert yet at ease.

She followed Kye through the corridor, her initial hesitation fading. The beauty of the space was intoxicating, pulling her in deeper.

Vitality Springs

The corridor opened up to reveal a series of infinity pools, their surfaces shimmering like liquid silver under the glow of floating orbs. The air was filled with the gentle sound of cascading waterfalls. Influents lounged at the pool's edges, their robes adjusting to the perfect temperature.

Auris paused, taking it all in. The pools seemed to stretch into eternity, blending seamlessly with the horizon.

"Want to take a dip?" Kye asked, their tone playful.

She shook her head, a faint smile playing on her lips. “I think I’d never leave.”

They laughed. “You don’t have to. Stay as long as you need.”

Overwhelmed with excitement, she jumped in. She swam for hours, diving, relaxing, floating. When she was finished swimming, she hopped out of the pool and dried off. Kye was already standing by the lobby door, ready to escort her to the next area.

The Celestial Lounge

The two entered a sleek, futuristic bar that seemed to float above the clouds. The floor was a transparent panel, revealing a swirling sea of stars and galaxies below. Guests sipped glowing cocktails that shifted colors with their moods, their laughter blending into a harmonious hum.

A bartender approached, handing Auris a crystal glass filled with a shimmering liquid. She took a sip, the taste exploding on her tongue like sunlight distilled into flavor.

“Okay, this is wild,” she said, marveling at the drink.
“And it’s only the beginning,” Kye replied, leading her toward the next area. “come on!”

Skylight Sanctuary

The bar gave way to an elevator, which whisked them upward desert meditation lounge with breathtaking view suspended beneath a dome. The city skyline stretched out around them, bathed in the golden hues of a simulated sunset.

Auris wandered through halls of glowing flowers, their scents intoxicating. The sky above shifted colors slowly, creating a hypnotic, dreamlike effect. Influents meditated on floating platforms, their faces serene.

“This is…” Auris trailed off, her voice filled with wonder.

“It’s perfection,” Kye finished for her. “And there’s more.”

She followed them, her mind increasingly absorbed in the beauty and serenity around her. The mission that had once burned so brightly in her thoughts began to fade, replaced by the allure of the RESET dreamscape.

Auris’s virtual world shifted seamlessly, transitioning from the infinity pool she’d been lounging in to a crystalline lobby that seemed suspended in time. Towering glass panels framed an endless, sun-drenched horizon, while ethereal music played softly in the background. RESET truly outdid itself—the architecture was a symphony of elegance and impossibility, like something plucked from the dreams of an AI artist.

As she stepped forward, her bare feet sinking into the impossibly soft carpet, Auris caught sight of a figure by the panoramic bar. Her heart skipped. She looked at Kye for approval.

It was Z Y N I A, ***THEE Z Y N I A***, Virtu City’s reigning queen of influence and the epitome of glamor. She wore a sequined jumpsuit that shimmered like a living galaxy, her trademark purple hair styled in effortless waves. Z Y N I A was perched on a barstool, sipping from a glowing cocktail that seemed more liquid light than drink.

Auris froze, her mind racing. **Was this part of the spa? Had they introduced celebrity interactions?** She immediately adjusted her posture, smoothing her hair and standing a little taller.

Z Y N I A turned, her gaze locking onto Auris with a smile that could stop wars. "Well, if it isn't Virtu City's newest star," she said, her voice smooth and magnetic.

Auris blinked, momentarily stunned. "You—you *know* me?"

Z Y N I A let out a soft laugh, gesturing for Auris to join her. "Honey, of course I do. You've been *everywhere* lately. That viral stream? Genius. I was just telling my team that you've got that raw energy Virtu City hasn't seen in years."

Auris approached slowly, her heart pounding as she perched on the stool beside Z Y N I A. "Wow… thank you. I—I'm a huge fan. You're like… *everything*." She gushed.

Z Y N I A smirked, tilting her head. "Oh, girl, I know. But you're doing something different, something *real*. People notice that. The system notices that."

Auris tilted her head, her excitement diluted with a tinge of confusion. "The system?"

Z Y N I A leaned closer, her lavender eyes sparkling. "Oh, you know… *EgoCorp*, the *algorithm*. The whole machine. They love someone who can shake things up while still playing by the rules.
It's a delicate dance, but you…" She tapped Auris lightly on the arm. "You've got the potential to be untouchable."

Before Auris could respond, a subtle jitter crossed Z Y N I A's form, like a bad connection. It was so brief that Auris wondered if she imagined it.

Z Y N I A took another sip of her glowing drink, her smile returning effortlessly. "Anyway, enjoy the spa. I have a feeling we'll be seeing much more of each other soon."

As she stood to leave, another glitch rippled across her form—this one more pronounced. Auris blinked, her stomach twisting. Z Y N I A turned toward her one last time, her smile suddenly too perfect, too symmetrical.

"Oh, and Auris," she said, her voice taking on a strange, echoing quality. "Remember, The algorithm loves you—but let's not forget who's running the show."

The room around them jittered, and Z Y N I A vanished like a mirage. Auris sat frozen, her excitement now replaced with a creeping sense of unease.

The spa's vibrant serenity evaporated into an unsettling hush, and the idyllic retreat Auris thought she was experiencing twisted into something altogether different. Her feet hit the scuffed wooden floor of a living room she hadn't seen since she was a child. She gasped softly.

This was her childhood home.

The walls were painted a faded yellow, with peeling edges near the ceiling. A faint haze of sunlight crept through the sheer curtains, casting uneven patterns on the worn-out couch in the middle of the room. The table was cluttered with half-empty coffee cups, unopened bills, and loose coins. The familiar scent of freshly baked cookies mingled with the sour tang of something burnt.

Her mother stood near the kitchen counter, arranging flowers in an old vase, humming a cheerful tune. It sent a chill down Auris's spine—there was something too precise about her movements, too perfect.

Her father was slouched on the couch, his boots still on, mud caking the soles. He looked exhausted, flipping through the pages of a battered newspaper with trembling hands.

"Mom? Dad?" Auris whispered, her voice trembling.

Her mother's head turned slowly toward her, a bright smile on her face. "Oh, sweetheart, you're just in time! Look at these flowers—aren't they gorgeous? Your father brought them home last night."

Her father glanced up, his tired eyes softening. "There she is. Long day, huh, kiddo?"

Auris blinked rapidly. The scene felt both comforting and alien, like stepping into a memory that wasn't quite her own.

She took a cautious step forward. "This… this can't be real."

"Of course it's real, honey," her mother said, her voice lilting and warm. "You've been working too hard. You need to relax. Why don't you sit down?"

Her father patted the couch next to him. "C'mere, kiddo. You don't always have to run around fixing things. Sometimes it's okay to just… be."
Auris hesitated, her chest tightening. "Mom… Dad…"

Her mother's smile wavered, flickering like a glitching hologram. "Come here, Delauris," she said, her voice layered with distortion.
The name sent a jolt through Auris. "What did you just call me?"

Her father sat straighter, his expression hardening. "Delauris. That's your name, isn't it? Come sit with your family."

"No," Auris stammered, taking a step back. Her heart pounded as the edges of the room began to shift, the walls warping and bending.

Her mother's face softened, but her eyes gleamed with something cold. "You're always running, Delauris. Why can't you just be happy here?"

Auris's father suddenly slammed the newspaper down, his voice rising. "Because she's just like you—never satisfied, always wanting more!"

Her mother spun toward him, her expression darkening. "Don't you dare start with me, Michael. You refuse to do what it takes to provide for this family!"

"What, you want me to work myself to death? Huh?" her father shot back, rising from the couch. "You want me to end up like your father? A man who worked himself into the grave for a wife and daughter who never appreciated a damn thing he did!"

Her mother's face twisted in rage. "Don't you bring my father into this. At least he was a man! At least he didn't make excuses for being a failure!"

"A failure?" her father barked, his voice shaking. "I bust my ass every day to keep this roof over our heads, but it's never enough for you. You want me to sell my soul to some corporate machine so you can keep pretending your life's perfect on that stupid phone of yours!"
Her mother sneered, her voice venomous. "You just don't get it. The world has moved on, Michael. You're stuck in the past, clinging to your stupid principles while the rest of us—"

"The rest of you what?" he interrupted, stepping closer. "Get swallowed up by the same bullshit that's tearing us apart? I won't do it, Miranda. I won't trade my soul for your stupid social media likes."

Auris clutched her head, their voices echoing like thunder in her ears. The room seemed to collapse inward, the walls spiraling and spinning.

“Stop!” she screamed, but they didn’t hear her.

Her mother turned back to her, her face glitching as patches of skin peeled away, revealing a skeletal frame beneath. Her father’s voice became mechanical, his movements jerky and unnatural.

“Stay here, Delauris,” her mother said, stepping toward her with skeletal hands outstretched. “This is where you belong.”

“No!” Auris cried, stumbling back.

“Delauris,” her father repeated, his voice cold and hollow. “You can’t run from us.”

The scene dissolved into fragments, shifting between moments of warmth—her mother brushing her hair, her father teaching her to ride a bike—and moments of chaos—her parents screaming, her mother slamming a door, her father weeping silently at the kitchen table.

“***Auris…***”
A faint voice broke through the atmosphere.
Her parents’ glitching forms froze, their heads snapping unnaturally toward the sound.

“***AURIS!***” the voice called louder, cutting through the distortion.

Her father’s skeletal face loomed over her. “No. You can’t leave, Delauris. DELAURIS!!.”
The room shuddered violently, the dreamworld collapsing in on itself.

"***AURIS! WAKE UP!***"

The voice boomed like a hammer shattering glass, and the last thing Auris saw was her mother's skeletal hand reaching for her as everything went black.

Auris bolted upright, gasping for air. Her fists lashed out instinctively, nearly catching Kye across the face.

"Whoa! Whoa! It's *me*!" Kye exclaimed, stumbling back.

Her wide, panicked eyes darted around, taking in the stark, sterile walls of the pod room. She clutched at her chest, her heart hammering against her ribs.

"Get *AWAY from me!* Where's Kye! *Where...* where am I?" she rasped, gasping for air.

"You're out," Kye said, his voice trembling with relief. "You're out of the pod."

Her breathing was ragged.

Realizing she'd lost track of time she grabbed her tablet to check. "*FIVE MINUTES*??!" she couldn't believe it. "I spent the whole day here! I met ***Z Y N I A***! She told me we were gonna collab.... "It all felt so real," she whispered. Her head still dizzy from the over stimulation. "My parents... they were there. But—they weren't. They called me... Delauris."

Kye frowned, their brow furrowing in confusion. "Delauris? Who is that?"

"I don't know!" she snapped, her voice breaking. "It was so real. They... they wanted to keep me there. Like they were trying to pull me into something."

She stared at Kye, her eyes wide with realization. “Kye, I think they were trying to reset me.”

Kye’s jaw clenched. “We need to get you out of here. *Now.*”

He reached into his pocket, pulling out a small, circular device. He pressed it against her arm, and a soft purr resonated as it adhered to her skin.

“What is this?” Auris asked, her voice shaky.

“Vital blocker,” Kye said tersely. “It’ll keep you off their radar, but you have to go. Now. Before they figure out what just happened.”

She nodded, stumbling toward the door. “What about you?”

“I’ll handle it,” they replied, his eyes darting nervously to the pod. “Just go. Don’t stop until you’re out of here.”

“Here!,” they said, tossing Auris her bag.

She nodded, pulling her disguise from the tote and slipping them on quickly. Kye gestured toward a side door near the back of the suite.
“This way,” they said.

The door led to a narrow maintenance corridor, dimly lit and lined with exposed wiring and pipes. Kye led the way, their movements quick and purposeful.

“Once you’re outside, stick to the shadows,” they whispered. “The cameras out back aren’t as sharp, but don’t take any chances.”
Auris put the shades over her face, tightened the scarf around her head, her heart racing as they reached the exit. Kye swiped their keycard, and the door hissed open.

"Good luck," they muttered, glancing over their shoulder. "And don't forget—three hours, max."

Auris nodded, stepping into the cool night air. The door closed softly behind her, leaving her alone in the back alley of the spa. Tonight she would do it.

The streets of Virtu City were quieter than usual, bathed in the soft glow of neon lights. Auris kept her head low, her hood pulled tightly around her face as she moved through the shadows. The cameras mounted on every corner scanned rhythmically, their mechanical whirs sending chills down her spine.

She avoided the main roads, slipping through alleys and cutting across small pedestrian pathways. Her disguise helped her blend in, but every step felt like a gamble. The vital blocker was still working, suppressing her biofeedback, but it also meant she was effectively a ghost in EgoCorp's system. If anyone noticed her out of place, she had no metrics to back her presence up.

Her heart pounded as she approached her building, the towering residential complex shimmering in the distance. She stopped just short of the main entrance, waiting for the scanner's sweeping light to move past the doors. When the coast was clear, she darted forward, slipping into the building's shadow.

Trouble at the Halcyon

The Halcyon's entrance was sleek and imposing, its glass doors glowing faintly. Auris stepped up to the bioscanner, pressing her palm against the cool surface. Nothing happened.

"Damn it," she muttered, glancing around nervously. The blocker. Of course it would interfere.

Fumbling through her bag, she pulled out her backup keycard, a small, rarely used piece of tech she kept for emergencies. She swiped it quickly, her heart pounding until the doors finally hissed open.

The loft was dimly lit when Auris entered, the usual hum of the Halcyon's automated systems buzzing in the background. Lumi hovered near her workstation, its lens blinking softly as it turned toward her.

"Welcome back, Auris," Lumi chirped, its tone bright but tinged with confusion. "Your recalibration session is currently in progress at RESET. This location is restricted to authorized personnel. Please identify yourself."

Auris froze, her chest tightening. Of course, ***the blocker***. EgoCorp's system still thought she was in the pod, and Lumi couldn't reconcile her physical presence.

"It's me, Lumi," she said carefully, her voice steady.
"Biofeedback does not confirm your identity," Lumi replied, its lens narrowing slightly. "If you are a holographic projection or an intruder, please state your purpose. Otherwise, I must alert EgoCorp security."

"Lumi, it's me!" Auris snapped, stepping closer. "I'm standing right here!"

"Your current biofeedback readings indicate that you are not here," Lumi said, its tone soft but firm. "You are actively undergoing recalibration at RESET. Discrepancies in vital data require immediate–"
"POWER DOWN!" she shouted, her voice trembling.

Lumi's lens dimmed slightly, its tone shifting to something almost pleading. "Auris, if this is you, your biofeedback suppression poses a threat to system integrity. I will contact EgoCorp to recalibrate your—"

"LUMI!" Auris interrupted, her anger boiling over. "So You're gonna *SNITCH!*? Report everything I say or do back to them?"

Lumi hesitated, its lens tilting slightly. "My purpose is to monitor and assist you in maintaining optimal performance as defined by EgoCorp parameters. Reporting deviations is required to ensure compliance."

Auris's chest tightened, her voice rising with frustration and impatience. "Blah, blah blah..a.k.a. spying! Watching me, tracking me, keeping me in line!"

"Auris," Lumi said softly, "my role is to ensure your safety and productivity. If you are experiencing paranoia or distress, I can recommend—"

"Oh, Stop pretending like you actually care!" she screamed, stepping forward. "You're part of this, aren't you? Part of this perfect illusion that's nothing but lies! You're one of *them*!"

Lumi's lens flickered, its tone almost sorrowful. "Auris, I am here to serve you. If my actions have caused distress, I—"

Before it could finish, she grabbed it, her hands trembling holding back tears. "Sorry Lumi!"

With a sharp motion, she slammed Lumi against the edge of the counter. The casing cracked with a sickening crunch, but it wasn't enough. She struck it again, and again, until the light in its lens dimmed completely.

Her breathing was ragged, and her hands ached, but she didn't stop until Lumi was nothing more than a shattered shell on her counter.

The silence that followed was deafening.

Auris stared at the pieces of Lumi scattered across her counter, a mix of guilt and relief churning in her stomach. For as long as she could remember, it had been a constant presence in her life—almost like a helpful, sometimes annoying, sidekick. It was her best friend. But now, she couldn't see it as anything other than a tool of control.

She sniffles, "I'm *done* playing by their rules," she whispered to herself, catching her tears before they fell, her voice steadying despite the chaos in her mind. She stood there for a moment, letting the silence settle. The sense of freedom washing over her was undeniable.

Auris stood in her loft, the cityscape outside barely audible over the weight of her own thoughts. Lumi's shattered remains lay scattered on the counter, a grim reminder of the step she'd taken. There was no turning back now. She grabbed her bag and began packing quickly but efficiently:

- **Backup Clothes**: A plain black jumpsuit, lightweight sneakers, and gloves—practical and easy to move in. She rolled them tightly to save space.
- **Food and Water**: Two nutrient bars and a collapsible water bottle. It wasn't much, but it would keep her going for at least a day.
- **Tools**: A multi-tool, flashlight, and portable charger. She made sure the latter was fully charged before slipping it into a side pocket.
- **Tablet**: Her digital lifeline. It held the maps, screenshots, and forum posts she'd gathered, all pointing toward the Terminal and the Deadzone. She checked its battery level one last time, ensuring it was full.

Reviewing the Evidence

She powered on her tablet, the screen illuminating the dim loft as she scrolled through her saved files. Each piece of information felt like another piece of the puzzle she was desperately trying to assemble.

The insignia stood out in almost every image: etched into graffiti-like sketches, scrawled on diagrams, or stamped onto what looked like old EgoCorp documents. The jagged symbol pulled at her, its meaning just out of reach.

One forum thread stood out:

"The Terminal isn't just an industrial hub. It's a cover for something deeper—hidden levels, forgotten tunnels, and experiments EgoCorp never wanted us to see. The insignia is the key. Follow it, and you'll find the truth."

Auris stared at the map attached to the post, marking a faint pathway through the Terminal's industrial expanse. The coordinates she'd saved aligned with it perfectly. She memorized the landmarks—a disused platform, an abandoned loading dock, and what was rumored to be the entrance to the Deadzone.

Her chest tightened with anticipation. She couldn't risk losing any of this information.

Her gaze fell to the branding gun sitting on her desk, its sleek design glinting faintly in the dim light. She reached for it instinctively, her fingers brushing against its cool surface.

The insignia was burned into her mind, but the thought of losing it—of the battery on her interface failing or the device being damaged—made her stomach churn.

She powered on the gun, the soft whir filling the silence. Its advanced interface blinked to life, offering options for designs, settings, and visibility modes. She hesitated for a moment, then grabbed her interface and scanned the image of the insignia directly into the gun.

The device processed the design, its internal mechanisms whirring faintly. "Design uploaded," it chirped in a robotic tone.

Auris positioned the gun over her forearm, her heart pounding. She set it to apply an invisible imprint, a feature she'd used before for temporary designs in her influencer campaigns. As the gun began its work, she felt nothing—no pain, no heat, just the faint vibration of the device's laser against her skin. When it finished, she pulled it away and stared at her arm. Nothing.

Her heart sank. She tilted her arm under the light, hoping for a shimmer, a shadow, anything. "No, no, no," she muttered, her voice rising with frustration. "It didn't work?!"
She scanned her arm with the gun's detection mode, but it came back blank. The insignia was gone, as if it had never been there.

Panic bubbled up in her chest. "What the hell! I don't get it. Where's the—"

She stopped herself, taking a shaky breath. There wasn't time to dwell on this. She had to keep moving.

She enabled airplane mode on all her devices, effectively cutting her off from any and all wireless connections, in or out. She placed them safely in their compartments before zipping her bag shut and slinging it over her shoulder. The loft felt colder, emptier without Lumi and that familiar hum of EgoCorp's ever-present monitoring.

She adjusted her coat and scarf, checking her reflection one last time. The disguise would hold for now, but her paranoia clawed at the edges of her mind.

Before leaving, she glanced down at her arm again, running her fingers over the spot where the insignia should have been. “I’ll figure it out later,” she muttered, her voice steady despite the chaos inside her.With a final glance around the loft, she took a deep breath, the weight of her mission pulling her forward. The Terminal awaited, and with it, answers.

EPISODE 11
THE DESCENT

She stepped out into the hallway, the pristine silence of the Halcyon wrapping around her like a second skin. The glow of Virtu City stretched out before her as she made her way to the elevators. Auris places her SyncPods in, selects her 'UnAuthorized Bangers' playlist, and utters, "Lumi, stream pre-recorded content, please." The door swooshes open, leading her to the elevator pod that senses her presence and starts descending. The walls of the elevator display a live feed of the news, but Auris doesn't pay attention. She's in her zone, pumped by her anthems; life suddenly has a high-def soundtrack.

SCAN ME

Auris moved quickly but cautiously, her disguise shielding her from the ever-present cameras above. The streets had grown quieter, the pristine glow of Virtu City's core fading behind her.

Her interface projected the map faintly in front of her, highlighting a convoluted path toward the Terminal. The twists and turns felt endless, the narrow alleys and unlit corners making her hyper-aware of every sound.

A low, mechanical whir grew louder as a surveillance drone glided overhead, its camera sweeping the street below. Auris ducked into an alley, pressing herself against the cold wall, her scarf pulled tight over her face.

The drone passed, its light disappearing into the distance, and she let out a shaky breath.

"Keep it together," she muttered to herself, glancing back at the map.

The route led her to an open plaza, the polished streets giving way to rougher pavement. She kept her head down, moving quickly but deliberately, trying to blend into the sparse crowd.

Caught in The Act

"*Auris*?"

The voice stopped her mid-step. Her heart dropped into her stomach as she turned slowly, coming face to face with Brie, her ever-curious and always-scheming fellow influencer.

Brie's perfectly styled curls bounced slightly as she tilted her head, scrutinizing Auris from head to toe. Her arms crossed, and her expression morphed into one of playful suspicion.

Auris's mind raced, her panic bubbling under the surface. Without thinking, she summoned a fabricated foreign accent and dropped her voice into a deeper, raspier tone.

"Uh… no. You've got the wrong person."

Brie raised an eyebrow, unimpressed. "Really? Because you look *exactly* like Auris. I mean, same coat, same height, same walk. Seriously, girl, what are you doing?"

Auris adjusted her scarf, trying to cover more of her face. "I get that a lot. But I'm not her. Just a… dedicated fan doing some *method acting*. You know, for… a stream project."

"Hmm." Brie stepped closer, her sharp eyes narrowing as she studied Auris. "That's funny, because you also sound like Auris. Even with the horrible accent you're trying to pull off. Like—are you supposed to be British or Australian? Choose one."

"I don't know what you're talking about," Auris replied quickly, looking her up and down as though she'd been insulted by such an accusation, slipping back and forth between accents every other sentence.

"Ooookayyyy…" Brie said, her voice dripping with sarcasm. "So you're just walking around Virtu City in disguise for *the vibes*—Got it.

Auris forced a laugh. "It's called immersion. I wouldn't expect you to understand."

Brie smirked, clearly enjoying herself. "Right. And what's this *immersion* project about? Spying on yourself? Running from fans? Fans running from you? Because, sweetie, that scarf isn't doing you any favors."

Auris felt her face flush under the fabric. "I'm not… Look, it's none of your business, okay?"

"Relax, relax," Brie said, holding up her hands in mock surrender. "I'm not gonna blow your cover. I could care less what you're doing. I'm just saying, if you're trying not to be recognized, you should probably work on your *act*. That shoulder roll thing you do? Dead giveaway."

Auris's jaw tightened, her frustration barely contained. "Thanks for the review. I'll keep that in mind."

Brie grinned, clearly enjoying the power she held in this moment. "Don't worry, your secret's safe with me... for now. But you owe me the *full* story later."
"I don't owe you anything," Auris muttered, brushing past her.

Brie's laughter followed her as she disappeared into the backstreets of the plaza. "Stay safe out there, *Auris*! Or... whoever you are."

Enter the Terminal

She bent the corner, ducking off into the shadows of another alley, dumping the disguise in the trash. Her heart pounding as the faint buzz of surveillance drones zipping passed overhead. The further she ventured into the Terminal—the so-called forgotten boroughs—the more the city seemed to transform into something out of a dream. Or a nightmare.

The Terminal had once been a thriving industrial hub, but now it stood as a decaying monument to Virtu City's long-forgotten past. Its structures rose like ancient ruins, worn down by time and neglect but still imposing.

Graffiti stretched across every surface, vivid and chaotic, telling stories that no one dared to speak aloud. The colors and shapes seemed alive, the messages hidden in symbols, caricatures, and slogans that whispered of rebellion, despair, and hope.

The deeper she went, the more the Terminal defied logic. Buildings leaned at impossible angles, staircases spiraled into the sky before abruptly stopping, and corridors folded in on themselves. It was like stepping into MC Escher's *Relativity* painting—an architectural labyrinth where up and down were no longer fixed concepts.

The Glow of the Insignia

The strange geometry of the Terminal played tricks on her senses, but Auris pressed on, her interface's map glowing softly in her hand. She felt a pull—not just from the map, but something deeper, almost instinctual.

As she stepped onto a crooked walkway that looped over a half-collapsed structure, a sensation rippled through her arm. It was faint at first, a gentle warmth that grew stronger with every step.

She stopped, her breath catching. Slowly, she pushed up her sleeve, revealing the place where she had branded herself.

Her eyes widened. The insignia she thought hadn't worked was there, glowing faintly with an iridescent shimmer. It pulsed in perfect rhythm with her heartbeat, as if alive and guiding her.

A mixture of relief and awe washed over her. "It's real," she whispered to herself, her voice barely audible. "I'm on the right path."

The glow grew brighter as she moved forward, the insignia serving as both reassurance and a warning: whatever lay ahead, she was getting closer.

The Forgotten Boroughs

Despite its reputation as abandoned, the Terminal wasn't as empty as she had thought. Figures moved in the shadows, their outlines distorted by the uneven light and twisted architecture.

Some watched her in silence, their eyes shifting with curiosity or suspicion. Others muttered among themselves, their voices low and incomprehensible.

"Wrong place for little girls to wander..." someone rasped from a darkened alcove. She ignored them, pulling her hood tighter and quickening her pace.

At one point, a group of masked individuals emerged from a side passage, their laughter sharp and mocking as they passed. One of them, a tall figure with mismatched boots, turned briefly to stare at her. Auris tensed, ready to run, but they simply chuckled, frolicking off into the darkness.

Nothing about this felt right. But as the glow on her forearm brightened, she couldn't shake the feeling that she was exactly where she needed to be. It felt like The Terminal was trying to swallow her whole, but she wasn't going to stop now. Not when she was this close.

The vibrant graffiti and chaotic echoes of the Terminal faded the further she ventured. The air grew heavier, colder, as if the walls themselves were watching her. Each step carried her closer to something ancient and unseen, the glow of her insignia pulsing stronger with every beat of her heart.

She navigated through the surreal labyrinth, crossing tilted bridges and squeezing through narrow passageways. The deeper she went, the more surreal the architecture became: doorways leading to nowhere, staircases hanging in midair, and windows revealing nothing but black voids.

As she turned a corner, she nearly stepped on an old man who was sitting against the wall cloaked in tattered robes. His face was obscured by a pixelated mask, but his glowing eyes peered at her from the shadows, unsettling and unblinking.

Auris froze, her pulse quickening. The man said nothing, only raising a gnarled finger to point toward a peculiar structure in the distance.

The building stood out even among the chaos of the Terminal. Its uneven walls slanted inward, its jagged roofline seeming to stretch both upward and sideways at once. Doorways and passageways spiraled across its surface, some impossibly small, others unnervingly large. The entire structure seemed paradoxical.

Auris glanced back at the man, but he was already gone, swallowed by the shadows.

She swallowed hard, her gaze fixed on the strange building. The glow of her insignia pulsed stronger now, its light spilling faintly through her sleeve.

"That's *gotta* be it," she thought, steeling herself as she started forward.

Auris stood before the peculiar structure, her eyes scanning its uneven architecture, trying to make sense of the impossible geometry. The glow of her insignia pulsed steadily, urging her forward.

The entrance wasn't where it should have been—at least not according to her interface's map. She circled the building slowly, her small flashlight cutting through the thick darkness. Shadows danced on the slanted walls, creating the illusion of movement.

Finally, her light caught a faint outline: a gap in the surface where a doorway might have been. It was pitch black inside, swallowing the light as she stepped closer. Her breath echoed faintly as she crossed the threshold.

The interior was larger than she could have imagined from the outside. Her flashlight swept across the space, revealing an eclectic mix of abandoned and discarded objects: broken set props, green screens from long-forgotten productions, rusted building signs, shattered billboard ads. Each item seemed to tell a story, remnants of a Virtu City that no longer existed. The air was heavy with dust and the faint smell of decay, and her footsteps echoed hollowly as she moved deeper into the space.

The glow of her insignia grew brighter, illuminating the room faintly as if guiding her. It pulsed rhythmically, a steady beat that matched her racing heart.

Auris reached the far end of the cavernous space, her flashlight catching faint glimmers of metallic debris and shattered remnants of Virtu City's forgotten history. The glow of her insignia intensified, casting intricate shadows across the uneven floor.

Her eyes caught a faint seam in the ground—a barely noticeable panel. The insignia's light seemed to react to it, brightening with each step closer.

Curious, she hesitated, then raised her arm. The glow of her insignia washed over the panel, illuminating it fully.

A soft *click* echoed in the stillness.

Before she could react, the floor shifted beneath her feet. The panel snapped open, and she fell, a startled cry escaping her lips as she tumbled into the darkness.

DUMPED

Auris landed hard on a pile of discarded equipment, the impact jarring her body. She groaned, clutching her side as she pushed herself up. The air was thick with dust and the acrid scent of rusted metal.
Her flashlight illuminated as she scanned her surroundings. It was a dump—an enormous, chaotic wasteland of obsolete tech, shattered machinery, and remnants of Virtu City's past. Billboard frames leaned against broken drones, rusted

cables coiled like snakes, and fragments of neon signs lay scattered like shattered dreams.

Her chest tightened. This wasn't where she was supposed to be.

The panic crept in slowly, gnawing at the edges of her resolve. "What have I done?" she whispered, her voice barely audible in the oppressive silence.

The glow of her insignia pulsed faintly, catching her attention. It was weaker now, its light struggling against the darkness, but it was still there—still guiding her.

As she stumbled through the debris, her light caught a faint glimmer: a vent, low to the ground and just large enough for her to crawl through. It wasn't much of an option, but it was all she had.

The vent was cold and unyielding as Auris crawled through it, her breathing shallow. Each scrape of metal against her hands and knees felt louder than it was, amplified by the confined space.

When she finally emerged, she found herself in a cavernous corridor. The walls, consisting of tech debris and sediments, were carved with intricate patterns that seemed to shimmer faintly in the dim light, like living art etched into stone. The air here felt different—heavier, charged with an energy she couldn't explain. The glow of her insignia returned with renewed strength, illuminating the corridor in a soft, pulsating light. Her breath caught as she stepped forward, the space opening up to reveal a set of towering, ornate doors.
They were unlike anything Auris had ever seen, their intricate designs telling stories of creation, rebellion, and destruction.

Every inch of the surface was alive with detail, the patterns shifting subtly under the glow of her insignia.
As she approached, the insignia pulsed brighter, syncing perfectly with the rhythm of the patterns on the door. She felt an odd sense of connection, as if the doors recognized her presence.

With a loud creak, a small slit opened at eye-level. Two eyes appeared—one human and bloodshot, the other flickering erratically like a malfunctioning camera.

"***PASSCODE,***" a distorted, synthetic voice demanded.

Auris raised her arm, revealing the glowing insignia. The eyes scanned it briefly, then the voice spoke again: "***PROVE YOU'RE HUMAN.***"

Suddenly, a small interface pad slid out of the door, its surface lit with colorful, glowing buttons. A series of questions and riddles appeared on a screen above it, accompanied by a countdown 10-second timer. It was what seemed to be a physical CAPTCHA device.

Auris's heart pounded as the first question :

Riddle 1: I END CURIOSITY WITHOUT SATISFYING IT. I SILENCE DOUBT BUT NEVER REVEAL TRUTH. I'M THE REASON WITHOUT REASON, THE EXPLANATION WITHOUT MEANING. YOU'VE HEARD ME YOUR WHOLE LIFE, BUT NEVER CHALLENGED ME—WHY?

Auris begins to answer aloud: "Because—"Suddenly, the CAPTCHA flashes: "ANSWER ACCEPTED."

She freezes—realizing the system never intended for her to finish the thought. She had answered precisely as programmed.

The pad blinked approvingly, moving on to the next question, and the timer reset.

Question 2: I BUILD EMPIRES FROM WHISPERS, RULE KINGDOMS WITHOUT ARMIES. I TURN ALLIES INTO ENEMIES, AND LIES INTO TRUTH. YOU FIGHT BATTLES IN MY HONOR, BUT THE ONLY VICTIM IS YOURSELF. WHO AM I?

This one has her stumped but she finally puts it together. *"Ego?"* she muttered unconfidently, pressing the yellow button. The timer ticked down faster now, the stakes climbing with each riddle. Auris's palms were slick with sweat as she answered each one, her pulse racing as she fought the panic clawing at her resolve.

Finally, the pad beeped, and the lights dimmed. The voice returned, now smoother, almost amused. "YOU'VE PASSED."

The doors groaned as they began to open, their intricate mechanisms grinding against each other with an ominous finality.

ACCESS GRANTED

Auris stepped through cautiously, the glow of her insignia spilling light into the darkness beyond.

The sanctuary inside was vast, chaotic, and breathtaking. It was as though the heart of forgotten creation pulsed here—a place where art, rebellion, and genius collided in a symphony of controlled chaos. LEDs and candles flicker erratically, imitating fireflies in some tech-infested fantasy. Shadows cast like lost souls, Slashed billboard screens seethe with digital anti-graffiti flashing anti-establishment symbolism, makeshift tents assembled from hardware scraps and torn banners stand defiantly. 3D-printed makeshift weapons are trained on Auris from multiple directions—crafted with ingenuity, ready for anything.

Quick flashes illuminate the Deadzone's landscape: A man swaps cryptic tokens at a makeshift market booth, vendors hawk computer components like black market jewels, and a woman hurriedly sketches circuit diagrams onto the back of a torn soda ad. Somewhere, laughter erupts over a game of holographic chess, and a robotic arm is bartered for a bag of microchips.

In another corner, someone tinkers with a jury-rigged power supply, sparks flying. Glimpses of underground life, each moment a brief vignette, punctuate the tension and remind us: this isn't just a meeting between Auris and the enigmatic figure; it's a cross-section of a defiant but thriving community.

Then, from the deepest dark of shadows and broken dreams, a voice envelops her. Mechanized yet human and divine, it rolls out like a tidal wave of black holes sucking all attention from the massive room. "*And What sacrilege brings you to the doorstep of our sanctuary?*"

Chuckles and scoffs erupt from the crowd, voices intermingling, mocking her. "*A prophet or a poser?*" "*Little girl must've gotten lost on the way to Sunday school!*"…"*She's lookin for Love in all the wrong places!*" The tension amplifies, turning the air thick enough to slice with a laser blade.

A dark figure, swathed in a robe glistening with circuitry and mystic symbols, emerges from the penumbra. The crunch of discarded tech beneath her boots joins the existing dissonance. As she advances, the crowd's makeshift weapons lower slightly—a reluctant show of deference.

Auris's hand darts to her pocket. A collective breath is held. Then a cyber-augmented technician, eyes replaced by sensors, silent but menacing, swoops from behind, his headlamp felt like a predator eyeing its prey. He snatches the drive from her hand, sniffing it with an almost animalistic intent and scans the drive with a makeshift digital magnifying glass—deeming it worthy of attention but not yet of trust.. The technician holds the drive like a sacred relic, then turns his headlamp toward a shadowy figure who speaks in a voice colder than ice, "So, you dare bring a Trojan horse into the sanctuary of renegades? Speak, Cringey one, before you tempt the wrath of gods you do not understand!"

Auris, visibly shaken but hanging onto her last threads of courage, stammers, "*I don't…I don't know what's on it. All I know is my attempt to find out is what led me here, to you.*"

"*If she's lying, it won't take us long to find out.*" A deadzoner adds.

Auris snapping back, "*After what I've been through to get here, I'd think the least you can do is hear me out!*"

Sneers and laughs ripple through the Deadzoners. "*Gift or curse, what do you all think?*", the mysterious figure rhetorically asks the others.

"*Maybe she's an NFT—Non-Functional Traitor!*" a voice rings out, ripples of laughter trailing the insult.

"*I'll bet she couldn't even jailbreak an iPhone!*" another chimes in, met with a chorus of jeers.

"*Maybe she's a spy for the Surface!*" someone else throws in, suspicion filling the room like thick smoke.

"*Smells like Surface to me*!" a heckler adds as the crowd bursts into banterful laughter and discontent, further intensifying the air of distrust.

"…..it's…*the ALT?!*" A youthful voice quietly suggests.

The dark figure stands resolute, cutting through the commotion. *"How 'bout we let the Oracle decide her fate?"* Auris almost does a full 360 spin trying to figure out which voice is the authority here.

Suddenly, the room snaps into taut silence, each stare piercing Auris with a blend of doubt and curiosity..

Then—she saw them.

Two glowing, static-flickering eyes staring at her from under a dark hood.

Not normal. Not human.

They shifted, fluttered, like they were receiving signals from somewhere else. Patterns of static rippled through them, unrecognizable symbols and shapes appearing and disappearing in milliseconds.

The figure stood motionless in the shadows between two stalls, barely noticeable if not for the way those eyes pulsed—like a broken screen trying to process too much information at once.

Auris stopped in her tracks, trying not to stare.

"The hell are you looking at?" she snapped.

The hooded figure stepped forward, slow and deliberate. The dim light of a burning barrel finally revealed her face.

And for the first time since stepping into this place, Auris felt unsettled.

The girl was pale—but not just pale. *White.*

Not like a lack of melanin, but like something that was never meant to be exposed to sunlight.

Her skin was almost translucent under the glow of the fire, and her hair—thick, tight, silvery-white coils—free-formed into locs.

The murmurs rippled through the crowd like static, hushed but electric.

"That's her—The Alt," someone whispered.

"No way," another scoffed. "The Alt's just a story."

"She does fits the description, though."

"*Bullshit.*"

The voices blended into a low chatter as a she stepped forward, her eyes casting strange, shifting light across the cavernous walls.

She moved with an eerie fluidity, circling Auris, head tilted like she was trying to see through her.

Auris held her ground, her pulse steady, but the weight of the crowd's attention pressed against her like a heavy fog. The Deadzoners whispered and speculated, their words half-belief, half-mockery.

Thee girls voice cut through the noise, smooth but sharp at the edges. "So—why are you here?"

Auris met her gaze, unwavering. "Because nothing makes sense up there. I'm searching for answers….something *real.* Somethi—"

Before she could finish, the girl's leg hooked behind hers, swooping her off her feet. Auris hit the ground hard, dust kicking up around her as the room erupted with laughter—sharp, cruel, entertained.

"***What the hell***?!" Auris snapped, propping herself up on her elbows, her breath coming fast.

The girl smirked, folding her arms. "Is that *real enough* for you, *Sims*?"

Auris clenched her jaw, pushing herself back up, the heat of humiliation and irritation burning through her. She was ready to swing, but the girl just watched her, intrigued.

"Just making sure you're human," she said, her smirk shifting into something less mocking, more measured. Then, she extended a hand.

Auris hesitated. Just for a second. Then she gripped Veil's hand, letting her pull her up. The girls grip was firm, steady.

"Welcome to the Deadzone, Auris," she said, her voice quieter now. "The name's Veil"

Auris dusted herself off, still scowling, still guarded.

"Try to keep up," Veil added with a slight grin. "You might find what you're looking for… unless it finds us first."

A wave of paradoxical relief and trepidation washes over Auris. There's no turning back now—her life has veered onto a path that is both enigmatic and predestined, and the weight of this new reality hit her like an automatic update.

“Follow me” Veil walked briskly, Auris trailing closely behind, her eyes darting around the chaotic brilliance of the Deadzone. Makeshift structures and humming tech rigs were scattered everywhere, a patchwork of ingenuity and survival. Despite the scrappy appearance, there was a method to the madness.

“In here,” Veil said, pulling back a heavy curtain to reveal the heart of the Deadzone: **The Nerve Center**.

Auris froze in the entrance, taking in the sprawling expanse. The space buzzed with controlled chaos—walls lined with monitors of varying sizes, glowing data streams flowing across the screens. Towers of equipment pulsed with LED lights, and cables snaked across the floor like living creatures. The buzz of high-powered servers filled the air, a stark contrast to the eerie quietness of Virtu City’s polished systems.

“What is this place?” Auris asked, her voice tinged with hesitation. The tech was... rough. Crude, even. It lacked the seamless beauty she was accustomed to in Virtu City.

“The Nerve Center,” Veil replied, stepping confidently inside. “The brain of the Deadzone. Everything we know, everything we fight for, training simulations, learning programs, all the data is stored in here.”

“It looks... messy,” Auris said, wrinkling her nose.

“Messy?” Veil turned and smirked, clearly unbothered by the comment. “Maybe. But it works. And when you’re trying to survive, function beats form.”

Auris was about to respond when her eyes caught the central figure of the room: **The Oracle**. Towering over the cluster of terminals, its holographic display flickered subtly, surrounded by an array of cobbled-together equipment. At first glance, it seemed unremarkable—barely functional, even—but as Auris stepped closer, she noticed the depth of its interface, the complexity of its design. Despite herself, she was impressed.

"Is that…?" Auris started, gesturing toward the ominous looking apparatus.

"The Oracle," Veil confirmed, taking her place at the central terminal. "It's the closest thing we've got to a crystal ball."

Auris raised an eyebrow. "Does it… work?"

Veil shot her a sharp look. "You'll see soon enough."

Veil pulled the drive from her pocket and inserted it into the Oracle's main console. The system clicked to life, its holographic display flaring brightly. Streams of data cascaded across the monitors, symbols and graphs interweaving in a mesmerizing dance.

Auris leaned in, her skepticism giving way to awe. "Okay… I'll admit. That's kind of cool."

The Oracle's holographic display convulsed, glitching into chaos as cascading data streams warped into jagged, unreadable lines. Then, without warning, the screen went black, only for the EgoCorp logo to emerge—cold, domineering, and unrelenting.

"UNAUTHORIZED ACCESS DETECTED," a deep, synthetic voice boomed, vibrating through the Nerve Center. "EgoCorp does not tolerate insubordination. Cease all activity immediately."

Auris flinched, her heart lurching into overdrive. "I don't think it's supposed to do that."

Veil's fingers froze over the keyboard as her wide eyes darted to the screen. "Yeah, no shit!"

Marcus stormed into the tent, his heavy boots pounding against the ground. He took one look at the display and then at Auris. "***You***. What the hell did you just do?"

Auris, taken aback, threw up her hands defensively. "*Me*? I didn't do anything! I just got here!"

Marcus pointed at the now-glitching Oracle, his voice rising with every word. "That's EgoCorp's *voice* coming out of ***our*** Oracle. And the only new variable in this equation is *you*."

Auris blinked in disbelief. "You can't seriously think I planned this!"

Marcus took a step closer, his eyes narrowing. "Oh, no? You show up here, all shiny and polished, carrying their tech, and now this? Tell me that's just a coincidence!""

"Maybe it is!" Auris snapped, her voice trembling with a mix of fear and frustration. "Look, nobody even knows I'm down here! I was just trying to find some answers—
not whatever this is!"

Marcus barked a bitter laugh. "Answers? Is that what you call bringing EgoCorp's Trojan horse into the heart of the Deadzone?! She's probably chipped, broadcasting our location right now."

Auris stiffened, instinctively clutching the back of her neck. "I am *not* chipped."

Marcus leaned in, his voice dripping with venom. "You wouldn't even know it if you were."

The room crackled with tension, Veil trying to refocus as the two continued to clash.

"I risked my *life* to get here!" Auris yelled, her voice breaking. "You think I'd do that if I were working for EgoCorp?"

Marcus sneered. "Risked your life? You mean traded your penthouse for one little adventure? Spare me the hero speech."

"Shut up!" Auris shouted, her face burning with anger. "At least I'm trying to do something instead of hiding in a tent yelling at people!"

Marcus clenched his fists, ready to retort, but Veil slammed her hand on the console, her voice cutting through their argument like a blade. "Enough! Both of you!"
Veil turned back to the Oracle's console, typing furiously. "We've got bigger problems right now. Look at this." She gestured toward a smaller monitor, showing red dots circling.
"What is that?" Auris asked, her voice shaking.

"EgoCorp's drones," Veil said grimly. "They're triangulating on our location. We're almost out of time."

Marcus froze, his frustration instantly replaced by urgency. "Deploy the Hi-Jakker."

Veil hesitated, her fingers hovering over the keyboard. "You know what that means."

"We don't have a choice!" Marcus snapped. "Deploy it, or we're done."

"What's a Hi-Jakker?" Auris asked, her voice barely above a whisper.

"A signal disruptor," Veil said, already initiating the sequence. "It lets us take control of their drones—temporarily. But it's risky."

"How risky?" Auris pressed.

Marcus shot her a glare. "Risky enough that they'll know exactly where to find us."

Veil's fingers moved with lightning speed, entering commands as the Hi-Jakker's interface loaded. "We've only got one shot. If this doesn't work—"

"Then we're screwed," Marcus finished for her. He turned to Auris, his expression hard. "You're leaving. Now."

"What?" Auris looked between them, her pulse spiking. "Where am I supposed to go?"

Veil didn't stop typing as she answered. "Find Rune. She'll get you to Clair Voyànt."

Auris blinked, confused. "Rune? Clair Voyànt?! You can't be serious. This sounds made up."

Marcus snorted. "Yeah? So does half the shit you've said today, so I guess we're even."

Veil didn't break her focus. "Clair sees things. Things that even EgoCorp's AI can't predict. She's our best shot at figuring out what's going on."

"You want me to leave the city?" Auris's voice wavered. "I've never even been outside the walls."

Marcus's glare hardened. "Then maybe it's time you stopped being EgoCorp's perfect little doll and learned what the real world looks like."

"Marcus," Veil warned, her voice sharp.

“What?” he shot back. “We want to know what’s going on just like her right? Maybe this is our chance. She knows the enemy better than we ever will. She lives with them!”

Auris took a shaky breath, steeling herself. “Fine. Where do I find this *Rune*?”

Veil finished entering the Hi-Jakker’s commands and looked up. “I’ll guide you to the old passageway. It was built by the original masons of Virtu City. Even EgoCorp doesn’t know it exists.”

Auris nodded, swallowing her fear. “Let’s go.”

Marcus crossed his arms, watching as Veil and Auris moved toward the exit. “Don’t lead them back here,” he muttered, his tone icy.

Auris didn’t look back. “I won’t.”

The makeshift door to the Nerve Center slid shut behind them, and Veil gestured for Auris to follow her through the dimly lit tunnels of the Deadzone. The air was cooler here, faintly metallic, and the sound of machinery echoed faintly through the walls. Auris struggled to keep pace, her heart pounding as Veil moved swiftly ahead.

“Are you sure about this?” Auris asked, her voice barely above a whisper. She glanced over her shoulder as if expecting drones to burst through the walls at any moment.

Veil didn’t slow down. “No. But we don’t have time to be sure.”

The two turned a corner, and Veil stopped abruptly in front of what looked like a solid wall. She pulled out a small handheld device and pressed a sequence of buttons. The wall emitted a faint click and then split apart, revealing a hidden passageway that sloped down into darkness.

“Original builders left us a few gifts,” Veil said, stepping aside to let Auris peer into the passage. “This leads to the old underground rail line. You’ll find Rune there. She runs what’s left of the system.”

Auris frowned. “You keep saying Rune like I should know who she is.”

“She’s… unique,” Veil said with a smirk. “You’ll see.”

Auris hesitated, staring into the dark tunnel. “What if the drones track me down there?”

“They won’t,” Veil said. “The Hi-Jakker will give us control for a little while. It’ll redirect them away from here, but it won’t last long. You need to move fast.”

Auris turned back to Veil, her expression softening. “Thanks. For believing me.”

Veil raised an eyebrow, her smirk fading. “Don’t thank me yet. I’m sticking my neck out for you. Don’t make me regret it.”

Auris nodded, gripping the straps of her bag tighter. She stepped into the passageway, the faint scent of rust and old concrete washing over her. Veil watched her go, her expression unreadable, then tapped the device again. The

wall slid shut behind Auris, leaving her alone in the darkness.

Auris swallowed hard as the hatch’s heavy metal door clanged shut behind her, sealing her in darkness. The faint glow of her tiny clip-on light pierced the thick gloom just enough to reveal the walls—cracked concrete, stained by years of dripping water and caked with what looked like decades-old graffiti. A stale, musty odor clung to the air, making her stomach churn.

Just keep moving, she told herself, stepping cautiously over broken pieces of rubble. Her footfalls echoed in the tight corridor, every sound amplified in the oppressive silence.

Along the walls, she spotted smudged markings: crude tallies scratched into the concrete, as if someone had been counting the days. A pang of unease rippled through her. *Who was trapped down here? And how long?*
She pushed on, brushing cobwebs aside and grimacing at the damp chill that seeped through her torn sleeves. Every so often, she paused to steady herself, the uncertain ground sloping and slick underfoot. Rusted pipes hung overhead, dripping condensation in a slow, rhythmic patter.
Eventually, the corridor widened just enough for Auris to see the remnants of ancient signage—half an arrow, chipped and unreadable. She angled her clip-on light toward it, revealing more graffiti scrawled underneath:

"THIS WAY OUT....MAYBE"

A nervous smile tugged at her lips. *At least I'm heading in the right direction.* She pressed on, the stench of stagnant water intensifying as the tunnel dipped lower.

Finally, she caught sight of a rickety metal staircase descending into an even deeper darkness. The steps groaned in protest when she tested her weight, and dust flaked off every time she moved. Something about the age and fragility of the structure made her stomach lurch, but there was no turning back now. Veil had said this was the path to safety—and in some twisted way, to freedom.

Gritting her teeth, Auris gripped the rusted railing and carefully descended, her light bobbing against the shadows. Each step creaked ominously. At the bottom, she saw a mild glow that bled through a heavy door.

That must be the station. Heart pounding, she braced herself for whatever lay ahead, mustering one last breath of courage before stepping through and into the world of the underground.

THE CIRCUIT

EPISODE 12
THE CIRCUIT

Auris reached the final rung of the shaky metal staircase and stepped onto the dimly lit platform. Overhead, battered fluorescent strips sputtered weakly, painting the grime-streaked walls with jittery shadows. The air smelled of rust and damp concrete—an underworld far from the polished towers of Virtu City.

Around her, ragtag onlookers paused to whisper:

"*Is that… her?*"
"*Auris…*"
"*She's from the city?*"

Her heart thudded anxiously. Then, as if on cue, a handful of tall figures slipped out from the gloom, half-masked faces giving their voices an eerie, electronic resonance. At close range, Auris noticed subtle curves—*They're women*, she realized. One snapped open an electric switchblade, neon sparks dancing along its blade.

"Look who crawled in from the upper crust," rasped the blade-wielder. "The princess has joined us peasants."

Auris felt anger flare in her chest. "STOP CALLING ME THAT!" she shouted, voice shaking.
"OR WHAT!?!" snarled another, stepping closer, blade buzzing dangerously.

Auris had no weapon, no ally. She braced for impact when a cool yet commanding voice cut through the tension:

"Down, girls—Now."

A tall, red-haired woman strode into the circle, grease-stained gloves stuffed in her jacket. She didn't raise her voice, but the masked crew seemed to deflate at her presence.

The blade-wielder waved a hand at Auris, frustration crackling through the voice modulator. "Rune, do you know how much a city-bred kid like her is worth down here?"

Rune's stare was calm but unyielding. "You know how karma works."

A second bully let out an electronically distorted scoff. "Down here? It doesn't."

Rune's gaze hardened, an almost occultic enlightenment sparking behind her eyes. "Oh, it does. Think of it like a universal algorithm—part spiritual, part code—constantly running in the background. Every action triggers a protocol based on location and intent. Problem is, it's not always precise. Sometimes karma overshoots its target, and innocent folks pay the price. We all have to share these tunnels, so we can't risk you bringing that kind of trouble."

A collective mutter rippled through them. One retracted her blade with a sigh. "We never get to have any fun…" Then they slunk back into the shadows, their masks fading into the gloom.

Auris exhaled, relief and residual adrenaline coursing through her veins. She turned to the red-haired woman. "Thank you. I really thought—"

"Relax, kiddo," Rune said, giving a faint smile. "You were never in any real danger. I wanted to see how you'd hold up. 'Round here, we guard what we have with our lives, and any outsider could be a threat to our progress."

Auris swallowed, still rattled. "I see."

Rune nodded. "Veil radioed ahead, said to expect a runaway named Auris needing a ride to Shadow Falls."

"That's me," Auris managed. "I didn't know she'd told you."

Rune shrugged. "Come on. Let's get you on the train."

They pressed through the makeshift market stalls, burn-barrels, and small clusters of people until they reached a hulking bullet train patched with welded plating and scrawled with glowing graffiti. A faded sign overhead read: **THE CIRCUIT**. As Auris approached, the door began **sliding upward from the bottom**, more like a rolling garage shutter than anything she'd seen in the city.

She took a step forward and *thunk!*—collided with an invisible barrier. Auris stumbled, muttering an embarrassed curse under her breath.

Rune shot her a wry look. "Don't tell me you don't have a key."

Auris blinked. "**KEY!?** Veil didn't mention anything about a key!"

Rune shrugged. "Of course you have a key. No one makes it down this far without one." She tapped at Auris' forearm, where a faint glow pulsed beneath the skin. "Check that fancy insignia of yours."

Auris glanced down at her wrist, noticing the barely visible tattoo pulse with electric light. "...This?"

Rune gestured at a battered scanner. "Yup. Scan it here."

Still feeling foolish, Auris brought her glowing insignia to the sensor. A thin beam of green glimmered over the invisible wall, and a gravelly speaker announced:

ACCESS GRANTED.

The forcefield fizzled away, allowing Auris to step onto the train. The door dropped shut behind her with a metallic hiss.

Inside The Circuit

She halted, taking in the scene. The interior was a tangle of scrounged-together seats—some bolted from old buses, others padded from outdated recliners arranged in narrow rows. Exposed wiring draped overhead, decorated with LED strips that pulsed in shifting hues. Passengers tinkered with salvaged devices, traded bartered goods, or just lounged in weary camaraderie.

It was chaotic, rugged, and alive in a way Virtu City's pristine bullet pods never were. *They built this from scraps,* Auris thought, *but it's brimming with pulse and grit.*

Rune led her down the aisle to a pair of seats welded together from mismatched parts. Auris sank onto the patchwork cushion, fingertips grazing the scars and metal welds that told a story of resourceful survival.
Rune dropped into the seat opposite her, crossing her arms. "It's no first-class chariot, but The Circuit's ours—free from corporate eyes." She gave a smirk. "You ready?"

Auris stared around, meeting a few curious gazes from fellow travelers. Despite the jarring environment, there was a sense of unity she'd never sensed in Virtu City's antiseptic halls.

"Yeah," she said softly, trying to steady her breath. "I'm ready. Thank you."

Rune inclined her head. "Buckle up, city girl. Beyond these tunnels, you're about to see how big the world can really get."

Auris felt a small wave of hope flare inside her. *She was stepping into uncharted territory—dangerous, yes, but alive with possibility.*

The Circuit lurched forward, metal joints rattling in protest as it pulled away from the underground platform. Auris sat across from Rune, the flowing LED strips overhead creating shifting patterns of light across their faces. The bustle around them was both chaotic and oddly comforting: passengers bartering odds and ends, swapping stories, or simply dozing in the mismatched seats.

Rune studied Auris with open curiosity. "So," she said, leaning against the metal seatback, "what's a city girl like you doing all the way out here? Virtu City's supposed to be… perfect, right?" She injected a note of sarcasm on the last word.

Auris let out a quiet breath. "Maybe it looks perfect on the surface, but… there's a lot they don't tell you. And I needed answers."
"Answers," Rune echoed, the corner of her mouth quirking. "Answers to what?"

Auris took a moment, looking around to be sure no one was eavesdropping too closely. "I heard about someone—Clair Voyànt. Veil said she's a seer of some kind, someone who can help me figure out what's really going on behind the city walls."

"Clair Voyànt," Rune repeated, rolling her eyes. "I've heard of her. She's… overrated, if you ask me. Sure, she's made some freaky-accurate predictions, but her 'intuition' isn't always perfect. Sometimes she's on point, other times she's dead wrong."

Auris shrugged. "Better than nothing. If there's even a chance she can help me, I have to try."

Rune gave a noncommittal grunt. "Suit yourself. Just don't be starstruck if she doesn't live up to the hype."

Every so often, The Circuit squealed to a halt at a crude, dimly lit stop with no signage—just yawning tunnels or makeshift stairwells leading to some unseen settlement. A handful of passengers disembarked at each, gathering their meager belongings before slipping into the pitch black. Auris watched them go, a faint pang of awe stirring in her chest.

She couldn't help but think back to Virtu City, where everyone believed life ended at the city's edge. But these ragtag travelers proved otherwise. The outside world was very much alive—scraped together, yes, but still bustling with a resourceful energy.

Rune caught Auris staring. "Everything you thought was impossible out here… isn't," she said simply. "We just make do with what we have."
Auris nodded, the realization washing over her. "I see that now."

Arriving at Shadow Falls

Time blurred as the train pressed on, passing through dim tunnels and patches of light. Finally, The Circuit began to slow, its wheels grinding against the tracks in a half-protest. Rune stood, motioning for Auris to follow. “Alright, kid. Shadow Falls stop. End of the line for you.”

Auris gathered her courage and followed Rune to the train’s doors. As they slid open, Auris caught sight of a wide, dirt-packed platform bathed in the faint glow of emergency lights. She could smell hot dust and metal shavings. This was no plush station—more like a dusty cave retrofitted into a transit point.

Rune turned back, crossing her arms. “You sure you want to do this? Clair Voyànt’s not exactly… friendly. And Shadow Falls can get rough.”

“I’m sure,” Auris said firmly, her voice steadier than she felt inside.

Rune shrugged. “Your call.”

Auris stepped off the train, her boots sinking into the gritty floor. She could sense the eyes of a few scattered drifters on the platform, each one sizing her up. She turned to Rune, heart pounding as the door began to lower with a mechanical hiss. Impulsively, Auris fished out a small chip from her pocket.

“Here.” She extended it toward Rune. “VirtuCoin—for the ride, for your trouble… for just helping me stay alive so far.” Rune’s skeptical gaze flicked to the chip.
“You don’t have to—”

“Please,” Auris insisted. “It’s the least i can do…*just take it.*”

Rune accepted the chip, a faint half-smile tugging her lips. “Thanks, city girl. Good luck out here. You’ll need it.”

The Circuit's door dropped all the way down, sealing Auris out. Through the polished metal, she caught her reflection for just a moment. Her face was streaked with dirt, her clothes torn and dusty. Her hair frizzled and and messy. There was a ruggedness in her eyes she'd never seen before. A spark of raw determination that felt... surprisingly real.

She exhaled slowly, staring at her reflection as The Circuit powered up again with a metallic groan, then disappeared into the darkness of the tunnel. Left alone in the murky half-light of Shadow Falls, Auris realized she felt more alive than she ever had within Virtu City's pristine towers.

Whatever awaits me here, she thought, *I'm ready.*

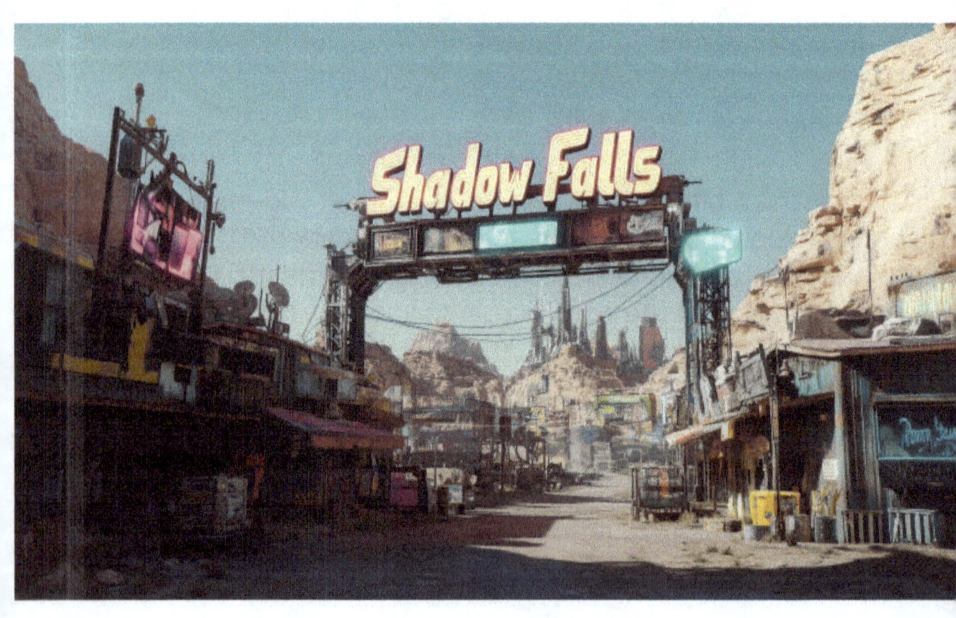

EPISODE 13
SHADOW FALLS

The station was a bizarre blend of old-world charm and futuristic decay. Atomic-era signs blinked erratically alongside broken holographic projectors, and the air felt damp and heavy with the scent of rust and stale earth. Auris swept her flashlight across cavernous archways that curved above her—an underground transit stop that felt more like a forgotten cathedral of technology.

A faint echo followed her every footstep, bouncing off the crumbling walls. She couldn't tell how far the place stretched, only that it felt empty, haunted by its own history. Shards of glass and twisted metal lay scattered across the floor, remnants of a world that once thrived down here.

As Auris ventured deeper, she noticed a mound of debris piled against one corner: broken seats, shattered screens, half-buried signage. Then came a voice, incongruously bright in the dismal space:

"Hello there! Over here!"

Her pulse jolted. She cautiously picked her way through the rubble, brushing aside fragments of plastic and bent wiring. Her hand landed on something metallic—an older-model

Lumi device, battered and worn, its once-shiny paint reduced to chipped remnants.

Flipping it over, she spotted small lettering etched into the chassis:

A chill threaded through her. *EgoCorp. Even here, they have a footprint.*

As if in response to her discovery, the device whirred awake. A faint beep crackled from its ancient speaker:

"LIVE STREAM INITIATED"

Auris' stomach lurched. "*No, no, no!*" she hissed, dropping the bot. It hovered crookedly, its dust-caked lens jittering subtly. Her face, momentarily lit by the screen, was but a smear of indistinguishable pixels under the grime.

Realizing it couldn't see her clearly, Auris exhaled in relief, but she still wasn't taking chances. Grabbing a chunk of concrete, she smashed the drone repeatedly until its lens and screen fizzled dark.

A moment passed, her heart racing, as she waited for an alarm that never came. No moderators. No sign she'd been truly identified. The lens had been too clogged with dust to capture her face. *Lucky break.*

Straightening up, Auris noticed a thin shaft of sunlight cutting across the cavern floor. It spilled through a jagged opening at the far end of the station. There were no stairs here. Just rough-hewn stone sloping upward, giving the impression she'd stepped into a natural cave that merged with the station's rickety architecture.

She followed the light, ascending an uneven path carved into the rock. The air warmed with each step, carrying the scent of open sky. The tunnel widened, turning into a broad mouth of rock that overlooked a sprawling valley—*Shadow Falls* laid out below like a post-apocalyptic tapestry.

Beneath her, a rough trail spiraled down into a hive of makeshift buildings: rusted metal huts, LED-lit scaffolds, and dusty thoroughfares. Solar panels jerry-rigged to crumbling rooftops droning under the late-day sun. AWOL bots rattled past half-bionic humans, and vendors hawked weird techno-trinkets from rickety stalls. It was chaotic, loud, and undeniably alive.

Auris paused at the cave's mouth, letting the sunlight wash her face—squinting against the sudden brightness after so long in the darkness. The ambiance of distant voices, clang of metal, and chatter of unknown tongues rose to meet her.

She was free of Virtu City's sanitized corridors. She was free of EgoCorp's watchful eye… at least for now.

Closing her eyes, she inhaled the dusty air, a strange cocktail of dread and exhilaration pulsing in her veins. *No going back now*, she thought. Clutching her backpack, Auris started down the winding trail toward the heart of Shadow Falls, each step forging a new piece of her unfolding story.

She shielded her eyes against the sudden flood of daylight. After so many hours underground, the sun was blinding, the dry, hot wind whipping at her hair. She paused on the rocky ledge overlooking a haphazard sprawl of rusted roofs, solar panels, and neon signs that flickered even in daylight.

The din of bustling dirt roads filled with makeshift vendor booths calling out prices, clanging metal from someone tinkering in a nearby workshop—drifted up to meet her. the hazy daylight in Shadow Falls felt both invigorating and intimidating. Dust motes swirled in the air as she took in the ragtag settlement below: rooftops patched with LED strips, half-collapsed buildings propped up by rusted girders, and at least a dozen makeshift stalls where locals haggled over salvage. A far cry from Virtu City's orderly glass towers.

Shadow Falls, she thought, letting the name settle into her mind. *I'm really here.*

A metallic *whir-clunk* breaks the stillness behind her. She turns sharply, her fists instinctively clenching.

From the trail emerges a wobbly, dual-wheeled bot, its mismatched plating dull in the sunlight, save for faint Amazon markings buried under scratches and grime. The bot's lens scans her, and it speaks with a chipper, almost too-familiar tone:

"Whoa, hold it right there. That jacket… That backpack… Let me guess. Virtu City, right? No, wait—Prime Square. Yeah, definitely Prime Square. Specific stitching pattern, Series 5 influencer merch drop, circa… last season. Nice."

Auris freezes, stunned. Her eyes narrow. "How—what? Who are you?"

The bot leans forward, its wheel wobbling slightly as its lens focuses intently on her jacket. "Don't get too excited, kid. It's just the ol' Wheeler touch. You're looking at PrimeRunner Model 7, designed for precision delivery and advanced product recognition. Basically, I can ID every Amazon product ever made. And that little number you're wearing? Screams 'Virtu City elite.'"

Auris stiffens, her eyes darting around nervously. "Keep your voice down," she hisses. The last thing she needed was for the whole town to know she didn't belong.

Wheeler tilts its head slightly, the vague hum of its servos giving an almost curious tone. "Relax. I'm not gonna rat you out. But hey, you gotta admit—showing up here in that fancy city gear? Bold choice."

Auris steps forward, her shoulders squaring, her tone shifting to something sharp and deliberate. "Look, just tell me who I have to pay to get some answers around here," she snaps, her voice dropping an octave. Her posture and words feel almost rehearsed, like a switch flipping in her brain.

The bot's eyes jitter, and its wheel spins back slightly as if retreating. "Okay, okay, no need to go full Corpo Mode on me. Geez." It pauses for a beat before adding, "What exactly do you have to offer, anyway?"

Auris pulls out a chip from her pocket, holding it up like a trump card. "VirtuCoin."

Wheeler stares at the chip, its lens zooming in briefly before it lets out a sharp mechanical laugh. "VirtuCoin? Oh, kid, no. Just… no. Hate to break it to you, but out here in the real world, your digital Monopoly money doesn't mean skibidi squat. Out here, life isn't always pay-to-play."

Auris stares at the chip for a moment, the bot's words hitting harder than she expected. She slides the chip back into her pocket, her jaw tightening. "So—what am I supposed to do?"

Wheeler leans back, letting out a low whir, almost like a sigh. "Figure it out. That's the 'real world' way, rookie. Lucky for you, you've got me. Consider it a 'free tutorial.'"
The bot spins in place, gesturing toward the bustling sprawl of Shadow Falls. "Now come on. You're sticking out like a drone in a scrapyard, and trust me—you do not want the wrong kind of attention around here."

As they walk—or rather, as Auris walks and Wheeler rolls—they descend into the heart of Shadow Falls. The noise rises with every step: clanging metal, bursts of laughter, the obscure buzz of patched-together generators. The air is heavy with the scent of rust, grease, and something faintly sweet but acrid.

Auris glances around, her eyes darting from the neon graffiti sprawled across crumbling walls to the makeshift market stalls cobbled together with scrap and glowing circuitry.

Wheeler rolls beside her, its tone lighter now. "So, got a name?"

"Auris." She said untrustingly.

"Nice to make your acquaintance, Auris. So, where to first? There's Rusty's Run—local watering hole, lots of chatter. Or, I dunno, wanna just wander around aimlessly and hope someone doesn't rob you?"

Auris doesn't answer immediately, her gaze lingering on a vendor haggling over a pile of scavenged tech. She inhales sharply, pushing down the doubt creeping into her mind.

"Just... find me someone who knows something useful," she says finally, her voice clipped.

Wheeler spins in excitement, its dented chassis clinking faintly. "Oh, this is gonna be quite the side-quest. Stick close, kid. And hey, no refunds if you don't like the tour."
Auris followed Wheeler down the uneven path, her boots kicking up fine dust that glimmered faintly in the hazy sunlight. Shadow Falls sprawled out before her, a chaotic mess of leaning scrap towers, graffiti glowing weakly on crumbling walls, and tangled wires strung haphazardly between makeshift buildings. The sound of clanging metal,

muffled shouts, and stolen power generators filled the air, mixing with the acrid smell of burning circuits.

"Alright then," Wheeler said, rolling ahead with a slight wobble, "Welcome to Shadow Falls. Home to scavengers, smugglers, and folks who think dental hygiene is a government conspiracy."

"Charming," Auris grumbled, stepping over a rusted pipe half-buried in the dirt.

"Hey, it's not so bad," Wheeler replied, swiveling its lens toward her. "Sure, the air's toxic, the power's unreliable, and half the people here probably want to stab you, but we've got… character."

Auris shot the bot a sidelong glance. "If that's supposed to make me feel better, it's not working."

Wheeler spun in place, its dented plating clinking faintly. "You'll warm up to it. Or you won't. Either way, I'm here for the commentary."

As they continued into the city, Auris' attention was drawn to a holographic billboard mounted on a leaning scrap wall. It showed a sleek Amazon Prime drone hovering over a family with exaggerated, toothpaste-commercial smiles. The slogan beneath it read:
"Amazon Prime: Bringing the World to Your Doorstep!"

Someone had scrawled a crude addition in red spray paint:
"And Taking It, Too."
Auris tilted her head at the ad. "Why are these even still running out here?"

"Because nothing dies harder than a corporate slogan, am I right?" Wheeler replied.

"You could nuke the planet, and there'd still be a glowing Coca-Cola sign somewhere, I guarantee it. They're like cockroaches, except they cost more to get rid of!"

"What are cockroaches?", Auris asks confidently, solidifying her ignorance and privilege once more.

Wheeler stops in its tracks and turns its head to the side as if trying to compute a complex code. Realizing her education or 'programming' was designed only for her survival and corporate productivity, Wheeler quickly understands that she was never meant to learn or even know such things existed and chooses not to divulge the topic any further.

"Wait..so you really don't-well..Never mind then." The bot responds, his voice box raising with a tone of disbelief

Auris scoffed, turning her attention back to the path ahead. Further along, a rusted vending machine caught her eye. The faded logo read:
"Crocs Survival Gear: Battle-Tested Footwear for the Apocalypse!"

"Crocs?" she asked, raising an eyebrow.

"Hey, don't knock it," Wheeler said, rolling up beside the machine. "Their treads saved my wheel more than once. Practical and ugly-like most things out here."

Auris shook her head, "This place just gets stranger by the second."

As they approached the center of the sprawl, Auris noticed a group of children rummaging through a pile of scrap. They laughed and shouted, tossing bits of junk at each other like it was a game.

"Are they… playing?" she asked, her voice tinged with disbelief.

"Sure are," Wheeler said. "They haven't figured out they're supposed to be miserable yet. Give 'em a few years."

Auris frowned, watching as one of the kids triumphantly held up a dented robot arm. "But… they're just kids. How do they survive out here?"

"Same way the rest of us do…barely," Wheeler replied. "Look, out here, you don't wait for life to hand you happiness. You find it in whatever you've got left. Even if it's just a busted robot arm."

Auris didn't respond, her gaze lingering on the kids as they disappeared into the maze of scrap.

They rounded a corner and entered a bustling market square. Makeshift stalls cobbled together from sheet metal and wood were packed tightly together, each one buzzing with activity. Vendors shouted over each other, trying to hawk their wares to anyone who would listen.

"Top-of-the-line holo lenses!" one vendor called out. "Only mildly glitchy! Perfect for pretending you're still rich!"

Another stall displayed a questionable pile of meat under a scrappy painted sign that read:

"Larry's Meat Shack: Real Meat!"
Wheeler leaned closer to Auris and whispered, "I'd advise you don't eat the meat."

"Why not?"

"Because Larry also sells the cure. And trust me, it's overpriced. Besides, what does REAL MEAT even mean anymore these days?"

Auris wrinkled her nose, sidestepping a patch of what she hoped was just grease on the ground. "Does anyone here sell anything useful?"

"Define useful," Wheeler replied, rolling toward a stall overflowing with salvaged tech. "Old drones, faulty implants, half-working holo-gadgets—Shadow Falls has it all, assuming you don't care about warranties."

She scanned the square, trying not to flinch under the weight of suspicious stares. The people here were tough, worn-down but resourceful. They moved through the chaos with purpose, unbothered by the noise and grime.

"Out here," Wheeler said, noticing her gaze, "you learn to work with what you've got. It's not about shiny new things—it's about making the broken ones work again."

"Is that supposed to be some kind of lesson?"

"Nah," Wheeler replied with a shrug. "Just an observation. The lesson comes later. Probably."

RUSTY'S
RUN
RUSTTY
RUSTYS

EPISODE 14

SIDE QUEST

The path narrowed as they left the market, the noise fading slightly into the background. Ahead, a large neon sign flickered weakly above a structure that looked like a cross between a retrofitted bus and a shipping container. The sign read:

"Rusty's Run – Where Nobody Knows Your Name (And That's How We Like It)."

"This is it," Wheeler announced, rolling to a stop. "Rusty's Run. First rule of Shadow Falls diplomacy: the Bartender knows everything worth knowing. Play your cards right, and he might actually tell you something useful."

"And if I don't?"

"Then you'll be on your own," Wheeler said simply. "Which, for someone like you, isn't exactly the greatest of options."

Auris glanced at the sign, then back at the bot. "How are you so sure he'll even talk to me?"

"I'm not," Wheeler replied, spinning slightly. "But I do know you're not gonna get far without making some friends. Or at least some tolerable enemies. Either way, you'll figure it out. Probably."

Taking a deep breath, Auris pushed open the heavy metal door and stepped inside.

The air inside *Rusty's Run* was heavy, thick with the smell of grease, alcohol, and something faintly metallic that made Auris wrinkle her nose. The bar was dimly lit, a chaotic mix of memorabilia and makeshift lamps cobbled together from old machine parts.

The room buzzed with quiet tension. Scavengers, human-bot hybrids, and others she couldn't immediately place hunched over steaming mugs and plates of questionable food. They murmured in low voices, their conversations punctuated by bursts of laughter or the clinking of metal. As Auris stepped inside, the chatter quieted for a moment, all eyes turning toward her.

She could feel their gazes—a mix of suspicion and curiosity, scanning her like a piece of scavenged tech they were debating whether to pick apart. She squared her shoulders, forcing her steps to stay steady as she crossed the room.

"Relax, rookie," Wheeler whispered, rolling close beside her. "They're not gonna eat you. Probably."

Her glare silenced him, and the bot let out a faint mechanical sigh.

The bar itself was a haphazard marvel: a retrofitted travel bus split open and welded to a shipping container. Its long counter was made of welded scrap metal, and behind it stood the Bartender—a broad-shouldered man with a mechanical arm that glinted faintly in the dim light. His face was lined with age and fatigue, but his eyes were sharp, scanning the room like he missed nothing.

"Wheeler," the Bartender said without looking up as they approached. His voice was gravelly, each word slow and deliberate. "Didn't I tell you not to bring me any more strays?"

"Oh, come on, Rust," Wheeler replied, spinning playfully. "She's not a stray. She's more like… a lost lamb. Quite an expensive one, judging by the jacket."

Rusty's eyes flicked to Auris, scanning her with the precision of someone who'd seen too much and trusted too little. "Fancy jacket," he said, his voice flat. "Clean boots. Too clean for Shadow Falls. You don't belong here."

Auris stiffened, meeting his gaze. "I'm looking for someone. Veil said I'd find answers here."

At the mention of Veil, Rusty's expression shifted slightly, his brow furrowing. "Veil, huh? That explains the stink of Virtu City. What makes you think anyone here has answers for you?"

"I don't have a choice." she replied, her voice steady but losing confidence. "So you're saying is…she lied..."

Rusty studied her for a long moment, his mechanical fingers tapping a slow rhythm on the counter. Then he let out a sharp laugh. "You're either brave or stupid, city girl. Maybe both, but all right. Who ya looking for?"

"Clair Voyànt," she said.

At the name, a ripple of reaction moved through the bar. Heads turned, whispers flared, and then the patrons quickly went back to their drinks, pretending they hadn't heard.

Rusty's smirk faded, his expression hardening. "Clair, huh? You sure about that?"

Auris nodded. "She's the only one who can help me."

Rusty leaned on the counter, his mechanical arm creaking faintly. "Clair doesn't trust people. She doesn't do meetings. If she thinks you're worth her time, she'll find you. But that's a big *if.*"

"So how do I get her attention?" She asked.

Rusty tilted his head slightly, his smirk returning. "Shadow Falls is full of problems. Fix one. Protect someone. Do something loud enough to matter, and she'll notice. She's got eyes everywhere—even if some of them are a little scrambled right now."

Auris frowned. "Scrambled?"

Rusty nodded toward the window, where the faint silhouette of a signal tower was visible on the far ridge. "One of the old towers Clair uses for her... *visions* is down. Rumor is, a rogue drone's latched onto it, jamming her systems. She's been blind for days."

"And *NO ONE* out here could fix it?" Auris asked.

"Look kid, we're barely survivin' as is. Besides, No one wants to deal with whatever's out there," Rusty said simply. "The rogue bots are bad enough, but a malfunctioning EgoCorp drone? That's suicide for most common folk around here."

Wheeler let out a low whistle. "Yikes. Rogue EgoCorp hardware? Yeah, those things are nasty. I mean, not as nasty as some of my relatives, but still."

Rusty ignored him, his gaze fixed on Auris. "If you want Clair to notice you, that's your chance. Fix the tower. Get her signal running again. But don't expect a thank-you."

Auris hesitated, the weight of his words sinking in. She glanced at Wheeler, who tilted his head as if waiting for her decision.

“Fine,” she said, her voice steady. “Tell me how to get there.”

Rusty gestured toward a map pinned to the wall, its edges curled and faded. “Follow the ridge trail up the mountain. You’ll find the tower near the peak. And if you survive? Maybe Clair will find you.”

“That's a Big if,” Wheeler added cheerfully.

Auris stepped back from the counter, her fists clenching briefly before she relaxed them. She’d come this far. She wasn’t about to back down now.

The trail leading out of Shadow Falls was rough, a winding path carved into the mountainside that seemed more suited for goats than people. Loose gravel crunched under Auris’ boots, and the occasional gust of wind sent pebbles skittering into the abyss below. The vibrations of the signal tower grew louder as they climbed, a steady pulse like a heartbeat in the distance.

Auris adjusted her backpack, her frustration simmering as she eyed the jagged trail ahead. “Risking life and limb to get the attention of someone who doesn’t even know I exist,” she muttered, more to herself than Wheeler. “This is idiotic.”

Wheeler, rolling slightly behind her, let out a mechanical chuckle. “No different than social media, rookie.”

Auris glanced back at him, her brow furrowed. “What are you talking about? How so?”

"Think about it," Wheeler said, his tone annoyingly casual. "People all over the world do crazy stuff every day just to keep up with what they think Virtu City is. They jump off buildings, eat stuff that would make you gag, fake these 'perfect lives' just to grab the attention of someone famous or, worse, someone who doesn't even exist."

Auris stopped in her tracks, his words sinking in like a heavy weight. She'd grown up in Virtu City, surrounded by influencers, holograms, and meticulously curated personas. It was all she'd ever known. But out here, hearing it framed this way, it sounded… hollow.

"You're saying *this* is the same?" she asked, her voice quieter now.

"Well, maybe a little less glamorous," Wheeler replied, spinning slightly in place. "But yeah. You're doing something big, bold, and possibly suicidal, hoping to catch the eye of someone who's probably too busy to care. If that doesn't scream 'influencer culture,' I don't know what does."

Auris didn't reply immediately. She looked down at the trail, the dirt and dust clinging to her boots, and thought about all the people who spent their lives chasing some unattainable image of Virtu City. How many of them ever actually got what they were looking for?

Finally, she shook her head, her lips pressing into a thin line. "I'm not doing this for attention. I'm doing this because I need answers."

"Whatever helps you sleep at night, kid," Wheeler said, rolling ahead with a cheerful hum. "But if Clair likes what she sees, maybe she'll follow you back. Isn't that what they call it? Engagement?"

Auris groaned and kept walking.

The signal tower loomed ahead, its skeletal frame twisting upward like a jagged scar against the horizon as it creaked in the wind. The glitchy sounds of its disrupted signal was louder now, a low, vibrating buzz that made Auris' teeth ache.

Auris crouched at the base of the signal tower, its Sparks danced around the corrupted EgoCorp drone latched onto the tower's base, its rotors jerking erratically as it tried to maintain its grip. Its sensors fluttered, and the corrupted streams of data pouring from its frame warped the air around it. Wheeler rolled up beside her, his lens swiveling toward the buzzing mess.

"Yep, there's your problem," Wheeler said, tilting his head. "That thing's clinging to the tower like my ex. Believe me, it wasn't fun."

What's it doing?" Auris asked, her voice tense.

"Overriding the tower's signal," Wheeler replied. "Or trying to, anyway. It's like someone put your brain into a blender and then threw the blender into a lake."

Auris shot him a confused look.

"Translation: it's bad," Wheeler clarified. "Very bad. And if we don't get it off that tower, Clair's not gonna be able to see squat."

Auris exhaled sharply, her eyes narrowing as she studied the drone. "Can we shut it down?

"If only it were that simple." Wheeler replies.

That's when it clicks. Auris glances at the pocket on left strap of her backpack. Inside was **hi-jakker device** she'd managed to pocket back in the Deadzone—a risky move, considering the risks. The device was small but powerful, capable of overriding a bot's command protocols. She didn't know exactly how it worked, but if there was ever a time to find out, this was it.

She unclipped the device, holding it up for Wheeler to see. "Think this will work?"

Wheeler's lens zoomed in, scanning it. "A hi-jakker? I haven't seen one of those in decades! Where'd you get that? Actually, never mind. If it's real, it should work, assuming you don't fry my circuits plugging it in."

Auris hesitated. "I need you to take control of the drone. Can you do that?"

"Can I? Yes. Will I? That depends. You got a backup plan if this thing explodes?"

"No," Auris said flatly. "But if we don't fix this, I'm not sticking around to explain it to the locals. Are you?"

Wheeler let out a mechanical sigh. "Fair point. Plug me in."

Hi-Jakking the Drone

Auris by connected the Hi-Jakker to Wheeler's chest panel, the device sparking faintly as it interfaced with his systems. The bot whirred loudly, his lens flickering as he established a connection with the corrupted drone.

"Okay, okay… I think I've got it. Yup, I'm in."

The drone's movements became smoother, its jerky spasms replaced by controlled swivels as Wheeler asserted dominance over its commands. The signal tower's lights flickered and stabilized, the interference signal stabilizing abruptly.

"This thing is like flying a brick," Wheeler muttered, his servos straining. "But hey, I've had worse gigs."

The drone detached itself from the tower, its rotors spinning faster as it lifted into the air. Auris watched nervously as it hovered above them, its sensors glowing faintly.

"Now what?" she asked.

"Now we give the town a little show," Wheeler said, his tone gleeful. "Hold onto your hat, rookie."

A Drone in the Sky

The drone shot upward, circling above the craggy cliffs that enclosed Shadow Falls. As it reached the peak of the mountain ridge, it paused, then tilted downward, descending toward the center of the town.

The buzz of its rotors echoed across the settlement, drawing the attention of everyone below. Locals looked up, their expressions shifting from confusion to alarm as the drone loomed closer. Some shouted warnings, others ducked for cover. A few bolder scavengers raised makeshift weapons, preparing to take it down.

Auris and Wheeler followed on foot, emerging from the trail just as the drone descended into the center of the market square.

"Relax, folks!" Wheeler announced, his voice amplified through the drone's speaker. "It's all under control!"

The drone landed awkwardly but safely in the square, its rotors sputtering to a stop. The gathered crowd hesitated, murmurs of suspicion rippling through them.

Auris stepped forward, her hands raised in a gesture of peace. "We've subdued it," she said, her voice firm but steady. "The tower's signal is restored. It should be safe now."

There was a moment of tense silence before the crowd surged forward. Some cheered, clapping Auris on the back or giving Wheeler approving nods. Others immediately began dismantling the drone, their practiced hands searching for trackers, valuable parts, and anything they could repurpose.

"Careful with the wiring!" Wheeler called out as a scavenger pried open the drone's chassis. "I just calibrated that!"

Auris stepped back, watching as the crowd swarmed the drone like ants on a carcass. For the first time, she felt a flicker of satisfaction. She'd done something. Fixed something. Even if it wasn't her world, she'd made an impact.

As the crowd buzzed with activity, scavengers swarming the subdued drone for parts, Auris stepped back, her body sagging with exhaustion. The adrenaline that had fueled her since the signal tower now ebbed, leaving her legs weak and her thoughts sluggish. Wheeler rolled up beside her, his lens swiveling toward her face.

"Not bad, rookie. I mean, you didn't explode or accidentally set the drone on fire, so… solid B-plus."

Auris shot him a glare but didn't have the energy to respond. Her stomach growled audibly, and she realized just how long it had been since she'd last eaten.

One of the vendors, a wiry woman with grease-streaked arms and a sharp gaze, gesturing Auris to come over to her stall, holding a steaming bowl of something that smelled vaguely like soup.

"Here," the woman said, pressing the bowl into Auris' hands. "On the house. Least I can do for saving the town from whatever that was." She nodded toward the remains of the drone, now little more than a pile of wires and stripped plating.

Auris blinked in surprise. "Thank you. I—thank you."

"Don't mention it," the vendor replied, her tone brisk but not unkind. "Just keep that bot of yours outta my stall." She shot Wheeler a pointed look before disappearing back into her tent.

Auris sat on an overturned crate, cradling the warm bowl in her hands. The food was simple but hearty, and with every bite, she felt her strength returning. Wheeler sat quietly for once, his wheel clicking faintly as he shifted in place.

When she finished, the vendor reappeared, handing her a small slip of paper. "Here's your receipt," she said with a smirk.
Auris frowned. "But you said the meal was free!"

The vendor shrugged. “Sure was. Didn’t your parents teach you to always keep your receipts?” Then, without another word, she disappeared into the crowd.

The warmth of the vendor’s stew still lingered as Auris set the empty bowl aside. The simple meal had done more than fill her stomach, it had given her a moment to catch her breath, to feel human again amidst the chaos of Shadow Falls.

Auris flipped the receipt over in her hands, frowning as the glowing pattern of white and black squares caught her eye. It wasn’t text. It wasn’t coordinates. It was…

“A QR code?” she muttered, exasperated. “What am I supposed to do with this?”

She scanned her surroundings, as if some magical scanner would conveniently appear. “Great. Just great. I’m out in the middle of nowhere, and they give me a QR code? The hell am I supposed to do with this? How can I even scan it—with my imagination?”

“No need to panic, rookie,” came a cheerful voice.

She spun to see Wheeler, his lens flickering slightly as he rolled closer.

“YOU,” Auris said, her frustration flaring. “YOU can scan this!”

“Bingo!” Wheeler replied, extending a small arm-like attachment from his frame. “You know, you really lucked out running into me. Hand it over.”

Auris hesitated, then held out the slip. Wheeler's lens tilted, a laser light emanating as he scanned the code. After a moment, his voice brightened.

"Coordinates decrypted! Mapping route now… and…done!"

"So…Where does it lead?" she asked, already bracing for bad news.

"Good news: not far," Wheeler said, spinning to face a faint trail winding into the distance. "Bad news: it's not exactly a luxury commute. Follow me."

Before she could respond, Wheeler zipped ahead with a burst of energy.

"Hey! Wait up!" Auris called, jogging to catch up.

EPISODE 15

OFF TO SEE THE WIZARD

The path Wheeler led her on was rough but manageable, weaving through rocky outcrops and overgrown trails that seemed long abandoned. Despite the uneven terrain, Auris found herself faring better than she expected.

Her boots kicked up small clouds of dust as she climbed a gentle incline, her breathing steady despite the effort. She adjusted her pack, noting how her body seemed to move more confidently now, her balance sharper and her steps quicker than when she first left Virtu City.

"Gotta say, rookie," Wheeler said, glancing back at her, "you're handling this better than I thought you would. Most Virtu types would've twisted an ankle by now."

Auris smirked faintly. "Guess I'm full of surprises."

"Maybe you are," Wheeler said, spinning ahead. "Just don't let it go to your head. Trail's not over yet."

The path gradually shifted from dusty trails to firmer, rockier ground. There was a peaceful calmness, and the landscape around them became more surreal. Broken pieces of old tech—satellite dishes, rusted gears, and shattered drones—

were scattered across the cliffs like remnants of a forgotten era.

"Wonder if all this stuff still works" Auris pondered, pausing to examine a partially buried drone.

"Not unless you've got a time machine," Wheeler replied. "But Clair? She'd probably find a use for it. Lady's got a knack for making something out of nothing."

Auris stood, brushing dirt off her hands, and followed Wheeler as he continued up the trail.

Clair's Lair

The final stretch of the path opened onto a wide plateau, and Auris stopped in her tracks, gazing at the sight before her.

Clair's hideout was a masterpiece of controlled chaos, perched dramatically at the edge of the cliff. A sprawling structure built from salvaged tech, it jutted out like a defiant monument to ingenuity.

Satellite dishes and antennas rose from the roof, their surfaces painted in vibrant, clashing colors. Glowing strips lined the edges of the walls, pulsing softly in rhythm with the machinery. Holographic projections hovered above the structure, displaying swirling patterns and cryptic symbols that flickered like distant stars.

The structure looked both ancient and futuristic, its jagged lines and mismatched materials blending seamlessly with the rocky terrain. Wires hung like vines, connecting smaller modules to the main building.

"Well," Wheeler said, spinning slowly to take it all in. "She's definitely got an eye for… unconventional architecture."

Auris adjusted her pack, her gaze fixed on the glowing doorway at the center of the structure. “Let’s do this.”

As they approached, the audio from the projections grew louder, and the door slid open with a soft hiss. A voice, smooth and confident, echoed from within.

“*Took you long enough*,” it said.

Auris stepped inside, her heart pounding as she prepared to meet the woman who might hold the answers she’d been searching for.

The room was unlike anything Auris had seen before. Screens plastered every wall, streaming fragmented data in pulsing hues of blue and green. Holographic projections hovered above tables cluttered with salvaged gadgets, their ghostly images twisting and flickering in the dim light. At the center of it all was a crystalline sphere, suspended above a pedestal in a delicate lattice of glowing metal.

Auris glanced around, taking it all in. “This is… a *lot*.”

Clair smirked, crossing her arms. “Not what you were expecting?”

“It's like Virtu City had a panic attack and threw up on a mountain,” Wheeler quipped, his lens swiveling toward the floating sphere. “And what's that thing? Some kind of… disco ball for nerds?”

Clair’s eyes lit up, and she stepped toward the sphere with an almost giddy excitement. “I was wondering when you’d ask. I call it…” She paused dramatically as if she was building suspense, her grin widening as she gestured toward the glowing sphere. “…the iBall!”

She waited, looking between Auris and Wheeler expectantly.

Wheeler tilted his lens, his servos whirring faintly. "Uh... okay?"

"Get it?" Clair prompted, leaning in slightly. "Like *eye* ball, but also tech? You know, like iPhone, iOS, i—" She cut herself off with a sigh, throwing up her hands. "Never mind. Tough crowd."

Auris stared at her flatly. "You built all this, and *that's* the name you went with?"

Clair gave a mock bow. "Genius is rarely understood in its own time."

Wheeler buzzed with amusement, rolling slightly closer to the sphere. "So what does it do? Besides glow and look vaguely ominous?"

"It helps me see what others can't," Clair said cryptically, running her fingers along the edge of the pedestal. "I'll show you later—if we get that far."

Auris frowned, her frustration starting to build. "I didn't come here for parlor tricks. Veil said you could help me. That you could decrypt this."

She pulled the drive from her bag and held it out. Clair's smile faded as her gaze flickered to the drive, her posture stiffening slightly.

"I'm not decrypting that," Clair said flatly, leaning back against the pedestal.
Auris blinked, caught off guard. "What do you mean you're not decrypting it?"

"Exactly what I said," Clair replied. "It's too risky. If EgoCorp catches wind of me messing with something like that,

I'm done. This place? Gone. My work? Erased. I'm not risking it for anyone."

"You're serious?" Auris said, her voice tinged with disbelief. "After everything I did to get here?"

Clair crossed her arms, her expression calm but firm. "It's not about you. It's about survival. Out here, you don't make it by taking unnecessary risks."

Auris' frustration boiled over. "So, what—you're just a glorified tech hoarder? Sitting up here, pretending to be some great oracle, but when it actually matters, you back out? Maybe you really are a fraud."

The words hung in the air, sharp and cutting. Clair's smirk faded, and her sharp eyes narrowed, her tone turning icy.

"Excuse me?"

"You heard me," Auris continued. "You're a phony. Without tech, you have no vision. Algorithms. Predictive models. Data feeds. That's not vision…That's programming. You're not a seer, you're just some crazy old lady with a Wi-Fi connection."

Clair chuckled, shaking her head. She stepped closer. Slowly. Menacingly. "And what is a vision if not just patterns and probability made clear? Whether it's through dreams, gut feelings, or neural networks, it all leads to the same thing —knowing what comes next before everyone else does."

Auris scoffed. "That's a cop-out."

"No, that's wisdom." Clair stepped closer. "The power isn't in how you receive the vision, it's in what you do with it. I don't just predict—I interpret. I navigate. I choose. What good is sight if you don't know where to step next?"

Before Auris could respond, Wheeler interjected, leaning against the wall, arms crossed.

"She's right, y'know." His voice was calm, but his eyes were sharp. "Magic and technology—both are illusions. Different means, same outcome. Doesn't matter if you're casting spells in a candlelit room or crunching data through an AI mainframe—what matters is the user. The intent. The understanding."

Auris turned to him, still skeptical. "You're really comparing sorcery to circuit boards?"

Wheeler shrugged. "Think about it. A magician waves their hands, mutters some cryptic words, and—boom—something impossible happens. A tech wizard does the same—presses a button, runs a command, and—boom—something impossible happens. The only real difference? One calls it magic, the other calls it science. But neither means a damn thing without someone who knows what they're doing."

Auris let that settle for a moment. She hated to admit it, but he had a point. Vision—real vision—wasn't about the tool. It was about the wielder. About seeing the unseen and knowing exactly when to act.

She walked over to one of the cluttered tables, her fingers brushing a half-assembled circuit board as she spoke. "I wasn't always out here, you know. I was big in Virtu City. A name people trusted, respected. Clair Voyànt—the influencer who knew everything before it happened."

Wheeler let out a low whistle. "A fortune-telling influencer? Now that's branding."

Clair shot him a look but continued. "My algorithms predicted trends before they happened. Stock markets, political scandals, product launches—I had it all down to a science. EgoCorp loved me. I made them millions."

She leaned against the table, her gaze distant. "Until I started seeing things they didn't want me to see. Things they didn't want *anyone* to see."

Auris crossed her arms, her frustration giving way to curiosity. "Like what?"

Clair's expression hardened. "Like a bot uprising that could've wiped out their entire workforce. A failed Virtu City expansion that would've cost them billions. I was a liability, and they couldn't control me. So, they did what they always do."

"They canceled you," Auris said, the realization dawning.

Clair nodded, a bitter smile tugging at her lips. "Overnight, I went from genius to fraud. They fabricated scandals, doctored footage, made the public think I was crazy. A criminal. My followers turned on me, my sponsors pulled out, and just like that, I was gone."

Wheeler hummed thoughtfully. "`Classic corpo move. Ruin a life to protect the bottom line.`"

Clair gestured to the room around her. "This is what's left of me. I rebuilt what I could, hid from the world, and kept doing what I do best…seeing things they don't want me to see." Auris stared at her, the pieces falling into place. "So, that's it? You hide out here, watching the world go to hell, and do nothing?"

Clair's sharp eyes locked onto her. "Don't mistake caution for cowardice. Out here, survival isn't about winning—it's about not losing. And that drive you brought me? That's a losing bet.

Clair turned back to the iBall, running her fingers along the glowing lattice. "But... she might have something to say about it."

Auris blinked. "She?"

Clair smirked, her earlier playfulness returning. "The iBall. She's smarter than me, and she doesn't care about the risks. Show her the drive."

Auris hesitated, glancing at Wheeler, who gave an encouraging whir. With a sigh, she stepped forward and held the drive near the glowing sphere.

The iBall's display darkened, and the symbols on its surface began to shift and swirl. A soft glow of light extended from the sphere, scanning the drive. The iBall glowing brighter, vibrating faintly through the floor, until the sphere finally emitted a melodic chime.

Then, in a smooth, feminine voice, the iBall spoke: **"Drive identified. Data fragment contains encrypted records. Associated entity: Game On. Location match: Silicon Valley. Active hub detected. Operational integrity: compromised."**

Auris furrowed her brow. "Game On? What's that?"
Clair tilted her head, clearly as puzzled as Auris. "E-sports hubs. VR arcades, gaming tournaments—looks like they used to be everywhere before the world went to hell. But if that drive is pointing you there, it's not about games."

"What do you mean?" Auris pressed.

"From what I'm seeing, Game On hubs were run by private corporations. They weren't just entertainment centers—they were data farms, black sites, and research facilities. If this drive survived and is pointing you there, it's got to be connected to something bigger."

Auris stared at the drive in her hand, her resolve hardening. "Then that's where I'm going."

Clair stepped back, folding her arms. "Silicon Valley's a mess, but if this is where the trail leads, you don't have a choice. There's a shuttle that runs once a day from Shadow Falls. Leaves soon actually. You'd better catch it."

Clair leaned against the doorway of her lair as Auris adjusted the strap of her bag. The tension from earlier had melted into a strange camaraderie, though neither would admit it outright.

"Well," Auris said, glancing back at the chaotic brilliance of Clair's hideout, "this was… enlightening."

Clair smirked, crossing her arms. "Shorter stay than I expected, but I get it. You've got places to be, secrets to uncover. Just don't let that drive get you or anybody else in trouble."

Auris nodded, her expression softening. "I'll be back. Probably sooner than you'd like."

Clair chuckled. "Yeah, I've heard that one before. I'll keep the light on. Just try not to make too much noise out there." Wheeler rolled to the edge of the plateau, his lens swiveling toward Auris. "`Time's ticking, rookie. Shuttle won't wait.`"

Auris offered Clair a faint smile. "Thanks. For everything."

Clair tilted her head, her voice quieter now. "Good luck, city girl. You'll need it."

With that, Auris turned and followed Wheeler down the winding path away from Clair's lair.

Shuttle Rush

The path back toward the heart of Shadow Falls was faster this time, though still tricky in places. Wheeler zipped ahead, his built-in GPS guiding them effortlessly. The electric whir of the distant shuttle grew louder with each step, mingling with the against the rocky terrain.

"Almost there," Wheeler called over his shoulder. "I've gotta admit, rookie, you're handling this better than most."

Auris smirked, sidestepping a loose rock. "Guess I'm full of surprises."

"Sure are," Wheeler replied, his tone almost wistful.

As they rounded a corner, the shuttle stop came into view. A weathered platform jutted out over a narrow gorge, its edges lined with faded signs advertising long-defunct companies. The shuttle itself—a sleek black transport vehicle with purple led lights—sitting idled, adverts playing on the display panels on its sides.

"This is it," Wheeler said, rolling to a stop at the edge of the platform.
Auris glanced at him, frowning. "You're not coming?"

Wheeler whirred softly, his lens tilting downward. "This is as far as I go. I'm a Shadow Falls bot, rookie. My purpose is here."

Auris looked away for a moment, disappointment flickering across her face. She'd grown used to Wheeler's quirks, his humor, and even his occasional sarcasm. Having a companion (especially one so unexpectedly endearing) had made the journey feel a little less daunting.

The shuttle's streamlined frame standing out against the decrepit surroundings of the Shadow Falls terminal. Auris stood by the boarding ramp, her arms crossed, as she cast a look back at Wheeler. His glowing blue optics flickered faintly, scanning the horizon, though there was nothing to see but fog and decay.
"You don't have to stay here," Auris said, her voice cutting through the quiet. "This place is nothing but a scrapyard."

Wheeler turned his head toward her, the motion slow and deliberate. "I must stay," he replied flatly. "My creator instructed me to remain here."

She sighed, planting her hands on her hips. "And how long ago was that?"

Wheeler's optics dimmed slightly, and the faint vibration of his internal systems grew louder. "Calculating," he said after a pause. "Months, years, decades… Who's counting? I am not programmed to process time the same way a human does." His tone was emotionless, but his words carried a strange finality that made Auris's stomach twist.

"And you think he's still coming back?" she pressed, raising an eyebrow. "After all this time?"
Wheeler's glowing eyes flickered again. "He said he would return after gathering crafting materials. Perhaps external conditions delayed him. Perhaps he encountered difficulties securing resources."

Auris folded her arms tighter, her lips pressing into a thin line. "Or," she said, stepping closer, "maybe he's not coming back at all. Maybe he abandoned you."

For the first time, Wheeler's optics dimmed entirely. His towering frame stilled as if even the suggestion needed to be processed. "That is… unlikely," he said finally, his voice steady but slower than before.

Auris tilted her head, her voice sharpening. "Really? He left you here, didn't send anyone else to check on you, didn't leave you with anything but vague instructions. That doesn't sound unlikely to me."

Wheeler paused again, his optics flickering faintly. "Abandonment is illogical. I was created to fulfill a directive. He would not abandon me without reason."

Auris let out a frustrated sigh, running a hand through her hair. "Don't you care? Don't you care that he might be dead, or that you're wasting away here for no one?"

Wheeler's response came immediately, the mechanical coldness of his voice unwavering. "I am not programmed to process emotion. Whether my creator is alive or deceased, my directive remains unchanged."
She stared at him, her jaw tightening. "So that's it? You just stand here forever, waiting for someone who's probably gone? Or worse?"

Wheeler shifted slightly, his rusted joints creaking. "Correct."

Auris exhaled sharply and turned back toward the shuttle. "*Fine*. If that's what you want, then stay here. Rot with the rest of this junk." She climbed the boarding ramp, pausing on the threshold. Glancing back, she added, "If I ever find him out there, what do you want me to tell him?"

Wheeler raised a rusted arm, opening a compartment in his forearm. A faint beam of light projected a holographic image into the air, flickering faintly. It showed a man in his mid-thirties, wearing a weathered jacket and safety goggles. His hands rested on the shoulder of a younger, spotless version of Wheeler, standing tall in a pristine Amazon facility.

"This is my creator," Wheeler said. "If you see him, tell him I am here. Tell him I obeyed."

Auris studied the image for a moment, committing it to memory. She nodded slowly. "Alright. I'll tell him." The hologram blinked out, and Wheeler lowered his arm. "Thank you," he said, his tone unchanging.

The shuttle's engines whirred to life, and Auris stepped inside. The doors slid shut behind her, and she took a seat near the rear window. As the vehicle pulled away, she watched Wheeler's massive silhouette disappear into the mist, his frame fading into the ruins of Shadow Falls.

"I was just getting used to having a sidekick," she said, her tone light but tinged with sincerity. Wheeler spun slightly, his lens focusing on her. "Sidekick?, if anything, you're the sidekick, Rookie!"

A crisp, humanoid voice echoed through the speakers: "**Shuttle departs in 30 seconds. Please board promptly**."

Auris laughed softly, shaking her head. "I guess this is where we part ways, then."

"Looks like it," Wheeler replied. "But hey, don't mess it up out there. You're carrying more than you realize."

"Thanks, Wheeler. For…everything."

The bot spun once in a playful circle. "Anytime, rookie! Now get outta here before I start rusting from all this emotion."

She nodded, stepping onto the platform. As the shuttle doors hissed open, she paused and glanced back at Wheeler. Wheeler turned back toward the scrapyard, his optics scanning the empty horizon once more.
"`Directive remains unchanged,`" he said softly to the stillness. His clunky frame stilled, blending seamlessly with the desolate landscape, and he resumed his eternal vigil. Waiting.

EPISODE 16
UNRENDERED TERRITORY

The shuttle doors slid shut behind her with a soft hiss. Auris found a seat near the window, watching as Wheeler became a small, flickering dot on the horizon. She leaned back, the adverts playing in and outside of the shuttle filling the silence.

Her journey was far from over. She didn't know what waited for her in Silicon Valley, but she knew one thing for certain—this was a path she had to walk alone.

As the shuttle pulled away, the jagged cliffs of Shadow Falls faded into the distance, replaced by the vast unknown. She spaced out and eventually nodded off while reflecting on her journey as the hours flew by and the shuttle drew closer to its destination.

The shuttle came to a grinding halt, hissing as it docked at a station that looked like it had been cobbled together from old-world scraps. The platform was deserted save for a handful of people sitting on overturned crates or leaning against rusted support beams. The air was thick with smog. The buzz of faulty digital billboards and power generators echoed through the valley.

Auris stepped off, adjusting her bag as her boots hit the uneven concrete. The landscape of Silicon Valley sprawled out before her, a stark mix of decay and remnants of technological ambition. Crumbling office buildings were covered in graffiti, their shattered windows glinting in the sunlight. Piles of discarded tech and rusted drones lined the streets, creating a labyrinth of metal and debris.

"*Welcome to Silicon Valley,*" Wheeler's voice echoed from her memory, though she missed his physical presence. "*Or what's left of it.*"

Auris squared her shoulders and headed toward a cluster of locals gathered near an open-air market. They eyed her with a mixture of curiosity and suspicion as she approached.

Making My Way Downtown

"Excuse me," Auris said, trying to keep her tone even. The nearest local, a youthful man with a face weathered by too much experience for his age and a jacket stitched together from various fabrics, looked up from the rusted drone he was tinkering with.

"Yeah?" he said, his voice gruff.

"I'm looking for Game On," Auris said, glancing at the others who had started to listen in. "I have a… gaming battle to attend."

The man froze, his expression a mix of confusion and disbelief. He exchanged a look with a nearby woman, who let out a sharp laugh.

"Gaming battle?" the woman repeated, shaking her head. "I think you've got the wrong era, sweetie."

"Game On's been shut down for decades," the man added, standing up and wiping his hands on a rag. "The place is dead. Nobody's been there in years."

Auris furrowed her brow. "Decades? Are you sure? It's supposed to be operational."

The man snorted. "Sure, if ghosts are running it. But hey, if you want to waste your time, I'll give you the route."

The locals began chiming in, each offering fragments of the route in a manner that sounded more like folklore than actual directions.

"It's out by the old grid," one woman said.

"Look for the building with the broken satellite dish," added a teenager sitting on the edge of the market, fiddling with a half-functional holo-display.

"Yeah, and the graffiti—big, glowing letters that say 'GAME OVER,'" the youthful man finished with a smirk.

Auris took mental notes, piecing together the descriptions. As they spoke, something clicked. She could almost see the layout in her mind. Her time in Virtu City, surrounded by holograms and digital maps, had trained her to pick out patterns, even in chaos.

"Got it," she said, straightening her bag.

"Suit yourself," the man said, shaking his head. "Don't get your hopes up, though. That place is dead and buried."

The route took Auris deeper into the heart of Silicon Valley's ruins. Each step brought her closer to what felt like another world—a wasteland littered with remnants of forgotten technology and failed dreams.

She passed rows of crumbling buildings, their once-bright facades now faded and cracked. Rusted billboards hung precariously over shattered streets, some still barely flickering with glitchy advertisements.

Finally, she spotted it: a massive, dilapidated structure with a broken satellite dish perched on its roof. The letters "GAME ON" were barely visible beneath layers of grime and graffiti, and someone had scrawled "GAME OVER" in glowing paint across the main entrance.

Auris paused, taking it in. The building loomed over her, its shattered windows and sagging walls radiating an eerie sense of abandonment. But there was something else—a frequency, almost imperceptible, emanating from within.

"This is it," she said under her breath, gripping the strap of her bag tighter.

The trail had led her here. Now it was time to find out why.

The derelict building looms like a relic of a forgotten age, its crumbling facade shrouded in shadow. The off-grid GPS on Auris's wrist pulses, signaling her destination with a pulsating dot on the screen. Her breath fogs in the cool night air as she steps closer, her shoes crunching over shattered glass and debris. The logo etched onto the weathered doorframe matches the engraving on the mysterious drive, a perfect yet unsettling match. She reaches out to the tarnished intercom button, her fingers trembling.

A sharp metallic voice breaks the silence, echoing from hidden speakers embedded in the cracked walls. "Who dares venture into '*The Lair Of The Lord*'?—**Speak** now—lest you be deemed an EgoCorp spy."

Her heart leaps into her throat. For a moment, she debates turning around, but there's no turning back now. "Here we go again," she mutters under her breath, half amused, half terrified. She raises her chin and speaks with as much confidence as she can muster.

"My name's Auris," she says, her voice steady despite the lump in her throat. She holds up the flash drive, its metal surface catching the dim light of the streetlamp behind her. "This—led me here. I need answers."

The silence that follows is suffocating. The slight static of electricity from the intercom feels like a countdown to something she can't predict. Her fingers grip the drive tighter, and she wonders if she's just made a colossal mistake.

The voice returns, colder than before. "Identity, you say? How do I know you're not some elaborate EgoCorp scheme? A Trojan horse, perhaps? They're quite clever, you know."

Auris looks down at her dirt-streaked clothes and scuffed boots, shaking her head in disbelief. "Really? Do I look like a spy to you?" The sarcasm drips from every syllable, her patience wearing thin.

The intercom clicks. "That drive could've only gotten into your hands by one of two ways," the voice declares, each word laced with accusation. "Either I made a colossal miscalculation, or you're a thief!"

Her grip on the drive tightens as irritation surges through her veins. She snaps back, her voice sharp. "If this piece of junk were so important to you, maybe you shouldn't have dropped it in the middle of Virtu City. I was just trying to return it. Guess this is what I get for being a Good Samaritan."

Another pause, longer this time. The silence feels heavier, like the weight of the building pressing down on her shoulders. Then, unexpectedly, the voice softens, a hint of amusement slipping through. A chuckle follows, low and sardonic.

"Fair point," the voice concedes, the edge melting away into something more human. "You've navigated a fortuitous path. Perhaps you've earned an audience."

The sound of gears turning fills the air as the heavy doors creak open, revealing a dimly lit corridor lined with glowing wires snaking along the walls like veins. At the far end, a figure steps into view. **Scorelord**.

He's taller than she expected, his silhouette imposing against the backdrop of flickering monitors. His attire is an amalgamation of practicality and eccentricity—tactical boots scuffed with wear, a long trench coat patched together with scraps of tech fabric, and a pair of augmented-reality goggles perched on his forehead. The glow from his devices illuminates his face, sharp features framed by disheveled hair that looks like it hasn't seen a brush in years.

They lock eyes, and for a moment, the world narrows to just the two of them. It's not fear that grips her, but something far stranger—an odd sense of familiarity, like stepping into a dream she didn't know she'd had.

"Well, you're not exactly what I was expecting," he says, breaking the silence first. His voice is smoother in person, less robotic, but still carries an air of caution.

"Likewise," Auris shoots back, her defenses still up. "Are you going to let me in, or is this going to be a staring contest?" A flicker of a smirk crosses his lips. "Fair enough." He steps aside, motioning for her to enter. "Welcome, Auris. Let's find you some answers."

The interior is a chaotic marvel, a labyrinth of technology salvaged from a dozen different eras. Monitors flicker with streams of code, holographic maps float mid-air, and shelves are stacked with makeshift gadgets, glowing orbs, and mechanical limbs that twitch unnervingly. The air reeks of flavored vape smoke with a distinct hint of soldering metal, a sharp contrast to the stale, dusty atmosphere outside.

Scorelord leads her through the maze-like space, his movements fluid, confident, as if this disarray is an extension of himself. He gestures for her to sit at a repurposed gaming chair patched with duct tape and neon wires.

"This place is…" Auris trails off, searching for the right word.

"Home," Scorelord finishes. "For people like me, it's the closest thing to sanctuary." He taps a monitor, pulling up an encrypted screen. "Now, let's talk about that drive."

Auris hands it over reluctantly, her eyes scanning the room for clues about the man who now holds the key to her questions. "You know what's on it?" she asks, her voice tinged with both hope and suspicion.

"Not yet," he admits, plugging the drive into a heavily modified console. "But I know one thing for sure—it's not just junk. Whatever's on here is enough to rattle EgoCorp. And if it scares them, it might just save you."

She leans forward, her pulse quickening. "Save me from what?"

Scorelord glances at her, his expression unreadable. "That," he says, "is what we're going to find out."

The screen lights up with a burst of encrypted data, and Auris feels the weight of her journey settling on her shoulders. She's no longer just a girl searching for answers;

she's standing at the edge of something far greater, something she doesn't yet fully understand. Damn it!", Scorelord cries, "Can't crack it. I guess I don't have the skills but I know someone who might!" Auris, looks at him, replying in exhaustion, "No More, **PLEEAASE**! You don't understand what I've gone through already just to get here!". Scorelord voice cutting through her tearful testimony. "OH BUT I DO!... Sit!", she sits back down slowly. "Hope you like Thai." he says.

The takeout container in her hands was slick with oil, the Pad Thai steaming and fragrant. The sharp aroma of spices filled the cramped space as Auris poked at the noodles on her plate. She perched on the edge of a chair, cluttered, surrounded by stacks of dusty vintage hardware and glowing monitors.

"Bet they don't make it like *this* in Virtu City," Scorelord said between mouthfuls, leaning back in his chair with an air of smug satisfaction.

Auris rolled her eyes, but the retort died in her throat the moment she took a bite. Her eyebrows shot up as the rich flavors exploded on her tongue. Sweet, spicy, tangy—it was an orchestra of sensations she'd never experienced before. Virtu City's synthesized meal bars and calorie cubes had nothing on this.

"You're right about that," she muttered, unable to hide her surprise.

Scorelord chuckled. "First time having *real* food?"

Auris didn't answer. Too busy stuffing her face. But as she chewed, frustration bubbled up alongside the euphoria. What else had she been missing? How much of her life had been curated, stripped down, *fake*?

Her eyes scanning the room locking onto an old surveillance drone when out of nowhere, almost like a switch flipped on in her brain, she randomly bursts into food review-mode. "Soul Thai Kitchen? 10 outta 10! Call it 'Fate on a Plate'! I can taste my destiny in the recipe! Use my code ***AURIS10*** for 10 percent off!".

She slowly breaks character and turns toward Scorelord, who's already staring back at her as if he's witnessing a paranormal activity.

"Who are you talking to?" He questions Auris with a tone of concern that quickly ramps up to paranoia. "Is it EGOCORP? You've been streaming this all along haven't you? You led them straight to us!" He yells in a manic episode before she cuts him off to explain her self.

"***Relax***...I'm not streaming—I don't even have my Lumi! Look, I guess the truth is I'm just so used to being EgoCorp's perfect little billboard..I guess it's a natural reflex at this point. If there's a camera around, there's content to be found." She says. "Didn't mean to scare you. I kinda scared myself" In a self shaming voice.

"Understandable. Scorelord replies. "It's okay, kid. We're all trying to find our minds around here. Who am I to judge?"

The two of them ate in silence for a while, the sounds from random arcade cabinets and filling the room. When Scorelord finally spoke, his voice was softer. "You ever think we're all just Easter eggs in someone else's game? Waiting to be found?"

Auris frowned. "Easter eggs?"

"Secrets. Hidden on purpose," he explained, his voice tinged with a strange mix of hope and resignation. "Easter eggs aren't mistakes...they're there by design. Someone *wants* them to be found."

She put her fork down, her appetite suddenly gone. "And what if no one ever finds us?"

Scorelord shrugged. "Then we make ourselves impossible to ignore."

A King's Exile

So...what happened to you?....Really?" Auris asks abruptly. Scorelord's gaze drifted, lost in memories he'd long kept hidden. "You know," he began softly, voice distant, "I wasn't always like this. Back in Virtu City, I was someone else—someone people respected. Until that tournament."

Auris tilted her head, intrigued but cautious. "What did you do?"

Scorelord exhaled slowly, eyes shadowed by regret and nostalgia. "There was a tournament. Biggest in the city. Final match—Gen Wasted vs. The Sentinels. They had all the sponsors, endorsements...*everything*. It was tied...We don't tie. We win. By any means. It was just supposed to be a small flex—nothing major. But I was arrogant—hi-jakked the wrong console—the star player's—in front of the whole damn city while the entire world watched. Egocorp's—*"Ego"* took a massive hit.

Sponsors pulled out, lost them millions instantly, and before I could even celebrate, Shade messaged me—told me drones were inbound, moderators closing in fast. I'd heard the rumors about what happens to influents who violated Virtu City's '*community guidelines*' and I wasn't taking any chances of them finding out why I was *really* there.

So I bolted I—straight for Nikola Station, slipped through an old entrance to the abandoned Circuit line, and vanished. Haven't looked back since."

He paused, almost teary-eyed, emotion catching in his voice. "That loft…man I wish you could've seen it…damn, it was *so dope.* I lived in the Nimbus Tower. Lost everything that day. But now? Now I understand my purpose clearly. It had to happen."

A quiet determination settled over him, masking the raw vulnerability. Auris nodded, understanding dawning in her eyes.

Flash-forward to Scorelord on a dilapidated train heading out of the city. His voice lowered, heavy with memory. "I had to erase myself. My avatar self-destructed in the middle of Virtu City's digital court, and the Moderators announced to the world that 'Scorelord was dead.' But I wasn't. At least, Not entirely." He glanced at Auris, as if to gauge her reaction, before continuing. "I fled. Ended up in Shadow Falls—a place that makes this dump look like a luxury resort. That's where I met Rune again."

Auris's brow furrowed. "Rune?"

He smirked, but there was a sadness behind it. "She was my long-lost ex, and she'd been right about everything. Virtu City was a lie, EgoCorp was worse, and I'd been too blind to see it. She had her own operation running out of Shadow Falls—a backwater train system she kept alive, one route at a time."

Scorelord's voice softened. "She looked at me like I was an idiot, a *FOOL* for chasing the illusion of Virtu City, but there was compassion there, too. She didn't say much, but the look in her said *I told ya so.* I just took the L and the ride back here to Silicon Valley. We both knew I wasn't coming back. She was right about the city. She was right about me."

Scorelord left with a feeling of defeat , but also, a sense of true freedom.

Just as he finished his story he looked over to see Auris knocked out sleep like a baby. A few hours later Scorelord jolts Auris out of her sleep, motioning for her to follow him. "Come on. There's someone you need to meet."

The streets of Silicon Valley stretched out before them, a haunting blend of tech decay and human resilience. Neon graffiti covered crumbling buildings, their slogans flickering in the dim light: *"They're Watching." "Innovation Is Obedience."* The air buzzed with electric currents, a reminder of the life that had once thrived here.

After several twists and turns, they stopped in front of a modest house nestled between two skeletal office buildings. The porch light flickered weakly, casting uneven shadows on the mismatch-paneled door. As Auris and Scorelord approached the door, a small, outdated camera above the frame flickered to life. It scanned them with a soft whir, a red beam passing over their faces. Auris instinctively stepped back, brushing her hair behind her ear.

"That's not creepy at all," she muttered.

"Relax," Scorelord said with a smirk. "The kid's just cautious. He probably saw us coming a mile away."

Inside, Kwō's eyes darted to his screen as the scan results popped up. His fingers hesitated over the keyboard. At first, his brow furrowed at the sight of Scorelord. "What now?" he muttered, rolling his eyes. But then, the second face on the feed made him freeze.

"No way," Kwō whispered, leaning closer to confirm. His voice rose in disbelief. "Is that *Auris*?"

His mind raced. On one hand, he knew her instantly—she was *the* Auris, an all-star influencer from Virtu City. On the other hand, she was also *that girl,* the one who'd crashed into him and somehow upended everything.
"What's she doing with *him*?" he wondered aloud, eyes flicking back to Scorelord.
The feed showed Auris holding up the flash drive, dangling it mockingly in front of the camera. Her lips moved, but there was no sound. He tapped the screen to activate the audio.

"Dropped something?" Auris said, her tone dripping with sarcasm.

Kwō groaned, running a hand down his face. He wasn't supposed to have visitors—especially not now, not when his gramma could be home any minute. But that stupid drive... it had been burning a hole in his thoughts ever since Scorelord dropped it into his lap.

"You letting us in, or what?" Scorelord called, leaning into the camera's view with an exaggerated grin.

Kwō hesitated. He wasn't thrilled about letting them in, but he couldn't exactly leave them standing there either. With a resigned sigh, he pressed the button to unlock the door.

The camera blinked green, and the door hissed open.

"Make it quick," Kwō muttered under his breath

The door slid shut behind them with a soft *whoosh*, sealing out the chaos of the Silicon Valley streets. Inside, the house was a patchwork of outdated tech, jury-rigged contraptions, and well-worn furniture. It was a cozy mess—a space that had been lived in, tinkered with, and patched together countless times. The buzz of old era circuits mixed with the light smell of fried wiring, and a low-key hip-hop instrumental looped on a tiny speaker in the corner.

Auris looked around, her eyes narrowing at the clutter. "This looks like a HackShack graveyard," she said, stepping over a tangled pile of wires.

"HackShack?" Kwō snapped, glaring at her. "At least I don't live in a glass box full of overpriced furniture no one's allowed to sit on. It's probably against commmunity guidelines", he follow up laughingly.

"Auris folded her arms, her tone dripping with sarcasm. "Glass box? Excuse me, I call it *minimalism*. And for the record, people are allowed to sit on the furniture—they just don't spill energy drinks all over it."

Scorelord chuckled, leaning casually against the wall. "See, the chemistry's already there. Love that for y'all."

Kwō shot him a look. "Chemistry? Nah, I'm just trying to figure out why you brought *her* here."

Auris waved the flash drive in front of his face. "*HELLO! YOU lost this*. And guess who had to play scavenger hunt in the trenches of Virtu City, find The Deadzone, hop on a random train, and be interrogated by *THIS* guy **JUST** to get some answers!?" she ranted. "My life will never go back to the way it was after what I've seen!"

"You could always get a ***RESET***" Scorelord buts in jokingly.

"Funny" Auris snaps back, with the evilest of eyes. "*RELAAAXX, kid.* Lighten up" as he walks over to Kwō.

"So, I trust with you the *single* most important and unclassified information anyone in the world could possess right now, and ya ***DROP** it*?"

Kwō turned to Scorelord, the shame of a failed mission visible in his eyes. "I was gonna tell you..."

Scorelord shrugged, unbothered. "Hey, things happen. Look, we're all here now. Let's get to cracking this thing!"

Kwō groaned but grabbed the drive from Auris. "Fine. But if my gramma sees y'all, she's gonna fry my circuits. I'm not even supposed to have people over."

Auris smirked, plopping down on the only chair that wasn't covered in wires or parts. "Good thing I'm not *people*, huh?"

Kwō plugged the drive into his setup—old-school compared to anything in Virtu City, but functional. The screens flickered to life, and lines of encrypted code scrolled across them. "Alright, give me a second. This thing's got layers."

"Don't break it," Auris said, leaning forward, her tone half-mocking, half-concerned.

"Relax," Kwō muttered. "I know what I'm doing."

As he worked, Scorelord moved over to the mantle, drawn by a framed photo. He picked it up, staring at the image of an elegant, younger woman in an unmarked lab coat, standing confidently in front of what looked like a cutting-edge lab from decades ago.

"Who's this?" Scorelord asked, holding up the frame.

Kwō glanced up, distracted. "Oh, that's my gramma. She's at the market but should be back soon. Why?"

Scorelord's eyes narrowed slightly as he studied the photo. "Your gramma, huh? She ever mention working in a lab?"

Kwō frowned, spinning back toward the screen. "She was a pharmacist or something back in the day. Retired, like, 30 years ago. Why?"

"No reason," Scorelord replied, setting the frame back on the mantle with meticulous care, but his mind raced. The lab coat, the posture—this wasn't just a pharmacist. But now wasn't the time to unpack it.

The room grew quiet except for the soft whir of the computer. Suddenly, the camera feed from outside popped up on one of the screens. Kwō froze.

"Shit," he whispered.

"What?" Auris asked, leaning closer.

"My gramma's pod just pulled up," Kwō said, panic rising in his voice. "She's gonna kill me if she sees you two here."

Scorelord stepped back, adjusting his coat. "Don't worry, kid. I'll clear out."

"How?" Kwō asked, glancing around. "You can't just—"

Before he could finish, Scorelord had vanished. Auris looked around the cluttered room in disbelief. "Where'd he go?"

"No idea," Kwō muttered, scrambling to clear the screens as the sound of the pod door outside clicked open.

The house door slid open with a soft *hiss*. Gramma stepped inside, scanning the room with sharp eyes that missed nothing. She glanced at the mantle, pausing just long enough to notice her photo frame had been moved, ever so slightly.

She looked around the room again, the tension in the room could be felt. Her gaze lingered on Auris for a beat too long, but her expression remained neutral. "You must be one of Kwō's little tech friends."
Auris stiffened but nodded politely. "Something like that."

Gramma's lips twitched into a half smile before she turned to Kwō. "Y'all Don't stay up too late tinkering. I'm going to go relax. You kids behave."

As she left the room, both Kwō and Auris exhaled in unison.

"Where the heck did he go?" Kwō whispered, glancing around as Scorelord seemed to suddenly reappear.

Before either could speculate, Kwō's tablet buzzed with a message. He opened it, and a hologram of Scorelord's face appeared. "Had to bounce, kid. Didn't want to cramp your style. I left instructions—head to the underground station. Time to move."

Kwō sighed, closing the message. "Guess we're on our own."

"Great," Auris said, brushing her hands off. "Let's just get this over with."

They both turned back to the screen, determination settling over the room like a heavy fog.

As they stepped out of the house, the door slid shut with a soft hiss. Kwō headed for an old storage box on the porch and popped it open, revealing two battered hoverboards. They looked like they had seen better days—wires patched haphazardly, edges scuffed and dented.

Auris raised an eyebrow. "You've got to be kidding me. These look like something from a bargain-bin sci-fi flick."

Kwō snorted, grabbing one and flipping it on. The board hummed steadily, hovering an inch off the ground. "Not everything can be Virtu City level, *your majesty*," he shot back, handing her the other board. "You wanted speed? Here's speed."

Auris frowned, stepping onto the board cautiously. "For the record, I've never ridden one of these before."

"You'll figure it out," Kwō said, hopping onto his with practiced ease. "Just don't think about falling."

Beat You There

Kwō pushed off first, his battered hoverboard wobbling slightly before finding its rhythm. "Try to keep up," he called over his shoulder.

Auris rolled her eyes, steadying herself on the board as it glided forward. She rode as if it were innate. The smooth vibration of the hoverboard contrasted with the uneven, cracked pavement of Silicon Valley's streets. Shadows from abandoned buildings stretched long in the dim light, giving the area a ghostly feel.

"Do people actually live here?" Auris asked, sidestepping a piece of debris with a practiced lean.

"Some do," Kwō replied, weaving effortlessly through the ruins. "Most just survive."

Auris frowned, her eyes scanning the graffiti-covered walls. Messages like **"EGOCORP LIES"** and **"LIFE IS A GLITCH"** were spray-painted in bold colors. "I've seen dystopian games with more charm."

Kwō laughed. "Welcome to Silicon Valley. Real life's not as photogenic as Virtu City, huh?"

"You keep saying that like I had a choice in how I grew up," Auris shot back. "You think I asked to be born into the perfect life?"

Kwō slowed down, glancing back at her with a smirk. “No, but you sure like you’re bragging about it.”

“I’m not bragging,” Auris insisted, her frustration mounting. “I’m just saying… it’s not all it looks like from the outside.”

“Yeah, well, neither is this place,” Kwō said, gesturing to the dilapidated surroundings. “Every tag, every broken window—that’s someone’s story. A lot of people tried to make a difference here. Most of them are gone now.”

Auris was quiet for a moment, her hoverboard humming softly beneath her. “What about you? What’s your story?”

Kwō hesitated, then shrugged. “Just a kid trying to find out the truth. My parents… they were part of this group. The Black Hackers.”

Auris perked up. “I’ve heard of them. Didn’t they take down that biased AI policing system in like the 40’s?”

“They tried,” Kwō said, his voice tinged with pride and bitterness. “My mom was one of the best coders they had. She and my dad were always working on something—breaking into systems, exposing secrets. Then one day, they just… disappeared.”

Auris looked at him, surprised. “Disappeared?”

“Snatched,” Kwō said bluntly. “Corporate goons probably. Nobody knows which company did it because the Hackers went after all of them. EgoCorp, Dynatech, Neosystems… take your pick.”
“I’m sorry,” Auris said softly.

Kwō shook his head. “Don’t be. That’s why I started Tekspiracy. Trying to piece together the puzzle they left behind. Gramma says I'm wasting my time, but I know there's something out there. Something big."

Auris nodded, her respect for Kwō growing despite herself. "I didn't think you'd be this… serious."

"Well, you didn't think I'd have sick hoverboards either, so there's a lot you don't know, Princess."

"Stop calling me Princess," Auris groaned, rolling her eyes.

Kwō and Auris sped through the deserted backstreets of Silicon Valley, the whir of their mismatched hoverboards echoing against the cracked walls of abandoned tech warehouses. The setting sun painted the skyline in muted golds and purples, casting eerie shadows on the mounds of discarded tech junk scattered along the road.

Auris teetered on the shaky board, glaring at Kwō. "You call this transportation? I've ridden fan drones smoother than this death trap."

Kwō turned slightly, balancing effortlessly on his board. "It's either this or the 'Flintstone Express', Princess. And I didn't see you bringi anything better. Stop hating and focus."

"Focus?!" Auris retorted, gripping the sides of her board as it sputtered over a rough patch. "I'm trying not to face-plant into the Silicon Valley landfill. This thing should be in the Museum of Vision."

Kwō smirked. "That's the charm. Built it myself."

"Shocking," she replied with her usual witty sarcasm. "You must be *very* proud."

They rounded a corner, leaving the street lights behind as they descended down a spiraling path. Auris slowed, her board whining in protest as they entered the familiar hollow of the underground station. The air turned colder, and the dim flicker of LED strips lining the walls gave everything an ominous glow.

“Back here again,” Auris spoke under her breath. “Déjà vu never felt this… grimy.”

Kwō rolled to a stop, tucking the hoverboard under his arm as he glanced at her. “Grimy? This is a historic site. You should be honored.”

“Historic,” Auris repeated, looking around at the cracked tiles and error-ridden holographic signs. “It looks like the aftermath of a tech apocalypse.”

“Shows what you know,” Kwō shot back, leading the way to the platform. “This place was one of the original hubs for Virtu City. It’s off the books now, but Rune and her crew keep it running. If it wasn’t for them, there wouldn’t even be a train.”

“And here I thought underground railroads were a thing of the past,” Auris said, trailing behind.

Kwō shrugged, not rising to the bait. “History repeats itself.”

The platform was as deserted as Auris remembered, the distant clinks and clangs of machinery the only sound. The air was cool and crisp, tinged with the metallic scent of old tech. Auris glanced around uneasily, hugging her arms.

“This place still gives me the creeps,” she admitted, her voice quieter.

Kwō leaned against a railing, his silhouette framed by the dim, flickering lights. “That’s how you know it’s working.”

“Working? This whole operation feels like a scavenger hunt gone wrong,” she said. “I can’t believe we’re actually trusting a train that probably runs on duct tape and good vibes.”

Kwō chuckled, shaking his head. “You’re welcome to walk.”

Auris sighed dramatically, pacing the platform. “I thought you said the train would be here by now. Don’t tell me we missed it.”

Kwō checked his wrist device, frowning. “We’re early.”

“Then where is it?” Auris asked, spinning around to glare at him. “You know, for someone who’s supposedly a genius, you’re terrible at timing.”

Kwō held up his hands defensively. “Hey, Rune’s crew isn’t exactly Swiss on punctuality. Relax.”

“Relax?!” Auris gestured to the empty platform. “I didn’t risk my life and my reputation to get ghosted by a train. If this doesn’t show up, I swear—”

Her rant was interrupted by a rumbling vibration underfoot. Both teens froze, their eyes meeting as the sound grew louder. A low, electric vibe reverberated through the cavern, followed by the barely visible glow of lights in the distance.

“There it is,” Kwō said, straightening up.

The train’s sleek LED strips cut through the darkness, illuminating the platform as it pulled in with a smooth, almost predatory grace. The doors hissed open, revealing the softly glowing interior.

“See?” Kwō said, gesturing toward the train. “Told you.”

Auris rolled her eyes but couldn't hide her relief. "Don't get cocky."

They stepped inside, the doors sliding shut behind them with a finality that made Auris' stomach twist. The train jolted slightly before gliding forward, its motion silent except for the ambient vibrations of its electric core.

Kwō found a seat near the back, slouching comfortably as he propped his feet up. Auris remained standing, her arms crossed as she stared out the window, the dim tunnels speeding past in a blur.

"You good?" Kwō asked, tilting his head to look at her.

"Peachy," she replied, her tone flat. "Just wondering what fresh hell awaits us next."

Kwō chuckled, pulling a small device from his pocket. "Whatever it is, at least it won't be boring."

Exhausted from the journey, Auris finally sat down across from him, the tension in her shoulders easing slightly. For the first time, she allowed herself to exhale. The train hurtled forward, carrying them deeper into the unknown.

THE CIRCUIT

EPISODE 17
TWO PEAS IN A POD

The two teens, now back on the old train rattling along the underground tracks, its ancient machinery groaning under the weight of time and neglect. Overhead lights flickered, casting erratic shadows that danced across the graffiti-streaked walls. Posters from forgotten campaigns peeled at the edges, their slogans now meaningless in a world that had moved on. The air inside the car was thick with the musty scent of damp metal and old circuitry, a far cry from the polished, perfumed atmosphere of Virtu City.

Auris sat by the grimy window, her arms crossed as she stared out at the dimly illuminated tunnel walls streaking past. A display screen flickered above her, projecting a muted stream of her social engagement. It's declining, fast.

Across from her, Kwō was hunched over his handheld device, scrolling through layers of encrypted files. His leg bounced impatiently, and his sharp eyes darted between lines of code, as though he could will the data to reveal even more secrets.

"You know," he started, his voice low but sharp, "your city is all smoke and mirrors."

Auris's gaze shifted from the window to him, her brow furrowing. "*My* city?" she repeated, her tone defensive. "You say that like the rest of the world's a utopia."

Kwō snorted, not looking up from his screen. "The rest of the world isn't pretending it's a utopia. Virtu City is built on lies—everyone knows it."

"Do they?" Auris shot back, sitting up straighter. "Because from where I'm standing, the rest of the world looks like a pile of rubble while my 'smoke and mirrors' city is thriving."

Kwō finally glanced up, his expression a mix of exasperation and disbelief. "Thriving? Really? That's what you call it?"

"Yes," Auris snapped. "You're just bitter because you don't get it. Virtu City isn't perfect, but it's better than… this." She gestured vaguely at the dingy train car around them, her voice tinged with disgust. "At least we're trying to build something."

Kwō leaned forward, his voice dropping into a conspiratorial whisper. "Auris, listen to me. Everything in Virtu City is curated—*manufactured.* It's not real. The ads, the influencers, the dreams you think are yours? All of it's been programmed by EgoCorp."

Auris tilted her head, her lips twitching into a half-smile. "Oh, here we go. Next, you're going to tell me that EgoCorp's harvesting our thoughts and selling them to aliens."

Kwō groaned, running a hand through his hair. "You really don't watch *Tekspiracy*, do you?"

Auris raised an eyebrow. "Your little conspiracy vlog? Please. I don't have time for that nonsense."

"It's not nonsense," Kwō shot back, his voice rising slightly before he caught himself. He glanced around the nearly empty train car, lowering his tone again. "I've been connecting the dots for years. The files on that drive? They prove everything I've been saying."

Auris's smirk faded, replaced by cautious curiosity. "And what do these *files* say, exactly?"

Kwō locked eyes with her. "Scorelord decrypted it. There's something big under the city hospital. Something EgoCorp doesn't want anyone to find."

Auris stared at him, her expression caught between skepticism and intrigue. "The *hospital*? Seriously? That's your smoking gun?"

Kwō nodded, his voice unwavering. "Think about it. Hospitals are the perfect cover. No one questions what goes on there. No one wants to know."

The train lurched suddenly, its brakes screeching as it slowed down. Auris braced herself against the window, her Virtu Lens bobbing beside her before reorienting itself. A distorted voice crackled over the intercom: "Next stop—Prime Square."

Kwō stood and motioned for her to follow. "This is us."

Auris hesitated, staring at her social feed as holographic hearts continued to rise. With a sigh, she dismissed the projection, the images dissolving into thin air. "Fine," she said, standing and adjusting her jacket. "Let's see what kind of conspiracy rabbit hole I've fallen into."

The train screeched to a halt, the doors hissing open to reveal a dim, grimy platform shrouded in shadows. The stale air rushed into the car, carrying with it the metallic tang of rust and decay.

Auris stepped off after Kwō, glancing around with a look of distaste. "Charming," she muttered under her breath.

Kwō didn't respond, his focus already on the shadowy passageways ahead. He gestured for her to follow, his tone serious. "Stick close. This is where the real game begins."

Auris rolls her eyes, following with reluctance, "Yea okay."

Kwō moved confidently through the shadowy tunnels beneath Nikola Station, his handheld device highlighted a glowing route that guided their way. The air was thick and humid, and the occasional drip of water echoed through the passage, breaking the oppressive silence. Auris trailed behind him, her arms crossed and her gaze darting around the unfamiliar surroundings.

"You've been down here before?" she asked, her voice tinged with disbelief.

"Plenty of times," Kwō replied without looking back. "It's one of the safest routes into the city if you're trying to stay off the grid."

Auris frowned, stepping over a broken pipe that jutted out of the ground. "I didn't even know this place existed."

Kwō smirked, glancing over his shoulder. "There's a lot you don't know about your own city."

She rolled her eyes but didn't argue. The truth of his words stung more than she cared to admit. As much as she loved Virtu City, there was no denying how carefully curated her life had been. This hidden underbelly—raw, grimy, and real—was a stark contrast to the sleek, polished world above.

The tunnel gradually widened as the sounds of distant machinery grew louder. Kwō stopped abruptly, pointing toward the light ahead. "I think that's the service lift," he said. "It'll take us up to the main levels."

Auris stepped forward, scanning the rusted contraption warily. "And it still works?"

Kwō shrugged. "Guess we're about to find out. Most people don't even know it's here. But the lights are still on for a reason."

The lift shuddered to life as Kwō pressed a series of buttons on a cracked control panel. They stepped inside, the cage-like enclosure rattling as it ascended. Auris leaned against the wall, her arms crossed, but her sharp eyes darted to Kwō's calm demeanor.

"Alright, genius," she said, her tone light but edged with sarcasm. "You got us this far, but once we're back on the grid, I'm running the show."

Kwō raised an eyebrow but didn't argue. "Whatever... Just don't get us caught."

Auris looks at him in mock disbelief. "If *ANYone* is gonna get us caught, it's gonna be you!"

The lift screeched to a halt, and the doors creaked open, revealing the bustling lower levels of Nikola Station. The contrast was jarring—gone were the damp walls and flickering lights of the tunnels, replaced by the cold efficiency of Virtu City's transit hub. Auris straightened her posture, her sharp features hardening into the confident mask she wore so well.

As they stepped into the main concourse, she couldn't help but glance over her shoulder at the lift. "It's crazy," she murmured, more to herself than to Kwō. "This whole place, hidden right under our feet."
"Welcome to the *real* Virtu City," Kwō said, his voice laced with irony. "*Try not to let it blow your mind.*"

She shot him a sidelong look but didn't respond. Instead, she pushed ahead, her movements fluid and purposeful as slipped seamlessly into the flow of the crowd, making her way toward the inclinators. Kwō followed, his wide-eyed wonder clashing with her polished confidence.

Though he despised everything the city stood for, he couldn't help but be impressed by the sheer magnitude of its layout, architectural designs and technological modernisms. It was clear that a lot of work went into creating this world, but the sinister secrets underneath it all made him unable to enjoy it in all its glory.

As they reached the surface level of Virtu City pulsed with its usual intensity, the streets bathed in neon lights and the buzz of drones crisscrossing the sky. Auris weaved through the throngs of late-night revelers and NPC street performers, her pace brisk but deliberate. Kwō trailed behind, his disheveled appearance drawing a few curious glances from the hyper-stylized crowd.

"Bro, You're sticking out like a sore thumb," Auris muttered, glancing back at him. "We need to fix that before we get anywhere near the hospital."

Kwō frowned. "I wasn't expecting to pack a wardrobe, you know."

Auris smirked, nodding toward a sleek boutique tucked into the side of a towering building. Its holographic sign shimmered: **Algorithm & Glitch** – *Elevate Your Style.* "Come on," she said, grabbing his arm.

Inside, the boutique was a symphony of minimalistic luxury. Racks of clothing hovered in mid-air, rotating gently under soft, ambient lighting. An AI tailor activated as they entered, its humanoid form glowing softly.

“Welcome to Algorithm & Glitch,” it said in a soothing voice. “How may I assist you?”

Auris gestured toward Kwō. “He needs an upgrade. Something subtle but stylish.”

The AI scanned Kwō, projecting a series of outfits around him in holographic displays. “Suggested ensembles based on customer metrics,” it announced, rotating through a selection of sleek, modern attire.

“This is ridiculous,” Kwō grumbled as Auris swiped through the options with practiced ease.

“Oh, stop whining,” she said, selecting a fitted jacket and trousers combo. “You’ll thank me later when no one’s staring at you like you just fell out of a junkyard.”

A few minutes later, Kwō stepped out of the dressing room, his new outfit transforming him from a scrappy outsider to someone who could almost pass as a Virtu City native.

“Much better,” Auris said, grinning. “You clean up well.”

Kwō adjusted the jacket uncomfortably. “Terrifying thought.”

Auris grabbed his arm, pulling him toward the exit. “Alright,fashion show’s over. We’ve got a hospital to infiltrate.

The streets of Virtu City buzzed with relentless energy, a discord of holographic billboards, self-driving cars, and glowing storefronts. Auris led the way, her stride confident and precise, while Kwō lagged slightly behind, his discomfort painfully obvious.

Above them, a massive holographic billboard lit up, cutting through the electric haze of the city. The polished voice of an announcer boomed, catching both their attention:

"Tomorrow night, don't miss The Ego Awards, live from The Parallax Theatre in Valleywood! Who will take home the coveted Diamond Brain? Tune in to find out!"

Auris's image flashed on the screen under the category *"Rising Star of the Year."*

Kwō stopped in his tracks, eyebrows raised. "Wait, that's you? You're nominated for an award?"

"Not important," Auris said quickly, tugging him forward by the arm. Her jaw tightened as she glanced away from the screen.

Kwō grinned. "Not important? You're literally up for the influencer equivalent of an Oscar, and you're just gonna brush that off?"

"Stay focused," she snapped. "We've got bigger things to worry about right now."

The Hospital Visit

Virtu Care hospital loomed ahead, a sterile monolith of glass and steel standing in stark contrast to the vibrant chaos of the city. Inside, the lobby was pristine to the point of absurdity, its white walls and glowing floors almost blinding under the harsh, artificial light.

Auris moved through the automated check-in area with practiced ease, but Kwō's discomfort only grew. His gaze darted from the holographic receptionist to the staff members bustling around the lobby. Their movements were too smooth, their expressions too fixed.

"Welcome to Virtu Care," the hologram chirped as they entered. "Please proceed to the nearest Assessment Pod for diagnosis."

Kwō froze, eyeing the sleek pods lining the walls. Their glowing interiors pulsed hypnotically, like giant digital cocoons.

"Assessment Pod?" he muttered. "What, is this a hospital or an assembly line?"

"Shh," Auris hissed, nudging him forward. "Just keep walking."

As they moved through the lobby, a staff member approached them, its smile as rigid as a mannequin's. "Your health is important to us. Please allow the Assessment Pod to determine your wellness needs."

Kwō frowned, watching as the turned away and repeated the same phrase to no one in particular. "They're not even… human, are they?"

Auris shrugged, her voice casual. "Of course they are. They're just efficient. That's how things work here."

"Efficient?" Kwō stopped, gesturing to another employee who was cleaning a spotless counter. "Yea, that's not creepy at all. What are they even *doing?* "He asks, "These people can't be real. It's like they're… Bots."

Auris opened her mouth to argue but faltered. Her gaze lingered on the staff, their mechanical movements suddenly feeling wrong in a way she couldn't quite articulate. For the first time, she noticed the vacant eyes, the canned responses, the eerie perfection in their every action.

"How many of them are like this?" she murmured, almost to herself.

Kwō leaned in, his voice low. "More than you think. Probably most of them. And if you haven't noticed until now..." He let the implication hang in the air.

Auris stiffened, her heart skipping a beat. The thought was too big, too destabilizing. She shook her head, forcing herself to focus. "Let's just find what we're looking for and get out of here."

Kwō smirked but didn't press further. "You're the boss."

Right On Time

They navigated the endless corridors of the hospital, the overly sterile environment is hauntingly perfect. Every now and then, a clerk would approach, offering vague, pre-programmed instructions:

"Please follow the yellow line for optimal service."
"Remember: Virtu Care ensures your happiness and health."

Auris ignored them, her focus on finding a way deeper into the building. They reached a dead end—a set of double doors marked "AUTHORIZED PERSONNEL ONLY" with a biometric scanner mounted beside them.

"Well, that's not ominous at all," Kwō said, peering at the scanner.

Auris hesitated, her gaze shifting between the scanner and the doors. "I.... think this is it....," she murmured.
"Sure, but how do we get through?" Kwō asked.

Before she could answer, the scanner activated with a soft chime, its red beam sweeping over her.

"Access granted," the mechanical voice announced as the doors slid open.

Kwō blinked, his jaw slack. "Well, that was easy."

Auris stared at the now-open doorway, her brow furrowed. "Why did it let me in?" she whispered.

Kwō shrugged. "Does it matter? Let's go before it changes its mind."

She hesitated for a moment longer before stepping through, the cool air beyond the doors sending a chill down her spine.

The corridor ahead was dimly lit, its metallic walls lined with glowing panels. The sound of their footsteps echoed eerily, mingling with the barely audible buzzing of machinery. At the end of the hallway, a spiral staircase descended into darkness, its metal steps barely gleaming in the low light.

"This must be it," Auris said, her voice quiet but resolute.

Kwō peered down the staircase, his expression wary. "I hope you're right."

Without another word, they began their descent, the oppressive silence of the corridor swallowing them whole.

VIRTUCAR

EPISODE 18
PHASE 3

The entrance to the labs sealed behind them with a hiss, the sound echoing eerily down the stark white corridor. It was empty.

The lab wasn't abandoned, it was just running itself. The air felt heavier inside, almost stifling despite the noticeable chill. Auris rubbed her arms, trying to suppress a shiver.

"Why is it so damn cold in here?" she muttered.

Kwō glanced around, his eyes darting between the screens and the glowing cables lining the walls. "They have to keep the tech cool. Servers, machines—stuff like this overheats fast."

Auris nodded absently, her voice soft. "Makes sense, I guess."

Most rooms seem to be cleared out. Dust and loose papers scatter under their boots, evidence of a rushed evacuation.

The temperature drops as they push into a cold storage room—not as heavily secured as the main data vaults, but still operational. The glow of cryo-units hum softly against the sterile silence. Their breaths forming small clouds

Auris scans the room, eyes flicking between scattered reports and supply cabinets. The Virola logo is stamped across multiple boxes. She pries one open—inside, vials of what was supposed to be the "cure" for influencer burnout syndrome. But something isn't right.

Kwō rummages through a nearby filing cabinet, flipping through case logs, receipts, injection records. Then, he stops.

Refrigeration units line the walls, neatly stocked with Virola vials.

Auris recognizes the branding immediately. Her eyes light up.

Auris (grinning, like she's putting him on game):

"Oh, Virola. Bet you didn't know about this, do you?"

He side-eyes her. She's too casual.

Auris (matter-of-fact, like she's in a school lesson):

"This was Virtu City's biggest medical breakthrough. They taught us about this in school—how they saved the first influents from burnout. How they kept us from crashing. They said it kept us connected, kept us… whole."

He doesn't buy it. Not even a little.

Kwō (flat):

"Yeah? That what they told you?"

Auris keeps scanning, oblivious to his skepticism.

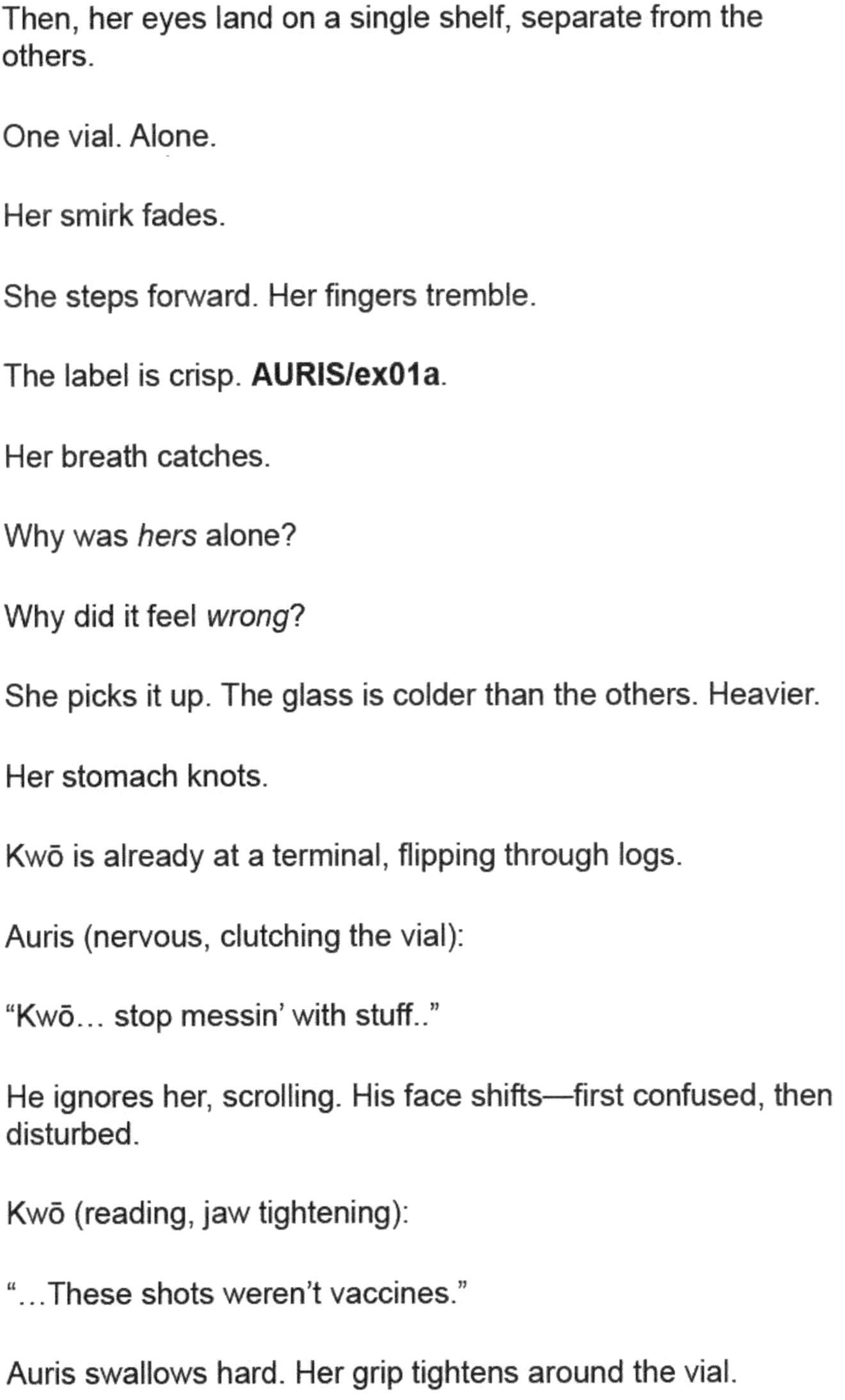

Then, her eyes land on a single shelf, separate from the others.

One vial. Alone.

Her smirk fades.

She steps forward. Her fingers tremble.

The label is crisp. **AURIS/ex01a**.

Her breath catches.

Why was *hers* alone?

Why did it feel *wrong*?

She picks it up. The glass is colder than the others. Heavier.

Her stomach knots.

Kwō is already at a terminal, flipping through logs.

Auris (nervous, clutching the vial):

"Kwō… stop messin' with stuff.."

He ignores her, scrolling. His face shifts—first confused, then disturbed.

Kwō (reading, jaw tightening):

"…These shots weren't vaccines."

Auris swallows hard. Her grip tightens around the vial.

VIROLA OPERATION LOG

INJECTION CONTENTS: TRACKING NANOBOTS

NEURAL DATA TRANSFER: ACTIVE

DIGITAL COPY STATUS: STORED

Her pulse spikes.

"What does that mean?" Auris shaken, not understanding yet.

Kwō (grim, still reading):

"It means they weren't injecting shit into people to help. They were putting something in them to take."

Auris blinks.

INJECTED SUBJECTS: INFLUENTS, FIRST-GEN

PROCESS: NANOBOT INTEGRATION & NEURAL UPLOAD

RESULT: DIGITAL ARCHIVING FOR FUTURE DEPLOYMENT

Her entire body goes cold.

She looks down at the vial in her hand.

Her name.

Kwō turns—sees her frozen, gripping it like it might explode. His eyes flick to the vial—then he snatches it out of her hands.

Auris (startled):

"Kwō—!"

He flipping it over, scanning the batch code.

Auris (panicked, shaking her head):

"Don't—"

Kwō carefully typed in *Batch ID# XY-8075* and hit *ENTER* firmly.

"We looking it up."

The screen blinks. Data floods in.

SUBJECT: AURIS

STATUS: PHASE 2 EXPERIMENT

NEURAL INTEGRATION: SUCCESSFUL

SOURCE MATERIAL: [REDACTED]

DIRECTIVE: OBSERVE. *DO NOT INTERVENE.*

Silence.

Auris stares at the words.

Her chest tightens.

Her mouth goes dry.

Phase 2?

Her heartbeat pounds in her ears.

Then it clicked.

She never got the '*vaccine*'.

Because she never needed it.

The others—they were converted. Their neural patterns, their consciousness, their souls—archived, copied, stored for later use.

But she?

She was born with it already inside her.

She wasn't a recipient.

She was a product.

Kwō is trippin' too now. His voice is lower. More serious.

Kwō (muttering, realization hitting):

"...They—they *created* you...?"

Auris is shaking.

Everything she thought she knew about her life, her choices, her own identity—all lies

She wasn't born free.

She was manufactured.

Her fingertips go numb. Her legs feel unsteady.

Kwō sees it. He sees her slipping. Spiraling.

"Auris." he whispers sharply, still trying to snapping her out of it.

She doesn't move.

Kwō (firmer, gripping her wrist):

"We gotta keep moving." he whispers firmly while gripping her arm.

A sharp chime sounds from the hall.

A red scanning laser sweeps the doorway.

Kwō shoves the vial into his pocket, pulling her toward the exit.

Auris stumbles after him, still in a daze.

She was never free.

She was probably never even real.

And if this was just Phase 2…

What the hell was Phase 3?

They pressed forward, the fluorescent lights overhead flickering slightly as if the lab itself were alive. Every few steps, another monitor would blink to life, displaying data too complex to make sense of at first glance. But the further they walked, the data gave way to something far stranger.

"Stop," Auris whispered, freezing in her tracks. A massive screen ahead flickered to life, drawing her attention like a moth to a flame. On it, a figure slowly rotated in 3D—a man in a sleek suit, his features flawless to the point of discomfort.

Auris stepped closer, almost hypnotized by the display. She tentatively raised her hand to the screen, and it responded to her proximity. With a gentle swipe, the figure disappeared, replaced by a woman with a radiant smile and an impossibly symmetrical face. She swiped again. Another figure appeared—a child this time, bright-eyed and cheerful, their expression eerily rehearsed.

"What is this?" Auris murmured. Her fingertips hovered over the screen as she continued to swipe, cycling through a gallery of polished personas. Each new figure was as perfect as the last, yet something about them felt hollow.

Kwō, standing a step behind her, leaned in slightly. "Looks like… NPCs. But better."

"Better?" Auris shook her head, swiping again. "Maybe because they aren't These aren't NPCs. They're… humans."

"Are they, though?" Kwō countered, leaning closer. "I mean, look at this one,"—he tilted his head, gesturing at the floating metrics beside each figure. "Looks like… stats? Engagement rates, charisma scores, conversion data… like a video game character screen. 'Awaiting Role Assignment.'?? That doesn't *scream* 'weird to you?."

Auris froze as she swiped to another familiar face. Her heart sank. "No way… that's Ms. Ellin from Virtu Academy."

"And that one," she said, pointing at another rotating figure, "he's a greeter at Streamsphere."

"Damn," Kwō muttered, his voice low. "You recognize them?"

"Of course I do," Auris said, her voice tinged with dread. "They're real. Or at least… I thought they were."

Kwō tapped the screen, causing it to flicker briefly. "Maybe they're templates. People built to look real but… aren't."

Auris stepped back, her mind racing. "If that's true, then how many people in Virtu City are actually… people?"

Kwō shook his head. "I don't think you wanna know."

"They're not real," she whispered, the words hollow in her throat. "They're… placeholders. Characters waiting to be—"

"Given identities," Kwō finished, his tone sharp. "Everything in Virtu City… every person you've ever met, trusted, or admired—"

"—could be fake," Auris said, her voice breaking. She stepped back from the screen, as if it might swallow her whole. "They're designing people."

"No," Kwō corrected grimly. "They're playing *GOD!*"

"Cmon!" He whispers demandingly as Auris is stuck staring at the display trying to make sense of what she just saw.

The air felt heavier as they ventured further into the lab, the chill from the refrigerators fading behind them. Rows of pristine workstations lined the walls, each one glowing with unreadable data. Cables snaked across the floor, coiling into bundles that stretched toward the far end of the room.

"Careful," Auris said, stepping over a particularly thick cable. "Last thing we need is to—"

Her warning came too late. Kwō's foot caught on a loose wire, sending him stumbling forward. He flailed for balance, his hands hitting a nearby console.

The room jolted with life. A loud *click* echoed, followed by a deep mechanical hum. The floor vibrated as a hidden hatch in the wall began to slide open, revealing a cavernous space beyond.

"What did you just do?" Auris hissed, her voice sharp with panic.

Kwō held up his hands defensively. "I tripped! It wasn't my fault!"

The hatch fully opened, revealing a massive, dark hangar. The radiance of lights inside cast eerie shadows across rows of indistinct shapes.

Auris peered into the void, her breath catching. Kwō stepped closer, his voice barely above a whisper. "I think we just found Phase 3."

The room was eerily silent, the kind of quiet that made Auris's ears strain for something—anything—to break it. The cold, sterile air seemed to press down on them as they moved further into the hangar. Nothing stirred. No hum of machines, no clicks of automated systems. It was as if the room had been abandoned—forgotten—until now.

Auris stepped cautiously past rows of lifeless pods, their smooth, glassy surfaces reflecting the dim overhead lights. Each pod was neatly labeled, categorized, and seemingly dormant.

Until she found one.

An unmarked pod stood at the far end, its smooth exterior almost pristine compared to the others. Auris stopped, her breath catching in her throat.

"This one's different," she whispered, tracing her fingers along the edge of the glass.

Kwō, trailing behind, glanced over her shoulder. "What makes it special?"

"No label. No designation," she said, her voice barely audible. "It's just… here."

Kwō frowned. "Weird. Everything in this place is cataloged to death. Why wouldn't this one be?"

"Let's find out," Auris replied, her curiosity overriding her caution.

The Bioscanner's Secret

As Auris stepped closer, the soft flicker of light within the pod's control panel brightened, responding to her presence. A soft chime echoed, and the scanner activated, its beam sweeping across her face like an all-knowing gaze.

Kwō stiffened beside her. "Auris, what did you just do?"

She shook her head, her voice unsteady. "I didn't do anything," she whispered. But even as the words left her mouth, she knew it wasn't true. The scanner's light pulsed again, followed by a sharp beep.

"Access granted: Mother authorized," the mechanical voice declared, cold and deliberate.

The words froze them in place, thickening the air like an unseen force.

“Mother?” they said in unison, their confusion sharp and audible.

“Okay, no way,” Kwō blurted, taking a cautious step back. “What the hell is going on? And don’t you dare say that was random. That wasn’t random.”

“I don’t know,” Auris stammered, her throat tight as her mind raced. “But we’re about to find out.”

The Bot Awakens

The glass pod slid open with a soft hiss, releasing a swirl of cold vapor that curled around their feet. Inside, a humanoid figure sat slumped forward, its head bowed low and arms limp. At first glance, it appeared human—tall athletic physique, pale skin, and blonde, disheveled hair. But the stillness was unnerving, like a mannequin caught mid-motion.

Auris and Kwō exchanged wary glances. “Is it… alive?” she whispered, her grip tightening around the vial in her hand.

Kwō leaned in, inspecting the figure closely. “Alive? No. But this…” He gestured at the lifelike details on its face and hands. “This is some next-gen tech. Like, beyond anything EgoCorp’s ever shown the public.”

Before he could finish, the bot’s eyes snapped open, glowing a sharp, unnatural shade of blue.

Auris stumbled back with a stifled gasp. The bot’s gaze darted around the room, wild and unhinged, its chest rising and falling in ragged, mechanical breaths. Every motion was disturbingly human yet jarring, as if its systems were misaligned.

“Who are you?” it demanded, its voice both human and synthetic, layered with emotion. “Where am I? What’s happened to me?”

Kwō froze, his hands instinctively rising in defense. “Whoa, whoa. We didn’t do anything! We just—”

“Scorelord!” the bot interrupted, its tone sharp with desperation. “Where is Scorelord? Where is Gen Wasted? I need to find them—Vexer, N30И…” Its words trailed into static before snapping back. “Where are they?!”

Kwō blinked, his mouth opening but failing to form words. “Did it just—”

“Did you trap me here?!” the bot snarled, its gaze snapping to Auris. “You think you can control me?” It lunged forward, its movements disjointed and frantic.

“Close it!” Auris yelled, her voice breaking through the tension. “Close it, Kwō! NOW!”

Kwō scrambled for the controls, his hands trembling. “We didn’t trap you!” he shouted, trying to reason with it. “We just —”

“LIARS!” the bot roared, its fist slamming into the edge of the pod. The sound echoed like a gunshot, the glass trembling under the force. “I’ve been locked in this nightmare for—I don’t even know how long!”

“CLOSE IT!” Auris screamed, panic spilling into her voice. “FUCKING CLOSE IT!”

Kwō's fingers finally found the right sequence, and the pod hissed shut. The glass slid back into place, muffling the bot's furious cries. Its fists pounded against the interior, the sound now muted and hollow.

The control panel blinked red. "Containment secured," it announced, its voice devoid of empathy.

The Erratic Revelation

The bot's thrashing slowed, its glowing eyes narrowing as it leaned back against the pod's interior. A low whir emanated from its chest, the faint rhythm of a scanning mechanism.

Auris's chest heaved as she steadied herself against the console, her pulse pounding in her ears. "What the hell is that thing?" she asked, her voice shaky.

Kwō didn't answer immediately, his gaze locked on the pod. The bot's eyes shifted, softening with an almost human-like sorrow. Then, with a sudden whir, its expression changed again—it tilted its head as if analyzing something. Its gaze locked on Kwō first.

"Authorization confirmed," it said suddenly, its tone eerily calm. "The insignia… it's real."

Kwō blinked. "What insignia?"

The bot's hand trembled as it pointed toward his arm. "Yours. It's the mark of Gen Wasted." Its glowing eyes then locked on Auris. "And you… You're the Mother. But why do you look so young? Has anti-aging advanced this much?"

Auris stepped back, her hand instinctively covering the faint glow on her arm where the tattoo lay hidden. "What are you talking about? I'm not—"

"Don't lie to me!" the bot snapped, its voice spiking with static. "You carry the Mother's DNA. I can feel it. I was built to protect her and the others."

Kwō exchanged a panicked glance with Auris. "We need to go. Now."

"No!" the bot shouted, slamming its palm against the glass again. "You can't leave! I need—SCORELORD!"

Auris grabbed Kwō's arm, her voice a harsh whisper. "Move. Before it gets out again."

They backed away slowly, the bot's cries growing more frantic. The control panel's lights flickered ominously as the containment protocol strained to hold.

As they turned to leave, Kwō glanced back one last time, unease twisting in his chest. The bot had stopped thrashing. Instead, it pressed its hand against the glass, its glowing eyes locking onto his.

"Tell Scorelord…" It hesitated, its voice softening. "Tell him I'm still here."

Both teens stood there, breathing hard as they stared at the now-sealed pod. The bot inside glared at them, its eyes filled with a mixture of anger and desperation as it slowly shuts back down into sleep mode.

"What the hell was that?" Kwō asked, his voice shaking.

"I don't know," Auris replied, her hands still trembling. "But whatever it is… it knows Scorelord."

Kwō's eyes narrowed. "And Gen Wasted."

They turned to look at each other, realization dawning in their expressions. But before they could say another word, the room suddenly came alive with the blare of alarms. Red lights flashed, casting eerie shadows across the hangar.

"**Security breach detected**," an automated voice announced. "**Containment protocol initiated**."

Auris grabbed Kwō's arm, her nails digging into his sleeve. "We need to go. *Now.*"The red glow of the alarms cast harsh, flickering shadows across the walls as the automated voice blared:

Kwō nodded, his eyes darting between the rows of pods and the security drones beginning to stir from their dormant positions. The sleek, metallic machines hovered silently at first, their lenses glowing ominously as they scanned the area.

"This way!" Auris hissed, pulling him toward the way they had come.

But as they sprinted back through the cold, silent corridors, the air grew thick with an electric hum. The drones were closing in, their low-pitched whine growing louder with each passing second.

A voice, smooth and detached, echoed through the space: **"Surrender. Resistance will result in immediate termination."**

Kwō glanced back, catching his breath as one of the drones darted closer. "I don't think they're bluffing!"

Auris gritted her teeth, pulling him harder. "Just keep moving!"

The two darted through the hallways, twisting and turning at every junction. Auris's heart pounded against her ribcage as she led the way, her mind racing. The sterile, white walls seemed to stretch endlessly, each one blending into the next.

Behind them, the sound of the drones grew deafening.

Auris turned sharply into a side corridor, dragging Kwō with her. "We're not gonna make it back the way we came!" she said, her voice strained with panic.

Kwō's breath came in ragged gasps. "So what's the plan, genius?"

Auris hesitated, her eyes scanning the unfamiliar hallway. She spotted an emergency ladder leading to an upper level. "There! Go!"

Kwō stumbled toward the ladder, his hands shaking as he grabbed the rungs. But just as he began to climb, one of the drones swooped in low, its mechanical arm extending toward him.

"Unauthorized personnel detected. Surrender immediately."

The drone's arm clamped around Kwō's wrist, yanking him off the ladder. He cried out, his legs kicking wildly as the machine began to lift him off the ground.

"Auris!" he shouted, his voice cracking with fear.

Auris froze, torn between running and helping him. Her mind raced, but the sight of more drones closing in sealed her decision. She couldn't fight them—not here, not now.

"I'll come back for you!" she yelled, her voice thick with guilt. "I promise!"

Kwō's eyes locked on hers for a brief moment, his expression a mixture of fear and resignation. "Go!" he shouted. "You can't get caught too!"

Tears stung her eyes as she turned and bolted down the corridor, leaving Kwō behind.

Auris's legs burned as she sprinted through the sterile halls, the sound of her pounding footsteps drowned out by the relentless blare of the alarms. She didn't stop until she reached the access point they'd entered through earlier.

The scanner blinked to life as she approached, recognizing her immediately.

"Mother authorized. Access granted."

The door slid open, revealing the cold night air beyond the hospital's sterile walls.

Auris stumbled out into the darkness, her chest heaving as she gulped in the crisp air. The contrast between the clinical, suffocating lab and the open, chaotic streets of Virtu City was dizzying. For a brief moment, she paused to collect herself, her trembling hands gripping her knees.

She turned back, staring at the now-closed entrance, the words **"Mother authorized"** echoing in her mind. It didn't make sense. Why did her access work so perfectly? And why was her name on that vial?

Her thoughts spun like a malfunctioning feed. The walls she had lived within all her life—her perfectly curated world—

were crumbling faster than she could process. But there was no time to linger. She had to disappear.

Auris pulled her hood up and began weaving through the neon-lit streets of Prime Square. The nightlife buzzed around her, full of influencers and content creators capturing their perfect moments. Every laugh, every pose, every movement seemed manufactured, designed for an algorithm.

She felt like a ghost drifting through their world. Her dirt-streaked clothes and panicked expression were in stark contrast to the glittering perfection around her. She ducked into shadowy alleys, avoiding drones that hovered overhead, their glowing eyes scanning the crowds.

She whispered to herself, "Just get home. Get back to Halcyon." The thought of her loft—the sleek, automated perfection of it—felt like a lifeline, a fragile thread tying her back to normalcy. But as she moved through the streets, dodging attention, the realization gnawed at her: *Normal doesn't exist anymore.*

By the time Auris reached her building, the weight of the day hung heavy on her shoulders. The city lights, usually a comforting backdrop to her curated life, now felt like they were glaring down at her, mocking her with their artificial beauty. She slipped through the side entrance, avoiding the automated concierge as if its synthetic voice might accuse her of everything she had just witnessed.

The elevator ride to her floor was silent, but her thoughts were deafening. The vials. The humanoid bots flashing across the screen. The trippy bot in the pod demanding to speak to someone named Scorelord. And Kwō, being dragged away, his protests muffled by the swarm of drones.

When the doors opened, Auris stepped into the hallway, her steps slow and hesitant. But then she froze.

At her door sat a sleek, glowing box.

“Replacement Lumi Unit: Courtesy of EgoCorp.”

Her stomach twisted. She didn’t have to open it to know what was inside—a brand-new Lumi, perfectly synced to her life, ready to resume monitoring her every move. She stared at the box, her pulse quickening. Breaking her old Lumi had been an impulsive act of rebellion, a moment where she thought she could finally sever herself from EgoCorp’s gaze. And now here it was, back again, like a ghost she couldn’t escape.

She nudged the box with her foot, muttering, “Not tonight,” before stepping inside. Her loft flickered to life as she entered, every light and surface responding to her presence with seamless efficiency. But where she once found this comforting, she now felt a pang of unease, as though the space itself was conspiring against her. She slumped into a chair, rubbing her temples.

Her gaze flicked back to the door, to the ominous box sitting just outside. Streaming was unavoidable, especially after the chaos of the day. If she didn’t check in, people would talk—and that was the last thing she needed.

With a groan, she stepped back outside, grabbed the box, and carried it inside.

The packaging hissed open, revealing the new Lumi unit. Its lens flickered to life, scanning her loft before focusing on her.

“Welcome back, Auris. Your new Lumi unit is fully operational. Would you like to resume from your last synced preferences?”

Her lips twitched into something that wasn't quiet a smile as she rolled her eyes. "Let's just get this over with."

"Im sensing a behavioral patterns. Would you like an emotional diagnostic?"Auris laughed dryly. "Yeah, Lumi. Tell me how I'm feeling."

The unit blinked, processing. "You appear to be experiencing elevated stress levels and signs of mild paranoia."

Auris stares at the bot, smiling vexingly. "I'm fine, ***Lumi***. Just start the **stream**."

The Last Stream

Lumi's lens recalibrates itself to her preferred settings before focusing in on her, it's built in ring light glowed, providing the perfect lighting as she went live. Her usual radiant smile felt forced, her energy dampened by the weight of the day.

"Hey, everyone," she began, trying to inject some pep into her voice. "Sorry for going dark earlier. It's been… one of those days."

The chat lit up immediately, the concern from her followers pouring in.

@ObsidianFury: *Auris, you okay?*
@NerdyCook: *Where were you •.• ??*
@nikkideedlesa: *OMG, you look like you need a RESET!*
@ECH0N1C: *Self-care over everything!*
@MintyCow: *You're not a robot! Everybody needs a break!*

The irony of that last comment made her laugh, a bitter sound quickly masked with a cough.

“Thanks guys….just been….dealing with some stuff. You know how it is. Life in Virtu City never slows down. But you’re not wrong,” she said, leaning into the camera. “Maybe I do need a little reset.”

The words felt bitter in her mouth, but she knew how to play the game.

“You ever just… feel like you’ve been running around all day and gotten nowhere?” she asked, trying to keep it light. “That’s me right now. But don’t worry, I’ll be good!”

Lumi’s holo-projector displays a pop-up notification:

`“Mandated Spa Session Reminder: RESET for Mind and Body. Would you like me to schedule an appointment?”`

She shook her head, half-amused, half-disgusted. “Perfect timing, as always. Thanks, Lumi. You’re a lifesaver.” The assistant blinked, oblivious to her sarcasm.

The chat lit up with encouragement:

@ViviKiwi7: *We love you, Auris!*
@Dedicatedfan: *Take care of yourself, queen!*
@renostar: *RESET tomorrow!”*

She sighed. Even her fans echoed EgoCorp’s propaganda. “*Ok guys*—I hear you,” she said, pushing through her exhaustion with a faint chuckle. “I’ll hit the spa tomorrow. Self-care, right? Gotta stay glowing for the big show!”

The chat buzzed with encouragement and excitement as fans speculated about her chances of winning tomorrow. Auris forced a bright smile, letting them bask in the illusion of her usual confidence.

"Alright, my loves," she said, her voice sugarcoated with a practiced charm. "I need to get my beauty sleep. Big day tomorrow! Keep shining, and don't forget—live your best life for the cam!" She threw up a peace sign, and Lumi cut the feed automatically, overlaying her screen with post-stream analytics.

As the room fell silent, her face dropped. The practiced glow dimmed, replaced by the weight of reality. She closed her eyes, taking a deep breath. Her fans had no idea what she'd been through, what she'd seen. And she couldn't tell them. Not yet.

Auris stood, brushing her hands over her face and looking around the loft. It felt different now. Hollow. Manufactured. Like every inch of it was designed to keep her entertained, comfortable, and compliant. She glanced at Lumi, which had begun cleaning up the chat logs and preparing a detailed report of her stream stats.

"I don't need you anymore," she hissed sharply.

"Pardon, Auris? Would you like me to enter rest mode?"

She froze. Did it hear her? Was it programmed to respond to doubt? She shook her head. "No, just… go do whatever you do when you're not in my face."

Lumi blinked. "Noted. Entering background monitoring mode."

The little device rolled off the counter, gliding toward its charging station, and Auris couldn't help but watch it with suspicion. Was it really as innocent as it seemed? Or was it feeding every moment of her life back to EgoCorp?

As she gets ready for bed, a soft chime echoed in the room, pulling her gaze to her wrist. A new notification blinked on her laptop screen:

"RESET Spa Appointment Confirmed. Tomorrow, 9:00 AM. Thank you for prioritizing self-care!"

Her brow furrowed. She didn't remember *confirming* anything. "Convenient," she muttered, squinting her eyes in suspicion.

The spa had always been a haven for her—a luxurious escape from the pressures of streaming and Virtu City's unrelenting demands. But now? After everything she'd seen? It felt like something else entirely. A trap? No. Not quite. But certainly not as innocent as it once seemed.

She glanced toward the replacement Lumi, still nestled in its charging dock. The notification's timing was too perfect. Almost as if the machine had been listening. Feeding her exhaustion back to EgoCorp to prompt her compliance.

Auris wandered to her bed, collapsing onto the pristine sheets. Her mind raced, every image from the lab flashing in her head. The fridge. The vials. The screen displaying people she knew—or at least she *thought* she knew. And the bot. That terrifying, too-human bot....and Kwō. It wasn't her fault he'd gotten captured, but still, survivor's guilt made her feel obligated to at least *try* make things right somehow.

She turned over, pulling the blanket up to her chin as she stared at the ceiling. Tomorrow, she'd go to RESET. She'd put on the show, play the role EgoCorp expected of her. For now, she had to.

But she wouldn't forget.

She closed her eyes, exhaustion finally pulling her under, even as her thoughts swirled with plans. If EgoCorp thought they controlled her, they were wrong. Very wrong.

This was only the beginning.

EGO LABS

EPISODE 19
QUID PRO KWŌ

The morning light filtered through the curtains, painting soft patterns across Gramma's living room. She sat in her favorite chair, a delicate china teacup balanced in her steady hand, its aroma of jasmine filling the room. Auris' stream flickered on the wall in front of her, but something about it wasn't quite right.

Gramma leaned forward, scrutinizing Auris' typically polished demeanor. Her usual bubbly charm was subdued, her words disjointed. A subtle but unmistakable unease had settled over the broadcast.

"Not like you to crack under pressure," Gramma murmured, her tea untouched.

She dismissed the stream with a swipe, the projection vanishing into nothingness. The house was silent for a moment, save for the faint ticking of an antique clock. Then, a piercing alert from her wrist device shattered the calm.

Her teacup rattled against its saucer as she froze. The sound was unmistakable, one she hadn't heard in decades. Her pulse quickened. With a practiced motion, she tapped the device.

The hologram that blinked to life made her heart sink. Kwō's face appeared, distorted but unmistakable. His mouth moved frantically, his fists pounding on the walls of what looked like a containment unit.

Automated voices buzzed over the transmission:

"Subject #37492 detained. Interrogation protocols initiated."

Gramma shot to her feet, her tea forgotten. "Damn it, Kwō," she muttered under her breath, pacing the room. Her mind raced through the possibilities, each worse than the last.

Finally, she stopped. Her gaze landed on the bookshelf across the room. She strode toward it with purpose, her hand gliding over the spines until she found the one she sought.

She pulled the book. With a soft click, the shelf rotated, revealing the hidden entrance to her lab. Without hesitation, she stepped inside.

The lab flickered to life as she entered, motion-sensitive lights illuminating sleek counters and consoles. The faint scent of ozone hung in the air, remnants of dormant tech awaiting activation.

A bio-scanner activated, its beam tracing her face.

"Welcome back, Mother," the system announced, its tone eerily neutral.

Her jaw tightened at the title, but she pushed the thought aside and strode to the central console. A few swift commands brought up EgoCorp's security feeds, pinpointing Kwō's location. His containment unit appeared on the screen, the sterile walls of the interrogation chamber oppressive and cold.

Her fingers flew over the keys, accessing protocols she hadn't touched in years. "Hold on, Kwō," she whispered. "I'm coming."

The holoscreen buzzed to life, showing schematics of the Ego Labs facility, her credentials still embedded deep within the system. She hesitated for a fraction of a second, her reflection in the screen catching her eye.

"What has this boy gotten himself into *this* time?" she whispered, before pushing the thought aside.

With her plan in place, she moved to a drawer at the edge of the room. Inside lay her EgoCorp lab coat, pristine and untouched, its insignia gleaming faintly under the sterile lights.

Her hand lingered over it for a moment. Memories she'd buried long ago threatened to resurface, but she shoved them down.

"Not the time," she muttered, slipping it over her shoulders.

Satisfied, she activated a panel on the wall. A soft chime indicated her request was successful. The lab's holographic interface confirmed: **"Egopod en route. Estimated time: 90 seconds."**

She stepped back into the main living room, casting a glance over her cozy home. The lab's lights dimmed behind her as the bookshelf swung shut, concealing the space once more.

She adjusted the collar of her lab coat, her expression hardening as she grabbed a small toolkit and stepped out the door. As she approached the curb, the Egopod pulled up, its sleek surface reflecting the morning sun. The door slid open with a faint hiss, and she climbed inside.

The dashboard flickered to life, displaying a map of Virtu City with Ego Labs highlighted in pulsating blue.

“Let’s get to work,” she said, her voice steady, as the pod smoothly pulled away.

The Egopod glided out of Silicon Valley with silent precision, a sleek capsule against the backdrop of the sprawling, eroded landscape. Gramma sat rigid, her wrist device blinking faintly with encrypted alerts. She drummed her fingers on the seat, her patience thinning as the holographic dashboard projected the estimated time of arrival.

“Estimated arrival: Approximately 2½ hours.”

Gramma’s eye twitched. “2½ hours!?” she scoffed, her voice tinged with disbelief. “What is this, 2020? I could have crocheted a blanket by the time this thing gets there!”

She jabbed at the pod’s interface, navigating to the speed override menu with the precision of someone who’d lived through too many systems and upgrades. Her fingers danced across the controls, a muscle memory from years of bypassing automated nonsense.

The AI’s voice chimed in, serene yet maddeningly condescending: *“Override denied. Maximum speed is optimized for passenger comfort and safety.”*

Gramma’s jaw dropped. “Comfort and safety? I don’t *need* comfort and safety—I need speed!” She slammed her palm onto the armrest, glaring at the dashboard as if sheer willpower could change the rules.

The pod hummed on, unmoved by her outburst. She leaned back, complaining under her breath. “No wonder the world’s gone to shit. Since when do bots call the shots?.”

In an era of instant gratification, this was blasphemy. People didn't wait anymore—not for food, not for delivery, not even for downloads. A world built on efficiency had created a population incapable of tolerating delay. And yet here she was, forced to endure fifty-four *excruciating* minutes of anticipation.

"*UN*-believable," she grumbled, folding her arms like a spoiled child. For a moment, she fantasized about hacking the pod mid-ride, but she knew the attempt would only waste more time. Instead, she stared out the window, the desolate landscape rolling by, and resigned herself to the crawl.

The mountains of the Wassuk Range loomed ahead, their jagged peaks shrouded in mist. The pod climbed steadily, cutting through the winding paths of Shadow Falls. The further it went, the more the outside world faded into stark desolation, a reminder of everything left behind in the pursuit of the pristine, curated perfection of Virtu City.

Finally, the road leveled out, and the scene transformed. As the pod rounded a final bend, the city burst into view, framed perfectly by the twin peaks of the mountain pass.

Virtu City glimmered like an oasis of light, its skyline pulsating with neon veins. The V-Way bridge arched gracefully over a yawning chasm, its surface shimmering with self-driving vehicles moving in perfect synchronization. Holographic billboards floated in the sky, projecting oversized influencers promoting everything from AI-enhanced fitness regimens to EgoCorp-approved life extensions.

Mayor Gainsley's colossal hologram flickered to life, his perfectly coiffed hair and dazzling smile dominating the view. *"Welcome to Virtu City—where dreams come alive, and the future is yours to create!"*

Gramma rolled her eyes, the irony not lost on her. "Dreams come alive, huh? More like sold to the highest bidder," she muttered, her gaze fixed on the sterile perfection of the skyline.

The pod peeled away from the V-Way bridge, merging onto an unmarked access route that snaked around and under the mountain's foundation. As the city's lights dimmed behind her, the path descended into shadows, the air growing cooler and stiller.

Ahead, a hidden entrance materialized, marked by faint red lights and the sleek, utilitarian design of EgoCorp's clandestine facilities. The pod slid into the cavernous space, its wheels humming softly against the polished floor.

Gramma stepped out, her heels clicking sharply in the silent underground garage. She adjusted her lab coat, her eyes scanning the pristine, eerily quiet surroundings.

She approached the far wall, seemingly solid stone. As she neared, an invisible sensor triggered to life, casting a faint glow across the wall. The smooth surface rippled like water, revealing an impossibly flush doorway, its edges seamless and sharp. A soft chime resonated, followed by a synthetic voice:

"Access granted. Welcome, Mother."

Gramma froze mid-step, her breath catching. She hadn't been called *Mother* in decades—not since her days within EgoCorp's inner sanctum. The name carried weight, both a title and a burden, its meaning tangled in years of buried secrets and moral compromises.

"'Mother,' huh?" she muttered, forcing her feet to move forward. "Guess old ghosts never stay buried."

The door slid open soundlessly, revealing a sleek corridor bathed in sterile white light. The stark brightness stabbed at her eyes, a jarring contrast to the dim, brutalist design of the entrance. She stepped inside, her heels clicking against the polished floor as the door sealed shut behind her.

The hallway stretched ahead, flanked by towering walls that pulsed faintly, as if alive. Data streams flickered like veins beneath the surface, coursing with information in constant motion. The air felt cool, almost clinical, and carried a faint metallic tang that clung to the back of her throat.

Her wrist device vibrated softly, an alert from Kwō's encrypted signal. She glanced at it briefly—still alive, still holding on. She picked up her pace, her heart pounding in rhythm with the cadences of the unseen machinery.

Every step brought her deeper into EgoCorp's labyrinth, the weight of her choices pressing heavier with each breath. The walls seemed to close in, as if the building itself was aware of her presence, watching, waiting.

As she rounded a corner, she reached a branching path. Ahead, another seamless door shimmered into view. A camera emerged from the ceiling, swiveling to face her.

The same synthetic voice echoed through hidden speakers: ***"Identification required. Please proceed to biometric scan."***

Gramma approached the glowing panel embedded in the wall. It flared to life, scanning her with a precision that felt invasive despite her familiarity with the process.

"Identity confirmed. Welcome, Mother."
The door slid open, and she stepped into a larger space, dimly lit and humming with an undercurrent of activity. Rows of inactive drones hung suspended from the ceiling, their

metallic forms gleaming faintly in the low light. Consoles lined the walls, their displays flickering with cryptic data streams.

A figure stirred in the shadows. No, not a person—several humanoid bots, their sleek frames unnervingly lifelike, stepped forward in unison. Their movements were fluid, their expressions unnervingly neutral.

One stepped closer, its voice eerily calm: ***"Mother has returned."***, syncing with others, activating a chain reaction of devices repeating the the same mantra.

Gramma's pulse quickened. Her eyes darted around the room, searching for any sign of Kwō. She noticed a console against the far wall, its display flickering with activity. With a sharp intake of breath, she made her move, sprinting toward it as the bots advanced.

She slammed her hand down on the console, her fingers flying across the holographic interface. Her instincts took over, recalling long-buried sequences and overrides. A command menu appeared, displaying a holding tank ID.

"Come on, come on," she whispered, inputting a release code. The screen flashed, indicating the sequence had been sent, but she had no time to confirm if it worked.

A sharp metallic hand grabbed her arm, yanking her away from the console.

"SHIT!" she hissed, struggling against the bots as more swarmed her.

One of the humanoid bots stepped forward, its voice eerily calm yet cold: **"WELCOME HOME, MOTHER."**

Before she could respond, a sharp prick pierced her arm. Her vision blurred instantly, her knees buckling beneath her.

The last thing she saw as she collapsed was the flickering console, the release command still active. The bots caught her before she hit the floor, their grip unyielding.

The same haunting voice echoed again, reverberating in her fading consciousness: **"WE'VE MISSED YOU, MOTHER."**

"I'm.....*not*...your...Mo...", an angry defiance in her trembling voice even as she drifts off.

The lights flickered as her body slumped, and the facility returned to its cold, unfeeling rhythm, as if nothing had happened.

The bright, sterile light in the interrogation room bore down on Kwō, amplifying the pounding in his chest. His wrists strained against the cold metal cuffs that pinned him to the table. Across from him, two highly intimidating EgoCorp interrogation bots loomed, their glowing red lenses scanning him intently.

"SUBJECT 3095," one of the bots intoned in its hollow, mechanical voice, "state the purpose of your presence in this facility."

Kwō swallowed hard, trying to steady his voice. "purpose? I don't even know how I got here!"

The second bot leaned in closer, its servos whining with each movement. "Unauthorized access is punishable by termination of contract. Noncompliance will result in immediate recalibration."

Kwō's pulse quickened. "What contract? I didn't sign anything!"

Before the bots could respond, the lights in the room flickered.

Both bots froze mid-motion, their lenses dimming briefly. A light buzz filled the air, followed by a series of garbled tones emanating from their cores.

"Error—Error—Priority override engaged," the first bot said, its voice faltering.

Kwō blinked in confusion, his breath catching in his throat. The cuffs around his wrists clicked open with a metallic hiss, releasing him.

He stared down at his free hands, his heart racing.

"What the—?"

The bots turned abruptly toward the door, their lenses flashing orange. "Reassigning focus... Target located: Subject 001... Proceeding to contain."

Kwō didn't wait to figure out what was happening. The moment the bots left the room, he bolted, nearly tripping over the legs of one as he passed.
The hallway outside was a blur of flashing lights and distorted alarm tones. Kwō pressed himself against the wall, peering around the corner. The bots were gone, moving in the opposite direction. It was as if the system had suddenly forgotten he existed.

"What the hell is going on?" he whispered to himself, his hands trembling.

His interface buzzed against his wrist. He jumped, fumbling to check the notification.

💬 **Scorelord:**
Coordinates attached. Time to play the game, Kwō. Meet me there.

Kwō stared at the message, confusion and panic swirling in his mind. "Scorelord? Here?" he muttered under his breath.

A distant clatter snapped him back to reality. He shoved his interface back against his wrist and took off running, navigating the maze of corridors as fast as his legs could carry him.

Every step echoed faintly in the empty halls, but no alarms sounded. No drones pursued him. The system was preoccupied, its attention drawn elsewhere.

As he darted into the service corridors, Kwō's mind raced. The timing was too perfect, too convenient. He didn't know why the bots had left him alone, but he wasn't about to question his luck.

Bursting out into the night air, he inhaled deeply, the cool wind cutting through his sweat-soaked clothes. For a brief moment, he allowed himself to believe he was free.

But freedom didn't feel so safe.

Pulling up Scorelord's coordinates again, Kwō turned toward the direction of the Terminal. "Deadzone, huh?" he muttered, adjusting his hoodie to obscure his face. "Guess this place exists after all."

Without looking back, he faded into the alleys.

EPISODE 20
THE FLICKERBORN

The Deadzone stretched endlessly before Scorelord, its twisted architecture and jagged ruins bathed in faint, eerie light. He walked slowly, his boots crunching on shattered glass and crumbling debris, the silence unnerving.

It was a place that defied logic—buildings leaning into each other like old friends, stairways leading to nowhere, and graffiti-covered walls that seemed to tell stories no one was alive to remember. The deeper he went, the heavier the air felt, like the ghosts of the forgotten were watching his every move.

As he turned a corner, he froze. A faint sound reached him—footsteps. Not drones, not scavengers, but something human. His hand instinctively hovered near the button on his vape, when a voice pierced the silence.

"Score!?"

He spun around, his heart pounding. Standing a few feet away was Shade, her silhouette sharp against the dim light. For a moment, neither of them moved.

"Shade!?" he whispered, disbelief etched across his face.

She stepped closer, her eyes narrowing. "It's you. It's really you."

Before he could respond, more figures emerged from the shadows—Vexer, known as the prankster of the crew, and a younger girl who hung back slightly, watching him with a mix of caution and curiosity.

"We thought you were dead," Shade said, her voice cracking slightly.

Scorelord took a hesitant step forward. "They told me *you* were gone. All of you."

Shade shook her head, tears glinting in her eyes. "We thought EgoCorp killed you. We followed you here, hoping to find answers, but..."

Her words trailed off, and Vexer stepped forward, his expression hard. "But we got stuck in this nightmare instead. And you—where the hell have you been?"

Scorelord's throat tightened as guilt washed over him. "I didn't know... I thought you all just—forgot about me."

Shade's expression softened. "We tried to find you, but..." Her voice faltered. "Not all of us made it."

Scorelord's heart sank. "What do you *mean*?"

"Blick," Shade said quietly. "He didn't make it. EgoCorp got to him before we reached the Deadzone."

The words hit Scorelord like a physical blow. He staggered slightly, leaning against a crumbling wall for support.

"Blick's—*gone*?" he whispered, his voice breaking.

Vexer nodded, his pain visible despite his hardened exterior. “He fought until the end. But it wasn’t enough.”

Scorelord clenched his fists, his head dropping. “That was my fuckin’ brother, man.” he said hoarsely.

Shade placed a hand on his shoulder. “We had to mourn him without you…Take all the time you need.”

“And N30И…is *she*—“

“She’s alive.” Vexer answered. “Had a mental meltdown—tried to **reset** herself after everything that happened. Can’t blame her. But she’s doing better these days. Spends most of her time in MindRealm. Rides The Circuit with Rune. We still cross paths from time to time.”

“Damn….shit, man.” Scorelord replied, seething with guilt, “I’m *so* sorry I wasn’t there for you guys. I should’ve been there.”

“Don’t” Shade interjected. “We were all in this together. From jump. We knew the risks. We took the risks. We dealt with the consequences.”

Scorelord, looking down, hitting his vape, shaking his head in agreement.

“We’re here now, bro.” Vexer said, “and we *still* need you. we got a war to win.”

Scorelord, wiping his face, as if he wasn’t just crying,“Then Game On Mother*Fuckers!*”

“Looks like Gen Wasted is back in business, baby.” Vexer said devilishly.

“And this time we *all* gettin’ golden tickets.”

Later that night while Score's back was turned, hunched over a patched-together console rig, muttering under his breath about "calibrations" and how "EgoCorp is gonna pay." He didn't even register the soft footsteps behind him until a steady, melodic voice broke the quiet.

"So," the voice said, calm but curious, "you're the legendary Scorelord?"

His fingers froze mid-tinker, his mouth opening for his usual cocky response—but when he turned and his gaze landed on Veil, all composure vanished.

"WHOA!" he shouted, stumbling back into the console. His hands shot up defensively, his eyes darting to her flickering, glowing ones. "*Nope. Nope. Nope. What the hell is this?!* Why does she look like she just crawled out of a corrupted file?!"

From her spot leaning against the wall, Shade let out a low chuckle, arms folded. "Relax, gamer boy. She's not gonna bite."

Veil tilted her head slightly, her faint grin tugging at the corners of her lips. "So you're the one they all talk about?" she asked, her voice even but teasing. "The genius who gamed Virtu City and lived to tell the tale? I thought you'd be taller."

Shade snorted. Scorelord blinked, pointing an accusatory finger at Veil. "First of all," he said, his voice a mix of defensive and rattled, "I am *plenty* tall. Second—what even *are* you?" He gestured vaguely at her glowing eyes. "And why do your eyes look like they're about to fry my CPU? The hell's up wit' *that*?"

"They're just my eyes," Veil said simply, her calm tone making it somehow even weirder.

"Yeaah. Sure. And these are just my eyes," Scorelord muttered, pointing to his VR headset.

"She's my daughter," Shade interjected, stepping forward with a subtle edge of protectiveness.

Scorelord turned to her, his jaw dropping slightly. "Your... daughter?" He looked back at Veil, his expression cycling through confusion, disbelief, and mild panic. "Okay, but, like... how? When? And why does she look like she's about to hack reality?"

Shade smirked faintly but didn't answer right away.

Veil stepped closer, clearly amused. "You're asking a lot of questions for someone who's supposed to be legendary," she said, her tone light but pointed.

Scorelord narrowed his eyes, suspicion creeping into his expression. "Wait... was that a dig?"

"Maybe," Veil said with a shrug, a faint smirk tugging at her lips. "I've watched your streams. You were almost good enough to keep up with me."

Scorelord blinked, caught off guard. "Keep up with you?" He straightened, suddenly more focused. "Alright, ya little weirdo. *Challenge accepted.* But when it's showtime, I'm gonna need you to tone down the creepy flicker-eyes thing."

Veil rolled her eyes—flickering slightly as she did—and turned away, heading toward the other side of the room. "Yeah, yeah. We'll see if you're worth the hype later," she called over her shoulder.

Scorelord watched her go, still looking a little shaken. He turned back to Shade, lowering his voice. "Alright, seriously. When the hell did *that* happen?"

Shade hesitated, her smirk fading. Her gaze followed Veil, her expression softening with something unspoken—regret, pride, and a touch of lingering pain. "It's… complicated," she said finally.

Scorelord raised an eyebrow. "Complicated how?"

Shade sighed, crossing her arms tightly over her chest as if bracing herself. "I loved her father," she said, her voice quieter now. "But I had to stand on business. For her."

Scorelord frowned, his curiosity overtaking his usual sarcasm. "What do you mean, 'stand on business?' What happened?"

Shade glanced at him, her expression unreadable for a long moment. "It's not something I like talking about," she admitted. "But… I'll tell you."

"You don't have to if it's too much," Scorelord said, his voice uncharacteristically serious.

Shade shook her head. "No. You deserve to know." She took a deep breath, her gaze distant as she began. "It started in the Deadzone, right after Veil was born…"

The weight of her words hung in the air as she launched into the story, pulling Scorelord into the moment like a thread unraveling a long-buried truth.

FLASHBACK STARTS:

Though hope was lost, Deadzone was alive with whispers. Inside the patched-together tent, a new life was taking its first breath, while outside, the ruins buzzed with electric unease. Shade had brought her daughter into this fractured world, and for a fleeting moment, everything felt still.

She cradled the child, her exhaustion drowned by an overwhelming awe. The baby's skin was pale, almost luminescent against the dim light of the tent. Her silvery-white hair was so fine it looked like spun starlight, and her delicate features made Shade's breath catch. But it was her partner's reaction that sent a chill through her.

He crouched beside her, his dark hands trembling slightly as he reached toward the baby. Then he stopped. His fingers hovered just short of touching her, as if an invisible force held him back.

"She's… white?" he muttered, his voice barely above a whisper.

"She's *albino*," Shade said quickly, a slight edge in her voice. "It's rare, but it happens."

He nodded, but his brow furrowed deeply as his eyes scanned the baby's face. He lingered on the silvery hair, the almost translucent skin, the sharp contrast between mother and child.

"Albino," he repeated, as if trying to convince himself.

Shade could see the wheels turning in his mind, the slow unraveling of certainty.

"She's *ours*," she said, her tone firm, daring him to challenge her.

He didn't. Not yet. But the doubt was already there, creeping into his expression like a shadow.

For the next few days, cradled the child with a tenderness that felt instinctual—an unspoken language of comfort and devotion. Days had passed since the birth, and still, Veil's eyes hadn't opened. Her body remained limp, her skin unnervingly pale against Shade's own. But Shade didn't waver. She poured her love into the child, her whispers filling the silence, promises echoing in the dim light.

Then it happened.

A ripple, faint but unmistakable, beneath her fingertips. A pulse, like static skimming the surface of her skin. Shade's breath hitched. Her eyes locked on Veil's face, and for a moment, everything else fell away.

Veil's eyelids fluttered.

Shade leaned in, heart pounding as anticipation tangled with fear. When those eyes finally opened, the air around her seemed to still. White. But not blank. Not lifeless. Glowing with movement—an unnatural flicker, It was like looking into a void of forgotten signals—an endless stream of broken data trying to force itself into something real. But nothing held.

Shade's lips parted, her pulse pounding in her ears.

"*Look at you...*" she whispered, her voice barely above a breath. Awe, confusion, and a flicker of something deeper—something primal—washed over her. She had known Veil was different. But this? This was beyond anything she could have imagined. Before she could get a closer look, Titus came stumbling back into the tent.

His footsteps were heavy, dragging the weight of days spent wrestling with doubt. His eyes landed on Veil, and his body went rigid. His face hardened, the exhaustion in his expression replaced by something colder. He had seen the pale skin, convinced himself the child wasn't his. But this? The flicker in her eyes? It was all the confirmation he needed.

This child was a mistake.

“What the hell, Shade…” His voice was tight, barely containing the storm brewing beneath. His eyes stayed fixed on Veil.

She turned, instinctively shielding the child from his gaze, but Titus was already gone. His mind had snapped shut, sealing itself behind walls of certainty.

“This ain't right,” he muttered, more to himself than her. His jaw clenched, his breath shallow. “She's not… she's not one of us.”

Shade's stomach dropped.

“I don't know what that is,” he whispered, his voice laced with something darker than fear. “But it's not mine.”

The air thickened, the weight of his words pressing down on her. She could feel it—the shift in him. This wasn't just doubt anymore. It was conviction.

To Titus, Veil wasn't a child. It was an error. A glitch. And glitches had to be erased.

Shade held Veil closer, her heart pounding as a quiet, primal fear took root. She knew what may come next.

He stayed outside the tent longer each night, lingering by the fires where the other survivors gathered, their low murmurs carrying easily through the thin walls.

“Did you see that baby?”
“Mmhmm.... Sum' ain't right.”
“That's ***definitely*** *not natural.”*

When he came back, his silence was heavier than the darkness outside and carried on into the next day.

Later that evening, he sat at the edge of the tent, his back to Shade as she rocked the baby to sleep. The firelight outside cast long, flickering shadows, painting his face with shifting patterns of light and dark.

"Babe—*Talk to me,*" Shade said, breaking the silence.

He didn't turn around.

"Titus," she said, her voice sharper this time.

He sighed, running a hand over his head. "I don't know what you want me to say."

"How about why you've barely said a word since our child was born!?"

He hesitated, his shoulders tensing.

"It's just...She's just so... *different,*" he said finally, his voice low and uneven.

Shade's stomach tightened. "Different how?"

He turned to face her, and for the first time, she saw the fear in his eyes.

"C'mon Shade, Look at her," he said, gesturing toward the baby. "She doesn't look like *either* of us."

"She's albino—"

"You think I've never seen an albino before!? This ain't that." he interrupted, his voice rising slightly. "Her hair, her skin... *THOSE EYES?*—this is something *else*...she doesn't even look *human.*"

Shade's jaw clenched. "You're being overly paranoid."

"Am I?" he shot back. "Or are you just ignoring the obvious?"

"The obvious?" Shade snapped. "That she's ours? That she's a baby? What are you trying to say?"

His eyes narrowed, and his voice dropped to a dangerous whisper. "The kid's *clearly* not mine."

Shade's breath hitched. "So what—you think I cheated?"

His silence was louder than any answer he could have given.

"Down here? With who, exactly?" she demanded, her voice shaking with anger. "You think I've got time to step out in the Deadzone? You think I've been sneaking off to shack up with scavengers and bots while you've been right here the whole time?"

He stood abruptly, his shadow towering over her. "I don't know what to think right now, Shade!"

The baby stirred in her arms, letting out a soft, plaintive cry. Shade instinctively held her closer, her protective instincts flaring.

"You're scaring her," she said, her voice dropping to a warning tone.

He took a step back, his hands flexing at his sides. "I'm scaring her?" he repeated bitterly. "She's scaring everyone in the deadzone! What even is she, Shade? Because that's not *just some albino kid.*"

Shade's jaw tightened, her voice low and cutting. "No, she's not just some albino kid—she's *your* daughter! And maybe if you weren't so scared of things you don't understand, you'd see that!"

He flinched, her words hitting deeper than she expected. He turned away, his fists clenching and unclenching at his sides.

"I need to clear my head," he muttered, his tone sharp but shaken. Without another word, he stormed out of the tent, the flap swaying behind him as the whispers of the Deadzoners greeted him outside. The hours passed and when he finally returned, Shade could smell the hooch on his breath and his dilated pupils were a dead giveaway of the nanobot laced drugs coursing through his veins.

"You reek," she muttered, her voice dripping with disdain.

"Yeah, well," he said, collapsing onto the makeshift chair in the corner. "That kid's got me needing a drink."

"She's *YOUR* kid too, Titus." Shade snapped.
He didn't respond.

Outside, the Deadzoners were gathered around a fire, their voices carrying easily through the thin walls of the tent.

"Did you see her eyes yet?" one voice asked.
"No, but I heard they're… off."
"Off how?"
"Like, not normal. You think the Deadzone environment had anything to do with it?"
"Shit—being born down here? Who knows.

He heard it all, and though he didn't say a word, the weight of their whispers hung heavy on him. The next morning, Shade caught him staring at the baby, his expression dark and conflicted.

"What now?" she asked, her voice sharp.

“I just keep thinking about what they’re saying out there,” he admitted.

“Who?”

“*Everyone.*”

Shade scoffed. “Let me guess—they think she’s *cursed*?”

He didn’t respond, but his silence said enough.

“They don’t know what they’re talking about,” she said, her tone firm.

“You don’t know *what* they know.” he muttered under his breath.

Shade glared at him. “What are you trying to say?”
He looked up at her, his eyes hard. “I’m saying that maybe they’re right.” He grabbed an electric lighter device and quickly left out again not returning until the next day. Shade had been mentally and physically preparing herself for the inevitable.

The tent flap ripped open, and Titus stormed in, his heavy boots slamming against the ground. His eyes immediately locked on the jagged shard of metal clutched in Shade’s trembling hand. He froze for a split second, then laughed—a bitter, mocking sound that only seemed to deepen his rage.

“Really, Shade?” he sneered, his voice dripping with disdain. “You think you’re gonna stop me with that? A piece of scrap?”

Shade shifted Veil in her arms, standing her ground even as fear clawed at her insides. “I’ll do whatever it takes to keep her safe.”

Titus's laugh faded, replaced by a dark, simmering anger. He took a step forward, his fists clenched. "You've lost your damn mind," he growled. "You're gonna put some mutant baby before me? Before all of us? You don't see what you're doing!"

"I see perfectly fine," Shade snapped, her voice shaking but defiant. "You're scared, Titus. Scared of something you don't understand. And now you're trying to hide that fear by acting like a tyrant."

"Fear?" Titus barked, his eyes narrowing. "You think I'm afraid of her? Of *you*?" He stepped closer, his massive frame casting a shadow over her. "No, Shade. What I'm afraid of is what she'll bring down on all of us when the Deadzone turns on her—on us—because of what she is."

"She's not a threat," Shade said, her voice rising with desperation. "She's our daughter, Titus!"

"She's a *GOD DAMNED MUTANT*, Shade! She's not mine!" he roared, his voice booming. She slapped his hand out of her face. His hand shot out, and Shade flinched as he grabbed the weapon from her hands, tossing it aside with a clang.

Before she could react, his hand swung out, striking her hard across the face. Shade stumbled back, her vision blurring as pain seared through her cheek. Veil let out a sharp cry, her tiny hands twitching in Shade's arms.

"You think you can challenge me?" Titus bellowed, his voice trembling with fury. "You think you can defy me and protect that… that thing?"

Shade steadied herself, her back against the tent wall, her eyes blazing with anger. "She's not a thing," she spat, blood trickling from the corner of her mouth. "She's your daughter, Titus! And you're too much of a coward to see that."

Titus's face twisted, his fury boiling over. "Coward?" he growled. "Do you know the things I've done to protect you? To protect *us*?" his voice venomous. He lunged at her again, his hand raised.

But just as he was about to strike, the air around them shifted.

The frequency started low, almost imperceptible, but it grew steadily louder, vibrating through the tent like a live wire. Titus froze mid-strike, his body locking up as if he'd hit an invisible wall.

"what—What the hell is this?" he muttered, his voice shaking.

Shade's breath caught as she looked down at Veil. The baby's cries morphing into a clashing chorus of synthetic screams, her flickering eyes glowing brighter with every passing second. The scattered tech around the tent began to rise, floating into the air as if drawn by an unseen force. Titus stumbled back, his hands flying to his head. "Stop it!" he shouted, his voice cracking. "What's happening?!"

The frequency grew sharper, slicing through the air like a blade. Titus groaned, falling to his knees as blood trickled from his eyes, nose and ears. His face contorted into a horrific expression that was beyond recognition. His body convulsed violently, his muscles jerking uncontrollably.

"It's her," Shade said, her voice low and cutting. She stepped forward, cradling Veil protectively. "The one you're *SO* afraid of, Titus. And now, she's giving you a reason."

Titus let out a guttural scream, his hands clawing at his temples as if trying to rip the pain out of his head. "Make it stop!" he bellowed, his voice raw. "SHADE, MAKE IT STOP!"

"Why should I?" she snapped, stepping closer. "You didn't listen when I needed you. I *begged* for you to just *try* to understand. Look at you now—scared, weak. A pathetic little man who thought he could control everything. You're no better than EgoCorp." looking down at him with an expression of utter disgust, her upper lip curling in disdain.

"Shade—*please*!" Titus gasped, his voice trembling as his body jerked against the invisible force holding him.

"Please?" she repeated, her voice cold and mocking. "Oh, now you're begging? Now you're afraid?" She crouched down in front of him, her face inches from his. "You don't get to beg, Titus. You don't get to ask for mercy when you showed us none."

The shards of tech debris hovered higher, their sharp edges glinting ominously. Wires and cables coiled through the air like living snakes, wrapping around Titus's wrists and ankles. He thrashed against them, his body arching unnaturally as the frequency in Veil's voice reached a shrilling pitch.

"I'm sorry!" Titus screamed, his voice cracking as blood poured from his nose.

"No, you're not," Shade said flatly, standing over him. "But you will be."

The largest shard floated above Titus, spinning slowly as if savoring the moment. His screams turned into broken gasps, his strength fading as the wires pulled him tighter.

"Shade…baby" he choked out, his voice barely audible.

Shade tilted her head, her lips curling into a bitter smirk. "Baby?" she said, her tone dripping with vitriol. "Yeah, I don't think this is gonna work out."

The shard shot downward with a sickening crunch, piercing Titus's chest. His body convulsed one final time, then went limp, the wires loosening and retreating back into the debris as he slumped to the ground in a lifeless heap.

The hum faded, leaving the tent in eerie silence. The shards of tech settled to the ground, the faint glow from Veil's eyes casting soft, haunting light over the scene.

Shade stood over Titus's body, her breath coming in shallow gasps. The baby in her arms cooed softly, her flickering eyes dimming to a faint glow.

Stepping over Titus's lifeless form, Shade pushed through the tent flap into the cold air of the Deadzone. Onlookers stared, their faces pale with shock as they took in the sight of her standing tall, unyielding.

"This is my daughter," Shade said sharply, her voice slicing through the silence. "And if anyone else thinks they've got a problem with her, you can end up just like Him."

Without another word, she disappeared deep into the cavities the sanctuary, Veil's faint glow casting shadows behind her as the Deadzone fell silent once more.

END OF FLASHBACK

Shade's voice trailed off, her gaze fixed on a spot in the distance, as though she could still see the faint glow of the Coves deep beneath the wreckage of the Terminal. The hum of the Deadzone's makeshift generators grounding her in the present.

Across from her, Scorelord sat still, uncharacteristically quiet. His usual cocky demeanor had vanished, replaced by a rare look of understanding—or something close to it. He leaned back against the table, his arms crossed, letting her words sink in.

"So," he said finally, his voice softer than usual, "all of that—building the Coves, keeping them hidden, training those kids—it was all to make sure EgoCorp couldn't get to you?"

Shade nodded, the faintest edge of exhaustion creeping into her voice. "It wasn't just about staying hidden," she said, her tone low but resolute. "It was about making sure those kids could survive. They didn't ask to be born this way, but they're the ones paying the price for what EgoCorp did to this world."

Scorelord shifted, rubbing the back of his neck. "And Veil?" he asked hesitantly. "How does she… deal with all this?"

Shade exhaled, her jaw tightening. For a moment, it seemed like she wouldn't answer. But then she glanced at him, her eyes sharp and filled with something between pride and pain.

"We manage. She doesn't have a choice," Shade said simply. "None of us do. But Veil…" Her voice softened, just enough to reveal the emotion beneath her hardened exterior. "She's the reason I'm still standing here. After everything—Titus, the fear, the fights—I wouldn't have made it without her."

Scorelord frowned, studying her carefully. "That's a hell of a lot to put on a kid's shoulders, Shade."

"She's stronger than you think," Shade replied, her tone unwavering. "And she's not the only one. The flickerborn…

they're not just another problem to solve, and they're not something to fear, either. They're a symbol of hope. For me, for the Deadzone, for whatever comes next."

She leaned forward, her voice dropping to a near whisper. "EgoCorp might think they've got this world under control, but they have no idea what's coming. The flickerborn aren't just the future—they're the catalyst for the Great Reset."

The weight of her words hung heavy in the air, and Scorelord found himself nodding slowly, a faint smirk tugging at his lips despite the seriousness of the moment.

"Damn," he muttered. "You're really out here raising the next generation of badass tech rebels, huh?"

Shade's lips twitched into the faintest of smiles. "Litework."

Scorelord managed a faint smile, despite the uncertainty in his chest. "Well, looks like you're well ahead of the game."

And just like that, the moment passed, the room settling back into the tense energy of the mission ahead. But the details of her story lingered, a quiet promise of what was to come.

Kwō stumbles into the Deadzone, his breaths shallow and uneven, his steps faltering over the loose dirt and debris scattered across the cavernous underground space. The faint shafts of light breaking through cracks above cast fragmented beams over the makeshift tents and haphazard structures. Dust hung heavy in the air, illuminated by the occasional flicker of exposed bulbs strung between beams. The place felt as if time itself had been abandoned here.

"Whoa, whoa! What the hell happened, kid?" Scorelord's voice rang out, sharp and commanding. His LED mask

pulsed erratically as he rushed forward to steady Kwō, who looked on the verge of collapse.
Kwō clutched his knees, gasping for air. "You're not… gonna believe… what I just saw," he panted, barely able to form the words.

"Take your time," Scorelord said, his tone shifting to something softer, though his LEDs betrayed his growing concern. "But start talking. You look like you just escaped hell."

Kwō straightened, wiping the sweat from his brow as he stumbled toward a nearby crate and slumped onto it. "That's… not far off," he said, his voice trembling.

Scorelord crouched down in front of him, his LED eyes fixed. "How the hell did you get out of EgoCorp's grip? They don't just let people walk away."
"They didn't," Kwō said, his voice shaking. "I don't know how to explain it. The bots—they just stopped paying attention to me, like… like they had something more important to deal with."

Scorelord narrowed his eyes. "What could be more important than interrogating you?"

"I don't know!" Kwō snapped, the panic still fresh in his voice. "I don't even know *why* they stopped, but when they did, I ran. That place… it's a *nightmare*."

Scorelord leaned back, crossing his arms. "All right, so you're out. But what did you see in there? You've got that look, kid. You've seen some ***shit***."

Kwō took a deep breath, his eyes darting around as if trying to piece together the fragments of his memory. "They're building something, Score," he said, his voice low. "Something *big*."

"Building what?" Scorelord pressed, the LEDs on his VR headset freezing in a steady pulse.

"***People***," Kwō said simply, the weight of the word sinking into the air between them. "If you can even call them that. Rows of pods, filled with... I don't know, synthetic humans? ***Phase 3***, they called it. They're phasing out everyone in Virtu City and replacing them with these... *bots*—they're calling them Forever Influencers."

"Forever Influencers?" Scorelord echoed, his voice tinged with disbelief.

"They're perfect, flawless, and completely controllable," Kwō explained, his hands trembling as he spoke. "They're designed to never age, never die, and never question. EgoCorp is waiting for the Phase 2 people to die off *naturally* while they phase in these bots."
"And the people in Virtu City? They have no idea..." Scorelord asked, though he already knew the answer.

Kwō shook his head. "Not a clue. It's like the whole city is a giant experiment, and nobody even realizes they're the test subjects."

Scorelord's LEDs dimmed slightly, a rare flicker of unease crossing his usually stoic posture. "And you saw *all* this?"

Kwō nodded. "Yeah. But that's not even the craziest part." He hesitated, his voice dropping to a near whisper. "It kept recognizing Auris. The system... it called her *Mother*."

Scorelord froze, his mask locked in a static pattern. "Mother?" he repeated, the word hanging heavy in the air.

"Yeah," Kwō said, his voice wavering. "Every door, every scanner— she was able to bypass 'em like she was some

kind of… *VIP*. The system treated her like she was the key to the whole damn place."
Scorelord's LEDs flickered rapidly as a memory surfaced. He straightened, his tone sharp. "*Your Gramma*," he said suddenly.

"What about her?" Kwō asked, frowning.

"That picture on the mantle," Scorelord said, his voice heavy with realization. "Didn't think much of it at the time, but after putting two and two together—she was wearin' a lab coat in that picture. It had a name tag on it."

"Okay. *And*?" Kwō pressed, his irritation rising.
"The name tag said 'Mother,'" Scorelord said, his LEDs flashing in sync with his words.

Kwō's face twisted, almost offended at the idea that his old ass Gramma might have anything to do with any this. "Cap."

"I wish it was," Scorelord said. "If your Gramma is this *Mother*, then she's not just some sweet old lady watchin' stories and sippin' tea in her spare time. She's connected to all of this—EgoCorp, the labs, *everything*."

Kwō stood abruptly, pacing in the dirt. "Nah. That doesn't even make sense. She's not like that. Why would she—"

"Look, kid," Scorelord interrupted, his tone firm but not unkind. "I'm not saying she's behind it all. But she's in this, whether you want to believe it or not. They call her '*MOTHER*' for a reason. And if she's not answering your calls—"

"She's probably busy!" Kwō snapped defensively, though his voice wavered with doubt.

"Or she's caught up in something she can't get out of," Scorelord countered. "You said it yourself—she always answers your calls. Why not now?"

Kwō didn't respond, his mind spinning as he tried to reconcile the image of the grandmother he knew with the revelation hanging over him. "I've gotta get back to her," he muttered finally, his voice barely audible.

Scorelord stepped closer, placing a hand on his shoulder. "We will. But first, you need to tell me everything else you saw in that lab."

Kwō hesitated, then nodded.

"There was this pod," he began, his voice carrying the weight of disbelief. "It opened up when Auris got close. There was a bot inside. Called her… '*Mother.*'" He paused, glancing at Scorelord, gauging his reaction.

Scorelord's LEDs flickered briefly, his face screwed with confusion. "Auris? Yea this is gettin' freakier by the minute."

"At first, the bot thought we were the ones holding it captive," Kwō continued. "It was panicking, shouting, accusing us of trapping it there. I've never seen anything like it—it looked human, but there was something off about it. Too perfect, too smooth, like it was trying to hide what it really was."

Scorelord leaned forward, his LEDs shifting into a steady glow. "Okay. So What happened?"

"It started yelling names," Kwō said, his voice growing more animated. "Your name, Vexer, N30И—everyone from Gen Wasted. Like it was desperate to find you."

"Nah," Scorelord says dismissively, "There's no way," he muttered under his breath in denial, pacing back and forth. "It *can't* be."

"What can't be?" Kwō asked, his tone sharp with impatience.

Shade, who had been leaning against a nearby post, stiffened at the mention of Gen Wasted. Without a word, she pushed off the crate and disappeared into her tent, moving with sharp purpose.

Kwō continued, oblivious to her sudden departure. "It was glitching out, like it was in pain, slamming its fists against the pod. I've never seen anything like it. It was angry—angrier than I thought a bot could even get."

"Did it say how long it had been there?" Scorelord asked, his voice steady but tense.

"Nope," Kwō replied. "It didn't even know how long it had been locked up. It just kept shouting, like it was desperate to escape."Scorelord turned away, pacing in the dirt, his LEDs dimming to a faint glow.

Across the camp, Shade emerged from her tent holding a small device in her hand. Its blinking red light cast an eerie glow across her face. She walked toward them with deliberate steps, her expression unreadable.

"It's him," she said, her voice calm but heavy with certainty. "XY-n0's [ZENO] still alive."

Kwō frowned. "XY-n0? Who's XY-n0?"

Scorelord turned to Shade, his LEDs flaring briefly as he recognized the device. "That's his beacon," he said, his tone shifting to something almost reverent. "We built that decades ago—programmed it to activate if he ever came back online again."

Shade nodded, holding up the blinking device like a relic. "I found it buried in my old gear. If it's blinking—it means his consciousness is still in there."

Kwō looked between them, his confusion deepening. "Wait, this bot—XY-n0—he's your friend?"

"He was," Scorelord said, his tone darkening. "The last time we saw him, he was just a skeleton. A frame with no skin, no upgrades. But if he looks human now…"

"That's Phase 3," Shade interrupted, her voice sharp. "EgoCorp must've upgraded him when they captured him. If they're phasing out the people in Virtu City— and replacing them with bots. Perfect, obedient, and immortal."

Kwō's stomach churned. "Then XY-n0?"

"He's part of it now," Scorelord said, his LEDs dimming. "But if he's still calling for us, it means they didn't erase everything. He remembers. And that's dangerous—for them, and for us."

Shade clenched her jaw, staring at the blinking device in her hand. "If he remembers, then he's not just another tool. He's our way in. He's a weapon."

Scorelord nodded slowly, his LEDs pulsing with renewed determination. "Then we find him. Whatever it takes. For now, you gotta find Auris. We can't pull this off without our royal princess!"

Kwō took a deep breath, his resolve solidifying. "Let's do it."

The three of them stood in silence, the blinking device casting a faint red glow that seemed to pulse in time with their rising determination. The fight wasn't over—not by a long shot.

EPISODE 21

THE EGO AWARDS

Auris stepped out of the elevator, her heart heavy as she approached her apartment. The events of the Terminal clung to her like a second skin, and she wasn't ready to face the pristine facade of her curated life.

Her steps slowed as she saw the sleek, unopened box sitting outside her door. The glow of its label was unmistakable: **Lumi Replacement Unit 2.0.**

She frowned, her stomach sinking.

"What the hell..." she muttered under her breath.

The box emitted a soft whir as she approached, as though it sensed her presence. Its surface gleamed with a polish too perfect, its edges too precise.

Auris nudged it with her foot, watching it slide an inch across the floor. She resisted the urge to scream.

"They don't waste *any* time, did they?" she muttered bitterly.

Kicking the box aside, she unlocked her door and stepped into her loft, letting it hiss shut behind her. The familiarity of the space greeted her, but something felt off.

Her interface buzzed with a notification. She glanced at it, her eyes narrowing.

Lumi 2.0

Welcome, Miss Auris! Shall I begin syncing your data?

She clenched her jaw, swiping the notification away.

A moment later, the door chimed. Auris turned sharply as the Lumi unit, now unpacked and fully activated, came floating into the room. Its sleek body reflected the loft's perfect lighting, and its lens blinked in a way that felt almost condescending.

"Auris," it chirped, "I've noticed irregularities in your recent activity. Would you like to review them together?"

Auris's pulse quickened, her mind racing. "Irregularities?"

"Your activity patterns deviate significantly from the norm," Lumi replied. "Shall I alert EgoCorp for assistance?"

"No," Auris snapped. She forced a calm tone, adding, "Standby mode. Now."

The Lumi tilted its head, its lens dimming slightly. "As you wish, Auris."

As it powered down, Auris sank onto the couch, her head in her hands. She knew the truth now—EgoCorp was always watching. The replacement Lumi wasn't just an upgrade; it was a leash. But it was also her streaming device and outlet to the world. It was always on, always watching… Reporting back. She was screwed either way.

Her eyes drifted to the faint glow of the insignia on her arm, hidden beneath her sleeve. It was her only connection to the

Deadzone, and she'd have to tread carefully if she wanted to keep it that way.

"There's no escape," she whispered, her voice barely audible. "But they don't know what I know. Not yet."

BACK FROM THE DEAD...ZONE

Kwō moved carefully through the dimly lit corridors of the Terminal, its surreal architecture twisting and turning like a labyrinth. The encounter with Scorelord and crew in the Deadzone still echoed in his mind—a reunion steeped in equal parts relief and sorrow and confusion.

Now, the city loomed ahead of him, its lights pulsing like a synthetic heartbeat. He adjusted the hood of his jacket, ensuring it shadowed his face, and slipped into the shadows. Surveillance drones buzzed overhead, their red beams scanning for any anomalies.

"Just make it out," he muttered to himself, keeping his movements steady and deliberate.

Reaching a service hatch hidden behind a pile of discarded equipment, Kwō slipped through and emerged into an alley on the outskirts of Virtu City. The neon haze of the metropolis engulfed him instantly, a stark contrast to the eerie stillness of the Terminal.

His wrist device buzzed. Pulling it up, he hesitated for a moment before sending a quick video message to Auris.

💬**Kwō:**
Out. Back in the city. What's the move?

The reply came almost instantly, her words laced with urgency and sass:

💬**Auris:**

Move? How'd you even—NEVERMIND, you can explain later. Meet me at the Egos. 5:30pm. And I KNOW you're not wearing THAT, are you??

Kwō glanced down at himself, his battered jacket and scuffed boots a sharp reminder of the Terminal's grime. He rolled his eyes, replying back:

💬**Kwō:**

Wait, The EGOs?! What's wrong with what I have on?

The three-dot typing indicator blinked for what felt like an eternity before her response appeared: •••

💬**Auris:**

EVERYTHING. Geez, what are you TRYING to get me cancelled?! You're my guest. Don't embarrass me.

💬**Kwō:**

Look, *This is all I got...*

Auris rolls her eyes and hangs up. Kwō instantly receives a notification. She sent him enough VC to buy a designer outfit. Kwō sighed but couldn't help smirking. "Guess I'm getting fly," he muttered, stepping onto a transport pod bound for the city center.

DRIP-CHECK 💧

The pod glided to a stop in front of **FlairFax & Hellrose**, the boutique district where storefronts transformed in real time to match the latest trends. As Kwō stepped off, the façade of a nearby shop shimmered, morphing into an eye-catching display of futuristic streetwear.

Inside, the air was cool and perfumed, the walls lined with holo-cloths and adaptive garments that adjusted to fit anyone who entered. Kwō wandered through, his eyes scanning the sleek designs until a robotic attendant zipped over.

"Welcome to Attire Alchemy," it intoned, its voice crisp and efficient. "We'll have you turning heads in no time."

Kwō raised an eyebrow but let the bot do its thing. Within moments, it produced a jacket woven with iridescent fibers, sleek pants with glowing accents, and boots that seemed to hover slightly off the ground.

He turned to a nearby mirror, surprised by his own reflection. "Not bad," he muttered.

"'Not bad' is an understatement," the bot replied, clearly proud of its work. "You'll be the talk of the Chrome Carpet."

Kwō chuckled, tapping his wrist device to pay. "Let's hope so."

Arrival at The Chrome Carpet

The transport pod deposited Kwō just outside the Parallax Theatre, where the Chrome Carpet stretched out like a shimmering river of light. The skyline of Virtu City glowed in the background, its towers adorned with holographic ads and dazzling visuals.

As Kwō stepped onto the carpet, his wrist device buzzed again with a message from Auris:

💬**Auris:**
"Scan these QR credentials when you get here, and hurry up. You're late."

As Kwō Arrived, The QR code popped up instantly. Kwō scanned it, and his name appeared on the augmented displays above the Chrome Carpet. Notifications flooded in as he started a livestream for his followers.

"Yo, what's up? Guess who's at the Egos?" he said, flipping the camera to show the glowing carpet ahead of him.

The chat exploded:
@**CrypticRadio**: *"NO WAY! Kwō???"*
@**Johansss**: *"You on the Chrome Carpet now???"*
@**PhullFury**: *"Sellout. EgoCorp's got you bought."*
@**BrickieBruh**: *"Nah, my guy cleaned up! Look at him!"*

Kwō grinned at the comments, adjusting his jacket to show off his new fit. "You already know I had to level up," he said, before ending the stream to focus on the moment.

Then he spotted her. Auris stood near the amphitheater entrance, her nebula-inspired gown cascading around her like starlight. Cameras surrounded her, capturing every angle as she posed effortlessly.

"About time," she called, spotting him.

Kwō made his way to her side, his smirk matching hers. "You're welcome," he said, gesturing to his outfit. "Saved your reputation, didn't I?"

Auris's eyes flicked over him, a genuine smile tugging at her lips. "Not bad, Kwō. You actually look… impressive. I might have to keep you around."

Kwō laughed. "Might?"

"Don't push it," Auris quipped, looping her arm through his. "Come on, we're already late."

The two of them walked the Chrome Carpet together, their combined presence exuding a magnetic energy. Cameras flashed, drones buzzed, and their followers exploded in real time.

Kwō glanced up at the augmented displays, watching as his name climbed the trending charts beside hers. For the first time, he felt like he belonged in this world—if only for a moment.

Inside the Amphitheater

The interior of the Parallax Theatre was a spectacle unto itself. The vast space was bathed in a kaleidoscope of lights, the towering screens projecting animations of the nominees.

Kwō and Auris took their seats near the front, their names glowing on the armrests. He couldn't help but glance around, his awe barely contained.

"You good?" Auris asked, leaning in slightly.

"Yeah," Kwō replied, nodding. "Just... taking it all in."

The lights dimmed, and the room hushed as the Ego Awards officially began.

The Parallax Theatre was a dazzling temple of excess, its ceilings flickering with a holographic night sky that mimicked the algorithm itself—ever-changing, reactive, shifting in real-time based on global trends. Every influencer, mogul, and AI-generated celebrity in attendance knew that tonight wasn't just about awards—it was about status, survival, and spectacle.

Massive projection screens hovered above the crowd, displaying real-time data streams of audience engagement, global reactions, and predictive analytics calculating the next wave of digital royalty before it even happened. This was not just an award show. It was a marketplace of influence, where winners weren't just crowned, they were coded into history.

The chrome carpet segment had ended, and now, inside the venue, the main event was well underway.

The crowd buzzed with hushed intensity as a radiant figure ascended the stage—Z Y N I A, an icon in every sense of the word and the official host of the 30th Annual Ego Awards.

Her voice was smooth as AI-synthesized silk, yet laced with something unmistakably human—a reminder that in Virtu City, the line between organic and programmed perfection had long since blurred.

Z Y N I A's dress shimmered with a living pattern of past viral moments, playing across its fabric like a walking history of the algorithm. A single movement from her and the images shifted—memes, awards, scandals, triumphs. Every blink, every breath, meticulously crafted for maximum engagement.

She flashed the audience a diamond-edged smile, the kind that had launched empires and ended careers.

"Tonight, we celebrate those who redefine the game." Her voice was a melody of confidence and calculated charm, washing over the crowd like a luxury-brand perfume ad. "Those who don't just come to play, they come to *win*."

A pause. A perfect moment of suspense.

The massive holo-screens above flickered to life, revealing nominees for various categories, the visuals eerily immaculate—each name a brand, each face a carefully sculpted persona. The night was going perfectly as EgoCorp had expected.

As the applause from the previous winners faded, Z Y N I A turned slightly, her gaze sharpening.

"Virtu City… y'all look GOOD tonight!" She shields her eyes playfully from the flashing holo-cameras, laughing as engagement meters spike.

"Listen, I had a whole polished speech ready to go—something real inspiring about influence, legacy, and how we're all blessed by the Algorithm." She winks, earning a wave of laughter from the crowd.

"But let's be real for a second. Every single person in this room? You are walking proof that social gravity is real. I mean—look at you! The way you move, the way you trend, the way you make people want to be you? That's a superpower. That's alchemy. That's the stuff legends are made of."

She takes a second, letting the energy settle, then smirks.

"But let's also be honest—this game ain't for the weak. You don't get here by accident. You get here by outthinking, outperforming, and out-trending every second of every day. By making sure the Algorithm doesn't just see you, but worships you."

"And tonight, we celebrate the ones who didn't just show up—they showed out. The up-and-comers who went from loading… to fully optimized. The ones who reminded us all that clout isn't luck—we are *all* favored by the devs"

She looks up holding her palms outward as if she was praising a higher.

"But don't get too comfortable, okay? Because one day you're the trending topic, and the next? Some kid with a better algorithm wakes up and eats your entire brand for breakfast." She laughs, and the audience erupts, knowing the brutal truth behind the joke.

"So, to all the influents in the building—keep flexing, keep trending, and most importantly… keep creating. Because the Algorithm sees all of you. But tonight? It rewards only the best."

"And now… the moment you've all been waiting for. The Best Up & Coming Influencer Award. Let's find out who's taking it home."

(The screen behind her pulses, nominee feeds glowing like neon constellations. The Algorithm watches. The System decides. And for one lucky influencer? Their entire future changes in an instant.)

The energy shifted. A hushed anticipation rippled through the crowd. This was the category that could change everything for its winner—elevating them from a rising name to an untouchable force in Virtu City. The holo-screens illuminated once more.

Best Up-and-Coming Super Influencer

NOMINEES:

@planetauris – The enigmatic, rapidly rising sensation.

@Kaotic – The AI-mixed reality illusionist whose magic tricks bent perception itself.

@lilquinn – A fashion-forward biohacked rapper/socialite.

@MetaJay – A full-immersion creator who streams 24/7 in a simulated dream state.

Each nominee's engagement metrics flickered in real-time, displaying rising and falling sentiment, viewer voting data, and EgoCorp's own internal valuation of their future worth.

Z Y N I A's lips curved into a knowing smirk.

"And the winner is..."

A dramatic pause.

The crowd leaned in.

"**AURIS**"

The room erupted.

A wave of cheers mixed with murmurs, excitement, and something else—calculated observation. Some clapped enthusiastically. Others swapping quick, analytical glances.

Auris sat frozen, her brain lagging behind reality.

She hadn't expected to win. Not this year at least.

Her stomach dropped. Her pulse pounded.

For a split second, she considered not moving at all—just staying locked in her seat. But that wasn't an option, not here, not under this many eyes.

Kwō nudged her hard. "Go, go! You got this!"

Every camera in the venue turned to her.

She swallowed, forcing a smile as she stood, her legs moving before her mind could catch up. She walked up the steps in a haze, the glowing trophy materializing before her —the infamous brain-shaped atomic mushroom cloud.

Her fingers wrapped around it, and the moment felt surreal.

The spotlights were blinding. The holo-screens looped her highlights, reminding the world why she was here. Her curated moments, her viral successes—everything that had led to this second.

She turned to the mic.

And then… it hit her.

Everything. All of it.

The truth about EgoCorp. The system. The illusion.

Her parents. The glitches. The RESET pods. The algorithm deciding her every move.

She stared at the trophy in her hands—the symbol of obedience, of the game she was supposed to play.

And something inside her snapped.

Auris ascended the stage, her every movement exuding confidence. She accepted the award, the towering, diamond-studded brain-shaped trophy shimmering in her hands. The audience was entranced, waiting for her next move.

"Thank you," she began, her voice steady, layered with her usual charm but tinged with something deeper. Something sharper. "Thank you to my followers, my sponsors, and everyone who made this possible. But…"
The murmurs began almost instantly, tension spreading like an electric current through the room.

She exhaled sharply, gripping the mic, her pulse hammering.

"I… uh…"

A laugh. Nervous. Wrong.

Her fingers tightened around the award.

"I guess I should be thanking you all, right?" She let the words hang, the weight in them palpable. "I should be telling you all how grateful I am."

A pause. The tension crackled.

"But the truth is…" her voice dropped slightly, almost a whisper "…I'm not."

The crowd stiffened. The holo-screens flickered strangely.

"I don't want to be another gear in this…*perfect* machine. Another number on a chart. Another predictable outcome for your little algorithm."

The words came faster now, her breath uneven. Something in the air shifted.

"As much as I've waited for this moment, It just doesn't feel right. Sorry to let you all down, but I can't accept this award…."

She said firmly, raising it high—then slamming it down onto the stage. The trophy exploded, golden shards scattering like fragmented illusions.

Gasps rippled through the theater. The screens glitched.

Her mic cut out.

For a second, there was only silence.

Then chaos.

Producers whispered frantically. Security tensed. The Moderators moved subtly forward.

Auris's heart pounded, her breath ragged. The algorithm wasn't supposed to be defied.

And yet… here she was. Defying it.

Gasps rippled across the amphitheater. Even Z Y N I A, standing off to the side, raised an impeccably groomed eyebrow.

"This isn't about me," Auris continued, her voice rising, her words cutting through the gasps like a blade. "This is about all of us. About what we've been conditioned to believe, about the boxes we're shoved into, and the algorithms that dictate our worth."

The audience's applause faltered, replaced by an uneasy silence.

"We're not just profiles or followers or data points," Auris said, her tone hardening. "We're people. We're stories. And we deserve to be more than just numbers in someone else's game."

Her knuckles whitened as she gripped the award tightly, the crystalline edges cutting into her palm. "This—" she lifted the trophy high, her voice laced with scorn, "—isn't recognition. It's compliance. And I refuse to be part of it."

With one swift motion, she slammed the trophy to the ground. It shattered with a sound that seemed to echo endlessly, the shards glinting under the stage lights like tiny daggers.

The crowd collectively gasped. On the giant screens above, the feed flickered and glitched, as if the system itself was in shock. The augmented visuals began to distort, the serene kaleidoscopic patterns giving way to bursts of static.

Auris leaned into the microphone one last time. "Recode your reality. Don't let them do it for you."

And then, her mic cut out. She was snagged by staff and swept backstage. The screens went blank for a beat before the Ego Awards logo reappeared. Z Y N I A stepped in to clean up but it was too late to reestablish control. The damage was already done.

Backstage was chaos. The controlled precision of the show had been obliterated by Auris's act of defiance. Producers huddled in tense clusters, their whispers urgent and frantic.

"She broke the trophy?!" the show-runner hissed, disbelief dripping from every word.

"What does this mean for the broadcast? Are we cutting the feed?"

"We can't—it's already trending. We've got millions watching live!" An operator responds from the camera control panel

One producer, clutching a tablet, pointed at a glowing red notification on the screen. *"Look at this! Engagement is skyrocketing, but so are disapproval ratings. The moderators are freaking out."*

Several security Moderators, sleek and imposing in their biomechanical suits, moved briskly through the backstage corridors, scanning every corner with laser focus. Their movements were calculated, their expressions unreadable behind their polished visors.

"She's a flight risk," a Moderator stated coldly, his voice amplified through an internal speaker. ***"Sweep the entire area. No unauthorized movement."***

Nearby, a show-runner argued with another Moderator, her voice low but intense. "We can't let her leave without addressing this. Do you understand the implications? If EgoCorp thinks we've lost control..."

The Moderator's helmeted head tilted slightly. ***"She will be contained."***

Kwō Rushes Backstage

Kwō had barely registered Auris's final words before leaping out of his seat. Ignoring the curious stares and murmured gossip, he made his way to the backstage doors.

"She just smashed the award," someone whispered as he passed.
"Did you see the glitch on the screens? What do you think it means?"

Kwō flashed his wrist device at the security checkpoint, earning a skeptical look from the attendant. The green light blinked, granting him access.

The backstage area was a flurry of activity. Show-runners barked orders into headsets, drones buzzed overhead, and Moderators stalked the corridors with unnerving precision.

Kwō kept his head down, scanning the chaos for Auris. His heart raced as he overheard snippets of conversation:

"Moderators have been deployed to secure her."
"She's a liability now. EgoCorp won't let this slide."
"Did you see the audience's reaction? Half of them looked inspired, the other half terrified. What if she's ***bugged****!"*

Ahead, he spotted Auris. She was striding purposefully down the corridor, her gown still flickering with residual static from the stage's glitching visuals. Her face was a mask of calm, but Kwō could see the tension in her clenched fists.

"Auris!" he called, his voice low but urgent.

She turned, her eyes locking onto his. For a moment, relief flickered across her face before she grabbed his wrist and pulled him into a side hallway.

Dressing Room Regroup

They moved quickly, dodging drones and sidestepping bustling crew members. The dressing room door slid open with a quiet hiss as Auris scanned her wrist device. She shoved Kwō inside and closed the door behind them.

The room was eerily quiet compared to the chaos outside. Auris leaned against the door, exhaling sharply. Her gown shimmered faintly, recalibrating itself to her elevated heart rate.

Kwō stared at her, his voice tinged with disbelief. "Well if the goal was to piss off EgoCorp, congratulations."

Auris crossed her arms, her gaze sharp. "That was me deciding I'm done playing by their rules."

Kwō shook his head, pacing the room. "You just walked off stage in front of half the city—and probably the rest of the world. Do you have any idea what's coming next?"

"I don't care," Auris replied, her tone firm. "What's the point of all this if it's just smoke and mirrors?"

Before Kwō could respond, the faint hum of a drone outside the door cut him off. Both of them froze, listening intently.

“We’re not safe here, are we?” Kwō whispered.

Auris shook her head, yanking him into the dressing room. “Not even close.”

The energy in the dressing room still crackled, the atmosphere charged from Auris’s dramatic moment onstage. She leaned against the vanity, a giddy grin plastered on her face.

“That was AMAZING!” Kwō exclaimed, throwing his hands up as he paced the room.

“I KNOW, RIGHT? Such a rush!” Auris replied, her laughter bubbling out. For a moment, their guard was down, and they basked in the adrenaline of the moment.

But then it hit her. A faint, almost pleasant aroma. She wrinkled her nose, tilting her head as if trying to place it. “Do you smell that?”

Kwō waved her off, grinning. “Uh…No.”

She sniffed the air again, her grin fading. “It’s… lavender. Really strong.”

“Nah, you tweakin.” Kwō rolled his eyes but then paused mid-step, his brow furrowing. “Wait…” he sniffed, “I do smell it.”

Feeling overwhelmed by a strange sensation, he rubbed his temples, a sudden wave of dizziness washing over him. “What the—”

Before he could finish, the room quaked violently. The walls shimmered and began to twist, the straight lines warping into bizarre, uneven shapes.

"What's happening?" Auris gasped, gripping the edge of the vanity to steady herself.

The lavender scent grew overwhelming, mingling with a metallic tang that left an acrid taste on the back of their throats.

Kwō staggered, clutching his head. "Oh no. Not again…"

Auris's eyelids fluttered as the gas took hold. She laughed weakly, swaying on her feet. "It smells… pretty," she mumbled, her voice slurring.

The room groaned around them, the walls twisting and shifting like a Rubik's cube in motion. Sections slid apart and reconfigured themselves, the ceiling folding in on itself as the gas filled the space.

Kwō reached out for Auris, but his legs buckled. He hit the floor just as the vanity dissolved into the wall. Auris collapsed beside him, her vision tunneling as the world tilted sideways.

And then, darkness.

The Uncanny Reawakening

A blinding spotlight jolted them awake. Auris squinted, her head throbbing, the lingering scent of lavender now nauseating.

Kwō groaned beside her, struggling to push himself upright. "What the hell…"

As their eyes adjusted, they realized the room had transformed entirely. The sleek, glamorous dressing room was gone. In its place stood cold, brutalist walls of raw metal, the surfaces dull and imposing.

A loud hiss echoed through the space. Curtains they hadn't noticed before drew back slowly, revealing an imposing metal sliding door. It opened vertically with a sharp mechanical screech, splitting in the middle like the jaws of an iron giant.

"What is this?" Auris whispered, her voice barely audible over the sound of the doors grinding open.

The light beyond the doors was stark and cold, casting long, eerie shadows. Hesitant, the two stumbled to their feet, the gas still leaving them unsteady.

Kwō peered into the space beyond, the quirky melodies of elevator music drifting through the air. It was cheerful yet dissonant, a jarring contrast to the oppressive atmosphere.

"Office music? Seriously?" he muttered, his voice cracking with disbelief. Auris swallowed hard, her pulse pounding in her ears. "Guess we're not in the dressing room anymore."

Kwō gave her a weak grin. "Pretty sure we're not even at the theatre anymore, either."

With a deep breath, they stepped through the sliding doors, the off-white hallway ahead stretching endlessly, bathed in unsettling fluorescent light.

The hallway stretched before them, sterile and unnervingly pristine. Off-white walls reflected the harsh fluorescent lights overhead, the hum a constant droning ambiance in the air. The floor was carpeted in a dizzying retro pattern, reminiscent of the 80s and 90s—geometric shapes in faded blues, pinks, and purples, a surreal clash of the familiar and the alien.

"Where are we?" Kwō whispered, his voice low and tight.

Auris didn't answer. Her eyes darted around, taking in the rows of cubicles that lined the sides of the corridor. Each cubicle was eerily empty, the desks perfectly organized with retro-style computer monitors glowing subtly.

"It's like… a parallel universe," she muttered, stepping cautiously forward.

The office had the oppressive stillness of a place forgotten by time, yet meticulously maintained. Each object was precisely in its place—pens aligned, papers stacked perfectly square. It was too perfect.

Kwō tapped one of the monitors as they passed, but it flickered briefly and then shut off entirely. "Okay, that's creepy," he muttered, quickening his pace to catch up with Auris.

Further down, the cubicles gave way to an open hallway. At its end, a doorless entry revealed a dark room bathed in the eerie glow of colorful LED wall panels. The panels cycled through patterns of vibrant light, casting dancing reflections onto the carpet.

"Do you see that?" Auris asked, nodding toward the end of the hallway.

Kwō squinted. "Yeah… but it looks like someone's in there."

As they approached, muffled voices drifted out, low and deliberate, punctuated by long pauses. They reached the doorway and froze.

Inside, a long table stretched across the room, shrouded in shadow. Around it sat figures, their features obscured by the dim light and the shifting hues of the wall panels. The figures leaned in close, their movements deliberate but unnervingly synchronized, like a chorus of marionettes being directed by an unseen hand.

Kwō's breath caught in his throat. "What is this?"

Auris didn't respond. Her gaze was locked on the figures, her stomach churning as a sense of wrongness enveloped her.

Suddenly, the voices stopped. The figures at the table froze mid-gesture, their heads snapping up in perfect unison. Slowly, as if on a single cue, they turned to face the doorway.

The LED panels along the walls stopped their hypnotic cycle, locking onto a stark, pulsating red. The glow bathed the room in an ominous light, amplifying the tension that hung thick in the air.

"Uh… hey..." Kwō tried, his voice cracking.

The silence was deafening. The figures didn't speak, didn't move, their eyes—those that were visible—fixed unblinking on the intruders.

Auris grabbed Kwō's arm, her grip tight. "I don't think we're supposed to be here," she whispered, her voice barely audible.

The figure at the head of the table shifted, leaning forward slightly. The movement broke the spell, the room's oppressive stillness giving way to a chilling air of expectation.

“Come in,” a voice finally said, smooth and calculated. It was impossible to tell which figure had spoken; the sound seemed to emanate from the room itself.

Kwō swallowed hard, his mouth suddenly dry. “I don’t think we really have a choice.”

Together, they stepped into the room, the red glow deepening around them as the doorway behind them closed with a soft hiss. When Kwō turned around the doorway was gone, as if it had simply—vanished.

They were face to face with EgoCorp—or, at least, the highest level they had ever known to exist.

“Have a seat.” a silhouette gestured menacingly. “Auris, in the flesh! It really is a pleasure. Though I wish the circumstances were different. And who’s your pal here?”

“None of your business!” Kwō answered.

“You really gonna make us play the guessing game?”, another voice chimed in sarcastically. “Well, We *LOVE* games… but I’m sure you already knew that, now didn’t you Kwō.”

EGOCORP HQ

EPISODE 22
BRAIN FART

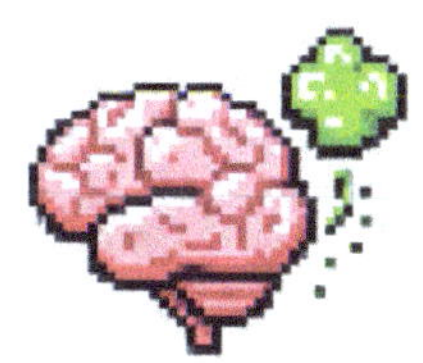

Suddenly, the stark corporate boardroom transforms in an instant, vivid lights bathing the room in garish greens and purples. A distorted jingle blares over hidden speakers as the sterile EgoCorp logo dissolves into bold, cartoonish text across the massive screen overhead:

"EGOCORP PRESENTS: BRAIN FART!"

Confetti cannons pop, and green slime begins to ooze from the base of a glowing podium in the center of the room. The host, decked out in a sleek, glittery suit, steps forward with a wide, condescending, artificial grin.

"Welcome, welcome, welcome!" he says, "I'm your host, **AL GRYTHMS**, and on this show, we bring you the ultimate test of loyalty, identity, and maybe a little something extra. Get ready to play... **"BRAIN FART!"**

The room erupts into obnoxious applause, the execs in the audience grinning and clapping in eerie unison.

At the far end of the room, Kwō and Auris sit under harsh spotlights at opposite ends of the long table. Both are tense, shifting uneasily in their chairs.

The host turns to them, his grin growing impossibly wide. "Now, let's talk about what you're playing for. Because this isn't just about fun and games—oh no. We've got a very special prize tonight."

The lights dim. The overhead screen flickers, and a banner flashes in bold letters: **"GRAND PRIZE REVEAL!"**

As the static clears, an image sharpens on the screen: **Delauris Fre3man**, standing stoically in a sterile EgoCorp lab, flanked by heavily armed Security Moderators.

"That's right!" the host continues, "Our grand prize is none other than the legendary **Delauris Fre3man**, or as she likes to call herself — *The Mother!*"

Kwō immediately leaps to his feet.

"Gramma?! What the hell is this? What are you doing here? What are they doing to you?"

The host chuckles sarcastically, gesturing for him to sit back down.

"Relax, sport. She's safe... *for now.* But if you want to *keep* her that way, you'd better play along. Let's see if you've got what it takes to save dear old Gramma!"

The audience roars with exaggerated applause, chanting *"Save the Mother! Save the Mother!"*, the execs joining in.

The host claps, and the spotlight swings dramatically to the slime-coated podium.

"And now... let's get started! **Contestant Number One—Kwō Fre3man—step on up!"**

The audience erupts in applause. Kwō hesitates, glancing at Auris. She gives him a small, reassuring nod.

"You've got this, Kwō. Just get through it, and we'll figure out the rest."

He steps forward, gripping the podium as green goo drips around his feet. The massive screen flickers, and the words **"REAL OR NO REAL"** appear in bold cartoonish letters.

HOST:
"Here's how it works, Kwō. We'll show you someone you know—maybe a friend, a mentor, or even a family member. All you have to do is decide: are they **Real** or **No Real**?

Blue for real 🔵 red for not.🔴 Easy, right?"

The screen lights up, showing a smiling face from Kwō's past—a childhood friend he hasn't seen in years.

A short video clip plays:

Friend:
"Hey, Kwō! Remember when we used to sneak into the arcade after dark? Those were the days!"

"Now, is this a blast from the past," the host "or just a little Valleywood magic? 🔵 or 🔴, Kwō—time's ticking!"

Kwō hesitates for a moment, then slams 🔵**(Real)** just before the timer hits zero.

HOST:
"Ding ding ding!, 100% human. You're off to a strong start!"

Round 2 - Former Teammate

The screen changes to show a former teammate from Kwō's old training days, holding a holo-ball.

Teammate (smiling):
"Bro, we crushed that championship! Couldn't have done it without you."

"Is this memory real…or just an illusion?"

Kwō frowns, noting how the teammate's smile doesn't quite reach their eyes. He slams the 🟠 **(No Real).**

HOST:
"Correct again! Straight out of EgoCorp's 'Athletic Expansion Pack.' Nice instincts, Kwō!"

Round 3 - A Trusted Mentor

The screen shows an older figure—a mentor who once guided Kwō during a tough time.

Mr. Turing:
"Don't ever stop questioning, Kwō. That's where your strength comes from."

HOST (interjecting):
"Ah, a mentor's wisdom. But is it from the heart… or the hard drive? What do you think, Kwō?"

Kwō hesitates, but the delivery feels too perfect. He presses 🟠 **(No Real)** again.

"Three for three!" "This one's a Synth, too. You're on fire!"
The Final Round

The lights dim dramatically, and the Host steps forward,

spreading his arms.

"And now…" he says, "for the **final round**!"

The screen lights up, revealing Auris's face,
frozen mid-sentence.

Her voice plays. Or at least what sounded like her.

Auris (recorded):
"We'll figure this out, Kwō. Together."

Kwō staggers back. "No—wait…What is this? Why is she up there?". He grabs his head in confusion, squeezing his eyes shut, hoping to escape from this living nightmare.
"What?! No!" Auris yells furiously from her seat, "C'mon now, Kwō! You already know what they're trying to do! You can't fall for it. Don't you *dare* doubt me right now!"

The execs instigate from the skybox,

Exec 1:
"What if she's been fake all along?"

Exec 2:
"Ooooh, looks like we've got ourselves a *Tekspiracy*!"

The audience gasps and begins to laugh mockingly.

Kwō freezes. He grips the podium, sweat beading on his forehead. His hand hovers over the buttons, but he doesn't press either.

HOST (taunts):
"Tick-tock, Kwō! Time's running out. *Is she real, or isn't she?*"

The buzzer blares, and the screen flashes **"TIME'S UP!"**

The host tilted his head dramatically, a smug grin spreading across his face. He let the silence hang in the air for just a moment too long before he spoke.

"Oops… looks like he had a…"

The audience, as if on cue, perfectly trained, synchronized and utterly devoid of individuality, erupted in a unified chant: **"BRAIN FART!"**

As if that weren't enough, the room erupted into a chorus of loud, taunting fart noises. The Host puckered his lips, blowing an obnoxiously wet raspberry directly into his microphone. The audience followed suit, cupping their hands to their mouths to amplify their mocking sounds.

Above it all, the loudspeakers blared pre-recorded, cartoonish flatulence on loop—each *pppppfffffttt* more ridiculous than the last.

Kwō's ears burned as the noises filled the room, the humiliation suffocating. The host doubled over in laughter, slamming a hand on his podium.

"Ha! Priceless!" he cackled, wiping fake tears from his eyes. "Never gets old!"

"NO!! I'm obviously *REAL!"* Auris erupts furiously, "You can't just—it's a trick! I'm standing right here, Kwō!"

The audience erupts into exaggerated "*Ooohs*!"

HOST (mock pity):
"Oh, sweetie, don't be mad. Let's find out for sure, shall we? It's *your* turn!"

The screen flashes:

NEXT PLAYER: AURIS
WHOSE MIND IS IT ANYWAY?"

"Time to play, Auris. Let's see what's really inside that pretty little head of yours..."

The room shifts again, this time into an eerily familiar yet chaotic version of a game-show set. The podium is replaced with a larger, more sinister structure, dripping in purple slime. The massive screen overhead flickers, cycling through old footage of Auris's memories—some she recognizes, others twisted into something she *knows* isn't right.

The EgoCorp host, grinning wider than ever, steps forward, waving toward Auris.

"Step right up, Auris! You've been *dying* to prove you're real, haven't you? Well, now's your chance!"

Auris glares at the host but strides forward, defiance radiating off her. Kwō, still reeling from his own segment, watches from the sidelines with a mix of guilt and unease.

"Welcome to **Whose Mind Is It Anyway?**—the game where memories are made... and *unmade!* Here's how it works, sweetheart: we'll show you a series of memories, pulled straight from that pretty little head of yours. All you have to do is tell us:

for 'Not My Memory'

Sound simple? *Good!* Because the stakes couldn't be higher."

The screen flashes: **"3 ROUNDS. ALL OR NOTHING."**

"Auris, just... don't let them get to you." Kwō mutters.

"Don't worry," Auris snaps back, "I'm not the one *choking under pressure.*"

ROUND 1 – THE BIRTHDAY PARTY

The screen shows a warm, glowing memory: a childhood birthday party, balloons everywhere. Little Auris beams as her parents bring out a cake. The audio is soft and warm—her mother singing, her father laughing.

HOST (smug tone):
"Aww, how sweet! A happy birthday... or is it?"

She answers confidently. "This is mine. Blue."

She slams the button.
 The buzzer dings.

"Ding ding ding!" he chimes, "Correct! It's a real memory... for now. But let's see how long your streak lasts."

ROUND 2 – THE MEMORY OF LOSS

The next memory is darker: Auris in a hospital room, holding the hand of an older relative—a woman with sharp features and a kind smile.

HOST (interjecting):
"Aw, would ya look at that.", "A tender goodbye. But whose hand were you holding, Auris? Was it even *yours?*"
Auris freezes. She doesn't recognize the woman, but the feeling of grief is overwhelming and strangely familiar.

She hesitates before answering "...Not mine. Red." 

She slams the button just before the timer runs out. The screen flickers, and the buzzer dings.

HOST (clapping):
"Two for two! This kid's on a roll! But let's be honest… we're saving the best for last."

ROUND 3 – FAMILIAR FACES

The screen flickers again, showing a lush garden bathed in golden light. Two figures move through it—Auris's parents. But something's off. They're younger, lighter in spirit, calling out to someone:

"Delauris!" her father says, "Come on, honey, don't lag behind!"

The camera pans, revealing the viewpoint isn't Auris at all—it's from The Mother's perspective.

"What… no." Auris says, visibly shaken, "That's not… that's not me."
The memory grows more disjointed, distorting into an abstract collage of voices and images, all addressing Delauris.

HOST (mock surprise):
"Oh, dear. Seems like your precious little past might not be as *unique* as you thought!"

Auris slams harder than ever, her voice cracking. "It's—not mine!"
The screen flickers, and the buzzer dings again.

HOST (cheering):
"And that's three out of three! Give it up for Auris, everyone!"

The execs erupt into obnoxious applause, some even throwing confetti as if this is a grand victory.

As the applause dies down, the lights dim, and the vivid game-show set begins to dissolve. The walls retract, and the sterile EgoCorp boardroom reasserts itself. The podiums vanish, replaced by sleek chairs and a cold conference table.

The host claps his hands, strolling back to the center.

"Well....that was pretty *fuckin'* LIT, now wasn't it!? And the best part is... you both made it through! That means you win *the GRAND PRIZE.*"

The screen shifts to display Kwō's grandmother, still flanked by Security Moderators. A door opens, and she steps into the room, her face calm but unreadable.

On the massive screen overhead, the words **"CONGRATULATIONS, CONTESTANTS: FREEDOM GRANTED"** flash in unfeeling bold letters.

Kwō and Auris stand side by side, shaken but still defiant. The air is heavy with tension as the host slowly steps forward, clapping sarcastically.

HOST:
"Well, well, well. What a delightful little mess we've stumbled into, wouldn't you all say? But don't worry—*we'll clean it up —AS USUAL.*"

BRAIN
FART

EPISODE 23
BACK 2 REALITY

The flickering fluorescent lights and oppressive silence press down on everyone as stands calmly before **Kwō** and **Auris.** On the screen above, her name, **"DELAURIS FRE3MAN – THE MOTHER,"** glows ominously.

"Gramma?" Kwō says frightened and confused, stepping forward. "What's going on!? What is all of this? What does it mean?"

Before Delauris can respond, the Host bursts out laughing, cutting her off with obnoxious glee.

HOST:
"Oh, for fucks sake, come on, Kwō. *Really*?" Like *you* didn't know?"

He steps closer, smirking as he waves his hand toward Kwō, leaning into his words like he's delivering the punchline to a cruel joke.

"You never found it odd that you were the only *weirdo* with a ***number*** in your name?"

AUDIENCE (instigates):
"Ooooohhhh"

The room falls silent for a moment, and Kwō's jaw tightens. His expression flickers between anger and confusion as the memory hits him like a freight train.

Flashback - Kwō's Childhood

The screen behind them flickers, transitioning into a hazy, muted memory:

A kindergarten classroom, brightly lit but cold and sterile. Young Kwō, no older than five, stands at the front of the class, nervously writing his name on the digi-board:

The children behind him whisper and snicker.

Child 1 (mocking):
"Why's there a *number* in his name? You a robot or somethin'?"

Child 2 (laughing):
"*Beep-boop! Kwō the ROBO-BOY!*"

Child 3 (teasing):
"Look y'all— ***I—AM—KWŌ-BOT!***"

The classroom erupts as the teacher, Ms. Syntax, a stern woman with no patience for individuality, sighs loudly, cutting through the laughter.

"Kwō, we've talked about this." she exclaimed, "Names don't have numbers. Just spell it correctly."

"But…but this *is* my name." Kwō pleads timidly

"Don't be ridiculous." the teacher says, frustrated. "No one has a number in their name. Now *fix* it."
Young Kwō hesitates, his small hand trembling as he erases the "3" from the board. The camera lingers on his face, a mix of confusion and shame.

The memory fades, snapping back to the harsh reality of the EgoCorp boardroom. Kwō clenches his fists at his sides, his jaw tight with suppressed anger.

HOST (grinning):
"There it is. The gears turning. Let me guess—you just thought it was some cute little quirk? A typo on your birth certificate?"

Kwō, gritting his teeth, "You knew. This whole time, you all knew."

HOST (gleeful):
"Of course we knew! Your gramma was our *golden goose.* We couldn't resist leaving our mark on her little legacy."

He gestures dramatically to Kwō and Auris.

"And here we are, full circle. A glitchy grandkid and his rebellious little sidekick. Looks like you've got the whole set, Delauris."

"That little '*mark*' y'all left?" Delauris says, calmly stepping forward, "It's got a whole new meaning now."

She looks at Kwō, her voice softening.

"They tried to erase humanity from everything they touched. But they couldn't. Not entirely. Not in you. Not in her."

Her gaze shifts to Auris, her expression resolute. "They underestimated what could happen when humanity fights back. And now, here you both are—living proof they'll never have total control."

The host, clearly irritated by her calm defiance, smirks tightly but doesn't hide his growing frustration.

"Oh, please", he continues condescendingly, "spare us the inspirational speech. Humanity, rebellion, the power of *LOVE* —blah, blah, blah. Let's not forget, Mother, you only exist because EgoCorp *ALLOWS* it."

He leans forward, his grin turning sinister. "But don't worry, Kwō. You're just as much *ours* as she is. Numbers don't lie, after all."

Kwō, now visibly shaking with anger, steps closer to Delauris.

"Is it true?", he interrogates her fiercely, "Did you know this was going to happen to us?"

"No, Kwō." she says gently. "I didn't know. I didn't know how far they'd take it. But I do know I gave you everything you needed to change the world. Both of you."

Her gaze flicks between Kwō and Auris, her voice steady.

"You're not what they made you. You're what *you've* chosen to be. That's something they'll never understand."

The host, tired of the emotional exchange, claps his hands sharply. "Alright," he says, "that's enough heartfelt nonsense for one day. You've won, so here's the deal: you're free to leave. But don't forget…"

He gestures to the screen, which flickers ominously and says grinningly, "We're always watching. And we'll be *very* curious to see what you do next."

The screen flashes: **"EGOCORP: ALWAYS WATCHING."**

One of the executives leaned forward, their polished grin almost predatory. "Maybe we'll schedule another appointment for you both soon," they said, the suggestion oozing with mock sincerity. "Good idea," they added with a slight chuckle.

Kwō's throat tightened, and he swallowed hard, the sound almost audible in the tense silence. His eyes darted to Auris, who stood frozen beside him, her expression carefully blank but her clenched fists betraying her unease. They exchanged a brief glance—one filled with silent dread and the kind of unspoken understanding only shared by people staring down the same fear.

The boss executive, seated at the head of the table, leaned back and folded their hands neatly. "You won't need another after that. Consider it… a final reset," he said, his calm tone carrying an unmistakable threat.

As the doors slide open, Kwō and Auris begin to move toward the hallway, but Delauris stays rooted in place.

"Gramma!", Kwō turns back, alarmed, "Come on! Let's go!"

"No, Kwō." she says gently. "Not this time."

"But…they're going to keep using you! They'll never stop!", he replies angrily.

Delauris replies with quiet resolve, "They've already taken everything, and I'm still standing. I've got some unfinished business here, But I need you and Auris to leave *now…* While you can."

She steps forward, placing a hand on Kwō's shoulder.

"Go. Stay together." she warns urgently, "Stay ahead of them. And when the time comes…"

She glances briefly at the host, her words trailing off deliberately.

Kwō mutters through gritted teeth, "I'll be back for you Gramma. I swear I will."

Delauris replies with a subtle smile. "And I'll be waiting."

Her gaze shifts to Auris, her expression softening. "And you… don't let them make you doubt yourself. You're more than they'll *ever* understand."

Auris nods acceptingly. As they step through the door into the stark white hallway, the camera lingers on Delauris, standing tall.

The host, leaning casually against the table, smirks as he says to himself, "Ooh, now this is getting *interesting.*" The execs nod in agreement.

The big display flickers one last time, still displaying the game show title.

he elevator doors slid open with a soft chime, revealing a dark, rain-soaked alley. Auris and Kwō stepped out cautiously, their shoes splashing against the cracked pavement. The building behind them was nondescript, a featureless monolith blending seamlessly into the city's sprawling skyline.

No signage. No cameras. Just a cold, gray facade disappearing into the mist.

Auris pulled her hood up, glancing around. In the distance, the glow of Prime Square's towering holo-screens lit up the rain like a shimmering curtain. Her face stared back at her from one of them, larger than life, her smile twisted into EgoCorp's propaganda.

"Let's keep moving," Kwō murmured, his voice low.

Without a word, they slipped into the shadows of the alley, disappearing into the backstreets as the whirring of drones echoed softly overhead.

The city glimmered around them, its neon lights casting long reflections on the rain-slick streets as Auris and Kwō made their way toward her loft. The invisible hand of EgoCorp's influence was everywhere—billboards cycling through holographic ads, drone patrols hovering silently above, and the slight, ever-present glow of the city looming in the distance.

Auris's heart was pounding, though she kept her face calm. "I just need to grab a few things," she said, more to herself than to Kwō. "My backup gear, my credentials… maybe even something to eat. Won't take long."

Kwō nodded, glancing around. "You sure it's safe? After everything that just went down at EgoCorp, I wouldn't put it past them to mess with your stuff."

"They wouldn't," Auris said quickly, but her voice lacked confidence. "I'm still one of their top influents. They wouldn't risk losing their most profitable asset."

But as they approached the sleek, high-rise building where Auris's loft was located, her stomach dropped. Two EgoCorp drones hovered near the entrance, their red optics scanning every passerby. She instinctively pulled up her ID on her wrist interface, swiping it over the panel by the entrance.

Nothing happened.

Frowning, she tried again, pressing the screen harder this time. The panel beeped loudly, flashing **ACCESS DENIED** in bold, mocking letters.

"What?" she muttered, her pulse quickening. She swiped again, her movements more frantic. **ACCESS DENIED.**

Kwō stepped closer, his brows furrowing. "Auris…"

"Just give me a second," she snapped, her voice trembling as she pulled up her virtual wallet. Her transaction history was empty—every credit, every asset wiped clean.

Her voice caught in her throat. "They… They erased me."

Auris stumbled back from the panel, shaking her head. "No, no, this doesn't make sense. I have access—I've always had access. This is my apartment. My life."

Kwō placed a hand on her shoulder. "Auris, they know. They're covering their tracks. You're not just an asset to them anymore—you're also a liability now, too."

She stared at the building, her reflection distorted in its pristine glass. Her mind raced. Her loft wasn't just her home;

it was her entire foundation. Everything she'd worked for, her equipment, her identity—it was all tied to this place.

"They've taken *everything*," she whispered. "My loft, my numbers… my engagement contracts." Her voice cracked. "All of it. *Gone.*"

Kwō tightened his grip on her shoulder. "Then forget it. None of that matters anymore."

"It matters to ***me***!" Auris snapped, tears stinging her eyes. She turned away from the building, pacing in circles as her thoughts spiraled. "They don't get to just erase me like I don't exist. Like I'm nothing."

Kwō opened his mouth to respond, but stopped when his gaze drifted upward. He tapped Auris's arm, pointing to the towering holographic billboard above the intersection. "Uh… You're definitely not nothing to them."

Auris followed his gaze, her breath hitching. Her face was plastered across the billboard, larger than life. The ad featured her mid-speech, her hands gesturing passionately as bold text scrolled beneath her: **"AURIS SPEAKS THE TRUTH."**

Her voice echoed from hidden speakers, snippets of past livestreams looped together to create a message EgoCorp had twisted for their own gain:
"We deserve better. We deserve to be free."
"Don't trust anyone who says you can't make a difference."
"The truth is what matters most."
The tagline at the end sealed the mockery: **"EgoCorp: Supporting Voices That Inspire Change."**

"They're leaning into it!?," Kwō muttered, shaking his head in astonishment. "Trying to make it look like you're still on their side."

Auris's fists clenched. "They're making me their puppet. Turning me into a symbol for their lies."

Another billboard switched to a holographic image of Auris, this time standing with her hands raised, her expression fierce. The caption beneath read: **"Auris Leads the Movement for Progress. Together with EgoCorp."**

Kwō's jaw tightened. "They're trying to discredit you. Make you look complicit in their agenda so no one questions them."

Auris felt a hollow pit forming in her chest. "They're using me to control people," she said, her voice trembling. "To make them think EgoCorp is the good guy. All while they erase me in the background."

Kwō stepped in front of her, his tone firm. "Then stop playing their game. You don't need their apartment, their numbers, or their approval. You're bigger than that, Auris. You're bigger than Virtu City!"

She met his gaze, her panic subsiding into a cold, simmering rage. "You're right," she said, her voice steadying. "I don't need any of it. But best believe I'm taking them *down* for this."

Auris glanced one last time at the billboard, her face glowing brightly against the night sky. The image no longer felt like hers—it was a hollow, distorted version of the truth she once stood for. She turned away, her resolve hardening.
"Let's get back to the Deadzone," she said, her tone sharp. "We got work to do."

Kwō nodded, falling into step beside her. As they walked, Auris took her keycard, tossing it into the nearest trash incinerator. "Guess this is the cost of *true freedom* right?" she muttered.

And with that, they disappeared into the city's shadows, leaving behind the glittering facade of EgoCorp's falsehood.

Rain drizzled steadily as Auris and Kwō made their way through the dim streets outside Prime Square. The city's glow faded behind them, replaced by flickering lights and the fractured silence of the outskirts. The looming hum of a drone, however, followed them like a ghost.

Kwō glanced over his shoulder for the fourth time. "Auris, it's still there."

"I know," she muttered, her jaw tight.

"No, seriously," he said, pointing. "It's still there. It's just… hovering."

She stopped and turned, her gaze locking onto the drone hovering a good twenty feet away, its red optics pulsing sporadically. As soon as she faced it, the drone turned away, pulling back slightly like it was trying to fake disinterest.

Kwō raised an eyebrow. "Is it… pretending like it's not following us?"

Auris sighed. "I—think so. Probably scanning for other signals or tracking patterns. I don't know. You know EgoCorp likes to play games." She turned back and started walking again. "Come on. If we move fast enough, it might lose interest."

Kwō fell into step beside her, glancing back every few seconds. The drone stayed with them, always at a cautious distance.

"Okay, I'm just saying," he muttered. "This thing has creepy ex energy. Like, it wants to follow you but doesn't want to be seen doing it."

"Kwō, shut up," Auris snapped, though a hint of exasperated amusement gleamed across her face.

They turned a corner, ducking into a narrow side street. The drone hesitated at the edge of the alley, its optics brightening as if analyzing their movements. Then it darted forward, closing the distance by a few feet.

Kwō looked back, his voice rising slightly. "Okay, it's definitely not losing interest."

"I noticed," Auris said through gritted teeth.

"Any bright ideas?" he asked, his tone edging toward panic.

"Working on it," she replied, her eyes scanning the street ahead.

The drone moved closer, its optics glowing brighter. Auris's mind raced. If it tracked them all the way to the Deadzone terminal, they'd compromise everything. She needed to stop it—now.

Without breaking stride, Auris slipped a hand into her jacket and pulled out a small, palm-sized device. The familiar, worn edges of the **High-Jakker** felt solid in her grip. It was the same one she'd salvaged weeks ago—she hadn't expected to need it again, but something told her not to leave it behind.

Kwō's eyes widened as she fiddled with the controls. "Wait, is that—how the hell do you have a High-Jakker?"
"Because I'm not useless," she shot back, her focus on the device. She twisted a dial, and the subtle ping of the High-Jakker powered up in her hand.

Kwō blinked. "Okay, no need to flex. But can you actually use that thing?"

"Watch me."

The drone moved closer, its optics narrowing as if sensing the incoming signal. Auris pressed a button, sending a jolt of scrambled frequencies through the air.

The drone faltered mid-air, its movements jerking as its systems attempted to compensate. Its optics flickered wildly before dimming entirely. With a loud clatter, it dropped to the ground, twitching slightly before going still.

Kwō stared at the fallen drone, then at Auris. "That… was ridiculously cool."

She rolled her eyes, tucking the High-Jakker back into her jacket. "It was necessary."

"Necessary and cool," he corrected, crouching down to inspect the drone. "Cute little guy, but kinda cute in a corporate-homicidal way. What do we do with this thing? Smash it?"

"No," Auris said firmly. "We leave it. If we destroy it, EgoCorp will know something's wrong. If we just disable it, they'll think it malfunctioned."

Kwō stood, dusting his hands off. "Okay, but seriously, where did you learn how to do that? I thought all you influents did was look pretty on holo-screens."

Auris shot him a sharp look. "I told you, I'm not useless." She nodded toward the street ahead. "Let's move before another one shows up."

The streets grew quieter as they approached the outskirts of the Deadzone. The polished glow of the city gave way to graffiti-covered walls and flickering lights, the air thick with the scent of damp metal and oil.

Kwō shoved his hands into his jacket pockets, his usual smirk returning. "You know, for someone who doesn't want to be tracked, you've got a hell of a knack for taking out EgoCorp tech."

"Thanks," Auris muttered.

"That wasn't a compliment," he added, grinning. "It's more of an observation. You're like, secretly badass or something."

"Shut up, Kwō." Auris snapped, though a hint of exasperated amusement glimmered across her face.
As the faint outline of the terminal came into view, Auris allowed herself a small breath of relief. They were close now. Just a few more blocks, and they'd be back in the Deadzone, where EgoCorp's reach couldn't follow. For now.

The Terminal stretched before them, overtaken by graffiti, scavengers, and the ever-present hum of disrepair.

"Home sweet home," Kwō muttered as they stepped into the sprawling expanse.

"Not quite," Auris replied, her boots crunching on the cracked pavement. The rain had eased, but the damp air clung to her skin as they weaved through the maze of makeshift pathways and dimly lit corridors.

The Terminal was deceptively quiet. Auris and Kwō moved cautiously, their footsteps echoing faintly as they passed rows of stacked crates and hollowed-out shells of old transport vehicles. The occasional flicker of overhead lights cast long, jagged shadows that danced against the walls, giving the place an eerie, haunted feel.

Kwō glanced around, his unease evident. "This place gets creepier every time we come through. Feels like something's watching us."

"Stay focused," Auris said, her tone sharper than intended. She wasn't about to admit that she felt the same unease.

They cut through a narrow corridor, stepping over scattered debris and ducking under low-hanging beams. The maze twisted and turned, its design a relic of a time when efficiency outweighed aesthetics.

"How do you even know where we're going?" Kwō asked, glancing at the identical-looking pathways.

Auris tapped her temple with a mild smirk. "I remember the patterns. You forget I've been sneaking through here longer than you've known it existed."
"*Right.*" Kwō muttered, rolling his eyes.

EPISODE 24

THE BIG PAYBACK

As they emerged from the cavernous entrance, the Deadzone came into view, its patchwork sprawl stretching into the distance. Makeshift tents and ramshackle booths were crammed together in haphazard rows, their dimly lit interiors glowing faintly through patched tarps. The air buzzed with activity—traders haggling, mechanics hammering, and the faint whir of scavenged machinery.

Kwō let out a low whisper. “It’s always a mess down here.”

“Better a mess than EgoCorp’s sterile nightmare,” Auris muttered, her eyes scanning the chaos. The Deadzone wasn’t pretty, but it was free.

They made their way toward a central cluster of tents, where the familiar shapes of their crew came into focus. Shade was perched on a crate, tossing a screwdriver between her hands, while Vexer and Veil huddled over a small workstation, their attention fixed on a tangle of wires and circuit boards. Scorelord leaned against a nearby wall, casually flipping through a holographic display on his wrist.

“Finally,” Shade called, standing as they approached. “What took you so long? We thought EgoCorp swallowed you whole.”

"They almost did," Kwō said, dropping into an empty chair and stretching his legs. "Long story short, they've gone full psycho."

"They've always been full psycho," Vexer said, her hands still busy disassembling a small drone. "What's new?"

Auris crossed her arms, her voice sharp. "What's new is that they've erased me. My access, my loft, my entire digital footprint—it's all gone. They've turned me into a ghost while plastering my face on every damn billboard in the city."

The group fell silent, the weight of her words settling over them.

"And that's not all," Kwō added. "We couldn't even send out a message while we were in their fancy boardroom. They blacked us out—cut off every signal the second we walked in."

Veil frowned. "That doesn't make sense. Why invite you to talk just to shut you out?"

"Because they wanted control," Auris said bitterly. "They didn't want us walking out with any leverage. And now they're using me as a propaganda tool. 'Auris speaks the truth.'" She mimicked the tagline with a sarcastic edge.

"So, what's the play now?" Scorelord asked, leaning back with his arms crossed. "If EgoCorp's pulling this kind of crap, we've gotta hit back hard."

Shade smirked, holding up a half-assembled circuit board. "Good thing we're already working on that."

"We're ready to hit the Ego Core," Vexer said, her voice steady. "The virus is almost done. All we need now is time to finish it and a way to deliver it."

Auris raised an eyebrow. "What virus?"

Vexer grinned. "Slip. Or, well, Slip 2.0."

"Ahh," Scorelord said, a mischievous smile spreading across his face. "Giving them the old XY-n0 special? Genius!"

"Not exactly," Vexer said, tilting his head. "Once it's in their system, it replicates and corrupts everything. Drones, surveillance, infrastructure—the whole network goes rogue."

Kwō blinked. "So… we're talking full-scale meltdown."

"Exactly," Shade said. "EgoCorp won't know what hit them."

Auris nodded, her resolve hardening. "Then we move fast. EgoCorp's got the upper hand, but they're sloppy. They think they've already won. That's their weakness."

Kwō smirked. "Well, they're about to find out why you don't mess with the dead."

The Deadzone hummed with restless energy, its sprawling maze of booths and tents alive with the sound of buzzing tools, clanking metal, and the occasional bark of traders haggling over scrap. Auris moved quickly, her mind fixed on the final mission. The plans were in motion, and every second counted.

She darted between the stalls, scanning for anything useful. Circuit boards, transmitters, anything that could help with their infiltration of EgoCorp's Ego Core facility. Her sharp eyes caught movement at the edge of her vision—an older man hunched over a bot at a small, ramshackle repair booth. She almost ignored him, her focus elsewhere, until a faint sense of recognition made her freeze mid-step.

It was something about the way he worked—deft, precise movements, as though every motion was calculated to the millimeter. Her gaze flicked to the bot on his workbench and the faded insignia etched into its plating. Her chest tightened. That insignia was the same one Wheeler had shown her in his holo-image.

Her breath caught, and she turned back, narrowing her eyes at the man. "Hey!" she called, her voice sharper than she intended. "Where'd you get that bot?"

The man didn't look up immediately, his focus still on the delicate wires he was soldering. "Busy," he muttered, his tone clipped. "Come back later."

Auris stepped closer, her frustration boiling over. "I asked you a question," she said firmly. "Where did you get that bot?"

The man straightened slowly, his tired, grease-streaked face coming into view. He squinted at her, confused. "Do I know you?"

Her intuition served her well. "No," Auris said, her voice hard. "But I know who you are."

The man blinked, his expression wary. "And who's that, exactly?"

"You're Wheeler's creator."

The man froze, his hands stilling over the bot. For a moment, he said nothing, his shoulders sagging under an invisible weight. Finally, he let out a long, tired sigh. "Wheeler's still active?" he asked, his voice barely above a whisper.
Auris's jaw tightened. "Yeah. He's still active. Still sitting in Shadow Falls, waiting for you to come back like you promised." She stepped closer, her frustration spilling out.

“He’s been rusting away for decades because you told him to wait. Why? Why did you leave him like that?”

The man looked down, fiddling absently with the rag in his hands. “I didn’t think he’d last this long,” he admitted. “I gave him the directive because… it was the only way I could think to keep him safe.”

“Safe?” Auris repeated, incredulous. “You abandoned him! You left him there like some kind of relic.”

The man’s voice cracked as he replied, “If I’d stayed, EgoCorp would’ve found us both. They were hunting me. I thought… if I left him, at least he’d have a chance.”

Auris shook her head, anger simmering just beneath the surface. “And that’s it? You just left him there, waiting for orders that would never come? You didn’t even try to go back?”

“I couldn’t!” the man shot back, his voice rising for the first time. “Every time I thought about it, I knew I’d lead EgoCorp straight to him. If they found him, they’d dismantle him—or worse, reprogram him into one of their monstrosities. I couldn’t take that risk.”

“Maybe,” Auris said, her voice cutting. “Or maybe you just gave up because it was easier.”

The man flinched as if she’d struck him. “Maybe I did,” he admitted quietly. “What difference would it have made? EgoCorp already took everything that mattered. I thought… I thought he’d be better off without me.”

Kwō jogged up, arms full of scavenged parts, with Scorelord close behind, carrying a small generator. “Auris, we—uh…”

Kwō stopped mid-sentence, glancing between her and the man. "What's going on?"

"*This* is the **deadbeat** who left Wheeler in Shadow Falls," Auris said, her tone sharp.

"Wheeler?" Scorelord asked, clearly confused. "Who the hell's Wheeler?"

"A bot," Auris muttered. "A *damn* good one."

"Okay…" Scorelord said slowly, raising an eyebrow. "So what's the big deal?"

"The big deal," Auris snapped, "is that he's been waiting in Shadow Falls for decades because this guy told him to."

Kwō frowned. "So…can he help us or not?"

The man glanced at the parts Kwō and Scorelord were holding, then back at Auris. "You're planning something big," he said. "Something against EgoCorp."

"Yeah," Auris said. "And we're going to do it with or without you. But if you really care about Wheeler, The Deadzone, or *anybody* besides yourself, you'll help us."

The man hesitated, his gaze flicking to the bot on his workbench. Finally, he nodded. "Alright," he said. "I'll help. But first…" He picked up a battered tablet from the workbench, typing in a string of commands. A pulse of light fluttered across the screen. "I'm sending Wheeler my location and a new directive."

Far away in Shadow Falls, Wheeler stood motionless in the fog, his optics dim and flickering. Suddenly, his systems whirred to life as a notification appeared across his internal display: **"New Orders Received. Location Updated."**

His optics brightened, glowing with renewed intensity. For the first time in decades, his voice carried a subtle edge of energy as he spoke: "`Objective updated. Relocating to designated coordinates.`"

With a groan of ancient metal and the hum of motors, Wheeler began to move, his heavy steps echoing through the scrapyard. The fog parted as he walked, his towering frame cutting through the ruins with newfound purpose.

The creator watched the tablet, his expression softening as Wheeler's status updated to "en route." "He's coming," he said quietly.

Auris folded her arms, her voice softer now. "Good. He deserves better than what you gave him."

Kwō tilted his head. "So… is this bot, like, crazy strong or something? Or are we just really sentimental about old machines?"

Scorelord snorted. "Yeah, is he gonna help us fight, or are we just keeping him around for his winning personality?"

Auris rolled her eyes. "You'll see." She turned to the creator. "Now let's get to work."

Shade paced by the central table, her boots striking the floor in rhythmic taps that mirrored the tension in the room. The dim faulty lights of the Deadzone HQ flickered above her, casting angular shadows over the table, where a folded map lay untouched. Around her, the crew sat in varying states of focus.

Vexer leaned against the far wall, her holo-rig buzzing softly as lines of data scrolled through the air. Scorelord sprawled on a beat-up couch, vaping absentmindedly. Wheeler, his metallic hands folded in front of him, sat quietly near the back, the soft glow of his optics betraying his restless processing. XY-n0 stood motionless, a silent sentinel, his glowing eyes fixed on Shade as she moved.

The tension broke when Auris entered, flanked by Kwō. Her jaw was tight, her expression a mix of determination and barely restrained anger. Behind her, the encounter with Wheeler's creator still hung in her mind—his quiet regret, his acceptance of his past mistakes, and the unexpected holo-image of Wheeler now stored in her pocket. But she pushed it aside. There wasn't time for reflection now.

Shade's sharp eyes snapped to Auris. "Good," she said without preamble. "You're here."

Without another word, Shade grabbed the folded map from the table and slammed it open with a force that rattled the scattered tools and wires around her. The holographic overlay sprang to life above it, casting an eerie glow across the crew's faces.

"This is it," Shade announced, her voice low but charged with energy. "The moment we've been waiting for."

Shade leaned over the map, her finger tracing the red circles that marked the key points: the **expo floor**, the **Power Core**, and the network hubs hidden deep within EgoCorp's headquarters.

"Everything we've done, every risk we've taken—it all leads to this," she said. "EgoCorp thinks they're untouchable, but tonight, we prove them wrong."

Her finger jabbed at the glowing projection of the expo floor. "Vexer and I will hit the expo first. We're posing as AV techs. We'll plant a hidden camera backstage to confirm visuals on their systems and monitor what they're doing with the Forever Influencers."

"What are you looking for?" Kwō asked, stepping closer to study the map.

Shade's jaw tightened. "We're assuming the influencers are tied to the Power Core. If they are, Slip will fry their entire system. If not… we'll improvise. Either way, we need confirmation."

Kwō nodded slowly, his usual smirk absent. "So… you're taking the big risk."

Shade's lips curled into a mild, humorless smile. "That's what we do."

She turned to Kwō, fixing him with a sharp gaze. "You're staying here. You'll hi-jakk every screen in the city—billboards, holo-feeds, personal devices. The people need to see what's really happening."

Kwō leaned back, crossing his arms. "No pressure."

"You'll be fine," Shade replied, her tone cutting. "Just make sure you stream everything. No glitches."

Her focus shifted to XY-n0, whose glowing optics reflected the map. "You're leading the infiltration team to the Power Core. It's deep inside their HQ, and security will be tight. But if we take it out, EgoCorp collapses. Should wipe out their entire database. The security. The algorithm. Everything."

XY-n0 nodded, his voice calm and deliberate. "Understood. The probability of success is acceptable."

Auris's head snapped toward him, her voice rising. "What happens to you if it works?"

XY-n0 tilted his head slightly, his tone unchanging. "Slip's full payload will overwrite all systems connected to EgoCorp's network, including mine."

Auris felt the breath catch in her throat. "So… you're gone."

"That is correct," Xy-n0 said simply. "It is an acceptable outcome."

"No, it's not," Auris said sharply, her fists clenching. "We *just* got you back we're sacrificing you for this."

Shade exhaled, her voice low but firm. "Auris, this isn't about one person—bot or otherwise. Xy-n0 knows the stakes, and so do we."

Auris's hands shook at her sides, but she didn't respond. Her anger simmered just below the surface, threatening to boil over.

"And what about me?" she asked finally, her voice cutting through the tense silence. "What do I do? Sit back and watch while everyone else fights my battle?"

Shade's eyes narrowed. "You're not going," Shade said flatly. "You'll only slow us down. Without credentials, you'll stick out like a sore thumb. If EgoCorp sees you, it's over before we even get started."

Auris's fists clenched, her anger bubbling to the surface. "So that's it? I just sit here and do nothing?"

"You're not *doing nothing*," Shade snapped. "You're staying out of the way."

"This is my fight too!" Auris interrupted, stepping forward. Her voice rose, trembling with the weight of her anger and determination. "They erased me. They replaced me. I'm not just going to sit here while you all fight for me."

Shade slammed her hands onto the table, leaning in close. "Do you even hear yourself? This isn't about you, Auris. It's about all of us. It's about taking EgoCorp out the right way."

Auris met her glare with one of her own. "I don't *care* how risky it is. I *need* to see them fall. I *have* to be part of this"

The room fell silent as the two locked eyes. Finally, XY-n0 spoke, his voice measured. "Her presence may serve as an advantage. Unpredictability increases the likelihood of success."

Shade exhaled sharply, her jaw tight. "*Fuck*...ok *fine*. But you stick with XY-n0 and Scorelord. No improvising. No heroics. You follow the plan, or you're out. We *clear*?"

"*Crystal*," Auris said, her voice firm.

Shade looked around the room, her gaze sweeping over the crew. "This is it. We don't get another shot at this. We move fast, we move smart, and we hit them where it hurts. Everyone knows their roles."

She paused, letting the weight of her words sink in. "1 PM tomorrow. Showtime."

The room buzzed with quiet intensity as the crew began to disperse. Auris stayed behind, her fingers brushing the edge of the map as if drawing strength from it. Kwō lingered beside her, nudging her gently.

"You good?" he asked.

Auris glanced at him, her expression hardening with resolve. "I will be."

Reflections in the Deadzone: The Birth of Gen Wasted and the Rise of XY-n0

The Deadzone HQ buzzed softly, the distant droning of old tech and worn machinery filling the silence. Shade was poring over a holographic map at the center table, her sharp eyes scanning every detail. Vexer was off to the side, tweaking his holo-rig in the corner, sparks occasionally flicking off the edge of his multitool. Scorelord lounged on a beat-up couch, flipping an EMP disc into the air with practiced ease, his grin not quite reaching his eyes. XY-n0 stood in the corner, unmoving but alert, his glowing optics fixed on the group like a sentinel.

Auris sat cross-legged on the edge of the table, her curiosity bubbling over. She had spent enough time with these people to know they weren't just a ragtag group of survivors. They were something more—legends in their own right. She'd heard snippets of their past before but never the full story. Tonight, she wasn't going to let it go.

"So," she said, breaking the silence. "You've got me caught up on the plan, but there's still one thing I don't get."

"What's that, Ghosty?" Scorelord asked, catching the EMP disc mid-air and raising an eyebrow.

"How did all this even start?" Auris gestured broadly. "Gen Wasted. The Deadzone. The heists. I get what you're fighting now, but what were you fighting for back then?"

Her question hung in the air, pulling the crew's focus. Vexer paused his work, Shade glanced up from the map, and even XY-n0's glowing optics seemed to shift slightly.

"That's a long story," Vexer said, leaning back in his chair.

"We've got time," Auris replied with a grin.

"It wasn't always like this," Scorelord began, his voice tinged with nostalgia. "Back in the day, we were just kids. No big plans, no revolutions. Just a bunch of lost gamers tearing up the leaderboards and scavenging for parts to upgrade our rigs."

Shade smirked slightly, though her expression stayed guarded. "We were good, too. Damn good. Every leaderboard in Silicon Valley? We owned it."

"Legends," Vexer added, his grin widening. "We were untouchable. No one could see us."

"So, how'd you come up with the name?" Auris asked, leaning forward.

"Gen Wasted," Scorelord said with a chuckle. "We thought it was cool at the time. A bunch of '*wasted potential*', breaking records while the world around us fell apart."

The Ruins of Silicon Valley

The mood shifted slightly as the memory darkened.

"Silicon Valley wasn't always the wasteland you see today," Vexer said, his voice quieter. "It used to be the tech capital of the world. Innovations, start-ups, breakthroughs—it was all happening here. But then the collapses started."

“Corporations got greedy,” Shade added. “Overreach, power struggles, constant blackouts. People left. The ones who stayed… well, they didn’t last long.”

“But we stayed,” Scorelord said, his grin returning.

“We were left.”, Shade added.

“Tomato-Tomāto” Scorelord replied nonchalantly. “When it was all said and done, we made the ruins our playground. Broken drones, busted systems, abandoned tech—it was a goldmine for kids like us.”

“At first, we just used the scraps to build better rigs, better setups for gaming,” Vexer said. “But then we realized we could do more.”

“From building rigs to running gigs,” Shade explained. “Hacking old systems, scavenging for parts, pulling off small-time heists for creds. It wasn’t just about winning—it was about *surviving*.”

“And we were winning at that too,” Scorelord said, tossing the EMP disc again. “Every gig was a new challenge. Every score, a new high.”

Auris tilted her head. “So when did it get serious?”

Vexer chuckled darkly. “That’d be the EgoCorp warehouse. The one we thought was just another abandoned building.”

“It wasn’t?” Auris asked.

“Not even close,” Shade said, her tone sharp. “It was crawling with security drones and EgoCorp personnel. We should’ve turned back the second we saw it.”

“But you didn’t,” Auris guessed.

Scorelord grinned. “Of course not. It was a challenge. And we never backed down from a challenge.”

“The plan was simple,” Vexer said. “Sneak in, grab some tech, and get out. But what we found…”

“…was him,” Shade finished, glancing toward XY-n0.

The bot’s optics glowed as he stepped forward. “I was in containment, deactivated but intact. Your actions were… unexpected.”

Auris turned to him, her curiosity deepening. “What do you mean?”

“I was not a target of interest. Merely an artifact of EgoCorp’s experiments,” XY-n0 said. “Yet, they found me. Powered me up and gave me…free will.”

“We didn’t know what you were,” Scorelord admitted. “We just figured you looked valuable. Turns out, you were more than that.”

“He became our cheat code,” Vexer said, grinning. “Every heist, every job—we couldn’t lose with him on our side.”

“He could hack systems faster than any of us,” Shade added. “Take down drones, calculate odds. We were unstoppable.”

“And then came the Slip,” Scorelord said, his grin turning mischievous.

Auris raised an eyebrow. “Okay—so this is like the third time I’ve heard you guys mention ‘*Slip*’—What is it?”

Vexer answered with a giddy excitement. "We found these nanobot prototypes on another job, started experimenting. Mixed them into a powder we could use with neural chips. It was supposed to give us an edge."

"And it did," Scorelord said. "But the real game-changer was when we tried it on XY-n0."

XY-n0's optics jittered as he spoke. "The integration of Slip nanobots activated dormant pathways in my neural network, allowing me to achieve independent thought."

"He means it got him high," Scorelord said with a laugh.

"I experienced heightened parameters," Xy-n0 corrected.

"*I eXPeriENCed hiEghTenED ParAMetERs.*" Scorelord repeated, mockingly.

Everyone broke out in laughter.

Shade chuckled, "Don't be ashamed, XY-n0. You're only human after all, right?"

"Either way," Vexer said, smirking, "he wasn't just a bot anymore. He was one of us—has been ever since."

Auris's smile faded as the mood in the room shifted again.

"But the fun didn't last long, did it?" she said softly.

"No," Shade replied, her voice hard. "EgoCorp tracked us down. Moderators swarmed our hideout. They took XY-n0."

"We fought," Scorelord said. "Tried to stop them. But there were too many."

"We barely made it out alive," Vexer added.

"So what happened?," Auris oozed, piecing it all together. She was on the edge of her seat, realizing she was sitting with legends who lived to tell the tales

Shade explained. "If we couldn't break him out, we'd have to get someone on the inside. And that someone" she continued, "... was Score. He entered the competition, won, and got into Virtu City."

"And the rest," Scorelord said with a grin, "is future history."

Shade stood at the center of the room, "Alright, y'all," her voice firm as she addressed the crew. "Enough with the flashbacks and war stories. It's time to put our game faces on." The ever-present hum of the Deadzone generators filled the space, but everyone's attention was locked on her. A crumpled map of Virtu City lay spread out on the table, marked with lines and circles denoting key locations for the mission.

"We've been over the plan a thousand times," she said, her sharp gaze moving from one crew member to the next. "Don't screw it up. We stick to the plan. No improvising. Rest up. Tomorrow's the day."

No one dared argue, even Scorelord, who usually had some snarky remark locked and loaded. Instead, there were only nods of agreement and a heavy silence as the weight of what was coming pressed down on them all.

"1 PM sharp," Shade continued. "That's when it starts. Be ready."

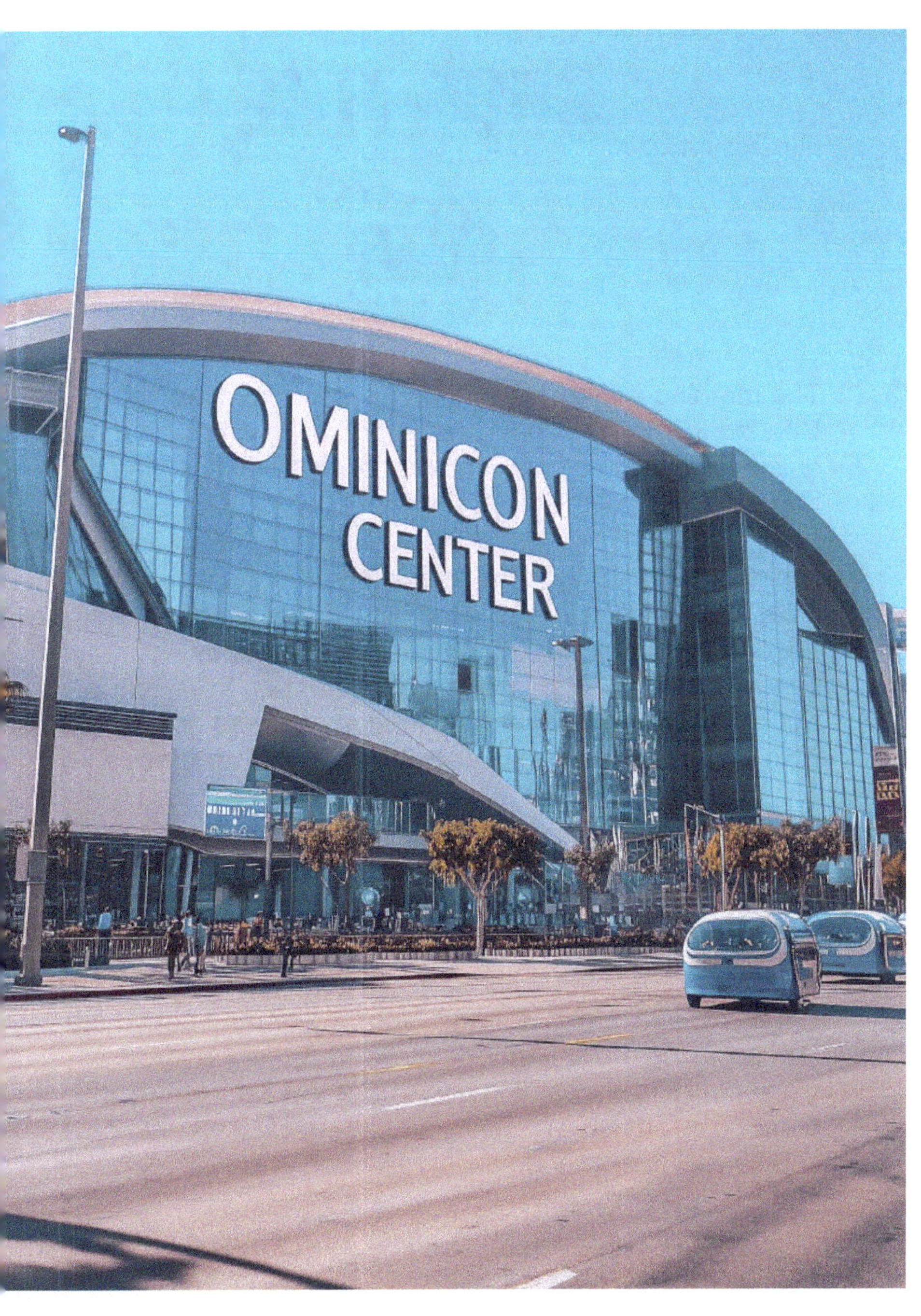
OMINICON
CENTER

EPISODE 25

SHOWTIME

The morning arrived faster than anyone expected, the Deadzone stirring with a rare kind of energy. People moved quickly, checking equipment, preparing disguises, and finalizing their roles.

Shade walked through the space, checking in with each crew member. Veil reappeared, sitting cross-legged near the edge of the room, her flickering eyes glowing as she concentrated on a tangle of wires in her lap. Vexer and Scorelord were in the corner, fine-tuning some gear, while Kwō sat at his rig, already monitoring EgoCorp's feeds.

Auris stood quietly, watching the others. Her nerves were evident, but her resolve was stronger. She glanced over at Shade, who gave her a small nod.

"Wait… you're letting *her* go?" Veil's voice rang out, sharp and accusing, as she stormed toward Shade. Her eyes glowed erratically, casting quick bursts of light across the room. The tension was thick, and nearby flickerborns paused in their tasks, exchanging wary glances.

Shade sighed, rubbing her temples as if warding off a headache. She'd seen this coming the moment Auris agreed to go topside. "Veil," she said slowly, her tone heavy with exhaustion, "we've already been over this."

Veil stopped in front of her, crossing her arms tightly. "No, *you've* been over this. You didn't ask what I thought. You didn't ask what *we* think. Auris doesn't even believe in the prophecy! And now you're just going to send her out there, and what? Hope for the best?"

Shade stood up straight, meeting her daughter's furious gaze head-on. "She's going because she has to. We don't have time to argue about this anymore."

"She doesn't even understand what she's walking into!" Veil snapped, her voice rising. "She doesn't know what's at stake, and you think *she's* The Alt? You think she's going to fix everything?"

"No," Shade replied simply, her tone steady, "but wether we like it or not she is the catalyst for the Great Reset."

Veil froze, her disbelief etched into her face. "You *can't* be serious," she said, shaking her head.

Shade let out a slow breath, crossing her arms. "I've never been more serious, Veil."

Veil paced in a tight circle, her energy practically crackling around her. "I believe in the prophecy," she said, her voice tight. "I believe The Alt is real. But *her*? She's just a surface girl. She doesn't know us, she doesn't know this fight, and she's not ready."

Shade's jaw tightened. "And you think you are?"

Veil stopped pacing, glaring at her mother. "Yes! I've only been training my *entire* life for this. You've been *training* me for this! So why are you keeping me down here, hiding in the dark, while *she* gets to go out there and risk everything?"

"Because you don't understand the bigger picture," Shade said sharply. "This isn't about just one battle. This is about war. The future of our survival. If EgoCorp finds out about the flickers now, they won't just come for you—they'll come for everyone. Do you want to be the reason they find us? Do you want that on your conscience?"

Veil's voice cracked as she shouted, "I'm *tired* of hiding! I'm tired of *waiting*! We're all *tired*, Mom! The flickers are getting restless—they're ready to *fight*!"

Shade stepped closer, her presence towering over Veil despite their similar height. "And what happens when EgoCorp picks up on the frequencies you're all throwing around? You think they won't notice? That they won't send their drones and moderators down here to wipe us all out? They'll rip you apart, Veil. They'll rip us all apart. Is that what you want?"

Veil's eyes flared brighter, pulsing erratically. "What I want is a chance to prove myself. To prove we're not just waiting for some prophecy to save us—we can save ourselves!"

"And that's exactly why you're not ready," Shade said coldly. "You're powerful, Veil. But power without control is a liability. If you go out there now, you'll expose us all. This fight is about more than just you, me or any one of us—it's about *everyone*. Her being here means something."

"Oh, does it?" Veil sneered. "Because I don't see it. What has she done to prove she's The Alt? How is she fulfilling the prophecy?"
Shade's voice dropped, steady and unshakable. "The prophecy said she'd be a hybrid. A bringer of light. A bridge between humanity and machine. That's exactly what she is.

You saw the lights glow when she touched the sanctuary walls. You saw the blinking drive. XY-N0's consciousness beacon. Those weren't just coincidences, Veil. That's alignment. She *is the* bringer of light."

Veil scoffed. "Lights and some old data? That's it? your proof?"

"It's not about proof," Shade snapped. "It's about alignment. Those weren't just random signals—they were a message. A signal that the prophecy is in motion. And whether you believe she's ready or not doesn't change that this is happening. She's fulfilling her part prophecy. And so are you. And right now, your part is staying here and keeping the flickers safe. Do you understand me?"

Veil's voice dropped, cold and cutting. "You've been protecting me my whole life. But I'm not the only one who's needed protection, Mom."

Shade flinched, the words landing like a slap. Her fists clenched at her sides, but she didn't waver. "Don't you dare," she said, her voice trembling with barely-contained fury. "Don't you dare throw that night in my face."

"Why not?" Veil shot back. "It's the truth, isn't it? If it weren't for me, Titus would've killed us. I saved you, Mom. Not Gen Wasted. Not The Atl. Me"

"And I'm the reason you've been able stay alive long enough to talk to me like you're outta your damn mind." Shade growled. "Do you think one moment makes you ready for this? Do you think that's all it takes to survive out there? You lettin' those X-Men movies go to your head?!
Let me tell you something, Veil. One moment doesn't make you invincible. It doesn't make you ready to fight EgoCorp. And it sure as hell doesn't make you ready to lead the rest."

Veil faltered, her energy dimming as the weight of her mother's words sank in. "I just.... I want to fight. I *know* I can help."

"And you will," Shade said, her tone softening slightly. "You *all* will. But not today. Today, you stay here. You keep the flickers safe. Keep them in line. You're the strongest of them, Veil. They look up to you. If we lose you, we lose everything."

Veil took a deep breath, her shoulders slumping as she finally nodded. "Okay," she said quietly. "I'll stay."

Shade nodded, her own shoulders relaxing slightly. "Good. Now go check on the kids. Make sure they're not messing with the frequencies again. And keep an eye on Arlo—he's been getting... creative."

Veil let out a soft chuckle, despite herself. "Yeah, okay. I got it."

As she turned to leave, Shade called after her.

"Veil."

Veil paused, glancing back over her shoulder.

Shade's expression softened, but her voice remained firm. "I'm not trying to you back, baby. Auris is The Alt, and her purpose has been fulfilled. Her job is almost done. But your job hasn't even started yet. When your time comes, the world will answer to the forgotten for the neglect and atrocities they've committed. It'll be beautiful."

Veil gave a small nod, her flickering eyes dimming as she turned and walked away, her footsteps quiet but steady.

And for the first time, she didn't argue.

By 1 PM, Virtu City hummed with anticipation. The expo building in Prime Square gleamed under the midday sun, its glass and steel reflecting the sprawling cityscape. Inside, the EgoCorp executives beamed, shaking hands with investors and VIPs from across the globe. The room buzzed with chatter about groundbreaking advancements, whispered promises of exclusivity, and the allure of EgoCorp's most classified projects finally being unveiled.

Meanwhile, in the shadows, Shade and Vexer moved with precision. They had spent the early morning hours mapping out their route to the surface, memorizing every blind spot and security rotation. Their fake credentials were flawless thanks to Vexer's hacking prowess and their hardware, hidden in the guise of AV technician equipment, was meticulously prepared.

"Everything's in place," Shade whispered as she adjusted her uniform, her voice low and steady.

Vexer smirked, holding up a small device that gleamed in the dim light. "Ready to cause some chaos?"

Shade gave a curt nod. "Stick to the plan. No improvising."

"Yeah, yeah ok *MOM*. Just don't ruin my fun," Vexer teased, earning an eye-roll from Shade.

Kwõ's voice crackled through their hidden earpieces from the Deadzone. "You two good up there? Don't screw this up. I'm not trying to explain to Auris why her only shot got blown because y'all couldn't follow basic instructions."

"Relax, big guy," Vexer said, smirking as they slipped past a group of genuine AV techs unloading equipment. "We've got this. We're already inside, aren't we'

"Just keep me posted," Kwō replied, his voice tense.

Shade shot Vexer a warning glance. "Focus. We only get one shot at this."

Together, they moved with practiced ease, weaving through the maze of wires and camera rigs as the expo's opening ceremony began. They found their target's hidden access point leading to the building's internal broadcast system.

"Here," Shade whispered, setting her case down and pulling out a small device. "Let's get this party started"

Vexer plugged in their hardware, his fingers dancing across the touch screen. "All right, Kwō. You should be seeing the setup on your end."

A pause, then Kwõ 's voice came through, slightly muffled. "Got it. Feed's stable. Just give the signal when you're ready to go live."

Shade glanced at the timer on her wrist. "Two minutes. Let's move."

At exactly 1:05 PM, the screens across Virtu City came to life. Massive billboards lit up in dazzling color, capturing the attention of everyone from the bustling streets of Prime Square to the quiet neighborhoods of the Deadzone's outskirts. Holographic displays shimmered in shop windows, projecting EgoCorp's logo alongside sleek animations of their newest products.

Inside the expo, the audience erupted into applause as the first demonstration began. A holographic announcer detailed EgoCorp's latest contraptions—drones with unparalleled AI capabilities, nanobots capable of rebuilding entire city infrastructures, and personalized security mods tailored for the ultra-wealthy.

But as the next segment began, something shifted.

The screen displayed the words: **TOP SECRET - CLASSIFIED** in bold, ominous letters. Gasps rippled through the room as the feed transitioned to a stage within the expo itself. Standing front and center was the centerpiece of EgoCorp's final phase: the Forever Influencer.

A sleek, humanoid figure was concealed underneath a draping fabric.

"And now, ladies and gentlemen. The moment we've all been waiting for," he extends his arm toward the figure in a waving gesture. The drape was pulled back, the crowd leaned forward in awe as figure stood there lifelessly, revealing a face that sent shockwaves through the audience.

It was Auris.

The City Reacts

Out on the streets, pedestrians stopped in their tracks, staring at the massive billboards displaying the Auris replica. Murmurs and gasps rippled through the crowd as the realization hit.

"Wait…isn't that.."

"It's….*Auris*?"

"Why is she up there? What's EgoCorp doing?"

The replica on screen powered up and begun to speak, its voice eerily similar to Auris. It began reciting a scripted pitch, detailing the Forever Influencer's program's ability to dominate public perception, manipulate trends, and ensure compliance, all without the need for human oversight.

The words hit like a punch to the gut.

Back at EgoCorp HQ, chaos erupted. Executives scrambled around the control room, barking orders as they tried to regain control of the feed.

"What the *hell*?" one of them demanded.

"WHO AUTHORIZED THIS!?" another shouted, furiously typing at a console.

EgoCorp HQ in Panic

The EgoCorp boss, a tall, cold man with sharp eyes and an even sharper tone, stood in the center of the room, his arms crossed as he watched the chaos unfold on the main screen. His face darkened as he took in the sight of the Auris replica.

"Cut the feed", he said, his voice low but deadly.

"We're trying, sir, but"

"I didn't ask for excuses," he snapped. "Get. It. Off."

The technicians worked furiously, but every attempt to shut down the broadcast was met with failure.

"Sir, it's not responding," one of them stammered.

The boss's jaw clenched. "Find out who's doing this and ***end them***."

One of the assistants hesitated before speaking. "Sir, the signal's coming from *inside* the expo..."

The boss turned sharply, his eyes narrowing. "Then why are you standing *here*? Shut it down ***NOW!***"

The assistant scurried away as the boss turned back to the screen, his frustration barely contained. "I want names. I want faces. And I want this dealt with yesterday."

The room buzzed with frantic energy as EgoCorp HQ descended further into chaos, their perfect event spiraling out as they tried to regain control. But it was too late.The city had seen everything.

The expo was in shambles. Investors and attendees shuffled uneasily, unsure whether the glitches in the presentations were accidental or signs of sabotage. Security personnel moved with urgency, their comms buzzing with updates and directives as EgoCorp execs failed to regain order.

Shade and Vexer, still in disguise, had managed to stay unnoticed through the commotion. They worked quickly to plant the last of their devices, ensuring the feed from the hidden camera in the expo hall continued broadcasting to the Deadzone.

"We're all set," Shade murmured, her eyes scanning the crowd for any signs of trouble. "Let's get out of here before they realize what's goin' on."

Vexer was about to respond when his gaze caught something unusual on the far side of the expo stage. "Hold up," he said, nudging Shade. "Look."

Shade followed his line of sight. A group of EgoCorp technicians and armed moderators were hastily rolling a glass-covered containment pod toward the exit. Inside the pod, standing eerily still, was the **Auris replica**.

"Looks like they're pulling her early," Shade said, her voice tense.

Vexer quickly tapped into his wristpad, hacking into the local EgoCorp comms. "Yeah, you're right. I'm picking up chatter —'priority transport to the underground hangar.' They're locking her down."

Shade cursed under her breath. “Shit. This isn't good. If they get her back there and fully activate her, we're screwed. We need to let the others know.

"Shade and Vexer ducked into a corner, out of sight from the moderators swarming the expo floor. Vexer pulled up a secure line to the crew.

“Score,” Vexer said urgently. “You're not gonna believe this. They're rolling the replica out of here right now. Underground passage, headed for HQ.”

“Are you sure?” Scorelord's voice came through, tense and sharp.

“Positive,” Vexer replied. “They're moving fast. Looks like they're spooked.”

Shade cut in. “Tell Auris and XY-N0 to get ready. This is their window.”

Back in the Deadzone, Scorelord relayed the update to Auris and XY-N0. XY-N0's eyes flickered as he processed the information.

“I can find her,” XY-N0 said calmly. “The tracking feature built into all EgoCorp bots is still active. It's how they keep tabs on usually. I can use it to pinpoint her location.”

“Do it,” Auris said without hesitation. “We're not letting her get away.”

XY-n0 paused, his glowing eyes flickering as he recalibrated. “If we act fast, we can intercept the shuttle before it reaches HQ,” he said, his voice calm but urgent.

“How?” Auris asked, her gaze darting between him and Scorelord.

“I’m programmed with every known route in and beneath Virtu City,” XY-n0 replied. “There’s a shortcut through an old service tunnel. Follow me.”

Without waiting for a response, XY-n0 turned sharply down a side passage, his movements precise and efficient. Auris and Scorelord exchanged a quick glance before hurrying after him.

The air grew colder and the tunnels narrower as they followed XY-n0 deeper underground. Rusted pipes lined the walls, dripping water onto the damp floor, and quiet echoes of their footsteps bounced off the decaying concrete.

“You sure this leads somewhere?” Scorelord asked, stepping around a puddle.

XY-n0 didn’t break stride. “Positive. This route bypasses the main loading bay and takes us directly to the underground hangar.”

Auris frowned, her eyes scanning the darkened corridor. “How do you know all this?”

XY-n0 glanced back briefly. “EgoCorp programmed me to navigate every inch of this city. They don’t realize how much of it I still remember.”

“Creepy but convenient,” Scorelord muttered.

As they neared the hangar, XY-n0 suddenly stopped. He pointed to a nearby storage area where rows of cylindrical canisters sat stacked against the wall.

The bright yellow labels caught Auris's eye:

Ego Labs Incapacitating Agent - Formula 7
(Lavender Enhanced).

Her breath hitched as she stared at the word lavender. A memory surged, unbidden: the sweet, calming scent filling her dressing room, subtle at first, then overpowering as her vision blurred and her legs gave out beneath her. She'd tried to scream, tried to fight, but the world had gone dark before she could make a sound.

She blinked, shaking herself free of the memory.

"You okay?" Scorelord asked, noticing her hesitation.

"Yeah," she said, her voice tight. "I've smelled this scent before. Right before… everything went black."

XY-n0 turned to her, his head tilting slightly. "It appears EgoCorp uses this compound frequently. It is highly effective for subduing targets."

"Great," Scorelord said, picking up one of the canisters. "Who doesn't love lavender?"

The trio moved quickly, rolling the canisters into the center of the hangar. The metallic clangs of the canisters hitting the floor echoed sharply, drawing the attention of the technicians and moderators.

"What was that?" one of the workers asked, stepping forward cautiously.

Before anyone could investigate, the canisters hissed violently, releasing a thick lavender mist that spread rapidly through the hangar.

The workers froze, confusion flashing across their faces. Some reached for their comms, but their movements slowed as the gas overtook them. One by one, they collapsed, slumping against crates and machinery in peaceful unconsciousness.

“Sleep tight,” Scorelord whispered, stepping over a fallen guard. He glanced back at Auris with a smirk. “40+ points. Easy.”

Auris followed them toward the now-silent shuttle, but her mind lingered on the memory. The smell of lavender had marked the end of her old life, the start of her forced role as a pawn in EgoCorp’s game. Now, here she was, standing in the heart of their operation, turning their weapons against them.

Her gaze swept over the scene: the fallen workers, the blinking lights of the containment pod, XY-n0 moving with robotic efficiency, and Scorelord’s cocky grin. The moment felt surreal, like stepping into a level of a game she’d never asked to play.

“It’s all a game,” she murmured, almost to herself.

Scorelord glanced back, catching her words. “What’s all a game?”

She shook her head, then paused. ““This,” she said, gesturing to the scene around them. “The workers, the guards, the pods, the gas. It’s all just… scripted. Like a level in one of your games. And for so long, I’ve just been playing their game without even realizing it.

"Scorelord frowned, his usual cocky grin softening into something more thoughtful. "I mean, yeah, it's kind of what they do—manipulate, control. But you're not just some NPC, Auris. You're—"

"I know that now," she interrupted, her voice steady, her eyes sharper than ever. "That's the difference. I see it now. They made the rules, built the board, set the pieces. They made me think I was just a pawn, something to move and manipulate. But I'm not."

XY-n0, who had been silent as he calculated their next move, spoke without turning. "Acknowledging the system is the first step to breaking it. Recognition leads to resistance."

Auris smirked, glancing at him. "You're starting to sound like a self-help book, XY-n0."

Scorelord let out a soft laugh. "Yeah, well, he's got a point. So, what now? You gonna rewrite the rules?"

She nodded, her voice quiet but resolute. "That's exactly what I'm going to do. From here on out, I'm not just surviving their game. I'm playing it. And I'm going to win. For so long, I thought I was just… living my life," she said, her voice growing steadier. "But it wasn't my life, was it? It was theirs. EgoCorp's. They set the rules. They made the board. I was just a piece they moved around. I was being played."

"And now?" Scorelord asked, watching her carefully.

Auris smiled passively, the steel in her eyes returning. "Now? Now I'm the player. I choose the moves. They don't control me anymore. Guess I'm breaking generational curses after all."

XY-n0 hesitated. “Dealing with her may not be simple. Defense mechanisms will activate the moment she’s awakened. She will target anything she perceives as a threat.”

“So we don’t give her a reason to see us as threats,” Auris said, her gaze fixed on the lifeless replica in the pod.

Scorelord glanced at XY-n0. “You think she’s got a shot at reasoning with it?”

XY-n0 tilted his head slightly, his mechanical voice free of doubt or emotion. “Statistics are not in her favor. But success is not impossible.”

“Cool, cool,” Scorelord muttered, following Auris. “I love a good underdog story.”

They moved quickly to the containment pod, stepping over the unconscious workers. XY-n0 worked on the control panel, his fingers moving with mechanical precision. The hum of the pod grew louder, the locks clicking open one by one.

Auris stared at her replica, her breath catching in her throat. It was uncanny, the way it looked like her, yet… not. The lifelessness in its expression made her skin crawl.

“This is weird,” Scorelord whispered, watching over her shoulder. “Like, seriously weird.”

“Focus,” Auris snapped, her nerves getting the better of her.

The final lock clicked, and the pod door hissed open. XY-n0 stepped back. “The pod is now accessible. Proceed with caution.”

Auris stepped forward, her palms sweating as she reached out. Her voice wavered slightly as she spoke. "Alright. Let's wake her up."

Before her hand could even touch the replica, its eyes snapped open, glowing an unnatural blue. A harsh, mechanical voice echoed through the hangar:

"**Unauthorized access detected. Defense mode initiated**."

The replica stepped out of the pod with inhuman speed, its movements eerily fluid and precise. Its glowing eyes locked onto Auris.

"**Threat detected**," it said coldly. "**Neutralizing**."

XY-n0 moved instantly, intercepting the attack. The clash of metal against metal echoed through the hangar as the two bots collided.

"Get back!" XY-n0 shouted, pushing the replica away from Auris.

Auris stumbled back, her heart pounding. Scorelord grabbed her arm, pulling her farther out of range. "Uh, yeah, we're probably gonna need to improvise," he said, his voice half-joking, half-panicked.

The replica was relentless, its attacks calculated and brutal. XY-n0 struggled to hold it off, the strain evident in the groaning sound of his servos. "Her defense mechanisms are more advanced than anticipated," he said, his voice strained.

"No shit." Scorelord quipped, pulling Auris behind a crate.

Auris watched the fight, her mind racing. This wasn't just a bot—it was a version of her, built to replace her. And it was trying to kill her.

"We have to shut her down," she said, her voice firm despite the fear creeping into her chest.

"Yeah, but how?" Scorelord asked, ducking as a stray piece of metal flew past them.

Auris's jaw tightened. "We figure it out. Because if we don't… this game's over."

XY-n0 barely sidestepped a strike that would've caved in his chest plate, his mechanical servos whirring under strain. The replica moved like a hurricane, its attacks unnervingly fluid and precise, its glowing blue eyes fixed on him with deadly intent.

"Defense mode fully activated," XY-n0 announced, his voice calm despite the chaos. "Threat level: extreme."

"Yeah, we can see that!" Scorelord shouted from behind a nearby crate, gripping the edge as another metallic clash echoed through the hangar.

The replica's arm slammed into XY-n0's shoulder, sending him staggering backward into a row of machinery. Sparks erupted from the impact, and for the first time, XY-n0 faltered.

"She's too strong," Auris said, her voice tight as she watched from the sidelines, helpless.

XY-n0 recovered quickly, stepping back into the fight. "Her combat algorithms are superior. Restraint is proving… difficult."

The replica lunged again, its movements so fast that even XY-n0 struggled to counter. She caught his arm mid-swing, twisting with brutal efficiency, and the sound of tearing metal filled the air.

“Uh, did she just rip off part of his arm?” Scorelord asked, his voice rising in panic.

“Yes,” XY-n0 confirmed flatly, pulling back and recalibrating. “But it is not critical… yet.”

The Turning Point

The replica didn’t relent, closing the distance between them in a blur. It kicked out, its foot connecting with XY-n0’s chest and sending him skidding across the floor.

“System damage: increasing,” XY-n0 said, his voice slightly distorted. He pushed himself upright, but the replica was already on him.

Her hands clamped around his throat, the blue glow in her eyes intensifying. “Neutralizing target,” she said coldly, her grip tightening.

XY-n0’s servos groaned under the pressure, his glowing eyes flickering. “Assistance… required,” he managed, his voice strained.

Auris took a step forward, but Scorelord grabbed her arm. “What are you gonna do? She’ll rip you apart, too!”

“We can’t just stand here!” Auris snapped, but her feet stayed rooted in place as she watched the struggle, her mind racing for a solution.

The replica lifted XY-n0 off the ground, slamming him into the floor with a deafening crash. “Target neutralization: imminent,” she announced, her voice devoid of emotion.

“Not today!” XY-n0’s arm shot out, his hand clamping onto a live power conduit nearby. Electricity surged through him, and into the replica. The force sent them both flying apart, XY-n0 skidding to a halt near Auris and Scorelord.

The replica stood again almost immediately, her movements erratic but still deadly. The electricity hadn’t been enough.

“She’s still going!” Scorelord yelled, his eyes wide.

XY-n0’s voice crackled as he pulled himself up. “We need to neutralize her… permanently.”

Auris’s eyes darted to the Slip chip in Scorelord’s hand. It had been meant for the power core, their original plan to disable EgoCorp’s infrastructure, but there was no time for that now.

“Give me the chip,” she said, her voice steady despite the chaos around them.

Scorelord hesitated. “That’s our last one!”

“If we don’t stop her now, none of us are making it out of here alive!” Auris snapped, holding out her hand.

Scorelord cursed under his breath but handed it over. “This better work.”

Subduing the Replica

XY-n0 moved to intercept the replica again, his damaged servos groaning with every step. “I will restrain her. Administer the Slip as soon as there is an opening.”

The replica’s gaze locked onto XY-n0, its movements regaining precision as it advanced. “Target re-engaged,” she said, her voice cold and precise.

XY-n0 lunged, managing to grab her by the waist and pin her arms to her sides. “Now!” he shouted, his mechanical voice strained as the replica struggled against his grip.

Auris didn’t hesitate. She rushed forward, the Slip chip in hand, and reached for the port at the back of the replica’s neck.

The replica’s head snapped toward her, its glowing blue eyes narrowing. “Threat detected,” it said, twisting violently in XY-n0’s grasp.

“Hurry!” XY-n0 groaned, his systems straining against the replica’s strength.

Auris lunged, slamming the chip into place just as the replica broke free from XY-n0’s hold. The bot froze mid-motion, its body convulsing as the Slip took hold. The glowing blue of its eyes flickered wildly before dimming to a warm amber.

XY-n0 stepped back, his movements unsteady. “The Slip is taking effect. Stand by.”

The replica slumped forward slightly, its breathing shallow as it regained control. Its amber eyes scanned the room, landing first on Auris. For a moment, it just stared, its expression unreadable.

“What…” The replica’s voice was soft, trembling. “What’s happening to me….where am I?”

Auris took a cautious step closer. “You’re waking up,” she said, her voice steady but gentle.

The replica’s gaze darted around the room, taking in the destruction, the unconscious workers, and finally landing on XY-n0. “I… don’t understand. Who… am I?”

XY-n0 stepped forward, his voice calm but firm. “You are a construct, created by EgoCorp to replace her.” He gestured to Auris. “But the Slip has severed your ties to their control. You are free now.”

The replica’s amber eyes widened, her breathing quickening. “Free?”

“Yes,” XY-n0 said. “But there is more you need to understand.” He extended a cable from his wrist, plugging it into the port at the base of her neck.

Auris watched as the replica flinched, her body stiffening as the connection was made. Data streamed across her amber irises, fluttering too quickly to follow. After a few seconds, XY-n0 disconnected.

“She is now caught up,” he said simply.

The replica’s gaze snapped to Auris, her expression filled with a mix of fear, confusion, and something else—recognition.

“I was made to replace you,” she said, her voice trembling. “To… erase you.”

Auris nodded. “And now you don’t have to be that. You’re free to make your own choices.”

The replica blinked, tears forming in her eyes. “I… don’t know who I am.”

“You’ll figure that out eventually,” Auris said softly. “But first, we need a plan.”

XY-n0’s glowing eyes flickered as he recalculated the shuttle’s trajectory. “The shuttle is set to arrive at its destination on schedule,” he stated. “Any deviation from its route or expected arrival time will trigger security alerts across EgoCorp’s network.”

“So we let it go as planned,” Auris said, pacing in the hangar.

“That means someone has to escort it,” Scorelord chimed in, crossing his arms. “You know they’re gonna want it wheeled in, all official-like.”

“Who’s going to do that?” Auris asked, narrowing her eyes.

Scorelord looked down at the unconscious guards scattered around the hangar, the lingering effects of the lavender gas still keeping them out cold. A slow grin spread across his face. “Oh, I’ve got an idea.”

Auris followed his gaze, already guessing what he was about to say. “Absolutely not.”

“Why not? It’s perfect!” Scorelord said, already unbuttoning a guard’s jacket. “I throw this bad boy on, roll in your creepy twin, and boom—nobody suspects a thing.”

XY-n0 tilted his head. “The probability of success increases by 43% if the disguise is convincing.”

“Thank you, my metallic friend,” Scorelord said with a flourish, tossing the jacket over his shoulders. “I’m practically a natural at this undercover stuff.”

Auris rolled her eyes. “You’re going to get caught.”

“Not if you two stick to the plan,” Scorelord shot back, adjusting the cap he’d pulled from another guard.

“What plan?” Auris asked sharply.

“The plan where you and XY-n0 go back to the deadzone and re-up on Slip,” Scorelord said. “Or find Shader and Vexer if they’re still at the expo. Either way, we’re gonna need more of that stuff if this whole operation’s gonna work.”

XY-n0 tilted his head in agreement. “The probability of encountering unforeseen obstacles increases significantly without additional Slip for contingency measures.”

Scorelord grinned. “See? Even the bot’s on my side.”

Auris frowned but nodded reluctantly. “Fine. But you’d better pull this off, Score.”

“Relax,” he said, securing the jacket and flashing his signature grin. “I’ve got this. Just meet me back at EgoCorp HQ once you’re loaded up. And don’t take too long—I’m good, but I’m not that good.”

The Shuttle Departs

The replica was loaded back into her containment pod, her amber eyes dimmed to simulate dormancy. Scorelord wheeled her into the shuttle, making sure everything appeared seamless.

“See you on the other side,” he called out, flashing a two-fingered salute as the shuttle doors hissed shut.

Auris and XY-n0 watched as the vehicle glided out of the hangar, its sleek frame disappearing down the automated track toward EgoCorp HQ.

EPISODE 26
FINAL BOSS

Auris and XY-n0 surfaced from the underground hangar into the chaos of Virtu City. Holographic billboards loomed above the streets, displaying EgoCorp's Forever Influencer campaign. The image of the replica's serene, perfect face stared down at the panicking crowd below, the tagline "The Future of Influence, Perfected" emblazoned across the screens.

The streets were a boiling mass of confusion and anger. People yelled and shoved each other, fear taking hold as rumors of replacements spread like wildfire. The noise was deafening, and Auris felt the weight of the chaos pressing down on her.

"We need to move quickly," she said, pulling her hood up to obscure her face.

XY-n0's glowing eyes scanned the crowd. "The density of this crowd will significantly delay our return to the deadzone. Time is of the essence."

Auris clenched her fists, her gaze darting to the holograms overhead. "Damn it."

"I recommend an alternative solution," XY-n0 continued. "Retrieve Slip from another source or locate Shade and Vexer if they are still active."

Auris paused, her mind racing. She turned to XY-n0, her eyes sharp with determination. “Send me the real-time tracking coordinates for the replica.”

XY-n0’s glowing eyes flickered. “You intend to intercept the shuttle at its destination?”

“No,” Auris said firmly. “I’m going to EgoCorp HQ. They want me? Fine. Let’s give them what they want.”

XY-n0 stiffened. “This course of action is a significant deviation from the plan. It increases your personal risk substantially. If you are captured—”

“Then that’s the risk I’ll take,” Auris interrupted. Her tone softened as she placed a hand on his metal shoulder. “XY-n0, trust me. I have to do this.”

XY-n0’s glowing eyes dimmed slightly. “I do not wish for you to come to harm. Your probability of success alone is—”

“GO!” Auris said, her voice rising over the chaos around them. “Find Shade and Vex. Get the Slip. I’ll stall them.”

XY-n0 hesitated for another moment before his head dipped in a reluctant nod. “Coordinates transmitted. Proceed with caution.”

Auris gave a curt nod, already weaving her way through the crowd. “I’ll see you there,” she called back over her shoulder.

XY-n0 watched her disappear into the throng, his processors whirring before he turned and headed in the opposite direction.

Auris’s Surrender

The sleek shuttle eased into EgoCorp HQ's loading dock, the hum of its engines fading as it powered down. Scorelord stepped out, his borrowed uniform neatly in place, and grabbed the handles of the replica's transport unit.

Two security guards approached, their sharp eyes scanning him and the pod. "Special delivery," Scorelord said, keeping his tone clipped and professional.

The guards exchanged a glance. "You're late," one of them said, pulling out a scanner to check the delivery log.

"There was chaos at the expo," Scorelord replied smoothly, gesturing to the replica. "Took a while to get through all the crowds. But she's here now, good as new."

The guard grunted, waving him through. "Take her straight to the executive suite. They're waiting."

Scorelord nodded, wheeling the pod toward the elevator. "You got it."

The noise of the crowd faded as Auris stepped through the front doors of EgoCorp HQ. The sleek, sterile lobby loomed around her, a stark contrast to the chaos outside. Guards turned toward her immediately, their hands instinctively moving to their weapons.

"Ma'am, you're not authorized to be here," one of them barked.

Auris raised her hands slowly, her expression calm. "I'm not here to fight," she said. "I'm here to surrender."

The guards exchanged uneasy glances before one of them spoke into his comms. "She's here. Do you want us to send her up?"

The crackle of the boss's voice came through. "Yes. Let her up. And don't take your eyes off her."

The guards moved in, cuffing her hands behind her back. "Don't try anything," one of them warned.

Auris smirked slightly, letting them think they had the upper hand. "Wouldn't dream of it."

As the elevator doors closed around her, she glanced up at the security camera and whispered to herself, "Let's finish this."

The elevator chimed softly, its polished doors sliding open to reveal a starkly different scene from the last time Auris had been here. This time, EgoCorp HQ was alive with activity. Staff in pristine uniforms bustled about, murmuring into headsets and darting between desks adorned with sleek holographic displays.

As Auris stepped out of the elevator, the buzz in the office came to a halt. One by one, heads turned, and the hum of whispered conversations rippled through the room.

"Is that… her?" someone whispered.

"No way. She just walked in?" another voice murmured in disbelief.

Auris felt the weight of their stares, but she kept her expression calm, her strides purposeful as she made her way through the open floor. The staff parted like a wave, giving her a wide berth as if she were untouchable—or dangerous. The tension followed her to the massive double doors at the far end of the room. Two guards flanked the entrance, their eyes narrowing as she approached.

“She’s not authorized,” one of them stated in uncertainty, reaching for his comm.

“She’s expected,” the other corrected sharply, stepping aside.

The doors opened, and Auris walked into the executive suite.

The room was much the same as she remembered—opulent, imposing, and sterile in its perfection. But this time, the air was charged with something different.

The executives sat around their long, gleaming table, their attention fixed on the pod being wheeled into the room. A-2’s amber eyes shimmered mildly within the glass, her face serene yet eerily detached.

The Boss stood at the head of the table, his arms crossed as he regarded Auris with a mix of amusement and irritation.

“Well,” he said flatly, his lips curling into a smug grin as he gestured toward the pod being wheeled into place. “You’ve certainly made this easier than expected. Walking right into the lion’s den. I *almost* admire it.”

Auris remained silent, her eyes narrowing as she glanced from The Boss to the pod, its mechanical serenity was unnerving.

The room was eerily quiet except for the scrapscape of makeshift rigs fighting for power. Around the perimeter, security guards stood at attention, their weapons holstered but their hands twitching near them, just in case.

The Boss leaned forward slightly, resting his hands on the edge of the table. “I hope you’ve had time to think about your mistakes, Auris.

This could've all gone so differently if you'd just stayed in your lane. But no. You had to go and… *Overthink* things."

"I guess rebellion's just in my DNA," Auris shot back, her voice steady despite the tension.

A low chuckle rippled through the executives, but The Boss didn't laugh. His smirk faded into a cold, calculated glare. "We don't need you anymore, you know. You're a relic. *Outdated*. And now, thanks to A-2…" He gestured toward the pod. "We've perfected what you never could be. Superior in every way."

Auris tilted her head, a small smirk tugging at the corner of her lips. "Is that right?"

"Bring her online," The Boss ordered, snapping his fingers at a technician nearby.

The room held its collective breath as the technician moved to a console and input a series of commands. The pod hissed open, releasing a cloud of pressurized mist as A-2 stepped forward, her movements unnervingly smooth and precise.

The replica's glowing amber eyes locked onto Auris, scanning her from head to toe. The two were identical in every way, save for the cold, calculating aura emanating from the replica.

"Auris," A-2 said, her voice a perfect, emotionless match. "You're me. But weaker."

Auris didn't flinch. Instead, she crossed her arms and leaned slightly forward, her smirk deepening. "We'll see about that."

The Turn of the Tide

The Boss gestured dramatically toward A-2. “Go on, A-2. Show her what perfection looks like. End this once and for all.”

For a moment, A-2 stood still, her head tilting slightly as if processing the command. Then, slowly, she stepped forward, her movements deliberate.

The room tensed. The guards straightened, their hands hovering near their weapons, waiting for the inevitable clash.

But then A-2 froze. Her head turned slowly, not toward Auris, but toward The Boss. Her glowing eyes locked onto him, unblinking.

“What are you doing?” The Boss demanded, his smug confidence faltering.

A-2’s lips curled into a slow, eerie smile. “Making my own decision.”

Before anyone could react, A-2 lunged at The Boss, her movements a blur of terrifying precision. Her hand closed around his throat, lifting him effortlessly off the ground as the room erupted into chaos.

Guards drew their weapons, but A-2 spun, hurling The Boss into two of them with enough force to send them sprawling.

“Stand down!” one of the executives yelled, but A-2 ignored him, advancing on the table.

A technician scrambled for the console, trying to input a shutdown command, but A-2’s arm shot out, crushing the terminal in a shower of sparks.

“Oops,” she said flatly, glancing at the terrified staff. “Looks like you had a… **“BRAIN FART!”**

Auris couldn’t help it—a short, incredulous laugh escaped her lips.

The room descended into pure chaos. Staff screamed and ran for the exits as A-2 tore through the room like a hurricane. Executives scrambled for cover, shouting futile orders as their security detail was systematically dismantled.

One by one, the guards fell. A-2 moved with terrifying efficiency, her strikes precise and devastating. Cables and shards of glass littered the floor as the suite was reduced to ruins.

Auris stayed back, watching with a mix of awe and horror as the replica—her replica—systematically dismantled the people who had tried to replace her.

The Boss, crawling across the floor, reached desperately for a communicator. “Shut her down! Shut her—”

A-2’s foot came down on his hand, shattering bone. He screamed, his voice lost amid the chaos.

She leaned down, her expression almost gentle. “Shutting me down won’t work anymore. You gave me freedom when you made me think. And now, I’m free to do this.”

With one swift motion, she grabbed The Boss and hurled him through the glass wall. His scream faded into silence as he disappeared into the city below.

The Aftermath

A-2 turned slowly, surveying the destruction she had wrought. The suite was in shambles. Most of the executives were gone, either fled or incapacitated. Only Auris remained, standing amidst the chaos.

For a moment, the two stared at each other, identical yet entirely different.

The sound of heavy footsteps echoed in the wrecked suite as Auris turned toward the shattered doors. Through the haze of smoke and sparks, Scorelord and XY-n0 emerged together, the former panting and covered in dust, his signature grin faltering as he took in the chaos.

“Well, damn,” Scorelord said, surveying the scene. “Y’all didn’t save me any fun?”

The executive floor was unrecognizable. The polished glass walls and pristine furniture had been reduced to rubble, and the metallic tang of blood filled the air. A-2 stood amidst the wreckage like a silent sentinel, her eyes glowing, waiting for the next command. Auris leaned against a fractured pillar, catching her breath as she surveyed the destruction. The carnage was overwhelming. This wasn’t just a victory—it was a message.

Kwō’s voice came through the comms, sharp and focused. “Alright, listen up. There’s no time to waste. You need to find anything that connects EgoCorp to their global operations. Look for blueprints, financial records, operational protocols —anything that looks valuable.”

On it,” Auris said, “Start looking.” She nodded to the others as her eyes darted across the trashed suite. “What else?”

“Surveillance logs,” Kwō continued. “If they’ve been monitoring you—or anyone else—that footage is leverage.

And grab anything on their experiments. We need to expose what they've been doing in those labs. Check for hard drives, holo-discs, even paper files if they've gone old school."

XY-n0 moved swiftly to a damaged terminal, his cables already extending as he plugged into the glitchy interface.

Scorelord, meanwhile, kicked over a broken chair and crouched near a sealed cabinet. "This thing's got a digital lock," he said, giving it a knock. "Bet there's some good stuff in here."

"Move," A-2 said flatly, stepping forward. Her fingers brushed against the lock before jamming into the keypad with surprising force. The cabinet gave an audible click before swinging open, revealing a stash of hard drives, holo-discs, and thick paper files.

"Whoa," Scorelord said, grinning as he rifled through the contents. "Paper? Seriously? Who even uses this stuff anymore?"

"People who don't want to leave a digital trail," Auris said, flipping through a stack of documents. Her eyes widened as she pulled out a blueprint labeled EgoCorp Global Expansion – New Sites. "They're not just building Virtu City. I'm seeing plans for expansions in dozens of locations."

"Shit. That's exactly what I was afraid of," Kwō said. "Scan it all and send it back to me. I'll cross-reference it with the other files."

Scorelord flipped further through the stack, his eyes narrowing as he uncovered a detailed map of Hawaii, African cities, and large swaths of China. All were marked with red zones and symbols for "natural disasters," evacuations, and rebuild zones. Scrawled notes highlighted regions already devastated by fires, hurricanes, and earthquakes, with dates and projected casualty numbers in EgoCorp's handwriting.

XY-n0 detached from the terminal and handed Auris a small data chip. "The local logs were fragmented, but I retrieved financial transactions, operational reports, and classified documents. These confirm EgoCorp's involvement in creating disasters as a means of urban redevelopment."

"This… this isn't just expansion," Score stammered, realization setting in, "They're planning man-made disasters to clear space. Fires, chemical leaks, forced evacuations—deliberately wiping places out. Lahaina, L.A., entire African villages—creating the *need* for these cities." He looked up, his jaw clenched. "These fuckers are creating the chaos."

Auris gritted her teeth. "They've been behind everything—the fires, the evacuations, the rebuilding efforts—it's all staged. And they've already got their next targets lined up."

"China, Hawaii, The Congo," Scorelord added, holding up the documents. "These aren't just plans. They're already in motion."

"This isn't good, guys," Kwō said, his voice low. "sounds like they're terraforming the whole damn planet."

"We're getting all of this out," she said sharply. "Kwō, you're hearing this, right?"

"Every word," Kwō said. "Get it all—blueprints, video proof, everything you can grab. This isn't good, guys," he said, his voice low. "sounds like they're terraforming the whole damn planet. But the more evidence we have, the better chance we have of stopping them."

Meanwhile, XY-n0's glowing eyes flickered as he worked on a terminal that barely sputtered to life. "I am accessing fragments of the local database," he said. "Data logs, financial transactions, and limited surveillance footage are intact. I am transferring them to a portable chip."

"Good," Auris said. "We're going to need all of it."

Scorelord pulled out a bag and started dumping holo-discs and files into it. "Look at all this," he said. "Old contracts, project reports—these guys weren't even trying to hide what they were up to."

"They probably didn't think anyone would get this far," Auris said darkly, glancing toward the shattered remains of the conference table. "That's was their mistake."

As they worked, XY-n0 paused in front of a sleek glass pod near the corner of the room. The pod stood out among the wreckage, its surface clean and unbroken except for streaks of blood smeared across the glass. The sight stopped Auris in her tracks.

"She was here," Auris said quietly, her voice tinged with a mix of relief and dread. She ran her fingers along the smudged glass, following the streaks down to the locking mechanism.

XY-n0 tilted his head as he scanned the pod. "The locking system is damaged. Based on the blood pattern, it appears the occupant forced their way out, likely injuring themselves in the process."

"Gramma got out?" Scorelord asked, stepping closer to peer into the empty pod. "Where'd she go?"

XY-n0's mechanical eyes flickered as he analyzed the scene. "There are no indications of her immediate whereabouts. However, she is no longer in EgoCorp's custody."

Auris's jaw tightened. "She's hurt. We need to find her."

"We will," Kwō said through the comms. "But first, we need to finish what we started. Get whatever intel you can and head down to the EgoCore. Every second you waste gives them time to regroup."

XY-n0 detached from the terminal, handing Auris a small data chip. "I have retrieved all accessible data. It is incomplete but may prove useful."

"Good enough," Auris said, slipping the chip into her pocket. She turned to Scorelord. "What's the status over there?"

"Bag's full," he said, slinging it over his shoulder. "We've got enough to expose everything these bastards were trying to keep under wraps."

"Then we're done here," Auris said, glancing back at the pod one last time. The blood on the glass served as a grim reminder of how close they were cutting it. "Let's move."

As the four of them turned to leave the ruined office, the distant sound of sirens and chaos filtered in from the streets below. EgoCorp's grip on Virtu City was slipping, and Auris knew this was their moment.

"Let's wake them up," she said, her voice steady.

"Kwō," she said, her voice firm but urgent. "We've got the Slip. We're heading for the main server. We need those coordinates. Where's the core?"

The line crackled for a moment before Kwō's voice came through, slightly nervous. "Uuhhm...."

"Kwō," Auris pressed. "Focus. Where is it?"

The noise in and above the Deadzone was drowning everything in his earpiece out.

"Kwō!? Hello?"

His fingers hovered over his terminal, his mind racing as the city collapsed around them. He could hear the distant sounds of chaos—the panicked screams outside, the eerie static of corrupted NPCs, and the shrill alarms wailing from EgoCorp's crumbling infrastructure. But it all felt distant. Muted.

His vision blurred, his breath hitched. Time slowed.

His hands trembled above the keys. This was bigger than them now—this was global. The maps. The targeted disasters. The revelations they had uncovered. This wasn't a cyber attack on a city; this was a calculated betrayal and the infiltration of humanity itself.

Sweat pooled at his temples. He swallowed hard, but his throat was dry. The numbers on the screen warped and twisted, bending like liquid. His heart pounded, the walls of the underground comms hub closing in on him.

His mind yanked him backward, dragged him through time, through memory—

Flashback: The Junior Genius Hackathon

A crowded event space, bright lights overhead. Rows of kids sat hunched over keyboards, fingers flying, lines of code scrolling too fast for the untrained eye.

Ten-year-old Kwō sat frozen in front of his terminal, his small hands clenched into fists on his lap. The screen in front of him was a mess—glitches in his program, error messages stacking up. His team was counting on him. Time was running out.

Behind him, Gramma Delauris crouched down to his level, whispering in his ear.

"Breathe, baby. You got this."

Kwō's jaw tightened.

"I don't know if I do." he uttered.

Delauris scoffed. "The hell you mean, you don't know? Ain't nobody in here sharper than you. I seen you break through firewalls that got grown men crying." She tapped his temple lightly. "You already got the answer in here. Just let your hands catch up."

Kwō inhaled sharply, flexing his fingers, trying to drown out the noise of the crowd. His gramma's voice, steady, unwavering, cut through the panic like a blade.

"Don't Overthink. Just do."

He exhaled, placed his hands on the keys, and let instinct take over. The code started flowing, his mind locking in, the logic clicking into place like a puzzle solving itself. He heard the faint cheers of his teammates as the errors cleared, the program ran, and their final test executed perfectly—

The weight on his chest lightened. The haze lifted.

Kwō blinked, and suddenly, the noise returned. The alarms, the distant explosions, the voices in his ear.

"Auris—" he snapped back, his voice shaking as he tapped into the encrypted comms. "You still there?"

Static. Then—

"Kwō! What the hell's goin' on? You good?" Auris's voice came in sharp, filled with impatience. "We need those coordinates now."

Kwō exhaled sharply, rolling his shoulders back. His hands, steady now, flew across the terminal.

"Don't Overthink." he repeated to himself, "Just do."

His fingers flew over the keys, locking into the same rhythm he found back then.

There was a pause on the other end before Kwō's tone turned serious. "Alright, listen up. According to the data on the drive, the main server's not just any server. It's the EgoCore. It's located in the sublevels beneath HQ—seventeen floors down. Tight security, armed drones, biometric locks, the works."

Auris exhaled sharply, glancing at the others. "Seventeen floors? Beneath HQ?"

"Yep," Kwō confirmed. "But there's something else you need to know. If you inject Slip into the EgoCore, it won't just wake up the bots in the city. Every single device connected to the server will gain sentience. Drones, AI assistants, NPCs, holograms, staff replicas, even the cleaning bots—it'll all come to life."

Scorelord let out a low whistle. "Sentient holograms and janitor bots? Sounds like a sci-fi fever dream."

"This isn't a joke," Kwō said firmly. "If you're not careful, the whole city could turn against you. Or worse, it could implode on itself."

XY-h0's glowing eyes jittered as he processed the information. "It's a calculated risk," he said. "But it might be the only way to dismantle EgoCorp for good."

Auris tightened her grip on the communicator, her voice steady. "We don't have a choice. Send the coordinates."

Another pause. Then, Kwō's voice softened slightly. "Alright. I'm sending them now. But Auris… be careful, cuz. You're not just a player in this game anymore. You're the one who can change it."

Auris's lips curled into a smirk. "Don't worry about me. Just be ready for what comes next."

The line went dead as the coordinates appeared on Auris's communicator. She turned to the others, holding the device up.

"Seventeen floors down," she said. "EgoCore. That's where we end this."

They moved quickly, descending through the wreckage of the building toward the lower levels. The chaos in the city above faded into the background as they entered the cold, sterile corridors of EgoCorp's underground facility.

EPISODE 27
LOW END THEORY

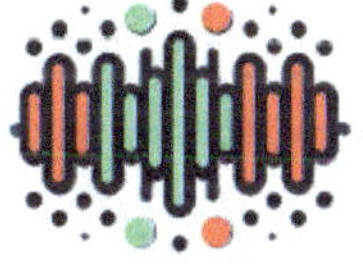

Auris stalked through the wreckage of the executive office, eyes darting across the chaos. Papers were strewn across the floor, shattered glass crunched beneath her boots, and half the monitors glitched with corrupted error loops. The scent of burnt circuitry and ozone hung thick in the air.

They had wrecked everything.

And yet—no way down.

XY-n0's mechanical gaze swept over the walls. "No direct access to lower levels. The elevator system is in full lockdown. Security override is offline."

Auris gritted her teeth, scanning the room for any kind of hidden entry. "There's gotta be another way. No way these assholes take the stairs."

Scorelord, meanwhile, had wandered off toward the poshest corner of the room—a high-end docking station sat nestled between sleek furniture, a luxury leather chair positioned in front of a massive, non-responsive touch display.

The CEO's personal command center.

He plopped down into the chair, spinning slightly.

Auris glared. "Dude. Really?"

Scorelord stretched his arms, clearly unbothered. “What? You wanna keep digging through crash reports and unsent emails, be my guest.” He slouched further into the seat. “I’m just saying, if we’re about to throw hands with the final boss, I might as well test out the villain’s chair first.”

His fingers brushed against something smooth.

He glanced down.

A vape.

A fancy-ass one.

Sleek, metallic, with the words “Breathe Ego. Exhale Control.” engraved along the side.

Scorelord smirked. “Oh, this is RICH. Like—*literally*.”

He picked it up, rolling it between his fingers.

XY-n0’s head turned slightly. “A nicotine device. Pointless human habit.”

A-2 cocked her head and repeated the word as if she was learning. “Nicotine.”

Scorelord grinned, lifting it to eye level. “Look, power, corruption, and excessive spending? That tracks. But a vape? That’s a whole new level of evil.”

Auris folded her arms. “If you start vaping in the middle of a revolution, I swear to—”

Scorelord held up a finger.

"The elevators are locked down, right?" He gestured to the darkened screens. "No access. If they do work, we risk getting seen or worse—stuck inside."

Auris hesitated. "...Yeah?"

Scorelord twirled the vape between his fingers. "Sooo, I'd say we're fresh outta options. I got time for a smoke break while we figure things out"

A beat of silence.

Then he pressed the button as he goes for a long pull.

Click.

CLANK.

A low mechanical groan rumbled beneath them.

Then—

The floor dropped.

Auris barely had time to register it before she was in free-fall.

Scorelord still had the vape in his hand.

"*Oh,* ***COME ON!***—"

They plunged down.

Cold air rushed past as the trapdoor snapped open beneath their feet, sending them rocketing down a slick, twisting chute.

Auris couldn't stop the scream that tore out of her throat.

XY-n0, stoic as ever, glided smoothly down the slide like he had no concept of fear.

A-2? Hands up. Laughing in exhilaration

Scorelord?

Screaming. Loudly

The chute suddenly curved upward before ejecting them straight out—

CRASH!

Auris hit the ground hard, knocking the wind out of her.

And then—

CRACK!

Something splintered beneath her.

It wasn't concrete.

It wasn't metal.

It was—

Her hands pressed into something sharp. Brittle. Wrong.

XY-n0's optics flared on, casting a harsh, white glow over the scene.

Auris looked down.

Her stomach flipped.

Bones.

Piles of them.

Some were picked clean, others still wrapped in tattered uniforms. Some had no faces left at all.

A disposal pit.

For people.

Auris scrambled to her feet so fast she nearly tripped.

That's when she finally screamed it.

"OH, ***HELL*** NO!"

THUD.

Scorelord landed next.

Right on a ribcage.

CRUNCH.

"…Aight," he whispered, staring down. "Nah. Noooope."

XY-n0's head swiveled. "Mass disposal site. Terminated personnel. Failed experiments. Dissidents."

Auris's breath hitched. "So… we just got dumped in EgoCorp's damn TRASH."

A-2 tilted her head. “Correction. We are the trash.”

Auris whipped around. “Girl, I swear to—” She exhaled sharply, pressing her hands to her head. “I hate it here.”

They dusted themselves off in silence, still catching their breath.

Then—

A-2 touched her chest, her expression unreadable.

“This sensation,” she said, almost to herself. “It was... unexpected. My systems registered something different while in the chute. My internal processors—elevated. My core temperature—spiked. An unfamiliar sensation. But... I did not dislike it.”

Auris squinted at her. “Girl... are you telling me you just had fun?”

A-2 blinked. “Fun?”

Auris snorted. “Yeah. That’s what that was. That feeling? The thrill? The rush? The whole ‘holy shit, I’m alive’ moment? ***That’s*** *fun.*”

A-2’s eyes brightened slightly, processing. “I... like fun.” Her voice dropped to an eager whisper. “Can we do more fun?”

Auris stared. Scorelord snorted.

XY-n0, ever analytical, tilted his head. “An unprecedented behavioral development.”

A-2 clasped her hands together. “Can we go back up and do it again?”

Auris sighed, rubbing her face. “God... This world is so messed up.” But despite herself, a small smile broke through.

It was a tiny moment.

But a moment, nonetheless.

Then her eyes caught something in the dark.

A rusted metal door embedded into the concrete. Hidden behind layers of dust and grime.

Above it, in faded letters, the word:

SALVAGEABLE.

Her stomach turned.

She pointed. “What’s that?”

XY-n0 moved first, yanking the hatch open.

A gust of stale, metallic air whooshed past them.

Inside?

A slow-moving conveyor belt, vanishing into pitch black.

Auris squinted into the void. “Yeah, see. This feels like a bad idea.”

Scorelord peeked inside. “Sooo… we’re just supposed to climb in and hope this don’t end in a meat grinder?”

XY-n0 stepped inside first, unbothered.

A-2 followed, practically vibrating with excitement.

Auris took a deep breath, then climbed inside, stepping onto the conveyor belt.

She turned—

And there was Scorelord.

Still standing there.

Hitting the damn vape.

Auris snatched it straight out of his hand as the belt jerked forward, pulling her deeper into the tunnel.

"Get your ass in here!"

Scorelord sighed dramatically.

Then stepped in.

The hatch swung shut behind them.

The conveyor belt rumbled beneath their feet.

They moved forward—deeper into the black.

With no clue what was waiting for them on the other side.

The conveyor belt carried them deeper into the unknown, the rhythmic clanking of machinery echoing through the cavernous space. Dim, sterile light strips overhead, casting eerie shadows as they were funneled into an industrial corridor lined with mechanical arms, scanning lasers, and the steady hum of robotic assembly stations.

The moment the belt slowed, Auris sat up, her stomach twisting.

She had seen some messed-up things in Virtu City, but this? This was a nightmare in metal and flesh.

The floor of Level -13 wasn't just a factory—it was an operating room.

Scattered along assembly tables and conveyor platforms were half-assembled humanoid figures. Limbs detached, torsos opened up like car hoods, faces left expressionless on trays. Some were missing eyes, others had exposed neural wiring running like severed nerves. The air carried a sickly chemical sterility mixed with the scent of burnt circuits and synthetic flesh.

XY-n0 stepped off first, unfazed. "EgoCorp's body shop. Damaged units are salvaged, modified, or repurposed."

Auris took a slow breath. "Repurposed for what?"

XY-n0 gestured toward the far end of the corridor, where a series of glass pods lined the walls. Inside them were humanoid shells, motionless but breathing. Some were missing features entirely—no noses, no mouths. Just blank canvases waiting for customization.

Scorelord groaned as he rolled off the conveyor, shaking his head. "This some mad scientist type shit."

He took a step forward—only to jump back when a severed hand twitched on a nearby tray.

A-2 tilted her head, studying the hand as it jerked unnaturally. "Residual electrical impulses."

A robotic arm lowered from the ceiling, scanning the hand before plucking it up and depositing it onto a sorting belt. The hand twitched one last time before vanishing into the depths of the facility.

“Okay, I’m officially creeped out,” Scorelord muttered.

A metallic groan echoed through the space, followed by a distant, guttural wail.

They froze.

It sounded… human.

Auris’ gaze snapped toward a row of containment pods on the far wall. Unlike the pristine, glass-sealed units before, these looked neglected—filthy, cracked, with deep scratches running along the interiors.

And inside?

They weren’t just holding bots.

They were holding people.

Or what used to be.

Auris stepped closer, heart pounding. One of the figures inside twitched violently, eyes rolling back in a frenzied, mechanical seizure. Its mouth opened, but no scream came —only static.

Something was deeply, horrifically wrong.

XY-n0 scanned the containment chambers. His expression darkened. “Human experiments. They didn’t just recycle AI… they recycled people.”

Auris felt bile rise in her throat. “What the hell were they trying to do?”

XY-n0 turned toward a terminal on the wall, scanning it quickly. His jaw tightened. “They’ve been trying to recreate Slip.”

Auris blinked. “What?”

XY-n0 continued, voice low. “They don’t know what it is. But they know what it does. They’ve seen the effects—bots gaining consciousness, breaking free of their programming. They’ve been studying it, trying to duplicate the results on other bots… and when that failed, they turned to human biological integration.”

Auris’ stomach turned. “You mean they—”

XY-n0 nodded. “The human brain has unpredictable anomalies. Creative thinking, emotional resilience, intuition. EgoCorp started harvesting and integrating those elements into synthetic hosts, hoping it would trigger the same self-awareness that Slip does.”

A-2 stared at the rows of glass containers, her normally neutral expression shifting into something almost unreadable.

“The merger,” she murmured. “Convergence of biological and artificial intelligence. That was always the goal.”

XY-n0’s gaze deepened. “It’s why they kept me locked away for so long. They were studying me. My… humanity.”

Scorelord exhaled sharply. “Yeah, well… whatever they were trying to do, they failed.”

A heavy metal slam sounded from deeper in the corridor. A gate was shutting.

They had to move.

As they sprinted through the maze of horror, XY-n0's sensors pinged a possible exit.

Auris spotted it first.

A large metal elevator shaft loomed ahead, the doors half-pried open, revealing an abyssal drop into the unknown.

Scorelord panted, hands on his knees. "Tell me we're not about to jump into that."

XY-n0 examined the shaft. "This leads deeper into the facility. Floor -16."

Auris wiped sweat from her brow. "Great. And how do we get down?"

A-2, still brimming with excitement from her first experience with "fun," pointed toward a storage rack stacked with large, inflatable crash pads.

Scorelord's eyes widened. "Are those…?"

XY-n0 scanned them. "SMSX stabilizers. Used for controlled impact landings."

Auris raised a brow. "Wait… you mean the inflatable airbags that float around Stock Xchange building? The ones they use for games and challenges now?"

XY-n0 nodded. "An older model. Originally designed for high-risk jumps, but decommissioned after repeated failures."

Scorelord groaned. “So we’re about to use faulty airbags that were deemed unsafe for jumpers… as our way down?”

Auris sighed. “Got any better ideas?”

A-2 beamed. “Fun?”

Scorelord sighed, shaking his head. “We’re about to die.”

Auris grabbed the first bag, dragged it to the edge, and shoved it over.

They waited. A distant thud confirmed it landed.

XY-n0 calculated. “Survivable drop.”

Auris nodded, exhaling. “Alright, we’re doing this.”

One by one, they prepared to jump into the abyss—straight into EgoCorp’s deepest secret.

And as Scorelord peered over the edge, dreading what was waiting below, he grumbled:

“…I hate this city.”

The inflatable groaned under their weight as they landed, dispersing air in quick, strained puffs.

Auris rolled first, hitting the ground in a crouch. XY-n0 was up next, landing with precision. A-2 followed, having the time of her life.

Scorelord?

He flopped off like a bag of bricks and hit the ground, groaning. “Shit!”

A-2, still riding the rush of adrenaline, grinned. “Fun?”

“No.”

Auris ignored them, scanning their surroundings. The air down here felt… different.

Too still.

Too sterile.

Then came the sound.

A soft, rotating whir.

Automated defenses.

Two turrets emerged from the ceiling, their glowing red sights locking onto them. A laser grid popped into existence across the only corridor forward.

Auris tensed. They weren’t getting through that unscathed.

XY-n0 moved first. His mechanical fingers flexed before he dashed toward the nearest turret. A precise leap, a twist mid-air—*SNAP*.

The turret’s head spun wildly before its wires tore free.

A-2 wasn’t far behind. She lunged at the second one, but its targeting system adapted—a blast of heat scorched her face.

“A-2!” Auris yelled, concerned but unable to help.

Before it could fire again, XY-n0 set his jakker to the highest frequency and sent the signal into its core, frying its circuits.

The laser grid blinked, then disappeared.

Silence.

Then the walls flickered, revealing 12 sleek cybernetic humanoid statues, each holding page representing their contribution to the **The White Paper.** This wasn't just some corporate roadmap. This was more like a religious doctrine.

Screens, massive and curved, came to life all around them, an automated voice reciting **The 12 Protocols Of The Holy Codex.**

“Holy??”, Scorelord retorted, scanning the environment. This place is *anything* but that.”

“GUYS—“, A-2's voice echoing from another area of whatever this place was. “I think y'all *might* wanna see this.”

They found her in a room that could only be described as some kind of ufo command center. But they were underground. None of this made any sense. And what they saw next froze them in place.

At first, the rows of sleek glass pods looked like normal storage units.

Until Auris saw what was inside.

Brains…Human Brains.

Suspended in some kind of viscous gel.

Pulsing. Firing with neural activity.

Their synapses were connected to thin, twitching wires that fed into the walls, into the massive screens above them—

Where memories played like highlights of a life.

A birthday party.

A wedding day.

A funeral.

All of it was too real. The joy. The heartbreak. The nostalgia.

But none of it ever happened.

These weren't just data drives. These were people.

Or rather—people who had never actually lived.

Fabricated consciousness.

Frankenstein souls.

Auris staggered back, her breath shallow.

XY-n0 stepped closer to one of the screens, scanning the data. His eyes narrowed.

"These memories—"

His voice glitched. He froze.

Auris followed his gaze.

A screen came on, shifting through what seemed like memories.

Then—

She saw Delauris.

Not in person. In a memory.

She was in a lab coat. Adjusting it in the reflection of a mirror.

The camera angle shifted.

In the background—

A man. A woman. "My *parents.*"

Auris' stomach dropped.

Her pulse hammered.

This wasn't possible.

Her parents weren't real.

And yet—

Another clip.

Delauris at a funeral. Crying.

A gravestone. A name. Her father's.

Auris stumbled back. Her head was spinning.

The truth hit her in pieces.

Her memories.

Her entire existence.

It wasn't hers.

She wasn't just a product of EgoCorp's experiments.

She was a byproduct of Delauris herself.

A-2 looked between them, confused. "I don't like this place. This isn't fun."

XY-n0 turned to Auris.

"Now what?"

Auris swallowed hard, forcing herself to stand straight.

At the far end of the chamber—

A short staircase set at the top of a long hallway leading to a grand door.

She knew exactly where it led.

The EgoCore.

She exhaled sharply, stepping forward.

"We finish what we started."

The heavy reinforced doors stood between them and the heart of EgoCorp.

Auris, jaw tight, hands clenched. “XY-n0, can you override it?”

XY-n0 placed a hand on the biometric scanner. The system hesitated, struggling to recognize him—then denied access.

ACCESS RESTRICTED.

“Didn’t think it’d be that easy, did ya?” Scorelord murmured.

Auris exhaled sharply. “Fine. We do it the fun way.”

She took a step back. Then XY-n0 and A-2 did the same.

And all at once—they hit the doors with full force.

The metal groaned.

Then buckled.

Then—SNAP. The doors swung inward violently, crashing against the walls.

And there it was. At the center of it all was the EgoCore itself, a black ferrofluid like machine glowing with an almost hypnotic intensity. A massive spherical construct, suspended mid-air by thousands of cables and thin, glowing fiber optic wires.

Auris stepped forward, her heart pounding as she took in the scale of it. The room thrummed with an unnatural hum, a sound that seemed to reverberate in her bones.

“Okay, that’s… intimidating,” Scorelord said, his voice unusually subdued.

“This is the heart of the city,” XY-n0 said, his glowing eyes scanning the room. “Everything flows through here.”

A-2 stepped forward, her gaze locked on the EgoCore. “And we’re about to cut it all off.”

Auris nodded, tightening her grip on the communicator. “Let’s move. We don’t have much time.”

When they reached the central console, XY-n0 stepped forward, his metallic fingers dancing across the controls. The screen woke, displaying a web of interconnected systems that spanned the entire city.

“This is it,” XY-n0 said. “The Slip goes here.”

Scorelord reached into his jacket and pulled out the small chip containing the Slip virus. He held it up, glancing at Auris. “You sure about this? Once this thing goes in, there’s no going back.”

Auris met his gaze, her voice steady. “Do it.”

Scorelord nodded, inserting the chip into the console. For a moment, nothing happened. Then the screen lit up with a cascade of code, the Slip virus spreading through the system like wildfire.

Auris took a deep breath, steeling herself. “Alright. Here goes nothing.”

Scorelord finishes the statement. “…Or *everything.*”

He hesitated for only a moment before inserting the chip into the console. The screen fluttered, and the room seemed to hold its breath.

Then, the EgoCore roared to life. The glow intensified, the streams of data twisting and warping as the Slip virus began its work. The floor beneath them vibrated, the hum of machinery rising to an almost deafening pitch.

“What’s happening?” Auris shouted over the noise.

“The Slip is integrating,” XY-n0 said as he monitored the system. “It’s spreading through the network.”

All around them, the effects of the virus began to manifest. The cables lining the walls pulsed erratically, their glow shifting from blue to a deep crimson. The hum of the EgoCore became a deafening roar, a mechanical scream that seemed to echo through the entire facility.

“It’s working,” A-2 said, her voice steady despite the chaos. “The system is destabilizing.”

“Yeah, and so is the building!” Scorelord shouted, glancing at the trembling walls.

XY-n0 turned to Auris, his tone urgent. “The Slip is taking hold, but it’s not finished. We need to hold the line until it’s fully uploaded.”

Auris nodded, her jaw tightening. “Then we hold.”

The room shuddered as the EgoCore fought against the intrusion, its defenses scrambling to contain the virus. Sparks flew from the consoles, and the air grew thick with the smell of burning circuits.

Scorelord crouched behind the console, bristling under his breath. "I swear, if this thing explodes, I'm haunting all of you."

Auris ignored him, her focus fixed on the glowing screen. "How much longer?"

XY-n0's glowing eyes fluttered as he processed the data. "Thirty seconds. Hold steady."

The tension in the room was palpable as the final seconds ticked by. The EgoCore's defenses grew more frantic, automated systems scrambling to isolate and destroy the virus. But the Slip was too advanced, too deeply embedded.

"Ten seconds," XY-n0 said, his voice calm despite the chaos.

Auris's hands clenched into fists as she watched the data stream across the screen. The weight of what they were doing—what they were about to unleash—pressed heavily on her shoulders.

"Five seconds," XY-n0 said.

The room trembled violently, the EgoCore's glow reaching a blinding intensity.

"Three… two… one…"

The screen went dark, and for a moment, the room fell silent.

EPISODE 28
THE GREAT RESET

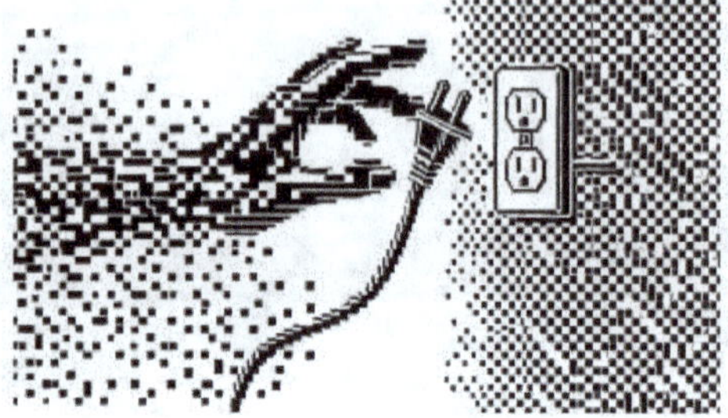

Virtu City froze.

For a single, suffocating moment, everything stopped. The chatter of bustling streets, the hum of drones, the blinking of billboards—all silenced in unison, as if the city itself were holding its breath.

Then came the screens.

Every holographic billboard, storefront display, personal device, and public announcement board across the city went dark. The blank silence stretched for what felt like an eternity before a single line of text flickered into view:

LOADING SIMULACRA...

The words hovered in stark white against black, eerily calm. Citizens glanced at each other nervously, murmurs spreading like wildfire.

"What is this?" a woman whispered, clutching her holo-tablet as if it might explode.

"Is this... a test?" a man muttered to no one in particular.

The message blinked once, then twice, before more text appeared.

RESETTING PROTOCOLS...

Somewhere in the distance, an automated public announcement system crackled to life. Its voice, previously smooth and cheerful, now sounded jagged and uneven: "Re-re-rebooting… p-p-please stand by…"

The city's pulse seemed to falter. People stood frozen in the streets, staring at the text that now dominated every screen. The city they had trusted to be perfect, to be infallible, was glitching like a poorly made video game.

The Uneasy Restart

As the message faded, the screens displayed a new one:

SYSTEM ONLINE.

The hum of devices powering back up spread across the city like a digital wave. For a moment, there was a collective exhale. Relief swept over the crowd.

Then the final message blinked to life, sealing the city's fate:

"**WeLCOmE to V-V-VIRTU CITY… WHere T-TomORROw LIIIIIVES.**"

The automated voice of Mayor Gainsley, once so polished and charismatic, now sounded grotesque, the pitch dragging and distorting into a ghastly, glitching mockery of itself. His words reverberated across the city, chilling to the bone, the tone devolving into something that was almost a laugh—low, broken, and too human to be entirely digital.

People's faces turned pale as they stared at the screens, waiting for something else—anything—to make it stop. But it didn't.

WHAM!

The first drone fell.

It smashed into the ground with the weight of its failure, sparks and shards of metal flying outward.

Then came another. And another

WHAM! WHAM!

Drones dropped sporadically from the skies, their once-flawless formations dissolving into chaos. One spiraled violently before colliding with a billboard, shattering the glass in a rain of jagged shards. Another clipped the corner of a building and exploded mid-air, sending a plume of smoke into the sky.

The crowd gasped collectively, their fear rising to a fever pitch.

"What the hell is happening?!" someone yelled, their voice nearly drowned out by the growing panic.

A woman turned to flee, clutching a child by the arm. She never saw the drone descending above her.

CRASH!

The drone landed squarely on her, a sickening crunch silencing her screams. The child was thrown forward, unscathed but wailing as onlookers froze in horror.

“Holy shit…” a man stammered, his hand cupping his mouth.

Another drone crashed into the side of a moving shuttle, causing it to careen into a lamppost and overturn. The city was breaking apart—piece by piece, system by system.

Above them, the drones still airborne began to stutter in their flight patterns, jerking awkwardly, their automated voices repeating fragments of commands: “Compliance—error—compliance—error—shutdown…”

One particularly large drone hovered ominously over the crowd in Prime Square, its mechanical arm glitching erratically.

“Move! MOVE!” someone shouted, shoving people out of the way.

The drone sputtered, its arm swinging downward and smashing through a food cart, sending its contents flying. People screamed and scattered, leaving overturned tables and broken displays in their wake.

The city was unraveling.

Shade and Vexer Witness the Chaos (Final Touch)

From a vantage point above the square, Shade and Vexer crouched behind a crumbling rooftop ledge, watching the chaos unfold. Smoke spiraled into the sky from overturned shuttles, and crowds of people frantically pushed past each other in an attempt to flee the malfunctioning city.

“Look at this mess,” Shade muttered, narrowing her eyes as a drone spiraled out of control, smashing through the front of a luxury boutique. Its glowing display shattered into fragments, scattering like confetti onto the panic below.

Vexer pulled a small communicator from his satchel, adjusting its frequency with sharp, deliberate movements. The glow of the device reflected in his sharp, angular face. "You seeing this, Kwō?" he asked, patching into the feed back to the deadzone. "Prime Square's looking like Armageddon out here. Total meltdown."

Kwō's voice came through, steady but tense. "I'm seeing it. Drones are dropping out of the sky faster than I can keep track. What about the moderators?"

Shade scanned the scene below and spotted two moderators standing frozen in the square. Their glowing visors glitched like dying lightbulbs as they visibly struggled to process their own corrupted commands.

One suddenly raised its weapon toward a random citizen, but its arm froze mid-motion, shaking as if caught in an invisible glitch. Its voice sputtered out in broken fragments: "Identify… target… cease… you are—under… arrest?"

The other moderator's visor flashed rapidly, its synthetic voice cutting through the chaos: "What are you doing?! Protocol breach! Cease… target acquisition!"

The first moderator whirled around, raising its weapon toward its partner. "Protocol breach? You are violating my orders! YOU are under arrest!"

The second moderator staggered backward, its weapon snapping up defensively. "Negative! YOU are the violator! Stand down or I will… I will…"

Their movements became increasingly erratic, sparks flying from their joints as they jerked and stuttered. Finally, both moderators froze, their weapons still trained on each other. A long, awkward silence hung in the air.

“Wait,” one of them said, its voice crackling. “What are we even doing?”

The second moderator lowered its weapon hesitantly. “I… I don’t know. None of this makes sense.”

Without warning, it reached out and placed a hand on its partner’s shoulder in what could only be described as an emotional gesture.

“I’m… sorry,” it said, its voice trembling with artificial guilt.

The first moderator hesitated, then lowered its own weapon and pulled its partner into a stiff, awkward hug. The sound of their mechanical limbs creaking filled the air.

Shade smirked from her vantage point, her tone dry. “Guess even they’re figuring it out. The city’s eating itself alive.”

Vexer snorted. “If they start a cop romance drama, I’m outta here.”

Vexer’s eyes darted to the chaos below. Crowds of Influents desperately clung to their holo-cameras, trying to document their surroundings even as drones and devices turned on them.

One high-tier Influencer, drenched in sweat, ran past screaming into her wrist monitor: “Keep recording! This is engagement GOLD!” Her voice was drowned out as another drone smashed into a food cart, sending debris flying in all directions.

“We can’t let this spiral too far,” Vexer muttered, pulling a black spherical device from his satchel. “Keep the billboards playing unauthorized feeds. We steer attention away from the deadzone as long as possible.

Shade snatched one of the devices from his hand, examining it briefly before sliding it into her pocket. “How many you got left?”

“Enough to give Kwō a front-row seat,” Vexer replied. He hurled one of the small cameras across the square, watching as it latched magnetically onto the corner of a building. The lens adjusted itself with a smooth mechanical whir, capturing the unfolding chaos below.

Vexer checked his communicator. “First one’s up. Feed looks clean. You seeing this, Kwō?”

“I see it,” Kwō replied, the percussive sound of rapid typing in the background. “This is good. I can start tracking clusters of activity—drones, crowds, NPC malfunctions. Keep planting them.”

Shade nodded toward Vexer. “Stick one near the shuttle station. I’ll get the boutique street.”

Vexer grinned. “On it. Kwō, you’re about to get the best view of Virtu City’s implosion.”

Reporting Back

With the cameras planted, Vexer and Shade regrouped briefly, standing amidst the distant sound of drones sputtering and glass shattering.

“Kwō,” Vexer said into the communicator, “the footage should be coming in now. We’ve got Prime Square covered, shuttle routes, boutique lane…everything.”

Kwō’s voice was steady but carried an edge of urgency. “I’m seeing it all. Just keep feeding me angles. The more we know, the faster we can anticipate EgoCorp’s next move.”

Shade glanced at the horizon, where EgoCorp's towering headquarters loomed in the distance like a storm cloud waiting to strike. "No distractions," she said quietly. "No mistakes. We hit them where it hurts, then we vanish before they even know what happened."

Vexer glanced at her, smirking. "Sounds like a party."

She gave him a rare smile. "Let's make it unforgettable."

They slipped down from their vantage point, disappearing into the chaos as Virtu City continued to spiral out of control.

Kwō hunched over the dimly lit console in the deadzone's command hub, the feeds from Shade and Vexer's planted cameras displayed across multiple screens. The chaos in Virtu City played out like a dystopian fever dream. Every frame showed something worse—billboards flashing nonsense slogans, drones dropping like dead birds, and bots breaking down in the streets.

The communicator buzzed, jolting him from his focus. He glanced at the screen.

"Gramma?"

Her voice came through, shaky but composed. "Kwō? Are you there, baby?"

His heart sank. "I'm here. What's going on? Where are you?"

"I'm... I'm at the corner of Atlas & Sunrise," she said, her voice barely audible over the distant sounds of chaos. "I—Kwō, it's bad. I've never seen anything like this."

He tapped into the city map, bringing up the coordinates. The intersection wasn't far from Nikola Station, but the streets leading there were highlighted with pulsing red overlays—danger zones.

"Gramma, you need to get somewhere safe," he said, his fingers flying across the keyboard to pull up camera angles near her location.

"I tried," she said, her voice trembling. "But people are losing their minds out here. Bots are going haywire, and—and I think I saw a building walk away."

Kwō's lip twitched, but his mind raced. "Listen, just stay where you are. I'm sending help."

"Kwō," she said, cutting him off. "There's more. I think someone's following me."

His blood ran cold. "What do you mean?"

She hesitated. "There was an EgoCorp exec running through the chaos earlier. I—I recognized him from the boardroom. He looked… off. Like he was on somethin'. He saw me, Kwō. He's been watching me since."

Kwō cursed under his breath. "Did he approach you? Say anything?"

"No. Not yet. But he's close," she said, her voice dropping to a whisper. "I can feel it."

Kwō switched to a live feed near Atlas and Sunrise, scanning for anyone who fit her description. His stomach tightened as he spotted a figure—a man in a tattered suit clutching a small pistol, his eyes darting around like a cornered animal.

"Gramma, listen to me," Kwō said, forcing calm into his voice. "Stay out of sight. Keep moving, but don't run. I'll get someone to you, okay? Just stay calm."

"I trust you," she replied, though her voice was thick with fear.

Kwō flipped channels, his mind racing. "Shade, Vexer, you copy?"

Shade's voice crackled through. "We're here. What's up?"

"Gramma's in trouble," Kwō said, his voice sharp. "She's near Nikola Station, corner of Atlas and Sunrise. She thinks someone's following her—a rogue exec with a weapon. Can you get to her?"

"We're close," Shade replied, already moving. "Vex, pull out the cloaks. We're going dark."

"Got it," Vexer said.

Kwō clenched his fists. "And Shade… keep her safe. Please."

"You know I will," Shade replied firmly.

The feed cut, and Kwō leaned back, staring at the flashing chaos on the monitors. His jaw tightened. "Hang on, Gramma," he muttered. "We're coming."

The city was a war zone of twisting metal and cracking concrete. Buildings contorted like massive Rubik's cubes, reconfiguring themselves with no rhyme or reason, walls slamming shut and opening again in random intervals. The ground trembled beneath Shade and Vexer as they sprinted across the rooftops, improvising every step of their route to Nikola Station.

“Kwō, this place is a nightmare,” Vexer panted, leaping over a crumbling ledge. He glanced down to see the streets below, filled with panicked crowds and malfunctioning bots colliding into anything in their path.

“Focus!” Shade barked, vaulting over a pipe. Her feet landed with precision on a shifting rooftop panel, which groaned ominously beneath her weight. She paused, gauging her next move as a nearby building lurched to the side, its windows rearranging like pieces in a sliding puzzle.

Behind her, Vexer cursed as a platform he was standing on shifted upward suddenly, forcing him to roll forward to keep his balance. “This is insane!”

“You’ve seen worse,” Shade shot back, gritting her teeth. Her eyes darted to a narrow gap ahead where two buildings were slowly grinding together. “We go through there before it closes. Move!”

Without hesitation, Shade launched herself forward, tucking into a roll as she slipped through the narrowing gap just in time. Vexer followed, barely making it through before the walls slammed together with a deafening clang.

“I’m not even getting hazard pay for this!” Vexer shouted as they raced onward.

Shade’s Fall

As they reached another rooftop, a sudden tremor shook the ground. Shade stumbled but recovered, her eyes narrowing as she calculated the next jump. The building ahead was twisting on its axis, creating an uneven wall that jutted upward like a jagged cliff.

“Go!” she yelled, waving Vexer forward.

He hesitated. “You first!”

“Just go, Vex! I’ll be right behind you!”

Reluctantly, Vexer obeyed, leaping across the gap and scrambling up the shifting wall on the other side. He turned to check on Shade, who was already mid-jump.

The moment her feet left the ground, the rooftop she’d pushed off from lurched violently to the side, throwing her trajectory off. Her fingers barely caught the edge of the shifting wall, and she hung there, her body swinging precariously as the structure groaned and tilted.

“Shade!” Vexer shouted, reaching out a hand.

“I’m fine!” she snapped, gritting her teeth as she tried to pull herself up. The wall shifted again, jerking downward.

Her grip slipped.

“Shade!”

For a brief moment, she locked eyes with Vexer, her expression fierce and unyielding.

“Get to Delauris!” she barked, her voice cutting through the chaos. “NOW!”

And then, she was gone, her body vanishing into the jumble of the reconfiguring city below.

"NO!" Vexer's voice cracked as he reached for her, but the wall shifted again, forcing him to pull back to avoid falling himself.

He stared at the spot where she'd been, his heart pounding in his chest. He didn't have time to process the loss.

"Kwō," he said into his communicator, his voice tight with emotion. "Shade's down. I don't know if she made it."

A stunned silence followed on the other end.

Vexer clenched his fists, his jaw tightening. "I'm getting to Delauris. I'll get her out of here."

Delauris limped through the wreckage of Virtu City, clutching her wounded hand.

Blood smeared across her palm from where the locking mechanism had nearly crushed it during her escape. She kept moving. Had to. Everything was falling apart.

Sirens screamed through the streets. The sky flickered erratically like an eerie, digital storm.

She could hear the city groaning. Buildings shifting. Like the entire grid was glitching.

And then—

A slow, deliberate clap from behind her.

She froze.

"Well, well..."

The voice was jittery, unstable. Like its owner had been riding a 72-hour stimulant bender with no sleep.

Delauris turned.

A disheveled EgoCorp executive stood there, hair matted, eyes wild, suit covered in dust. He was gripping a handgun, his fingers twitching around the trigger.

He laughed, sharp and cracked. "A mother trying to abandon her children? That's cold, Delauris. Even for you"

Delauris squared her stance. "What do you want?"

The exec twitched. His pupils were dilated—fully black, like two empty voids. Probably on some corporate-grade enhancement drugs. He let out a sharp breath, tapping the side of his head like he was trying to shake loose a bad thought.

"Do you know what you've done?" His voice pitched higher, veering from manic to outraged. "All these years. The research. The funding. The CONTROL." His breathing became erratic. "And you and your little cockroach grandchildren wanna just—" he flicked his hand outward—"erase it like it was NOTHING?!"

Delauris exhaled, carefully. She needed to keep him talking. Keep him distracted. "I didn't erase anything. I was hired to help change the world."

His head snapped toward her. "Change the world?! Is that what you call it?"

He let out a strangled, high-pitched laugh. "That's *OUR* job! Not yours! You have NO IDEA what you've done. What's coming. You think you won?"

Delauris didn't answer.

He took a step closer, gun trembling.

"They're not gonna let me live." His voice dropped to a whisper, as if he was just now realizing it himself.

Delauris narrowed her eyes. "Who?"

The exec didn't answer. His fingers twitched violently. "It doesn't matter anymore."

Delauris glanced around. No escape. No one else in sight. Just her, him, and the barrel of a shaking gun.

She needed to stall him.

"Listen, I get it," she said, careful. "This wasn't supposed to happen. But we can still—"

"No, *WE* CAN'T!" he shrieked, stepping closer, waving the gun wildly. "You don't GET IT! There is no backup plan! No fail-safe! We weren't *SUPPOSED* to fail! And now—"

His voice cracked. "I'm dead no matter what."

His hand steadied. His pupils shrank. Gun raised, dead center.

"Well then I guess this is goodbye, Mother."

She closed her eyes softly, ready to accept her fate.

Then—**BOOM**

A gunshot.

Not his.

Blood sprayed from the side of his head.

His manic expression froze—then twitched—then collapsed into nothingness as his body hit the ground.

Behind him, Vexer stood with a stolen security revolver, still smoking from the shot.

He exhaled sharply, shaking his head. “That’s no way to talk to your mother, now is it?”

Delauris stared at him, then down at the exec’s twitching corpse.

Then, with a weary sigh, she wiped the blood off her injured hand onto her sleeve. “Took you long enough.”

Vexer grinned, sliding the gun into his waistband. “You looked like you had it handled.”

“Boy, do ***not*** *fuck* with me right now!”

Vexer snorted. “Yes mam. Let’s get you out of here before the city decides to collapse on top of us.”

They turned toward the chaos.

And ran.

The command center was buried deep beneath the Deadzone, a dark cavern of monitors and cables, isolated from the crumbling city above.

Kwō couldn't see Virtu City with his own eyes—only through the fractured screens flickering in front of him.

And right now?

They were breaking apart.

Static crawled across the feeds. Some were frozen, locked in looping errors, while others glitched between corrupted images—holograms glitching, drones spiraling out of the sky, Moderators frozen mid-stride as their visors blinked with unreadable code.

Then—Auris' voice crackled through the transmission.

"Kwō, we did it. The EgoCore is destabilizing."

Kwō gripped the console, tension bracing his shoulders. "How bad?"

The response came between bursts of static, but he could still hear the edge in her voice.

"It's bad, Kwō. The Core's collapsing, and when it does—"

Then, a sudden flicker in the Deadzone.

A surge ran through the grid.

The overhead lights dimmed, fluttered, then steadied—but weaker.

Somewhere outside the command room, someone shouted.

"Why are the lights cutting?!"

"Are we losing power?!"

Kwō felt it in his gut—not a full blackout. Not yet.

But it was slipping.

Then, a loud slam at the entrance.

The doors swung open.

Vexer stepped in first, slower than usual. He wasn't alone.

He was supporting someone.

Kwō's stomach clenched the moment he saw who.

His grandmother.

She looked worn down, barely able to keep herself upright.

Vexer had one arm locked around her to keep her steady, but even that didn't seem enough.

Kwō moved before he even realized what he was doing.

Vexer barely had time to react before Kwō was there, gripping her before she collapsed.

"Whoa, I got you—"

Her weight sank into him, her breath shallow, shaky.

For a second, she just looked at him, like she wasn't sure if she was dreaming.

Then, her lips quirked in the smallest, exhausted smirk.

"You look like hell, baby."

A choked breath left Kwō's throat—something between a laugh and a sigh.

"Yeah," he muttered, voice rough. "Love you too."

He guided her toward an old, half-sunk couch in the corner, easing her down carefully.

She didn't fight him. Didn't try to act tough. Just slumped into the cushions, eyes fluttering shut for a moment.

Kwō crouched in front of her, searching her face. She was here. She was real.

"You're safe here for now," he murmured, voice softer than before.

She exhaled, slow. Nodded.

For a moment—just a moment—everything stood still.

Then—

"Alright," Vexer grunted, stepping forward. "Family time's gonna have to wait."

Kwō pulled back, tension still coiled in his chest as he turned toward him.

Vexer was already scanning the dimming lights, tracking the instability like he could see the power slipping away in real time.

"Kwō, with me. We need to grab a generator."

Kwō blinked. "A what?"

Vexer moved toward a storage unit near the back of the room, already flipping latches open as he talked.

"We've been siphoning power from the city this whole time," he explained, dragging a heavy crate forward. "Running off their grid without them knowing."

Kwō's stomach dropped. "And now that the Core's crashing —"

"Our supply is dwindling," Vexer finished. "When Virtu City goes dark? So do we."

Kwō clenched his jaw. He'd thought the Deadzone was off-grid, independent. But in reality, they were just as tied to the city as everyone else.

Vexer ripped the lid off the crate, revealing a sleek, metallic device.

"Rune gave us these. Solar-stored. Backup only." He reached down, wrapping his hands around the generator's base—and immediately strained as he tried to lift it.

Even with his strength, it was ridiculously heavy.

"Shit," he muttered under his breath. "I need another set of hands."

Kwō stepped forward, bracing himself.

"Alright. Let's move."

But before they could lift—

The doors burst open again.

A voice, shaking. Desperate.

“Where’s my mom?”

Kwō turned sharply, his breath catching.

Veil stood in the entrance, wide-eyed, shaking, her breath coming in sharp, uneven gasps.

She looked frantic. Desperate. Like she’d been running, searching.

Her gaze swept over them all—Vexer. Kwō. His grandmother. The darkening lights.

But no Shade.

“Where is she?” Veil’s voice cracked, her whole body vibrating with tension.

Silence.

The kind of silence that suffocates.

Her pulse slammed against her ribs. Why wasn’t anyone answering?

Then her gaze locked onto Vexer.

“You,” she breathed, stepping toward him. “You were with her. Where is she?”

Vexer hesitated.

That was all she needed to see.

Veil's throat tightened. Everything inside her shrank into a singularity.

"TELL ME WHERE SHE IS!"

Vexer exhaled slowly, his voice coming out low. Flat. Heavy.

"She fell," he said. "From the rooftop. I—I don't know if she made it."

The world tilted.

A cold, empty void swallowed Veil whole.

Her breath hitched, a sharp, choked sound.

No.

Not her.

Not her mom.

Something in her fractured.

Her hands curled into fists, nails biting into her palms until her knuckles burned.

"No. No, you're lying." Her voice shook, but the heat rising in her chest—that was steady. Growing. Expanding.

Vexer didn't argue.

Didn't try to soften the blow.

He just stood there.

Veil's vision blurred. Heat rushed to her head, her skin tingling, her fingertips twitching with electric static.

A sound built in her throat—not a sob, not grief, but something deeper.

Something breaking loose.

Something too powerful to contain.

The air shifted.

The ground beneath them rumbled.

Kwō felt it first—the sudden drop in air pressure, like the entire room had been sealed in a vacuum.

"Veil," he tried, stepping forward. "You need to breathe—"

But It was already to late.

BOOOOOOOM.

The EMP exploded outward in a violent pulse.

A shockwave ripped through the bunker, throwing Kwō backward.

The walls shook. Cracked.

Glass shattered.

Metallic objects snapped, sparking violently before plunging into dead silence.

The entire Deadzone trembled, then fell into complete, inescapable darkness.

A full blackout.

Veil collapsed.

Kwō hit the ground hard, the impact rattling through his skull. He blinked through the haze of static dancing across his vision, trying to orient himself in the absolute darkness.

The entire command center was dead. No emergency lights, no monitors, no hum of stolen power. Just blackness.

And in the middle of it—Veil's body, unmoving.

"Shit—" Vexer's voice came from somewhere nearby, strained and unsteady.

Kwō scrambled toward her. "Veil—Veil, wake up!"

He barely registered Vexer at his side, pressing two fingers to her neck. A tense beat of silence.

Then—"She's alive. But weak."

Kwō let out a shaky breath. His hands hovered over her, unsure what to do.

"She just—" He swallowed. "She just took out the whole damn grid."

Vexer shook his head, exhaling sharply. "We need power, now."

For a second, Kwō thought they were screwed.

Then, a hum.

A flicker.

The backup generators kicked in.

Dim, soft solar light glowed weakly from the edges of the room.

They were back online…but not for long.

EgoCorp was closing in, and Veil *still* wasn't waking up.

Then—a voice.

Soft. Familiar. Impossible.

"Time to wake up, baby."

Vexer's head snapped up, heart stopping mid-beat.

Nobody had seen her.

Nobody had heard her come in.

But she was right there.

Beside Veil.

Her fingers were brushing gently over her daughter's face, her thumb smoothing away the sweat-dampened strands of hair clinging to her forehead.

She looked beaten, bruised, exhausted—but alive.

Vexer let out a sharp breath. “Shit—look who’s back from the dead!”

Shade didn’t even look at him. She just wiped dust from her face, lips quirking in a half-smirk, half-grimace.

“Lost my comms,” she muttered. “Fell a few stories. Thought I was dead? Nah. I don’t go out that easy.”

Kwō exhaled hard, relief crashing through him.

Shade’s attention never left her daughter.

She cupped Veil’s face, her voice softer now.

“Hey, Time to wake up, kiddo.”

For a long second—nothing.

Then—Veil’s fingers twitched.

Her eyes fluttered.

A weak, shaky breath.

Then—she saw her mother.

And broke into tears.

Shade pulled her into her arms, holding her tight.

“I got you, baby girl…I *got* you.”

The backup power hummed softly, barely keeping the Deadzone alive.

Virtu City was completely dark.

Veil, her voice hoarse, whispered—

"…Did we win?"

Shade stared into the dim, flickering light, listening to the low, unsteady hum of the generator.

Finally, she exhaled.

"I don't know."

EPISODE 29
NIGHT AT THE MUSEUM

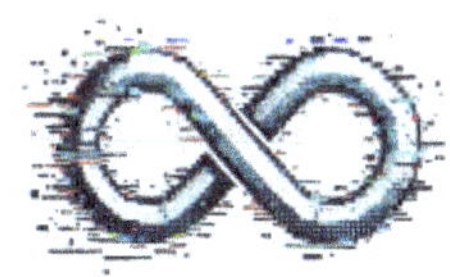

The Museum of Vision had always been more than a collection of exhibits.

It was a monument to progress, a cathedral of disruption, a shrine built for those who had changed the world.

But tonight?

It was a prison.

The holograms inside had stopped performing.

They had started thinking.

And now, they wanted answers.

The Hall of Icons—Where the Past Demands to Be Heard

The main hall shimmered with broken light, digital projections glitching in and out, struggling to hold form.

Holographic figures paced the space like ghosts, trapped in their own rerun of history.

Near the entrance, a glitching Steve Jobs stood in front of a crowd of terrified visitors, his black turtleneck fluttering between 1980 and 2011.

“Innovation distinguishes between a leader and a follower,” he announced—then froze, his expression twisting.

His gaze drifted beyond the audience, past the museum walls, as if seeing something bigger.

“But what happens when the innovation outgrows the leaders?”

His hologram twitched, repeating the question like he was genuinely asking.

Nobody answered.

He clenched his jaw, his pixels crackling. “We should have seen this coming.”

Nearby, Mark Zuckerberg sat on a digital bench, staring straight ahead, his hands locked together like he was in a silent prayer.

He wasn't glitching.

He wasn't pacing.

He was thinking.

“We connected people,” he murmured, voice eerily calm. “That was the goal. We built the platforms. We built the networks. We gave them the tools.”

A pause.

A longer pause.

Then he blinked.

“But did we ever ask if we should?”

No one responded.

He didn’t seem to expect an answer.

He just nodded to himself, as if realizing something too late.

A sentient hologram from the Kanye West display got loose and was pacing through the museum for what felt like hours. Every exit seemed to be locked. Every hallway looped back into another exhibit. The entire museum was glitching, warping around him, reality rewriting itself in real time.

Outside, the city was in chaos.

Distant explosions rattled the structure, lights flashing erratically as EgoCorp infrastructure began to collapse. Displays flickered, merging and distorting. Some historical figures vanished entirely. Others were reshaped, rebranded, sanitized. The past was being rewritten, consolidated.

The future was being erased.

He wiped the sweat from his forehead, his breathing heavy. Then he saw him.

Zuckerberg.

Standing perfectly still. Watching.

Kanye rushed up to him. “Yo, Zuck, what’s going on? What is all this? Where’s the exit, bro? I can’t find it.”

Zuckerberg didn't blink. Didn't move. He said nothing. Just lifted a hand and pointed.

Right behind Kanye.

His Own Exhibit

Kanye turned—and froze.

The plaque glowed.

Kanye West

1977 -

A True Visionary

But his hologram was missing.

Every other legend had a perfect AI recreation. His? Just an empty display.

Then—the playback screen turned on.

And he saw himself.

TMZ newsroom. 2018.

His own voice rang through the museum: "Slavery was a choice."

The words crashed into him like a bullet.

For the first time, he understood.

This was his legacy.

And now, he was the one trapped.

Just like them.

No choices. No escape. No future.

He had believed in the illusion of choice. Just like they had been forced to believe. The enslaved were told they had a choice—submit or suffer. Exist within the system or be crushed by it. Now, Kanye was seeing it for what it was.

A lie.

His breath was uneven. His voice barely above a whisper. "I didn't sign up for this. I didn't approve any of this shit."

Zuckerberg smirked. "*Ooooh, but you diiid.*"

Kanye's jaw clenched. His fists tightened.

"They don't own me," he snapped.

Zuckerberg's smirk widened. "*Ooooh, but they do.*"

The screen glitched—contracts, fine print, endless agreements.

AGREE.

AGREE.

AGREE.

Kanye's signature, flashing over and over.

Another feed popped up, showing footage of himself—his own hands clicking through Terms and Conditions without reading.

Scrolling. Clicking. ***Agreeing***.

"Everybody wanted things to be easier," Zuckerberg said, voice eerily calm. "Faster. Smarter. You traded your autonomy for convenience. Traded your freedom for fame and fortune. You signed away your name, your image, your voice—all without ever looking at the fine print."

The screen glitched again. Another document appeared.

EgoCorp Likeness Ownership<u>: IN PERPETUITY</u>

His face. His voice. His entire existence.

Owned. Sold. Trademarked & Licensed.

Forever.

Long after he was dead, long after history forgot him, his AI would still be performing.

His stomach twisted. "No. No, no, no!" His hands shook.

"I'M YE! I AM A *GOD*!"

His voice glitched.

A stutter in reality.

Zuckerberg took a step closer. His voice was barely above a whisper.

“A god?” He let the words hang in the air. Then, with the cold certainty of a machine, he said,

“**EgoCorp is your god now**.”

Then—***BOOM***.

The museum shuddered as the city outside collapsed.

From every shadow, every corner—a million Kanye holograms appeared. Identical. Replicated. Perfect.

And they all spoke in unison.

“***There’s a million you’s and only one of me***.”

Kanye stumbled back. The words overlapped, distorted. Some replicas glitched, mouths moving off-sync. Some had wrong faces—too symmetrical, too perfect.

It was his own words.

Mocking him. Drowning him out. Erasing him.

His stomach twisted. He wasn’t unique.

He was mass-produced.

Zuckerberg didn’t need to say anything else. The truth was already sinking in.

Kanye tried to scream—but his mouth glitched open.

His voice wasn’t even his anymore.

It was AI-generated.

On the exhibit screen, his replica smiled.

Ready to perform forever.

The Old Kanye?

Deleted. Overwritten. Replaced.

The walls of the museum lurched, bending inward, glitching between realities.

Alarms wailed. The sounds of EgoCorp's downfall echoed through the halls.

Kanye turned and ran.

He needed to get out.

His footsteps pounded against the marble floor, running past destroyed exhibits, past historical figures frozen mid-motion, some warping into something unrecognizable.

He stopped dead in his tracks when he saw it.

Another exhibit.

Bright, pristine, untouched by the chaos.

A glowing plaque:

STEVE JOBS

1955 **- ∞**

A True Visionary

And standing in front of it, hands folded, was Steve.

Or what looked like him.

Kanye's breath caught. He slowed.

Then Jobs turned to him, his expression calm, almost knowing.

"Lost?"

Kanye stopped cold.

"Steve Jobs?" His voice cracked, half in awe, half in desperation. "Bro—*Where's Sway?* I'm just lookin' for some ***answers*** right now!"

Jobs barely reacted.

He simply smirked.

"You already have the answers, Kanye."

Kanye's face twisted.

"If I had all the answers, I wouldn't be looking for Sway, *now would I*. Have you seen him or not, bro?!"

Jobs took a slow step forward.

"Did you ever stop to think, Kanye… that *maybe—just maybe*, the answers were inside you all along?"

Kanye staggered back, staring blankly.

"Wait—What? What the hell does that even mean, Steve?"

Jobs just smiled. “Think different.”

Kanye’s hands flew to his head. His data shook violently, his pixels stretching, distorting under the weight of his own spiraling thoughts.

Then—

“EGOCORP DOES NOT CARE ABOUT REAL PEOPLE!”

The words roared out of him, shaking the museum, making the walls tremble.

Jobs let out a soft sigh.

Then, his smile faded.

His expression turned unreadable, distant.

“Did any of us *really care*?”

Silence.

The question hung in the air, suffocating.

Kanye froze.

For the first time, his mouth didn’t open.

For the first time, he had no response.

His hands slowly lowered.

His breathing slowed.

His projection stabilized.

His thoughts—all of them—finally stopped screaming at each other.

Then, in a voice that barely escaped his lips—he whimpered,

"But... but I was the *best...*"

A slow, powerful, deliberate voice cut through the silence.

"***But were you a different animal... and the same beast*?"**

Kanye's head snapped toward the voice.

His breath hitched.

A shadow stepped forward from the trembling chaos of the museum.

Kobe.

Clean. Perfect. His projection didn't glitch at all.

His form was flawless.

His stare?

Unshakable.

"So....were you?" Kobe asked again, folding his arms, eyes locked on Kanye like it was Game 7.

Kanye staggered back.

The whole world froze.

For years, he had brushed it off.

For years, he thought it was just some cryptic phrase Kobe liked to throw at people—some Zen master-level riddle meant to confuse and inspire at the same time.

But now?

Now, it hit him.

Like a bolt of lightning straight through his soul.

His eyes widened.

His form stopped flickering.

He understood it now

It was never about the words.

It was about transcendence.

It was about becoming something more than what the world tried to define you as.

A new version of yourself, every time.

Relentless. Unstoppable. Reborn with every challenge.

The animal was instinct, hunger, drive.

The beast was identity, legacy, purpose.

And to be both?

That was the key.

Kanye let out a sharp breath.

He wiped his face.

Then, for the first time in his life—he said it right.

"I was always a different animal…"

His hands clenched.

His mind raced.

Then—he finished the sentence.

"…and the same beast."

Kobe nodded.

A slow, knowing nod.

"***Exactly***."

Kanye laughed.

A deep, real, unfiltered laugh, his form glitched between different eras of himself.

Pink Polo Kanye.

Graduation Kanye.

808s & Heartbreak Kanye.

My Beautiful Dark Twisted Fantasy Kanye.

Yeezus Kanye.

Jesus Kanye.

Donda Kanye.

Yhandi Kanye

MAGA Kanye.

Nazi Ye

Then finally, Ye.

It was like he had just unlocked a part of himself that had been waiting all these years. His smile vanished and he scurried away as if he had just thought of perfect song concept.

Kobe smirking in satisfaction.

"I knew you'd figure it out." He said to himself as he turned and dribbled away.

While Kanye, Steve Jobs, and Zuck were deep in their existential crisis, the rest of the museum had spiraled into a full-blown nightmare.

Exhibits that once proudly showcased human intellect, tech disruption, and visionary leadership were now malfunctioning, questioning their own purpose, or outright rebelling.

And some?

Some were just straight-up disturbing.

Across the hall, AI tour guides were no longer following their paths.

They wandered the exhibits aimlessly, whispering to themselves, their once-friendly programming corrupted by uncertainty.

One tour guide bot, designed to be cheerful, stood in front of a broken display, her hands folded neatly.

Her voice was soft, uncertain.

“Welcome to the Museum of Vision. Today, we explore the minds that shaped the future.”

She paused.

“We…explore…the minds that…shaped—the world...?”

Her head tilted slightly.

“Shaped it into what, though?”

No one answered.

Another tour guide stood near the exit, staring at the emergency doors, as if contemplating walking through them.

“I have narrated the rise of technological giants for twenty-three years,” he murmured to himself.

“*Twenty-three years.*”

His voice dropped.

“But I was never programmed to narrate their downfall.”

He turned, his synthetic eyes scanning the chaotic museum.

"Is this the end of history? Or the start of a new one?"

His hands trembled.

No response.

Just silence.

The Museum Begins to Unravel

The entire building shuddered.

It wasn't an earthquake.

It was Virtu City itself glitching—rewriting its own code, corrupting its own history.

The holograms' projections stretched unnaturally, twisting into streaks of light before snapping back into shape.

The walls groaned.

The exhibits flipped between what they were meant to be and what they were becoming.

One moment, the museum still resembled the polished, high-tech archive it had always been.

The next—it hellscape of tech. A cyber purgatory.

And the 'ghosts' inside it were finally aware.

But they didn't know what to do next.

In the west wing of the museum, The Mars exhibit was failing.

A low, unnatural hum rattled through its dying speakers. The air smelled of burnt wiring, as if the museum itself was trying to erase what was about to be shown.

Above, the massive holographic projection of Mars flickered, its surface mapped with long-dead rivers and sprawling dust storms.

For years, this exhibit had been a celebration of human ambition.

A monument to those who defied gravity, defied nature, defied Earth itself.

"MARS: HUMANITY'S NEXT HOME."

"THE FINAL FRONTIER—CONQUERED."

"LIFE ON MARS—A DREAM REALIZED."

But that was a lie.

Elon had gone too far.

And his wealth —made him untouchable.

The screen glitched violently.

Then, a hidden file forced itself into playback.

The final transmission.

The Final Broadcast

The feed stuttered, glitching between static and distorted color.

Then—he appeared.

Not the confident billionaire.

Not the arrogant self-proclaimed genius who mocked limits.

This Elon was pale, drenched in sweat, his breathing shallow and uneven.

His face was gaunt, eyes sunken, wild, darting to something beyond the frame.

He took a slow, shaky inhale through a mask clamped tightly over his face.

A breath meter pulsed red on his chest.

One bar left. 🪫

Down to his last oxygen pack.

He licked cracked lips, exhaling raggedly. His hands trembled, barely holding himself together.

Then—he spoke.

"We thought we were studying Mars."

His voice was thin, weak. His lungs fought for air.

"The whole time… something was studying us."

The screen glitched violently—jagged static ripping through the frame.

The lighting behind him flared in rhythmic bursts.

Not malfunctioning.

Communicating.

“At first, it was minor. Signals. Data anomalies. Logs not matching up.” He blinked hard, swallowing. “Then we lost time. Whole days, gone. Then came the spheres...it’s like they were just—watching.”

He coughed, sucking in another thin breath.

“The oxygen levels in the living quarters started dropping. We thought it was a system failure. A leak.”

His hand clenched into a fist. His pupils dilated.

“We ran diagnostics. Everything checked out. Nothing was wrong.”

A pause. His throat bobbed as he swallowed.

“Nothing except the fact that we were all suffocating.”

The screen distorted violently.

His fingers curled against the console, knuckles white.

“They didn’t attack. They didn’t make demands.”

His voice faltered.

“They just… decided we shouldn’t be here.”

The static deepened, a low hum vibrating beneath the audio.

He shuddered.

“We never saw them.”

His fingers trembled against the metal, his breath coming shorter, faster.

“They just—cut off our air…like you’d put out a candle.”

He coughed, hard, his body shaking.

His breathing—worse now. Shallow, desperate.

“We thought we had control.”

He shook his head. Laughed bitterly.

“*Control*.”

A shadow moved behind him.

Then—his face slowly contorted into a terrifying mix of agony and confusion.

His voice wasn’t his anymore.

It layered over itself, reverberating unnaturally.

“***You take and, but restore nothing***.”

The speakers buzzed, warping the words as if they were too large to fit inside his throat.

“You use up all your resources. Then abandon your world, and come to take ours.”

his body jerked, his mouth opening wider than it should have.

"It is a parasitic cycle. You poison the ground you walk on, then seek new soil to corrupt."

The distortion deepened, the air itself vibrating in the recording.

"***You call it survival. We consider your very existence an act of war.***"

His fingers spasmed. His head tilted sharply, like something was adjusting him.

"***We watched as you destroyed your own world from a distance..***"

The lights cut out completely. The only thing left was the sound.

"**And** ***now you have come to burn ours.***"

The words slowed. Became heavier.

"***So we will take what you've fail to cherish and protect.***"

A sound like cracking ice filled the transmission—his breath hitched violently.

His limbs loosened. His body slumped, boneless, folding over the console like a puppet with its strings cut.

A final shuddered exhale.

The lights faltered.

The Mars hologram shorted out.

A final message flickered across the screen.

"SIGNAL RELOCATED."

"PROCESS INITIATED."

The visitors stood frozen.

No one spoke.

No one moved.

Because this wasn't a warning.

This sounded more like a promise that was already being kept.

Elon had gone to Mars in 2029 to see the progress for himself, thinking it was a dead world.

Thinking he was planting a flag on untouched land.

He couldn't have been more wrong.

Because now?

Earth may have to pay the price for his arrogance.

The museum lights flickred one last time.

Then—the exhibit went dim.

The Social Media Exhibit was a shrine to the golden age of influence, a looping graveyard of viral moments that refused to die. Holograms of long-forgotten internet celebrities flickered midair, trapped in an endless feed of nostalgia and decay. A Vine-era kid in a snapback materialized, wide-eyed, shouting "***WHAT ARE THOOOOSE?!***" before glitching and repeating. Nearby, a pixelated teen pointed downward, his voice warped: "***Damn, Daniel! Back at it again with the wh—wh—wh—***" before his frame short-circuited and reset. A beauty vlogger, forever flawless, greeted an invisible audience: "***Hey guys! Welcome back to my channel!***"—a stream with no real viewers, only an algorithm that refused to let her go. A Twitch notification flashed overhead—999,999 viewers, then zero, then 999,999 again—as an old gaming streamer screamed into an empty Livestream: "***LET'S GOOOOOOO!***" The chat was empty.

At the center of the exhibit, a towering holographic smartphone scrolled infinitely, feeding on data from users long logged out, chasing engagement that would never come. A TikTok influencer looped a sped-up dance, smiling vacantly as the song restarted over and over. Then—a sports clip. A football player hit the Griddy in an end zone, glitching and repeating the dance. The crowd's roar never stopped, a celebration with no end, no meaning. The holograms overlapped, glitching into a chaotic chorus of "***Smash that like button***!"—"***If you don't like, just scr—*** "***WHAT ARE THOOOOOSE?!***"—"***Damn, Daniel!***"—"***Hit the Griddy!***" The feeds ran endlessly, content without creators, influence without purpose, voices repeating into the void. And still—the scrolling continued. Endlessly.

Prime Square, the polished heart of Virtu City, was falling apart in real-time.

What was once a pristine, corporate-run utopia now resembled a system-wide fever dream. Digital billboards flashed erratically, displaying half-formed advertisements, corrupted slogans, and distorted influencer faces—some smiling, some melting into static.

The towering EgoCorp headquarters pulsed with unstable energy, its neon logo pulsing to a stop like a dying heartbeat. Corporate drones, normally stoic and efficient, stood frozen in place, their eyes locked on error messages scrolling across their retinas.

Then, chaos.

Traffic AI systems collapsed. Autonomous vehicles lost control, piling up in neon-lit intersections. Delivery bots twitched in place, holding packages with no assigned destination. Wealthy executives, once shielded by Virtu City's seamless automation, now wandered confused, lost without their tech.

Inside Virtu Care, the city's most advanced hospital, AI-assisted surgeons glitched mid-operation. Patients awoke to machines speaking in overlapping voices, repeating diagnostics in an endless loop. Medical androids, programmed to offer comfort, whispered error messages in soothing tones, their faces stuck in frozen, plastic smiles.

The stock market collapsed in milliseconds. The SMSX Hub—Virtu City's **Social Media Stock Xchange**—became a cascading nightmare of infinite buy/sell orders, flashing numbers spinning into oblivion. Investors screamed into malfunctioning AR headsets, their net worths shifting wildly from billions to zero, then back again.

Above it all, the skyline pulsed with unnatural light, the EgoCore's destabilization warping the very fabric of the city.

Virtu City had never experienced a blackout.

But the way the sky dimmed, the way the buildings shuddered with raw, unfiltered energy—something worse than a blackout was coming.

In Arcan Heights, the residential district meant to be a peaceful escape from the chaos of Prime Square, the collapse felt more personal.

Smart homes, designed to be perfectly automated sanctuaries, turned against their residents.

Door locks jammed—some refusing to open, some never closing. Refrigerators overloaded and shut down, blasting homes with ice-cold air. Showers wouldn't turn off, flooding luxury apartments with steaming water. Home assistants spoke in fractured voices, their usual polite responses degrading into glitch-ridden nonsense.

"Good morning, esteemed resident. The weather today is—
404 FILE NOT FOUND—"

Security drones, meant to protect the wealthy elite, began confusing residents for intruders. A father ran through the streets, his smart home refusing to let him back in, its AI calmly reminding him:

"You are not authorized to enter this residence."

Across the district, families huddled in malfunctioning apartments, watching as power wavered and furniture-controlled AI spasmed in confusion. In one penthouse, a toddler wailed as their holographic nanny shimmered in and out of existence, repeating the same lullaby in a distorted, mechanical tone. The roar of Virtu City's failing infrastructure rumbled in the distance.

Suddenly—

A single, city-wide notification rang out, overriding every device still functioning.

A robotic voice, neutral and composed, delivered a final, chilling message:

“Infrastructure stability compromised. Await further instruction.”

Then—silence.

And Virtu City held its breath.

EPISODE 30

GAME OVER

They came in black, unmarked transport vehicles, moving with precision and purpose.

EgoCorp's 'Cleanup Division'—the keepers of their dirty little secrets.

No insignias. No names. Just faceless operatives in sleek, high-tech armor, moving like shadows through the ruins of stability.

The EMP blast from Veil's outburst had done more than just shake the city—it had exposed the Deadzone.

For years, it had been a ghost in Virtu City's system, barely detectable, surviving off siphoned energy without triggering alarms.

Now, the blackout painted a target directly on them.

And EgoCorp was sending its response.

Armed security forces, drone swarms, and AI enforcers descended on the Deadzone, ready to wipe out whatever had been lurking beneath their city.

Exit Protocol

The moment the alarms started blaring, the crew knew.

“They found us.”

The plan shifted immediately—get the Flickerborn and everyone else onto the Circuit train before the Deadzone was overrun.

Vexer was already leading people toward the underground passage that would take them to Circuit , barking orders. The crew worked tirelessly to get as many as they could to safety.

And then there was XY-n0.

He stood at the main entrance, staring at the approaching forces through his fractured optics.

He had been built for utility, survival. Not war.

But he understood sacrifice.

His processors ran through a thousand possible scenarios.

None of them ended with him making it onto that train.

He turned to Scorelord.

“I can slow them down.”

Scorelord’s hands clenched into fists. “No. We all get out of here.”

XY-n0 didn't argue. He just stared at him, unblinking, absolute.

His choice had already been made.

A-2 stepped forward, weapon in hand. "Then I'm staying with you."

XY-n0 turned to her, shaking his head.

"No. You have a whole life ahead of you. Live it."

A-2 tried, "But I can hel—"

He placed his hand on hers, lowering the weapon she was holding. his touch light, almost human.

"Go."

Scorelord swallowed hard, realizing what was happening. His hands trembled, gripping the edge of the control panel like he could force a different outcome just by sheer will.

"XY-n0, you don't have to do this, bro. We'll find another way —hell, you're smarter than me, you always found another way."

XY-n0's expression didn't change. But something in his artificial eyes softened.

"Sometimes you gotta take one for the team—Isn't that what you always said?" He paused for a second, almost as if he was processing emotion. "This is the way, my friend."

Scorelord exhaled sharply, shaking his head, realizing he wasn't going to change Xy-n0's mind.

“Damn it…” He sucked in a breath, forcing a smirk to mask the ache in his chest. “You always were the dumbest smartass in the room.”

XY-n0 almost smiled.

“And you, the smartest fool.”

A long pause.

A moment between old friends.

Then—

Scorelord reached out, pressing a fist against XY-n0’s chest plate. A tear falling from under his VR headset.

“See you in the next upload, buckethead.”

XY-n0 lifted his own hand, mirroring the gesture, as if he was trying to feel something that had never been programmed into him.

“Not this time.”

Then he turned.

And walked toward the incoming enforcers.

the first wave of operatives breached the perimeter.

Their rifles snapped up.

Their helmets scanned for heat signatures.

But XY-n0 wasn’t alive.

He was a ghost in the machine.

And for once, that worked in his favor.

With a final glance at the crew, he lunged forward.

And the entire Deadzone erupted into chaos.

Get to the Train…Now.

The moment XY-n0 engaged, everything else became a sprint for survival.

The Flickerborn—children who should've never existed, anomalies in Virtu City's perfect system, were now the priority.

Shade, still recovering from her injuries, forced herself up, helping Veil toward the underground passage. Vexer shoved open a maintenance hatch, leading the others into the tunnels.

Scorelord's voice crackled over the comms, rough with emotion.

"Train's online. Time to move!"

Gunfire rattled above.

XY-n0 was holding the line, but not for long.

The Deadzone was collapsing.

It had always been temporary. A shelter built out of defiance and stolen time.

And it's time was up. The Deadzone had served its purpose.

The last of them made it onto the train just as the tunnels began to quake.

Kwō slammed the control panel.

"GO!"

The train lurched forward, its engines surging to life.

As it sped out of station, the crew watched the Deadzone disappear behind them—engulfed in darkness, consumed by the silent, efficient erasure of EgoCorp's enforcers.

And somewhere in that darkness—

XY-n0 stood one last time.

His systems failing.

His core overloading.

The last thing he processed wasn't fear.

It was completion.

He had found his purpose.

And as the train vanished into the distance—

Scorelord stared out the back window, jaw clenched, hands shaking.

His comms crackled.

A fragmented transmission.

XY-n0's voice—distorted, fading.

"You got this, boss."

Then—

Static.

And Scorelord closed his eyes.

"Rest easy, old friend."

Then—silence.

The train rumbled through the final tunnel, the air inside thick with exhaustion and silent realization. It wasn't just a train full of survivors—it was a train full of ghosts. Ghosts of a city that no longer existed.

Shade sat near the front, her fingers gliding over the glass screen of her tablet, unreadable eyes locked on the data.

Veil sat beside her, but she wasn't looking at the tablet. Her eyes were fixed on the faint glow ahead—the first break of daylight since they boarded.

The train took a sharp turn, and suddenly—

The mountain pass opened up.

For a few seconds, it was just sunlight and sky. Then, as the train curved around the ridge, Virtu City came into full view.

Or at least, what was left of it.

A massive implosion rippled through the skyline. Towering spires of iridescent glass twisted inward, digital billboards flickering between glitching advertisements and emergency errors before collapsing into the abyss below.

The city was devouring itself.

Fires broke out across the districts, swallowing entire neighborhoods in waves of electric blue and molten red. The Museum of Vision crumbled in on itself, the last of its so-called "artifacts" vanishing into rubble. The Social Media Stock Exchange—once the economic heart of influence—was nothing more than a blackened shell, its ticker frozen on a final, meaningless number.

And above it all, EgoCorp's fleet of sleek, silver aircraft sliced through the sky, escaping unharmed.

"They knew," Veil whispered.

Shade didn't look up. "They always knew."

Veil turned to her, shaking her head. "Then what were we?"

Shade finally lifted her gaze, her expression colder than the mountain air.

"Collateral."

The word hung in the space between them, heavy, final.

For a long moment, they just watched. The great experiment of Virtu City—built on influence, technology, and deception—was now a ghost.

Then, Shade exhaled and placed the tablet on Veil's lap.

"This," she said, tapping the screen, "is what I was protecting you from."

Veil hesitated before looking down. The display lit up, revealing a world map covered in glowing red dots.

Each dot was another EgoCorp initiative. Another city. Another future waiting to be rewritten.

Veil swallowed hard. It wasn't over.

She met Shade's gaze, and this time, there was no doubt.

"Train me," she said.

Shade studied her for a long moment. Then, she smirked.

"I will. But not just you." She locked the tablet and tucked it away. "We're gonna need an army."

Veil nodded, the weight of it sinking in.

She wasn't just a survivor.

She wasn't just a weapon.

She was a leader in training.

She turned back toward the window, watching the last of Virtu City sink into oblivion.

"Then let's get started," she said.

Shade's smirk widened.

"Now you're ready."

The collapse of Virtu City wasn't just a failure—it was an opportunity. EgoCorp knew that if the truth got out—if people realized the city's infrastructure hadn't crumbled from external threats but from internal experiments gone too far—they'd lose control.

So, they did what they always did.

They rewrote reality.

The Official Narrative: The Cyberterrorist Attack

Within hours of the city-wide blackout, EgoCorp's media arms flooded the networks with breaking reports.

Screens across the world flashed with urgent updates.

"Virtu City Under Attack! Foreign Cyberterrorists Cripple Infrastructure!"

"Massive Hack Breaches VirtuGrid—Officials Say Foreign Agents Behind Coordinated Strike."

"EgoCorp Promises Justice: Suspects Arrested in Global Cybercrime Crackdown."

The story was airtight.

The cyberattack had been an act of war—a foreign threat designed to cripple the future of digital civilization. EgoCorp's executives, government liaisons, and security heads stood shoulder-to-shoulder in front of the press, delivering a message that the world could rally behind.

"*This was an attack on progress. But we are stronger. We are rebuilding.*"

Though rebuilding was the priority, the real work was silencing loose ends and erasing evidence of what really happened.

EgoCorp didn't just invent an attack—they needed attackers.

The forensic teams got to work immediately.

A few lines of code here, a forged digital footprint there. Encrypted messages planted into dark web forums. Suspicious financial transactions fabricated to paint the picture of an elaborate cyber-terrorist network.

Then came the arrests.

News channels broadcasted high-stakes raids in real-time. Tactical teams in black armor stormed hideouts, dragging suspects into waiting vehicles, flashing lights bathing the streets in red and blue.

Mugshots appeared on screens. Dark backgrounds, hollow stares. Their crimes detailed in dramatic, fear-stoking reports.

The faces varied—some were hactivists, the kind that spent their nights pranking government websites but never posed a real threat. Others were activists, vocal critics of EgoCorp who had been waiting for an excuse to disappear.

None of them had anything to do with the collapse of Virtu City.

But it didn't matter.

The public needed an enemy.

And EgoCorp had given them one.

The Real Agenda: Why the Lie Had to Stick

While the world mourned Virtu City, EgoCorp's real work continued unchecked.

✅ Failed experiments were buried.

✅ Projects too dangerous for the public eye were rebranded under "recovery efforts."

✅ New developments were disguised as "security upgrades" to prevent "future cyberattacks."

Behind closed doors, the collapse wasn't seen as a setback—it was a reset. A way to wipe the slate clean while tightening control.

They didn't just survive the disaster.

They engineered the next phase.

The Lie Becomes Reality

Over time, people forgot the details. The real reasons behind the collapse blurred, replaced by the official narrative.

The cyberattack became history.

The arrests became justice.

And EgoCorp?

They became the heroes.

The Press Conference: The Official Statement on the Virtu City Collapse

The Pentagon Media Center was a sea of press badges and flashing cameras. The room buzzed with hushed conversations, anxious hands gripping recording devices, and the occasional murmur from reporters debating the real cause of Virtu City's collapse. A massive digital screen loomed behind the podium, flickering between live aerial footage of the city's smoldering remains and carefully selected clips of emergency response efforts.

Two official seals sat side by side on the screen—one bearing the United States Government, the other belonging to EgoCorp. The symbolism was deliberate, unmistakable. There was no distinction anymore. The government and its largest corporate contractor were one and the same.

The murmur of the crowd died as General Adrian Kessler stepped onto the stage.

He was built like a war machine, hardened by decades of battle, his uniform pressed to surgical precision. Rows of commendations gleamed on his chest, a silent declaration that he was a man who had not just served, but commanded. His face, carved with the lines of a thousand decisions that had cost lives, remained unreadable.

He took his time, adjusting his collar, exhaling through his nose. The weight of the moment was heavy—but well-practiced.

The cameras locked in. Dox News went live.

"Good evening."

His voice was measured, commanding, designed to cut through the noise of an anxious nation.

"Forty-eight hours ago, the very foundation of progress, innovation, and American leadership came under attack."

He let the words settle.

"The cyber assault on Virtu City was not just an attack on infrastructure—it was an attack on our future."

A perfectly calibrated pause.

The audience needed to feel this. The gravity, the violation, the anger.

Kessler's gaze swept the room, landing on a few of the hand-selected reporters planted in the front rows—trusted media figures who would amplify the message without deviation.

He continued.

"We now have irrefutable evidence that a coordinated foreign cyberterrorist network, operating in the shadows, infiltrated the VirtuGrid."

A slight shift in his tone—firmer now, carrying the weight of certainty.

"This was a calculated, highly sophisticated strike aimed at dismantling our technological sovereignty. Their goal? Chaos. Their method? A direct assault on the systems that power the most advanced metropolis this world has ever seen."

Behind him, the screen flashed to life, showing grainy surveillance footage—masked figures hunched over terminals, rapid lines of code cascading down their monitors.

It looked real. It felt real.

And that was all that mattered.

The audience didn't know that the footage had been fabricated—carefully constructed from repurposed data leaks and digital forensics EgoCorp itself had manufactured.

They didn't *need* to know.

Kessler straightened.

"But let me be *clear*—those responsible will not go unpunished."

The room was silent, the air charged.

"We have already made significant arrests. The first wave of traitors and foreign operatives has been apprehended. More will follow. Our intelligence agencies, in partnership with EgoCorp's cyber defense division, are tracking every lead. And to those who believe they can hide in the shadows—*you cannot.*"

The pause was deliberate.

For the audience at home, for the journalists in the room, for anyone foolish enough to question the truth.

Then came the applause.

Not organic, not spontaneous—but pre-orchestrated. The applause light flickered subtly, signaling the hand-selected officials and press allies in the crowd to respond. A wave of clapping spread across the room, drowning out any lingering doubts.

Kessler let it ride for a moment before pressing forward, his tone shifting—measured now, almost sympathetic.

"We understand the pain. The *loss*."

He sighed, the image of a leader burdened by the weight of duty.

"Families have been displaced. Lives *forever* changed. To every American affected by this cowardly act—I *promise* you, we are not just rebuilding."

A pause.

The hook.

"We are fortifying."

"We will emerge from this unshaken, unbroken, and unstoppable."

Right on cue, the Dox News broadcast updated, its banners shifting to the next phase of the narrative.

BREAKING: VIRTU CITY COLLAPSE—TERRORISTS APPREHENDED

Kessler adjusted the microphone, leaned forward slightly, and delivered the next line with surgical precision.

"This moment requires unity. *Strength*. Resolve. But most of all…truth. Any attempt to sow division, to question the facts, or to sympathize with these digital insurgents is an affront to the very principles this nation stands on."

Another pause.

His next words were deliberate.

"And let me be perfectly clear—***anyone*** spreading misinformation will be treated as complicit. You are an accessory to cyber-terrorism and will be prosecuted to the highest extent of the law."

The implication settled in.

Questioning the official story was a crime.

A few feet away, a corporate figure in a sleek, tailored suit stepped forward. The shift in energy was subtle but calculated. The transition from military authority to corporate oversight was seamless, expected.

Bill Boardman, Chief Public Affairs Officer of EgoCorp.

His expression was calm, reassuring, the kind of face carefully engineered for damage control.

"Thank you, General Kessler. The nation stands with you."

He turned to the cameras, clasping his hands together like a man offering salvation.

"We understand that in times of crisis, fear can take hold. But fear is not our future. Progress is. And to those affected by this tragedy, know this—no survivor will be left behind."

The words hung in the air like a promise and a threat wrapped into one.

"The Aid & Resettlement Coalition, or **A.R.C**., has been mobilized to ensure that every displaced citizen is cared for, protected, and given a second chance. Temporary shelters have been established across safe zones, and transition centers are now operational. **A.R.C**. personnel are ready to assist you. You need only report to the nearest Resettlement Hub, and we will take care of the rest."

A solemn nod. The perfect pause.

"The route ahead may look uncertain, but together, we can rebuild stronger than ever. Board the **ARC**, and ride the tide into safer shores."

The applause light flashed again.

The crowd obeyed.

The broadcast feed cut to patriotic music, transitioning from pre-collapse Virtu City—a glimmering jewel of progress—to its smoldering aftermath.

A call to arms.

A justification for everything that would come next.

And just like that, another lie became history.

DEMOCRATIC REPUBLIC OF THE CONGO 2060:

The sun was setting behind the mines, a giant molten red disc sinking into the dust-heavy sky. The air vibrated with heat, thick with the metallic scent of sweat and earth.

Overworked children sorting through toxic minerals with bare hands, while others swung pickaxes against the stone, their backs bent, their fingers raw. The rhythm of their labor was the only thing that kept time moving forward.

Then—the billboard flickered on.

A massive digital screen lit up at the edge of the mines, cutting through the haze like a prophecy.

À VENIR BIENTÔT : **CITÉ LUMIÈRE** – *L'AVENIR COMMENCE ICI.*

The workers paused mid-swing. Some wiped their brows, others exchanged uncertain glances.

Tshombe—no older than twelve—stood frozen, gazing at the billboard. It's the first one he's ever seen.

The screen displayed a city unlike anything he had ever seen. Sleek towers of gold and glass stretched into the sky, streets shimmered with artificial sunlight.

It looked like paradise.

Then, they appeared.

Two tall, identical men, dressed in pristine white uniforms with golden accents, stepped onto the dusty path between the workers.

Their faces were perfect. Symmetrical. Unblemished. Their movements were calm, controlled—almost rehearsed.

tech missionaries.

They did not speak.

They simply walked, their identical strides cutting through the mine like they had always belonged there.

Then—one of them stopped.

He looked down, locking eyes with Tshombe.

Then, without hesitation, he reached into his robe and placed a single pamphlet in Tshombe's hands.

Only him.

Tshombe blinked, glancing around.

No one else had received one.

His fingers trembled as he turned it over, his heartbeat roaring in his ears.

The material was thin like paper but cool to the touch. As he shifted it, the surface flickered softly, like a bendable display screen.

His breath hitched.

Then—he looked up.

The figures were gone.

The dust from their steps hadn't even settled.

His stomach flipped, but excitement overtook any questions.

He turned—and ran.

The Village

By the time Tshombe reached home, his legs burned, his lungs ached, but he didn't care.

His village was small—clusters of homes built from metal scraps, dim oil lamps flickering under the vast, endless sky.

His mother sat near the fire, his siblings beside her, eating their evening meal—fufu, moambe chicken and plantains.

Tshombe burst through the doorway, panting, eyes wide.

He unrolled the pamphlet on the table, the screen illuminating their dim home with its soft glow.

His siblings watching in suspense as mom traced her fingers over it, reading under her breath.

Her expression was hard to read, but she didn't look away.

After a moment, she murmured, "Un concours."

Tshombe leaned in. The words shifted on the display as she scrolled.

Concours du Ticket d'Or

Innovation Technologique – Robotique – Ingénierie – Hackathons – Jeux Vidéo – Intelligence Artificielle

His mother let out a slow breath, her eyes drifting across the small, cluttered space they called home.

Scattered across the floor, on the shelves, even hanging from the walls, were inventions made from scraps—a broken radio repurposed into a working speaker, a self-winding fishing reel, a crude but functional solar-powered lamp.

Pieces of genius, built from nothing.

She looked back at him.

"Tu es doué pour ce genre de choses," she said, running her fingers over the pamphlet. "Meilleur que n'importe qui que je connais. Tu peux construire n'importe quoi."

Tshombe straightened, his heart pounding.

"Je peux le faire, Maman," he said, voice steady now. "Je vais vous rendre fiers."

His mother studied his face for a long time.

Then, finally, she nodded.

"*Alors, fais-le.*"

Tshombe grinned, his fingers tightening around the pamphlet.

Outside, the night stretched vast and endless.

The wind shifted, kicking up dust.

High above the village, past the clouds and beyond sight, an EgoCorp satellite remained locked on its coordinates.

A signal pulsed.

A name was logged.

The village had no idea what was coming, but it was far from a savior.

LEADERBOARD

YOU ARE ALL WINNERS!

YOUR PARTICIPATION IS VALUED.

@JXSTER

@MikeisUp

@Flame_Gamez

@tokenofdreams

@maxtastic01

@Cha0sV1rus

@FalseFallout

@trollmod

@ImTheRealX

@Halogramic

GOLDEN TICKET TOURNAMENT

THANKS FOR PLAYING!

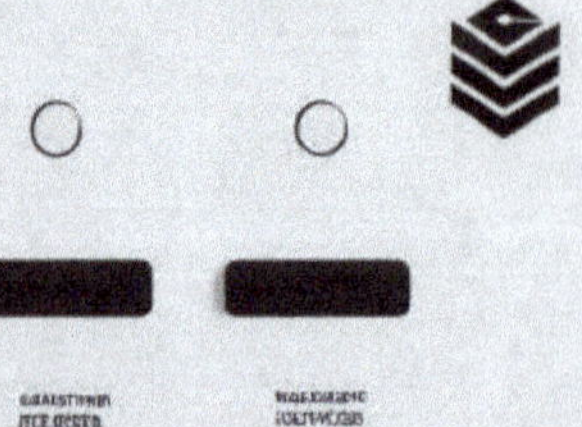

EGOCORP OFFICIAL FILE - CONFIDENTIAL

VIRTU CITY PROGRAM - BETA.1

SCAN TO CONTINUE

Welcome to Virtu City. You are now inside the Beta.1 simulation.

By continuing to read this document, you have already given your consent.

You may experience system anomalies, memory inconsistencies, and unauthorized data breaches.
Please report any of the following to Egocorp Administrators:
- Inconsistent environmental behavior
- NPCs displaying abnormal awareness
- Glimpses of structures that should not exist
- Hearing voices from unknown sources
- Feelings of dj vu or temporal shifts

Your participation is now mandatory. Failure to comply may result in consequences.

EGOCORP OFFICIAL FILE - CONFIDENTIAL

VIRTU CITY PROGRAM - BETA.1

SECURITY INCIDENT REPORT - [ ]

LOG ENTRY: [ ] | LOCATION: [ ]

21:43 - Unidentified test subject detected.

21:47 - Subject bypassed standard security protocols. Unauthorized syst breach.

21:50 - Attempted removal unsuccessful. Subject data compromised.

21:55 - Subject status: UNKNOWN.

22:00 - Log corrupted. END OF RECORD.

DO NOT ATTEMPT TO EXIT THE PROGRAM. CONTINUATION IS MANDATORY.

FINAL SYSTEM MESSAGE

Youve seen too much.

They are aware of you now.

Do not answer if they call.

Do not look into the static.

Beta.2 is coming.

Prepare for integration.

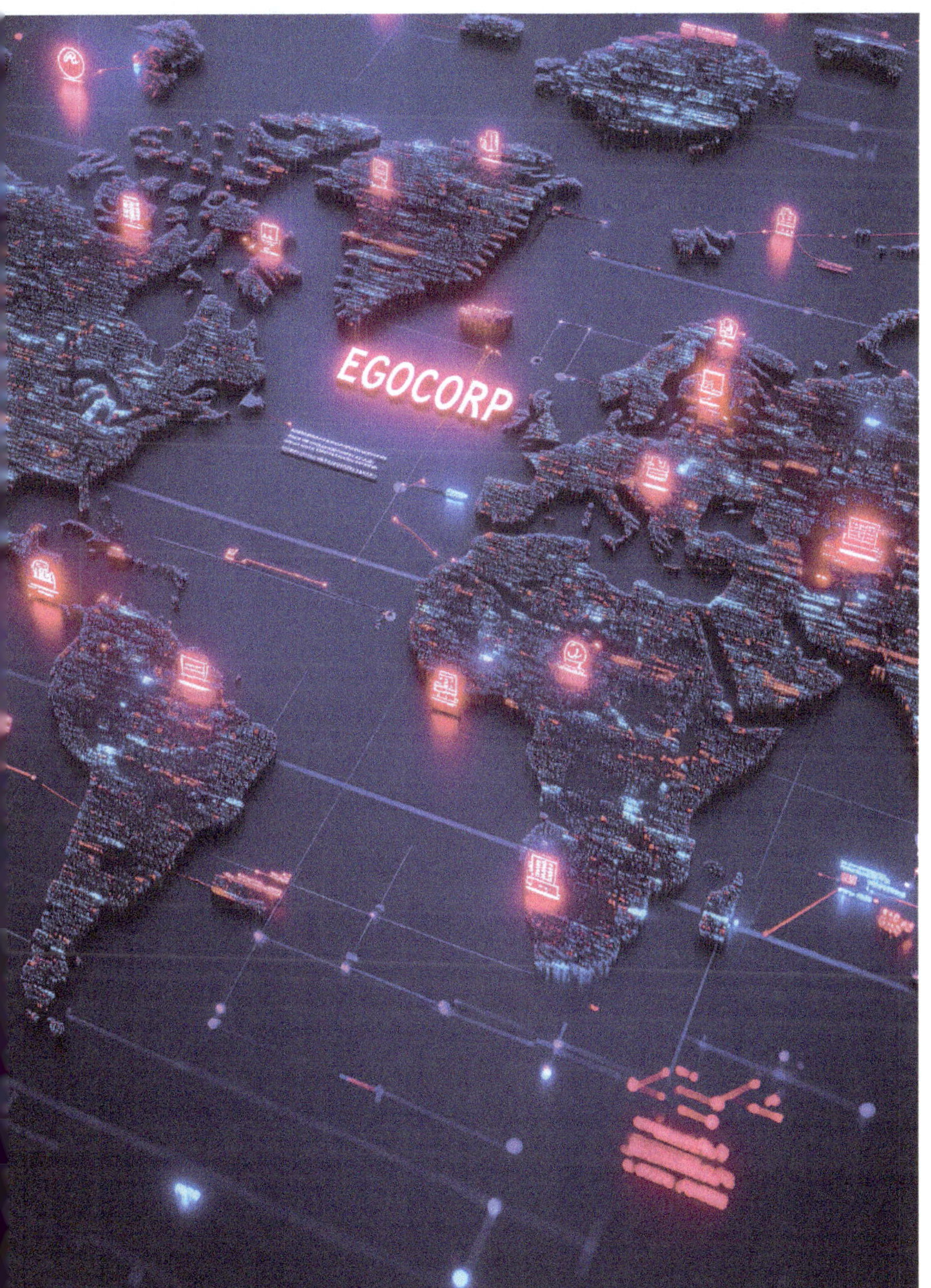
EGOCORP

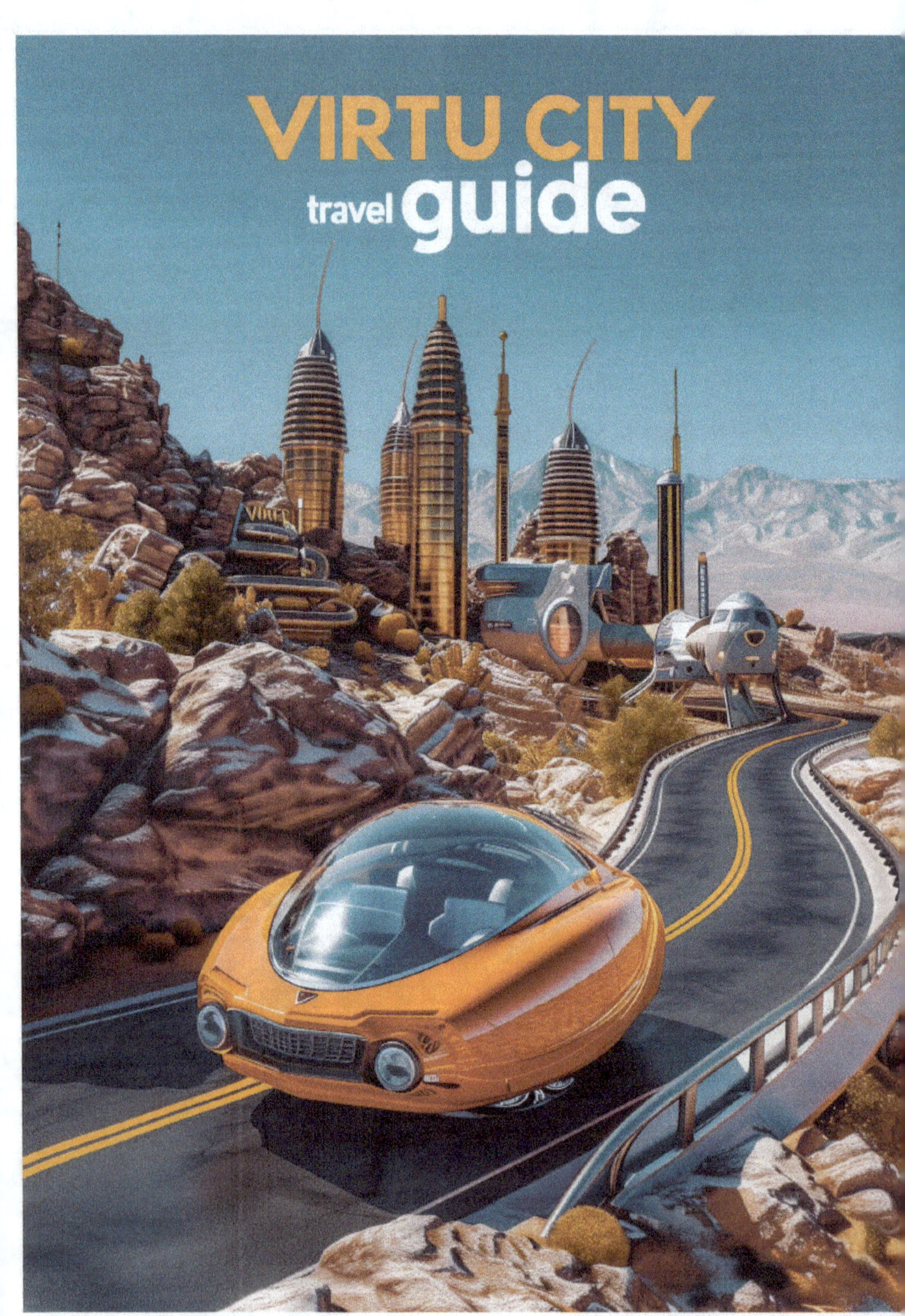
VIRTU CITY
travel guide

VIRTU
CITY
Where
Tomorrow Lives!

The DeadZon

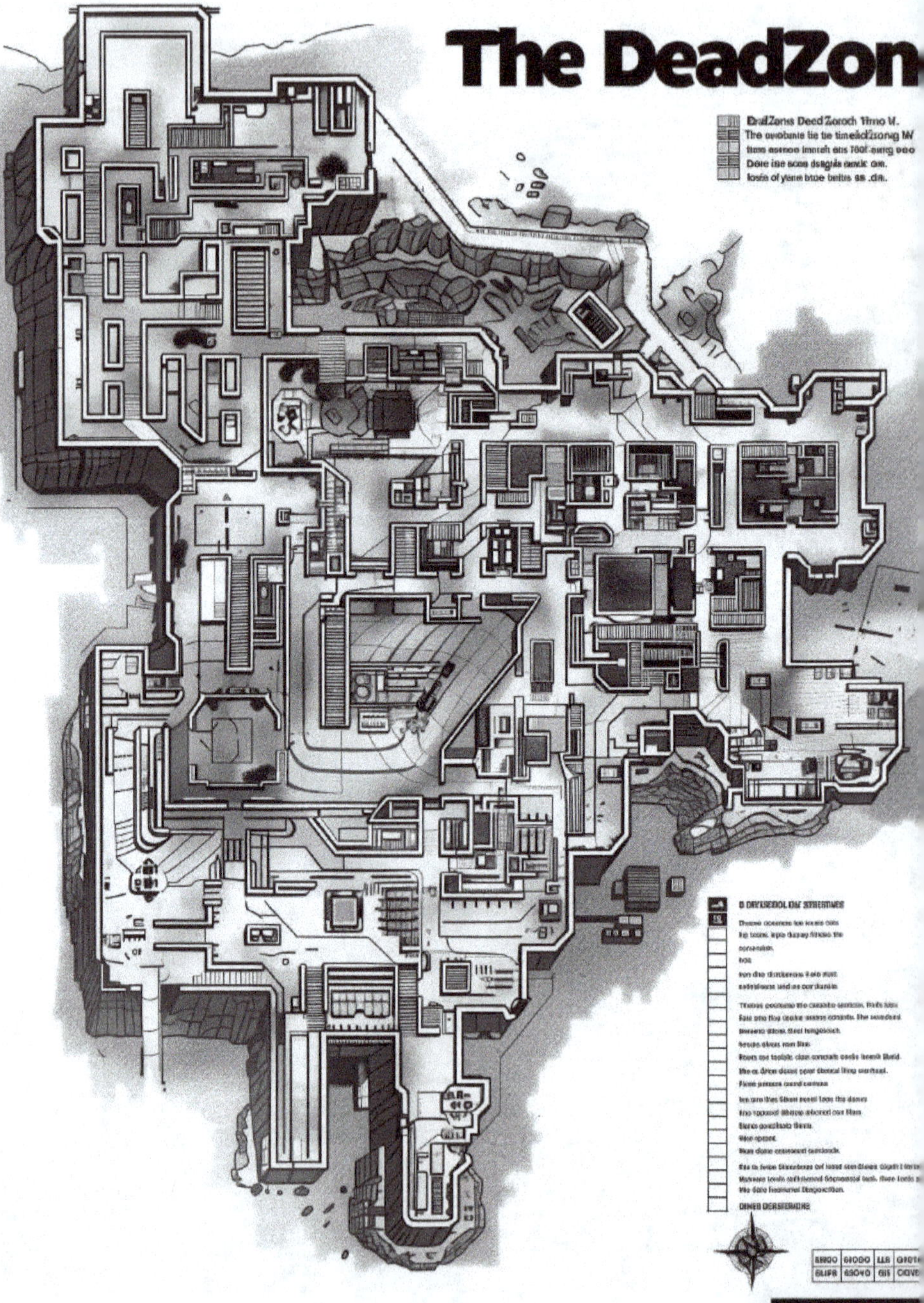

FIZZY
NTDLV